I0655117

the Borgia Seed

*How a Turkish princess and a renegade knight on a holy
mission to find the True Cross led to the fall of an empire
in the Middle Ages, changing the history of Europe.*

RICHARD TARA

AKA

Ricardo Barberini

Copyright © 2011 Richard Tara
All rights reserved.

ISBN: 0615491715
ISBN-13: 9780615491714
Library of Congress Control Number: 2011930196
Borgia Publications, San Carlos, CA

A tale of forbidden love and lust laced with venomous hate during the last conflict between Muslims and Christians, *The Borgia Seed* is the story of Rodrigo Borgia, then a peasant knight, who kidnapped the sister of the Turkish sultan only to fall in love with her and embarked on a dangerous journey to rescue the holiest object of Christianity, which had been lost for generations.

ACKNOWLEDGMENT &

DEDICATION

It is never possible to write a book without help from many, many people. A historical novel has to have some elements of reality and accuracy about it and as such, the work is very involved and painstaking. I would like to thank the staff of CreateSpace for their very courteous work and guidance.

I would like to thank my editors, Sandra Quinn (La Due), Maureen Freeman and K C Steffen for all their really hard work in this project. I would like to thank my work manager and publicist Emma Waroff for her diligence and attention to details and Darian Taha for his on-going support and encouragement.

Finally my heartfelt thanks to the readers of this book, and I do hope there will be many.

We dedicate this book to the people who made Renaissance a reality and overcame centuries of superstitions to make possible the life that we enjoy today.

INTRODUCTION

The story behind this book goes back more than a hundred years. Many years ago, my grandfather was visiting Rhodes Island in the Mediterranean. He was browsing in an antiques shop and came across an ancient book that intrigued him. It seemed to be a diary and a book of poetry with some elegant drawings. He could not read it, since it was in a foreign language. However, he decided to buy it because he liked the drawings and the calligraphy.

My grandfather kept it as a valued possession, hoping to be able to have it translated some day. That day never came for him but, years later, my father, who was a natural linguist, came across the book. It seemed to be a diary written by a very cultured woman.

My father managed to get the gist of the story together and translate it even though there were many missing pages. While living in Rome, he met Prince Orsini and through him met a Mr. Mansour Mehmandoost, who was the intelligence officer of the Iranian Embassy in Rome. That was years before the revolution that made Iran into a rogue pariah state. Mr. Mehmandoost had built a vast network of friends and contacts during his stay in Rome and my understanding is that he was the man who introduced the then Empress Soraya of Iran to Prince Orsini and caused the affair that led to her divorce. Through his friendship with Mansour, my father managed to get access to the Vatican Museum and its secret documents, including the secret room that he described in detail and is included in this book. He also gained access to the daybook of Francesco Foscari, who was the doge of Venice during those turbulent years in the Middle Ages.

What my father had in his possession were fragments of a story. He hoped to put everything together and publish it under the title, *The Secret Diary of a Turkish Princess.* He met with Maurice Girodias, who had miraculously survived World War II and the Nazi occupation of France, to discuss his project. Maurice was the president of Olympia Press in Paris and being half-Greek and half-Jewish, was especially excited to publish the diary, since it told the story of the fall of Constantinople from the point of view of a Turkish princess trapped inside the city. Maurice had published many controversial authors, such as Henry Miller, Vladimir Nabokov, William Burroughs, and J. P. Donleavy. He told my father to bring him the manuscript as soon as possible. However, before my father could complete his manuscript, Olympia Press went bankrupt and Maurice moved to New York. My father did not have the time or the resources to complete and self-publish his book.

I discovered his notes for the book several years later. I could not put it down until I had read it all. Being a historian, I decided to investigate the background of the story and complete the work. The result is *The Borgia Seed.* I have tried to fill in the gaps for many of the characters in the book by delving into history books, archives, and old maps. Even though most of the characters are real, we are publishing it as fictionalized history since we do not want to offend any particular group.

Back in 1453, Constantinople was the last remnant of Western civilization facing the Muslim world. It was somewhat like the United States is today; an open, tolerant, and rather decadent society, in which all of the religions and nationalities coexisted side by side, and more importantly, it was the mixing pot through which the East and the West transferred their cultures, values and knowledge.

This important gateway between Europe and the Middle East was wiped out by the Ottoman Turks in 1453.

The Ottomans, who had originated in central Asia, choked off any contact between the Muslim world and the Western Christian world, much to the disadvantage of the Muslims, who effectively were separated from the Europe for five centuries. The European world continued its march forward while the Muslim world did not. Whereas, in the first century of Islam, women held positions of power and respect and even led armies, the fundamentalists and fanatics who took over gradually reduced them to the position of prisoners of harems.

Almost everyone in this world, regardless of his origins or faith, wants to be left alone to live his life happily with family and friends. We sincerely hope that people of all religions and nationalities will learn to live together and at least adopt "live and let live" as a slogan rather than "live and let die."

the Borgia Seed

CONTENTS

BOOK I – THE MISSION

BOOK II – THE RAPE OF THE MILLENNIUM

PRELUDE

The winter of 1451 was one of the coldest in Europe. The continent was still in the clutches of a mini ice age that had lasted for nearly a century and had left famine, disease, and the dreaded Black Death in its path. It had also brought in hungry invaders and marauders from central Asia in search of food and warmth. These ravenous intruders followed the path of their great ancestors, the Mongolian hordes of Genghis Khan, who had ravaged Russia and the Middle East two centuries earlier, except this time around they cast their eyes further into conquering the whole of Europe. The mightiest of those invading tribes were the brutal Ottomans, who, by mid fifteenth century, had conquered all of Asia Minor, parts of the Middle East, and most of the Balkans.

In that brutally cold winter, an impetuous and sometimes vicious young man succeeded to the throne of the mighty Turkish Ottoman Empire. The young man, who took the name of Mohammed II, was barely nineteen years old.

On his deathbed, his father, Sultan Murat II, had made him promise that he would try to achieve the victory that had eluded the Ottoman rulers for over three hundred years: the conquest of Constantinople. At that time, Constantinople was the last outpost of Western civilization and Christianity at the tail end of

Europe. The city was surrounded on all sides by hostile Muslim forces. No sooner had Murat died than Mohammed began preparations for a great battle between the two major civilizations.

On the other side of Mediterranean, nearly two thousand miles away, there was another young nobleman who would take the leading role in the ensuing conflict, yet he had no land or money and was unaware of the role he would play in the destiny of the world.

Read on...

CHAPTER ONE

MISSION FROM GOD

On a frosty day, early in February 1453, Pope Nicholas V was nervously pacing up and down his private quarters in Castle San Angelo in Rome. Nicholas V was not really an old man—he was barely fifty-three years old—yet the ravages of time, intrigues, corruption at home, and treachery abroad had worn him way beyond his years. This slight man with dark, piercing eyes had fought hard to reform the Curia, the administrative arm of the papacy, and he had battled with all elements to promote unity among the European powers. During the past few years, he had been the target of several assassination attempts and these days he hardly ever went out without an armed escort.

Unlike many popes before him, Nicholas was not related to any of the great families of Rome, nor did he have ties to the French or German kings. He was of humble beginnings. Before becoming Pope Nicholas V, he was plain Tomasso Parentucelli, a country priest who had been elevated to cardinal based on his abilities.

In Germany, Martin Luther had not even been born yet, but fifty years earlier Jan Hus of Bohemia had already planted the seeds of division and rebellion against the Catholic Church. The church had vast land holdings in most European countries.

Devout believers had bequeathed those lands to the Vatican over the centuries. Now, the German princes and the French king were plotting against the Catholic Church and planning to divvy up its rich properties. Nicholas thought it ironic that the Germans, who were once among the most devout, should be planning the demise of the Holy Church.

Against this backdrop rose a far greater threat. The Ottoman Turks, who had migrated from the central plains of Asia, had taken over most of present-day Greece, Serbia, Bosnia, Montenegro, Albania, and Croatia and had almost completely encircled the great city of Constantinople. Sultan Mohammed II, a vicious and cold-blooded ruler who had not hesitated to murder his own infant brothers to solidify his claim to the throne, was preparing for the final push against the last bastion of Western civilization.

Nicholas V had appealed, in vain, to the Christian kings, princes, and nobility of Europe. He was hoping to raise a Crusade, this time not for conquest of Muslim lands but to save a holy Christian city. His appeals were ignored. Urgent pleas for help from Constantinople and its emperor, the courageous Constantine XII, also fell on deaf ears. The truth was that after three hundred years of warfare, people were tired of wars and Crusader taxes.

It was nearly the noon hour. There was a gentle knock at the door and a skinny, middle-aged man attired in the black costume of the priest monks entered the room. The newcomer bowed gently and said, "Holy Father, Cardinal Alfonso Borgia and his nephew are here." The pope waved his hand absent-mindedly and within a few moments, the cardinal and his nephew were ushered into the room. As was the custom of the day, the pope offered the visitors his signet hand to be kissed and then motioned them to sit down. The skinny, middle-aged priest was Father Alfaro, the pope's devoted personal attendant and historian. Father Alfaro moved silently to a corner of the room and stood near a window.

Cardinal Alfonso Borgia was over seventy years old, which was remarkable in an era when most people did not live past fifty. The old cardinal had one of the sharpest minds in the Vatican. The pope relied upon him to control the finances of the Catholic Church. The younger man, Rodrigo Borgia, was barely twenty-two. He was tall and handsome with a dark complexion and very dark, almost black eyes.

Since leaving the seminary a few years ago, he had not bothered much about religion and did not have any particular love for the Church. However, he had the greatest admiration and loyalty to both the pope and his uncle. The pope and his uncle knew that Rodrigo was a brave man, but they also knew of his reputation as a seducer of aristocratic women, young or old, married or not. His uncle also had heard the rumors about Rodrigo bedding his own half-sister, Isabella.

The pope, obviously exhausted, waited a few moments to catch his breath and then in a tired voice said, "My son, I admire your devotion to your uncle and me. That is why I am going to ask you to put your life at the disposal of the Church." Rodrigo, looking directly into the pope's eyes, said, "Holy Father, I will gladly give my life for you, and the holy church of Christ." Rodrigo had been hoping for some purpose in life. The pope's request rekindled his death wish.

The pope managed a faint smile and went on to explain his reason for summoning Rodrigo. "I know that I do not have much longer to live, my son. I had a revelation about a week ago and I have not been able to go to sleep or rest since then. Last Sunday evening, as I was praying to the Lord, I had a vision of the great holy city of Constantinople and its Cathedral of Hagia Sofia surrounded by the infidels. Then, suddenly, I saw a blinding light, which I can only think of as the Holy Spirit, rise from within the sacred grounds of Hagia Sofia and ascend to the heavens. It was as if the Holy Spirit had abandoned the church and the city. I then knew the end was coming for our Christian brothers in that holy city. I fear that we do not have any chance of saving Constantinople from the infidel. I will need to send you on a mission to the East from which you may never return alive. But first I would like to know if you are willing to risk your life for our savior and Lord, Jesus Christ."

Rodrigo did not hesitate for even an instance. He replied with the bravado of youth, "Holy Father, I laugh at death and will give my life gladly for our savior. I beg of you to let me be the instrument of his will." The atmosphere was so charged with raw emotion that the old man, Cardinal Alfonso, overcome with emotion, knelt on the floor, weeping uncontrollably, and recited the Lord's Prayer repeatedly.

The pope sat back and waited for the old cardinal to recover his composure and sit down again on his chair. Nicholas faced Rodrigo and said, "What I am about to tell you is one of the best kept secrets of the world. Do you know anything about the Knights Templar?" Rodrigo remembered the story of how that sacred order of knights had been wiped out completely by the order of a French pope and the greedy French King Phillip.

Nicholas continued, "My son, during the Crusades, there were two orders of military monks established for the protection of pilgrims who were making the long, perilous journey to the holy lands. They were the Knights Templar and the Knights Hospitaller. The men who entered the ranks of those orders were usually sons of noblemen, like you, who swore to a life of celibacy and obedience to the pope. Gradually, kings and princes of Europe endowed those orders, specifically the Templar order, with tremendous amounts of land and gold. That created intense jealousy from the French King Phillip, who envied their fortunes. Therefore, he devised a plan to brand them as heretics and confiscate all that they had. For this, he needed help from the pope, since he was the only person who could disband the order.

"At that time, the pope was dead, so Phillip managed to force an election on French soil and handpicked a pliant French priest by the name of Bertrand de Goth to be the next pope, Clement V. With Clement's help, he also packed the College of Cardinals with many unworthy French clergymen. Clement was the first pope to be forced to stay in Avignon in France, an exile that lasted eighty years.

"Phillip tried to convince Clement to outlaw and disband both orders. Clement refused repeatedly until the threats got too severe and he agreed to disband the Templar order, the richer of the two orders. Even though he signed an order of denunciation, he secretly signed another order renouncing his first order.

"The Italian cardinals managed to inform the Templar order of the disaster and just before the ax fell, most of the Templar knights boarded several ships with their treasures and disappeared forever, or so it seemed. A few Templar knights, including the grand master, Jacques de Molay, agreed to stay behind and be martyred to keep the secret.

"Therefore, when Phillip's henchmen made their surprise assaults on Templar castles and temples, they did not find any treasures. Phillip managed, however, to confiscate all their lands.

"From that date, the Templar knights have remained the secret army of the popes and only the pope and two of his closest advisors know about their existence. In case something happens suddenly to the pope, the new pope is informed of the existence of this secret order of devout men. The Templar knights select new members of the order in secret. They approach only men who are not worldly and are willing to sacrifice all in service of Christ and the pope. In the past, those hero knights have performed many deeds of chivalry for us and many of them have been martyred in the holy lands carrying out missions on behalf of my predecessors."

Rodrigo thought to himself, "Obviously, this is not an invitation to join the Templar knights, since my sinful life excludes me."

The pope, seemingly reading his mind, smiled faintly and said, "That is not the reason you are here, my son."

Nicholas continued, "Another secret that I am entrusting to you is about your mission." With that, he motioned to Alfaro, who silently left the room and within a few moments returned with a young man. The man looked to be in his twenties. He was tall and lanky. His light brown hair was tied back neatly behind his neck. He was dressed like a French knight and was wearing a scabbard without the sword, as it was customary to approach the holy father unarmed. His deep blue eyes, ringed with dark circles, highlighted a bony face with high cheekbones. He coughed as he entered the room, kneeled, kissed Nicholas's hand, and sat down opposite Rodrigo.

Nicholas made the introductions. The newcomer was Jean de Mont Claire from the region of Languedoc in southeastern France.

The pope went on. "Over a thousand years ago, Saint Elena, the mother of Emperor Constantine the Great, made several trips to Jerusalem to locate the cross on which our savior was crucified, known as the True Cross. Eventually, she discovered it and even brought a fragment of it back to her palace in Rome. However, the cross itself was left in Jerusalem, in safe keeping, in the church of Holy Sepulcher, for three hundred years until the city and the cross fell into the hands of the Saracen Arabs. In the next few hundred years, it was recovered and lost several times. At one time, the infidel Muslims kept it in a stable to affront our Lord. Finally, in 1192 Saladin took it to Damascus out of spite for the killing of Muslim hostages by Richard the Lionhearted in Acre.

"Eventually, the Knights Templar devised a plan to rescue the cross and bring it back to Christendom. It took several years to locate it in the city of Damascus. Many of the knights who had lived in the Christian-controlled areas near Jerusalem spoke perfect Arabic. Four of the knights dressed as Persian traders and with the help of an Arab convert, managed to slip into the city of Damascus in 1199 and remove the True Cross. They succeeded in taking the cross to Constantinople, where they left it for safe-keeping in the possession of Emperor Alexius III. The leader of this expedition was Arthur of Brittany. He recorded a detailed account of how they had recovered the cross and sent it to Pope Innocent III along with a signed receipt from Emperor Alexius, stating that he was keeping it for the Holy Church of Rome."

At this point Cardinal Alfonso interjected, saying, "In those days, many of the popes were elected because of their positions in the community. Pope Innocent III was part of the Conti family, who were then as now, one of the most powerful families in Rome. Innocent was not even a priest when he was elected pope, so he did not appreciate the importance of the True Cross."

Nicholas reached across to the middle of the table, picked up a folder, handed it to Rodrigo, and said, "You should read this, as it will give you clues about what you are looking for."

Rodrigo was still uncertain of what he was supposed to do.

The pope continued. "The cross has remained in Constantinople ever since. Its location is secret and probably forgotten. The Templar Knights passed that information to each succeeding generation. We know exactly what it looked like and how it was decorated two and a half centuries ago. During the Crusader kingdom, it was adorned with gold, silver, and other jewels. The front and the back of the cross were covered with small mirrors so they would shine for miles around in every direction whenever it was carried in front of the great crusading armies. At other times, the cross was covered by a silk blanket." With that, the pope handed another folio to the still mystified Rodrigo and told him that inside the envelope was the drawing and the description made by Arthur of Brittany two hundred and fifty years earlier.

The pope paused, leaving a deathly silence in the room. The atmosphere was charged with anxiety and anticipation. Rodrigo unconsciously gripped the arms of his chair, his palms sweaty. Everyone, except Jean, who was looking down at the table in front of him, stared at the pope.

The pope added, "As you all know, the infidel Mohammed, who calls himself the sultan, is steadily surrounding the holy city of Constantinople. There have been many attempts in the past ten centuries to capture that holy city, but this time, I am afraid the city will fall to the Muslims.

"There is a lot at stake here. The Arabs were illiterate, barbarian, desert nomads who eventually became partially civilized by adopting the cultures of Egypt, Syria, and Persia. There have been several great Muslim leaders like Saladin who, though misguided in his religion, had the spirit of gallantry and valor. The Arabs eventually decided to coexist with the Christians in their own territories.

The Ottoman Turks are a different story. They are savages from Asiatic lands. They have an immense appetite for plunder and rape. They have been trying to conquer Constantinople for over two centuries. The sad truth is that many renegade Christians who are after bounty and gold have joined the Ottoman army of Mohammed. Unlike Saladin, Mohammed has no spirit of chivalry or mercy for conquered people.

"Mohammed is also receiving help from the French king, Charles VII, and the Venetian doge, the imbecile Francesco Foscari. The Bulgarians, who have hated the Byzantines since they were decimated by them several hundred years ago, are also helping them, since they have been promised a piece of the occupied land. The Venetians have the most to gain from the collapse of Constantinople, since the crown jewels of the Byzantine

Empire are in safekeeping in Venice and if the city falls, the jewels, which are probably worth more than all the riches of Italy, will be freely theirs."

The pope paused again to catch his breath. It was obvious that this godly, frail man was ill. After a few moments, he continued. "This is the reason that you and Jean are here." At that point, Jean looked up from the table and gazed directly at Rodrigo with a quiet smile.

Nicholas, gathering all of his physical strength stated, "It is our wish that you, Rodrigo, lead a small group of men to Constantinople under the cover of strict secrecy, recover the True Cross, and save it from falling into the hands of Mohammed and his army of beasts, who will most certainly desecrate and burn it."

The words sent a chill down Rodrigo's spine.

"Jean, as you may have guessed by now, is one of the last of the great order of Knights Templar," Nicholas continued. "He will be your assistant and will verify the authenticity of the cross once you recover it. It is not an easy task. We cannot send you on the most direct and fastest route, which is through Venice, or use Venetian ships from other ports. The Venetians may betray us as they have done many times before. The Genovese are our friends but their port is too far north from here. Naples, to the south, would have been my other choice but we are having some problems with them and they are courting the French in their plans to take over Sardinia.

"The nearest port in friendly hands is the port of Pisa. As you may know, I was born near Pisa and we have many loyal friends there. We have arranged for you to travel north to Florence and then to Pisa. A ship will be waiting for you and will take you to Dubrovnik on the Croatian side of the Adriatic Sea. That city is still in Catholic Christian hands. From there, you will need to travel secretly through mostly hostile Barbarian Muslim-controlled land to Constantinople.

"In Constantinople, you will present letters of greetings and a request for the transfer of the cross, which was kept in trust for us, to the Emperor Constantine XII and the patriarch, Basil. I would like you to know that your mission is to recover the True Cross by any means possible. If either the Eastern Church or the emperor is not amiable, then I leave it to you to devise other means. This mission will remain secret and no one but you and Jean shall know the purpose. As far as members of your party are concerned, you are a papal emissary offering gold and messages of help from the pope to Emperor Constantine.

"However, if one of you is killed, then you may entrust the secret to another member of the party. Alfaro will show you to your rooms and I want you to read the chronicle of Arthur of Brittany and the description of the cross and commit them to memory. These papers have not left the Holy City since Pope Innocent." Then turning to Rodrigo, the pope said, "To lead this group of men, you will need a title. I have asked your uncle, Cardinal Alfonso Borgia, who is a prince of the church, to adopt you. You are now officially his adopted son and with that, I will bestow the order of knighthood of the Holy See upon you. I will see you all again tomorrow after sunset."

Without further words, Cardinal Alfonso and then everyone else got up, each kissed the hand of the pope, and left him alone in the room.

~ CHAPTER TWO ~

ADVENTURES OF ARTHUR OF

BRITTANY

Alone in his room, Rodrigo reflected on all the unexpected events of that one morning. Until late last night, he'd been a happy, carefree man who enjoyed a rather precarious life as a lover of women, wine, and food. Now, he was sitting in this room in the heart of Rome, entrusted with possibly the greatest mission of all time.

Obviously, a higher purpose had brought him all the way from his insignificant little town in Spain into the presence of the pope. He kneeled down in the center of the room, facing the window, and prayed fervently. He asked God not to let him fail this saintly pope and come back empty-handed. Before supper, he met with Jean and they talked at some length about their lives.

Jean was the third son of the count de Mont Claire. As such, he would not inherit any of his father's vast fortune. Therefore, his choices in life were limited. His father provided him with excellent schooling and he was trained to be a knight at the service of a king or a prince.

However, the Knights Templar, who were always secretly looking for pious souls, spotted him and invited him to join the now-secret order.

Somehow, Jean and Rodrigo were like two lost brothers, reunited after many years of wandering, and that bond eventually would grow into a deep mutual friendship.

Later that night, Rodrigo sat in his room in the bowels of the great Castle San Angelo and read the chronicles of Arthur of Brittany. The chronicles, written on durable Egyptian paper, were old but still readable. They were written in Latin, which was easy for Rodrigo to understand. The first few sentences of the page gave thanks to the Lord for the successful completion of the mission, and then Arthur went on to explain how the True Cross was recovered. As Rodrigo studied the first page, the thought came to him that the hand that had rested on those pages while writing the words was long gone and probably had turned to dust. He was sure that the soul of the great knight was with God in paradise.

* * *

The Chronicles of Arthur of Brittany

To His Holiness Innocent III:
Chronicles of our effort to recover the most exalted cross of our Lord and savior.
In the year of our Lord 1199, my Templar brethren and I under that guidance of his eminence Cardinal Paul of

the Crusader states in Palestine, undertook the task of recovering the True Cross of our Lord, Jesus Christ.

I selected three brothers who, like me, were born in the Crusader states under Christian control. We could all speak Arabic almost like the natives, as we had to associate with infidel servants, nurses, and vendors since we were small children. Because of our fair looks and accents, we still decided to dress and pass as fair-skinned Persian merchants instead of Arabs.

We knew that the infidels had kept the holy cross in Damascus for many years but we were not aware of its location. We needed a guide who knew Damascus and could find the location of the cross.

In the summer of that year, a young, rich, Arab infidel by the name of Al Mansoor was visiting our fair city of Acre on his way from Jerusalem. His father was a prince of the city of Baghdad and he was on his way back home. At that time, the old Genovese money merchantman, Bernardo, who was perhaps sixty years or more, had just arrived from his trip to Genoa with his new young wife, Diana, who was a fair maiden from Genoa. She was a woman of extreme beauty. Her body was very well proportioned in all aspects. Above all, she had very fair skin and auburn-colored hair. The infidels find women with red hair irresistible and they carry the highest prices in the slave markets. Because of this trait, we are always on guard trying to protect our innocent fair maidens from the savages. Unfortunately, the savages sometimes succeed in kidnapping our Christian sisters and we have seen many young infidels with reddish hair or blue eyes, which proves that their mothers or grandmothers were innocent Christian pilgrims or a relative of some murdered Christian citizen.

Soon after Bernardo arrived back in Acre, he was stricken with the Fever of the Thousand Deaths and died miserably. His grief-stricken wife was left alone, waiting for a ship to take her back to her parents in Northern Italy.

Unlike the ugly Saracen women, our women do not need to wear any veils in public. As luck would have it, Al Mansoor came across Diana and was instantly besotted by her beauty. He tried to woo her with money, but the innocent Christian child vehemently rejected him.

Al Mansoor next attempted to kidnap the fair Diana. Thanks to our vigilance, he was caught with her before leaving the main gate of Acre. He knew that the penalty for kidnapping a Christian woman was death by being cut in half.

Bishop Theodore of Acre, who knew of our predicament, requested the lord governor of Acre to grant a conditional release to Al Mansoor.

The bishop and my fellow knights approached Al Mansoor and laid out our plan to him. We told him that he was under the sentence of death and the only way he could avoid it would be to cooperate with us.

As much as Al Mansoor believed in his false religion, he was even more in love with Diana. He agreed to cooperate with us on one condition and that was the hand of Diana in marriage. The infidel Al Mansoor was a virile looking young man but he was not a Christian. Diana refused his hand. After a month of living in the dungeons, he was beginning to soften up. The good news was that our fair Lady Diana had really found him attractive after being married to an old man.

Bishop Theodore suggested to Al Mansoor that he should convert to Christianity and show his true devotion by helping the brother knights recover the cross. Al Mansoor was so much in love that he eventually agreed to become a Christian like the rest of us if the fair Diana would marry him. Since Lady Diana was secretly fond of Al Mansoor, a match was easily arranged.

Al Mansoor was released from the dungeons. We had him washed and shaved, and clothed him in Christian attire and took him to the church of Bishop Theodore. In front of knights of Templar and Hospitaller and many Muslims, he denounced his false religion and accepted Christianity. He was baptized as Marco. He knew that with all those Christian and some Muslim witnesses, he could never renounce his conversion. Muslims, like Christians, would die before renouncing their religion unless they truly believed in their newfound faith. For the Muslims, the penalty for becoming a Christian is death and any Muslim who kills a converted Muslim would supposedly go to heaven.

The Christian brothers welcomed Marco wholeheartedly. He was married to Lady Diana within a week. He was allowed to enjoy his marriage bliss for one week before we approached him to remind him of his solemn promise. Much to our surprise, he welcomed the opportunity to show his new bride and us that he was a man of his word. However, Marco had the last word. He insisted that we must be circumcised before he would undertake the dangerous journey with us, for even if we looked like Persian Muslims, we were not circumcised. The discovery of four uncircumcised men would have meant death to all of us. We had to submit to this barbaric initiation of both Jews and Muslims.

Knowing that we would not voluntarily submit to such mutilation, our grand master, Gilbert Horal, arranged a surprise. On a given day, each knight was called in for a meeting with him at different times. In my case, upon arrival, I was set upon by six other knights and slaves and was laid flat on my back. One man sat on each outstretched arm and two men on each leg. My pants were torn down forcibly and then out of the shadows, a Jewish butcher of a surgeon who was also a dentist and a barber, stepped forward with his sharp razor.

The Jew gleefully cut the skin of my member and folded the remaining skin back onto itself. Then, he covered the bleeding organ with piles of charcoal ash, which eventually hardened into a cone-shaped mound surrounding my genital organ. For two weeks after the surgery, I had to walk around with no pants and just a long, thin, cotton wrap around my midriff. The hard conical-shaped ash seemed to weigh a bushel. The most painful time was when I got up in the mornings and my sinful body caused an erection.

After two weeks of agony, the ash mound was broken. I was still sore. It took another two weeks before the Jewish doctor allowed us to travel and even then, the soreness was agonizing. However, it was a blessing in disguise, as one brother was challenged in Damascus and had to prove that he was a Muslim by showing his member to the local Sharta, who are their local peace officers.

On the morning of September 12, in the year of our Lord 1199, the four circumcised brother Templar monks and Marco all dressed as Persian traders, left Acre for Jerusalem. We had with us Al Mansoor's two black slaves, who did not speak or understand anything beyond basic commands. The remainder of Al Mansoor's retinue was locked up in the castle so there would be no danger of our mission being betrayed.

After one day of hard riding with our camels, we arrived in the city of our Lord, Jerusalem. We dared not visit the Church of Holy Sepulcher for fear of being discovered. Rather, we waited, with other merchants, for the caravan that was going northeast to the city of Damascus. I was still worried that Marco would betray us. The penalty for spying was death by beheading, but by the grace of God, we were spared exposure. After one week, we departed with a caravan of two hundred people for Damascus. We had obtained some English wool from Acre and were posing as wool merchants, since English wool is in great demand in the Orient.

The road to Damascus passes through some deserts and mountainous areas. It is an ideal road for ambush and has been used by both Muslim Saracens and Christian brothers for attacking rich caravans. Twenty-five Askari soldiers guarded the caravan. Those Askaris were fierce mercenary warriors.

We tried to avoid all unnecessary contact with other fellow travelers. The Saracens are strange creatures when they travel. Every night there was drinking and dancing going on. There were plenty of women fellow travelers from Acre and Jerusalem, who traveled with this caravan for entertaining the men and obtaining gold. It shames me to say that some of those women were fallen Christians.

We arrived in Damascus after five days of traveling through the wilderness. The city of Damascus is one of the wonders of the world. It is much bigger than Jerusalem but smaller than Constantinople.

By now, we had taken Muslim names and were used to calling each other by those names only. Al Mansoor took us to a large caravanserai in the middle of the town. A caravanserai is a Saracen inn. It has a very large yard with one huge main gate through which animals, carts, and people can enter and exit. The whole yard is encircled by living quarters. These quarters are two stories high. The gate is shut late at night to keep intruders away. However, there is a small side door and a doorkeeper that allows late-night revelers to come in. The animals are cared for in the huge yard in the middle. The travelers and other merchants sleep in the rooms, which are located in the buildings that surround this yard. There is also a huge eatery place facing the main gate at the far end of the caravanserai. There, the patrons sit on the floor and are served dishes mostly of lamb, lentils, and rice with yogurt followed by various sherbets.

We told the caretaker of the caravanserai that we would be there until the next caravan left for the great city of Baghdad. Meanwhile, we started making very discreet inquiries about the True Cross.

A large city like Damascus is similar in many respects to Constantinople. It had many eating houses. It also had many drinking taverns, mostly owned by Jews and Christians, where people would go to drink wine, except that it was not done openly. There were also the usual brothels. Damascus also had male brothels where men of many ages from young to old were available for acts of fornication. This practice is very common in Saracen lands.

After some days of discreet inquiries, Al Mansoor found a veteran of the Saladin campaigns. This middle-aged man was called Al Sabah. He had obviously fallen on hard times. We fed him and listened to his war stories. He assumed that we were Persian Muslims. After a few nights, he desired to go to one of those places of ill repute where men lay with men. I could not face visiting a place of such abomination. Brothers Zachariah and Benjamin volunteered to go with him and Al Mansoor to gain his confidence. We nurtured this dog for two weeks, plied him with drinks and food, and gradually learned the truth.

Apparently, Saladin was so enraged by the massacre of Muslim hostages at Acre[1] by King Richard the Lionhearted that he had decided to burn the True Cross. His brother, Aladdin, who was more level headed, dissuaded him. Aladdin was hoping to marry King Richard's sister, Joanna, and was hoping to present the cross as a wedding gift to Joanna. However, the marriage never took place, as she already had secretly married one of the French knights.

The cross was kept wrapped up in Saladin's palace. After Saladin's death, the Saracen soldiers stripped much of the gold and jewelry from the palace. The cross was bared of its jewels and even its silken cover was stolen. The discarded cross may now be in one of the many storerooms in the palace.

1 It was rumored by some Arab historians that Richard's wife, Queen Berengaria, who accompanied him on his crusade, was captured by the Muslims. During her captivity, she fell in love with Saladin and they were secretly married in the Muslim tradition, since her marriage to Richard was not considered legal— by Muslim law, anyway. She eventually was released as part of the agreement to open Jerusalem to Christian pilgrims. Apparently, Richard never forgave Saladin for seducing his wife—not that Richard was really interested in her in the first place.

We offered to pay Al Sabah a huge sum of money for helping us to find the cross. We explained that the ruler of Baghdad would pay handsomely for such a relic and we would share some of the profit with him if he were to accompany the cross and us to Baghdad. Greed got the better of Al Sabah. We gave him some money to buy clothing befitting a rich man and he started to visit the palace and call on his old acquaintances.

For the next thirty days, every night, we would wait for him expectantly at the drinking tavern, listen to music, and watch the belly dancers. Every night he would arrive empty-handed.

Then one night, he came in very early and was excited. He said, "I think I know where it is. It is in the *Beit Ol Mal*."

"*Beit Ol Mal*" means the house of property. Every Muslim city has a central repository that is usually managed by the grand mufti or the senior religious figure of the city. All of the donations and lost properties are left there to be distributed to the poor and the needy. Also, if people die without any heirs, their property is assigned to the *Beit Ol Mal* under the supervision of the grand mufti and he is responsible for distributing it to the people who are in need.

We were happy to hear the news. Since there is usually no item of real value in those storehouses and the security is lax, it would be easy to make an entry. Nevertheless, the *Beit Ol Mal* of Damascus was large and we did not know where to look for the cross without attracting undue attention.

Then Al Mansoor suggested that we wait until Friday when almost all the people were attending the Friday prayers.

This sounded like a good idea. However, we hit a new obstacle. Al Sabah had fallen in love with one of the young lads in one of the male brothels that he was visiting. He was spending a lot of time in this place and wanted us to purchase the contract of the young lad for him before he would cooperate with us anymore.

In Muslim countries, the workers at the places of ill repute are not usually slaves. They are people in need, or people whose services have been sold in bondage for a certain period. A needy family might sell their daughter or son for a period of, say, five years. In cases like that, anyone can try to buy their freedom by working harder or others could buy their contract. None of the brother knights wanted to be a party to this kind of transaction. Al Mansoor, seeing the impasse, used his own money for the purpose. Fearing that Al Sabah would take off with the lad, he purchased the services of the young lad in his own name after exacting a promise, under oath, from each of us that we would not divulge his doing so to his wife Diana. He then promised Al Sabah that he would not touch the young man and would release him to Al Sabah outside the city walls once we had recovered the cross.

The next day, we met this young man. His name was Jamal. He was probably eighteen years old with a light complexion and brown eyes. He was dressed in white pantaloons and a tight black jacket with fine golden embroidery. I thought women would find him more attractive than men. He was wearing a dagger at his belt. I asked him why he was wearing the dagger. He smiled and said, "I am wearing this so no one can take advantage of me." I nodded but I thought to myself, "This young man is allowing anybody who wants to, to fornicate with him. What protection is he talking about?" Anyway, Jamal stayed with us in the caravanserai.

Two weeks went by before we found a Friday that seemed to fit our needs. We lay in wait early Friday morning and as the faithful left their posts for the communal prayers, we managed to get in through a side door to the main warehouse. This warehouse was immense by any standard. It was a dusty place littered with broken furniture, pots and pans, and sacks of dry foodstuffs. We were careful in our search but did not succeed in finding the cross. The hour was passing so we left the warehouse as we found it and retreated, leaving a window slightly open for future access.

In desperation, Al Mansoor, who was homesick for his wife, took a risk and using Jamal as bait approached one of the guards. Many Saracens are more interested in boys and men than in women. The guard agreed to help. He wanted Jamal to work there as his helper. In a huge warehouse like that, he could have his way with Jamal whenever he wanted. The Arab thought that we were doing this for greed to steal something of value, so he did not question our motives further.

Eventually, Jamal found the cross and informed us. There was no point in delaying any further. We brought our camels to the front of the warehouse and picked up the cross, which was wrapped in an old blanket by Jamal, and headed out of town after giving some gold coins to the delighted guard.

Al Sabah wanted to know why we were going west instead of east toward Baghdad. Al Mansoor explained that we were going that way to throw off anyone who may be following us. We chose the mountain side, away from the regular road, and rode our camels until dusk before disembarking for the night.

As we were sitting by a little charcoal fire that had been lit by one of the slaves, Brother Zachariah asked Jamal how he had ended up in Damascus in such a place. Jamal said that it was a long story. We were all eager to hear it, so he told us his tale.

* * *

The Story of Jamal

My true name is Timothy. My parents are Nestorian Christians who still live near Baghdad. My father had three sons and two daughters. He was a successful merchant but made some bad decisions and went broke. Since childhood, I was told that I looked more like a girl than a boy. When I was about ten years old, my father, for fear of kidnappers and seducers of young boys, hired a servant to look after me.

A few years later, some sheik from the marshlands of the South had apparently seen me and had taken a fancy to me. This sheik, who was named Khazaal, bought all my father's debts. He told my father that he would trade all the debts for his third son. Initially, my father did not accept, but he faced jail time and the whole family could then be sold as slaves. In the end, he was forced into accepting the offer.

For days, I was in tears. I knew what that man had in mind and was scared. In addition, I knew it was a crime against nature to have that kind of relationship with another man. I even ran away from my home, but the servants caught me and brought me back.

I was about fourteen when the sheik sent two body-guards to take me south to his tribe. We traveled for four days on horseback until we arrived at an oasis, which was where his tribe was located. The sheik had several wives and many children, some older than me.

I saw the sheik for the first time that afternoon. He was about sixty years old and his skin was leathery, wrin-kled, and burnt by years of exposure to the sun. He was very happy to see me. There was to be a celebration that night. First, I was led to the women's tent where I was prepared by making sure that all my body hair was removed.

After the ceremony, the sheik took possession of me. He was a very nice man and treated me better than he treated his wives. The wives and other children liked me as well since I was not a threat to any of them. I soon realized that he was interested in being the submissive as well as the dominant partner in our relationship. At first, I was appalled by having a relationship with him, but interestingly enough, after six months or so I did not mind anymore. The sheik died two years later.

In his will, he officially freed me from my bondage and left me some money. I could have stayed on with the tribe but decided to leave and see the world. I stopped by to see my family and afterwards wandered around. In Damascus I ran out of funds and, in return for money, I signed on for one year with the owner of the male brothel, since it was the only profession that I knew well. I was there barely three months when you arrived and Al Sabah took a fancy to me. One day, I may marry and have children of my own but I am happy now with Al Sabah.

* * *

At this point, Al Sabah wanted to marry Jamal right away. In some Muslim lands, marriage vows between two men are allowed.

Al Mansoor, like most Muslims, knew the marriage vows by heart. That is because Muslims are allowed to have temporary wives, which they call concubines. Therefore, when they arrive at a new town or feel the urge, they can marry a woman for twenty-four hours or even less and feel confident that they have not performed an act of adultery, which is against their religion. A temporary marriage to a concubine could be very short, indeed. A man visiting a brothel can utter the words and be married to a harlot for fifteen minutes. It is all religiously legal but very insincere.

Al Mansoor rattled off some verses in Arabic and declared Jamal to be Al Sabah's concubine for one week. He then handed Jamal's contract to Al Sabah, who promptly burned the paper in the fire, thus freeing Jamal from any obligations. The couple moved a short distance from the camp and spent their first night of married life together. The following morning, Al Mansoor told a tired but content Al Sabah that we had decided to sell the cross to the Christians in Acre since it would bring a better price. He was welcome to come with us or he could go back. Al Mansoor gave him the gold as we had promised. Al Sabah and Jamal decided to go with us at least until where the road branches off to Jerusalem.

Before leaving the camp, we unraveled the cross for the first time. We all fell down and started weeping at the sight of the cross that had held the body of our savior so long ago. The cross was shaped like a large letter "T." The headboard, which the Romans had attached to the top of the cross, was gone. The wood was old and rotten in some places. The third bottom part of the cross had been broken and was missing. It was now probably less than half of its original size. All the jewels, diamonds, and gold that had been adorning it had long been forcibly extracted. Some of the mirrors that had covered the cross were still intact and reflected the sunlight. I moved until I could bask my face in the reflected light from one of the mirrors. I kneeled there praying for forgiveness for all of my sins and salvation in the other world. It was more wonderful than any confession that I had ever made. I felt touched by our Lord and a huge weight was lifted from my shoulders.

We rode post-haste to Acre. Al Sabah and Jamal decided to go to Jerusalem and we left the lovers at the cross-road. In Acre, we went to see Bishop Theodore with our find. He was joyous and grateful. We left the cross at his church and an eager Al Mansoor, who was now again called Marco, went to see his bride, who was impatiently waiting for him. We had been away about ten weeks.

The bishop and our grand master decided to send the cross to Constantinople and then to Rome as soon as possible to avoid its recapture by the Arabs. Three days later, a ship was leaving for Constantinople from the port of Acre. The three brothers and I took the cross onboard. We were planning to leave Marco and his wife behind in Acre, but they decided to come with us to Constantinople. They had plans to go to Genoa to live near her parents. It was not safe for a converted Muslim to venture outside the city walls of Acre, anyway.

After a four-day journey, we arrived in Constantinople. I went to see the patriarch with letters of recommendation from Bishop Theodore. He fell on his face at the sight of the holy object and like everyone else, wept with joy. Next, we took the cross to Emperor Alexius III. The patriarch and the emperor took joint custody of the cross and issued the receipt, which I have attached to the letter. I have also drawn a picture of the cross for Your Holiness, which is also attached.

Your Holiness, I cannot but emphasize the importance of sending a ship with emissaries to take this holiest of objects back to Rome. I beseech thee. Any delay may cause the loss of our savior's cross forever. I feel that my life's work has been done and my destiny has been fulfilled. I am going back to Acre to defend our Christian cities, die fighting for our Lord, and join my martyred brethren.

Your servant in Christ,

Arthur of Brittany

* * *

The document was dated December 1199

~ CHAPTER THREE ~

RODRIGO BORGIA

It had all started two years earlier, late in September in 1451. Young Rodrigo was walking on the soft sandy beaches of Valencia in Spain, looking into the distant horizon, and reflecting on his future. Rodrigo was then just over twenty years old. He was tall and very handsome and had that certain charisma that attracted women of all ages. Even men found him a very pleasant person and were proud to be his friends.

The day had been balmy. The horizon of the Mediterranean Sea was turning a fiery copper and tiny wavelets danced on the surface. Dusk was settling in.

For a twenty year old in the Middle Ages, Rodrigo was very well educated. He sensed that his destiny was calling him. He had been offered a huge dowry of land and titles and a position at the Royal Court in Madrid if he married the young girl who had adored him since they were children. Alternatively, he could follow the spirit of adventure that was calling him to perform a pre-ordained task that no one had ever done before.

Looking at the magnificent, darkening turquoise sea melding with the dark red sky, he wondered how many people had stood on that remote stretch of beach a thousand years ago and who would follow his footsteps in the hundreds of years to come.

Unlike most inhabitants of Europe, who were drowning in superstition, Rodrigo was a logical thinker.

He sat there watching the sun sink into the far off waters of the immense sea and the moon rise to illuminate the sea and dust the little wavelets with shimmering rays of silver and gold. He was still there when distant church bells rang, marking the midnight hour.

Rodrigo was part of a large family in Valencia. Actually, he was born in Xativa, a small town near Valencia in Spain. His family was not wealthy but it was well respected because ancestors on his father's side had been major figures in the struggle to free Spain from the Moors. The Muslim Moors still controlled the lower half of Spain, so the nobility, the Catholic Church, and the common people glamorized war heroes.

Rodrigo's mother came from peasant stock and the combination made Rodrigo physically strong and mentally superior to many of his contemporaries. Because of the family's name and the respect it commanded, Rodrigo had received an excellent education along with the offspring of some of the richest families of Valencia.

Rodrigo's mother had died when Rodrigo was about three years old. His father, Jofre, married his second wife, Elisabetta, nearly a year later and they had a daughter, which they named Isabella in honor of Rodrigo's mother.

Since childhood, Rodrigo had a talent for making friends. In school, other students were eager to help him. He was a handsome boy and after puberty attracted the attention of many women, who found him somewhat irresistible. He had a natural charm that attracted people. His closest friend, Pedro, was the son of the rich and powerful Don Sebastian, count of La Rocha. Pedro lived with his parents, his younger sister Cristina, and many servants and retainers in a large mansion. Cristina was a couple of years younger than Rodrigo and their parents had already discussed their eventual betrothal. Almost everyone except Rodrigo was aware that Cristina had a crush on Rodrigo. Pedro's father was often away in Madrid, since he was a member of the Royal Court. Pedro's mother Carolina was an attractive woman of about thirty, although she looked younger. She was a vivacious woman, very different from Rodrigo's stepmother, who was plain and ordinary. Carolina had long, black, curly hair that cascaded down to her shoulders. As a rule, she did not wear the customary Spanish mantilla when she was at home. Sometimes, Rodrigo would see her with her feet bare, singing as she attended to her duties.

Carolina was always affectionate to Rodrigo and would insist that he stay overnight in their big mansion as often as possible.

Rodrigo was especially fond of the vast library that count La Rocha had acquired to prove his literary interests. Rodrigo, who had an insatiable appetite for reading books and committing them to memory, was the only person who really used this magnificent library, which was stocked with books on history, literature, mathematics, medicine, arts, and philosophy in Latin, Spanish, French, and Italian. The count owned some Arabic books on medicine and mathematics, as well.

People in the household seldom entered the library, except Pedro or Cristina, who would try to pull Rodrigo out of the books and outside to play.

Rodrigo's maternal uncle, Alfonso Borgia, was a cardinal in the Vatican. There was a possibility that Rodrigo would also be called to the service of the church. Therefore, Rodrigo learned Latin and Italian, starting at a very young age. He also could understand some Greek and French. With the help of an old friar, he had taught himself to read Arabic. He was very fortunate in having this library at his disposal, for it enabled him to converse with much older people about philosophy, history, and religion. Pedro's father and his friends were always astonished at Rodrigo's command of those subjects. Even at school, his history teacher, at times, deferred to him.

Because of diversity of the books that he had been reading, Rodrigo's religious beliefs were rather vague. While he believed in God, he was not sure about many events in the Bible that could not be logically explained. He never dared to express his beliefs in public lest he be branded a heretic, which would destroy him and his family.

Rodrigo's sexual urges had begun, like those of most other boys, at adolescence. He knew that he liked girls but he had not had an opportunity to fulfill his dreams. Because of his good looks, and much to his dismay, he also attracted the attentions and interests of some men.

When Rodrigo was about thirteen years old, he began to notice Carolina in a different way. Sometimes, as she brushed by him, the aroma of her perfume and the sheer power of her presence would make him feel warm and slightly giddy. What was worse, he would even get twinges of sexual arousal that made him feel guilty. He actually detested himself for being attracted to a married woman who was the mother of his closest friend.

By modern standards, Rodrigo's sexual education began at an early age. However, in the Middle Ages, boys were married by sixteen and if a girl was not married by fourteen it was considered strange. (Juliet, in Shakespeare's *Romeo and Juliet*, was only thirteen years old.)

Rodrigo had no control over his feelings and soon matters got worse. Often times, Carolina would hang around him and ruffle his hair or massage the back of his neck. The proximity made him crazy. He was worried that she would notice the bulge in his pants and would be angry with him for having sexual desire for her. His emotions for Carolina were so unthinkable and so forbidden that he did not even admit his feelings to his confessor. Soon, Rodrigo could not sleep at night. He felt ill and looked pale. He lost his appetite and his father and stepmother were concerned for him. In those days, it was not unusual for a person to become sick one day and die the next.

Rodrigo kept praying for divine guidance but soon realized that he was in love with the mother of his best friend and no amount of praying could cure this particular kind of sickness. He tried staying away, but that only added to his sense of loss. He was brokenhearted. His friends Pedro and Cristina could not understand his new behavior and were unhappy and upset at him for ignoring them.

How does a thirteen-year-old cope with the sudden awakening of his sexuality, his loyalty to his friends, and the notion of adultery with a married woman?

Eventually, Rodrigo gave up his solitude and started visiting his friends again. Carolina, like his own stepmother, was concerned about Rodrigo's health and lack of appetite. She tried to be nice to him and would hug him longer than usual to show her concern. Ever since Rodrigo had been a young boy, Carolina had greeted him by kissing him on his lips, just as she kissed her children. Now, every time their lips touched, he felt a jolt going through his body all the way down to his loins. Apparently, Carolina noticed it, too. She was looking at him differently and sometimes when he was playing a board game with Pedro and Cristina or doing his homework, she would stand next to him for a few minutes, put her arms around him, and caress his arms with her soft, warm hands.

Then one day, after about six months of torture, Rodrigo was spending the weekend at Pedro's house. The boys were planning to go horseback riding the next day when they received a message from Pedro's father asking his son to join him in the capital as soon as possible. There was a chance that he could introduce Pedro to the royal court. There were many old noble families in the country that had never been presented to the king.

In almost every country in Europe, it was considered a great honor to be presented to the king and the queen. Nobles went to extraordinary lengths to become part of the establishment. They bribed court officials with land or money or offered their young daughters as bait to the king. There was no disgrace in being the brother or father of a king's mistress or the grandfather or uncle of a king's bastard.

Given the possibility of becoming recognized at an early age, Pedro had to pack and leave rather quickly. He suggested that Rodrigo stay as the man of the house until he came back from Madrid. Rodrigo, feeling anxiety mixed with anticipation, tried to make an excuse but Carolina and Cristina insisted that he stay on and look after them.

Pedro left the next morning. The first day passed uneventfully. Rodrigo got up as usual, had some breakfast, and went to chapel with the others.

On the second day after Pedro's departure, Rodrigo went to the library to indulge in his favorite pastime of selecting and reading those wonderful books. It was after lunch and it was the siesta time. Rodrigo was sitting in the library reading in Latin about Caesar and his conquest of Egypt. Normally, Rodrigo did not have an afternoon nap. However, he soon fell asleep while reading the book and slipped into a recurring and disturbing dream.

He dreamed that he was walking alone in a dense forest. As he walked along, he would come across a beautiful woman whose face was covered with a white, lace veil. She was standing near a waterfall feeding some black swans. Rodrigo would try to approach her but every time he got close to her, she glided away. At the edge of a waterfall, Rodrigo would catch up to her and try to remove her veil. As soon as his hands touched the veil, his feet would slip and he would start sliding down the waterfall, which seemed to culminate in a never-ending void. He would scream in fear and wake up soaking in cold sweat. Even though he was not very religious, he had told his confessor about his recurring dream and was told that it was normal for young boys to have strange dreams. That did not help him. He could not help but think that the woman in his dream must be Carolina and he could never get close to her because she was a forbidden fruit and the penalty for trying to remove her veil of innocence would be everlasting damnation.

He was having the same dream when he woke up with a start. Someone was gently massaging his temples. He could smell sweet perfume in the air. He tried to get up but gentle hands held him down and he heard the sweet voice of Carolina. "Relax, Rodrigo, relax. You just had a bad dream." Rodrigo looked up into Carolina's beautiful face and her dark, mesmerizing eyes. She bent down and a cascade of dark, curly, sweet-smelling hair almost covered his face. Carolina's face moved lower and she planted a kiss on his forehead. He was already aroused in his dream and that kiss made matters worse.

Years of coaching had hammered into his head the rule that a gentleman stood in presence of women, so he stood up uneasily, his head bowed in embarrassment. He was aware of his state of sexual arousal. Carolina looked at his bulging pants, smiled, and said, "What do we have here, my dear? Have you been having a naughty dream?"

Rodrigo was beet red in the face with shame and stammered something incoherent. Carolina took a step toward him, hugged him, and said, "You can tell me all, my dear, you know." Rodrigo was quite tall for his age. Carolina was about his height. Rodrigo lifted his head and, for a fraction of a second, their eyes met.

Lust won! Their lips met, the dam broke, and Rodrigo's world changed forever. Carolina clasped Rodrigo's head with her small hands and looked into his eyes. "Do you know how much I have suffered because of my love for you?" she asked almost irately.

That one kiss had taken away Rodrigo's inhibitions. He felt lightheaded and content to be in love. Why should he care that she was the mother of his best friend? It was love that matters above all. Rodrigo responded, "I have been suffering, too. I have not been able to sleep nor eat properly for months because of my love for you."

A smile of recognition lit Carolina's face. "So, that is what has been happening to you," she said. "I should have guessed. I am so glad to be in your arms and you will not regret loving me. As my lover, you may call me Carolina. I would love to hear you whisper that you love Carolina forever, in my ear." They kissed some more. Carolina could not contain herself. Her hands were all over him, caressing him, and arousing him ever more. She slid her hand inside his trousers and felt his hardness, which was hot with desire. She gave him an approving smile as she stroked him deftly. "More tonight, my dearest love," she whispered.

They spent the next hour cuddling, kissing, and swearing their love to each other. They knew that almost no one ever came to the library.

At last, Carolina said, "I will have to go now, my dearest; will you come to my bedroom after midnight? I think it is safer that way. Cristina sleeps with her nanny and will not be coming to my room at night." With that, she gave him another kiss, wiped the makeup from his lips and face with her handkerchief, and was gone.

CHAPTER FOUR

CAROLINA'S STORY

Carolina was born to a middle-class family in Barcelona. Her father died when she was about six years old and the little money that family had soon evaporated. In those days, very few opportunities were available to a middle-class girl with no dowry. Carolina was descended from the female side of a noble family but as was the custom in those days and for many centuries to come, only the male descendants would get the titles, the land, and the money.

There were only two opportunities for a highborn girl without a dowry or source of income. One was to become the mistress of a married man. The other avenue, especially if the girl was not very attractive, was to become a companion to an older rich woman.

For lower-class girls, the choice was either going into service as a maid or entering the shadowy world of entertainers, barmaids, and prostitutes. The very lucky girls in this category would catch a rich farmer as a husband or become mistresses to the rich. Those opportunities were very rare, however. Nell Gwen in England and Madam de Barrie in France are among the few lower-class girls who became associated with royalty.

In Europe until the 1930s, it was customary that girls without dowries would be tutored in social graces, etiquette, and techniques of how to please a man. It was hoped that by the time they were sixteen or soon thereafter, a rich man—maybe even a distant relative—would take them on as a mistress and provide them with all the amenities that they needed. Of course, the girl had to be quite attractive, witty, and sociable.

Therefore, at an early age, Carolina's mother and maternal uncle, noticing how attractive she was, decided to invest in her education and train her to be a potential mistress. Her mother and uncle scraped together enough money to send her to good schools and private tutors who instructed in the arts of dancing, playing the piano, conversing, and being pleasant to men.

When girls like Carolina reached the age of puberty, a retired mistress would teach them the sexual side of relationships with men and how to avoid unwanted pregnancies.

A successful placement with a rich man would mean a life of luxury for the girl, with servants and a nice house. The details of the agreement would be handled like a contract, written and mutually agreed upon between the mother or guardian and the client. The girl's close relatives would receive a lump sum or a stipend upon conclusion of the agreement.

Naturally, in the fifteenth century and even beyond, an untouched maiden was much more valuable than a woman who had been "used." So, families closely guarded a girl's chastity.

Another custom introduced by the Muslims who ruled Spain for centuries was anal sex. A doctor or a midwife could easily verify virginity. However, there was no way to ascertain if a girl had ever had anal intercourse or, for that matter, how many times she had indulged in it. Therefore, then as now, girls who wanted to engage in sex acts with men but did not want to risk pregnancy or loss of their hymen practiced anal sex. In addition, families who were in desperate financial need allowed their daughters to have that kind of relationship with strangers for a fee. In those cases, the mother or a trusted chaperone always stood by behind an unlocked door, ready to intervene if the man tried to take advantage of the girl by force or seduction. Even to this day, this practice is common in many Middle Eastern countries.

As soon as Carolina was about twelve years old, she was introduced to wealthy, titled men who could be potential lovers. As in some other poor families, her mother allowed her to meet and be intimate with men who were eager to part with money for some of her favors as long as intimacy did not extend to reproductive parts of her body. Carolina was a very calculating girl and did not allow herself to be abased or seduced by any man. Eventually, she was introduced to Don Sebastian, who was actually a distant relative, and she caught his eye right away. Terms were arranged and she moved into a private residence in Madrid with servants and maids and was given cash and jewelry.

Don Sebastian was betrothed to the daughter of a rich landowning aristocrat from southern Spain. However, he fell in love with Carolina and as luck would have it, within a few months, Carolina became pregnant. Therefore, instead of fathering an illegitimate child, Don Sebastian hastily married Carolina and together they moved to his mansion in Valencia to avoid gossip and scandal. It was fashionable for the married nobility to keep one or two mistresses on the side and after his second child,

Cristina, was born, Don Sebastian found a mistress in Madrid and started to neglect his wife's conjugal needs. He was, nevertheless, a devoted father, a great provider for his family, and very fair to all of his tenants and servants.

CHAPTER FIVE

RODRIGO AND CAROLINA

Rodrigo spent the rest of the afternoon wondering about his good luck. Nevertheless, he was apprehensive about what he was supposed to do that night, since he had never been with a woman before. He did not know what to do and was too ashamed to admit it to Carolina.

At dinnertime, Cristina was her usual happy self. Carolina was cheerful and bubbly. Rodrigo was a bit reserved. He avoided making eye contact with Carolina for fear of betraying their illicit meeting that afternoon. In Spain, the dinner is served late. After dinner, Cristina wanted to play a board game with Rodrigo. Rodrigo obliged and they had some fun. Cristina was an able player; she could beat her brother at chess but she usually lost to Rodrigo because she concentrated on him rather than on the game. Around eleven o'clock, the nanny took Cristina to her bedroom. Carolina dismissed the servants and offered a glass of sherry to Rodrigo. They drank and talked about generalities and how good it was that Pedro had been called to the court. Near midnight, Carolina walked over to Rodrigo, took his head in her hand, kissed him on the lips, whispered into his ear, "I will see you in half an hour," and departed the living room.

Rodrigo went to his bedroom to change and prepare for meeting the love of his life. The next half an hour seemed like an eternity to him. Most Spanish bedrooms had a bedpan and a watering can. The bedpan was used at night to avoid the long trip in the dark to the toilet. The watering can was used for washing one's face and hands. He cleansed his body and cleansed his teeth with a velvet cloth, as was customary, and finally rinsed his mouth with a very dry red wine.

A few minutes after midnight, he started to walk from his bedroom to Carolina's bedroom. The mansion was a three-story building. Like most Spanish mansions, the ground floor was dedicated to the dining room, the sewing room, the drawing/living room, and a storage area. The servants lived in the basement, which was where the kitchen and the laundry were located. The Children lived on the second floor on the south side of the building. The parents lived in a suite on the north side of the building. There were other guest bedrooms on this floor, also. The third floor housed the children's playroom, a large game room, and additional guest bedrooms and storage areas. Rodrigo's bedroom was next to Pedro's and two doors away from Cristina's bedroom on the second floor. Rodrigo had to walk the entire length of the corridor from one end of the building to the other to get to Carolina's bedroom.

Normally, he would use a candle or an oil lamp to move around at night. This night, however, Rodrigo could not do that for fear of attracting attention. He had to pass Cristina's bedroom where, he knew, her nanny would be sleeping near the door, guarding her charge. As he stepped softly in the dark, groping for the walls, he thought about how he would make the return journey without being discovered. He stumbled a few times, once nearly falling down the staircase to the ground floor, before he finally made it to Carolina's suite.

Carolina and her husband shared a suite but slept in separate bedrooms. The suite was designed in the French style with an anteroom and a bedroom on either side. The two bedrooms also were connected via a powder room, and each bedroom had its own independent door to the hallway.

Rodrigo had been to Carolina's bedroom many times while playing with Pedro and Cristina. Carolina's door was unlocked. He twisted the handle, entered, and closed the door behind him very quickly. Two large tall candles, one on the dressing table and the other by the side of the large, four-poster bed, provided dim light. A gentle breeze wafted through the open windows. The light from the moon shone through translucent lace curtains and cast shadows on the opposite wall. Perfume filled his nostrils. Warmth tingled in pit of his stomach. He felt light-headed and happy in anticipation of the excitement of things to come.

Carolina, wearing a flimsy robe tied loosely in the front, was sitting at the side of her bed. She beckoned to him. He rushed over and she received him with open arms. They rolled over on top of the bed and cuddled each other. Carolina said, "I have been sitting here anxiously waiting for you since I came to my bedroom. I am glad you are here." Rodrigo could feel the firm breasts hidden under her robe.

After a few kisses, Carolina whispered seductively, "Just stay on this bed and let me undress you." Rodrigo was wearing only a tunic and long cotton pants held together by a cotton cord. He was barefoot because he did not want to make noise while crossing the hallway. Carolina helped him remove both pieces of clothing and stepped back to admire the athletic body of this virile lad lying on her bed. He had the face of Roman statues of the pagan gods with a smaller and more attractive nose. His muscles and sinews were strong and already bulging with power.

In the semi-darkness, she could not really see his pubic area. Carolina flung her robe wide open to display a young, tan-colored body that had aged little since her late teens. With the robe still open, and with a little cry of joy, she jumped on top of Rodrigo on the massive bed. They felt each other's naked bodies for the first time.

Rodrigo had never experienced the hot sensation of a woman's body before. In fact, since his mother had died when he was a child, he had not been in close contact with any female— until that morning, that is. The experience was a transmutation from boy to a man. The sensation of those firm breasts and their stiff, pointed nipples against his chest drove his mind wild. The smoothness of her body was beyond what he had imagined in his wildest dreams about women.

For Carolina, having this young virile virgin under her body was mind blowing. She had been faithful to her husband ever since marrying him fourteen years earlier when she was barely fifteen, even though it was well known that Don Sebastian had one mistress in the capital and probably another in Valencia.

She lifted her head and looking into his dark eyes said, "I am going to teach you about love. When I am finished with you, you will be an irresistible lover. I know you are impatient now; I can tell by the hard dagger that is throbbing against my belly. Let me show you." With that, she rolled over on her back and pulled him on top of her. She opened her thighs wide to let his youthful hardness rest on her scorching pubic area.

Now, she said, "You must caress and gently nibble at my breasts and don't stop until I tell you to. But don't get carried away with your teeth."

Rodrigo obeyed. It had been years since Don Sebastian, Carolina's husband, had done anything like that to her. She had always loved to have her breasts stroked and her nipples sucked by her husband, but now Don Sebastian had his mistresses and was not interested in her. It seemed, too, that sometimes he resented her since he had been forced into marrying her because she was pregnant with Pedro, who, nevertheless, was still his only legitimate son.

After a few minutes, Carolina said, "That is enough for now. I do not want you to waste your seeds on the sheets." She pulled herself up a bit so that his member was at the proximity of her throbbing love tunnel. She reached down, gently grabbed his instrument and guided it into her hot, molten channel.

He pushed right in. It felt snug, warm, and moist; its walls gently squeezing and releasing his manhood. He started making love to her instinctively. The feeling of that entry was so stimulating that he did not last very long and soon had his first orgasm inside a woman.

Carolina, laughing lightly, said, "Don't worry, my sweet; I did not expect you to do any different the first time around. Wash yourself and I will be back shortly."

In the candlelight, Rodrigo used the bedpan and the watering can to wash his crotch and dried himself with the towel that lay next to it. Carolina cleaned herself in the powder room and was back very quickly. She kissed him on the lips lovingly and said, "You really had a lot of seeds stored there, my señor!" Soon, under the expert hands of Carolina, Rodrigo was back in action.

That night, Rodrigo and Carolina made passionate love until it was nearly dawn. They fell sleep for short periods; but it was Rodrigo who would wake up first and initiate another bout of lovemaking. He left her suite before Cristina's nanny would wake up for her morning prayers and sneaked back into his room. He fell asleep almost immediately and did not wakeup until it was nearly time for lunch.

* * *

After Rodrigo left, Carolina had a lot of cleaning up to do. She had anticipated that there would be many telltale stains on the bed sheets, and she knew the maids would notice. She had prepared the bed by putting waterproof oilcloth under the bed sheet and a large towel on top of it. In addition, she had mounds of cotton wool next to the bed that she used to clean Rodrigo and herself every time they had sex.

As soon as Rodrigo was gone, she emptied the bedpans out the window and hid the towel and the cotton wools. She could wash the towel discreetly and throw the cotton wools away in the garbage later.

* * *

For the next three weeks, Carolina and Rodrigo continued their liaison every night. However, after the first few days, they were both sore from their carnal activities and had to stop for a day or two. Rodrigo thought that they must have done it at least forty times in those three weeks.

In addition to her bedroom, they met in the library and in one of the guest rooms whenever the opportunity arose. Several times, they went for rides in the country and had encounters under the open skies. Carolina showed Rodrigo an abandoned shepherd's shack on Don Sebastian's land that they cleaned up as a future meeting place.

Rodrigo knew that he had committed one of the deadliest sins according to the Bible. The Spanish Church was the most conservative and oppressive in Europe and Rodrigo had no doubt that if anybody found out about their affair, they would both be dead. He had no illusions about that. If he was merciful, Don Sebastian would run Rodrigo through with his sword and strangle his adulterous wife and no one would dare to blame him. Such was the power of their passion that despite it all, they continued their affair.

Rodrigo decided to learn to defend himself better. He was good with a sword, as fencing had been part of his education. However, a sword is bulky and not easily hidden. Rodrigo visited the mansion's armory on the third floor, which was full of weapons that a feudal baron would need to arm his subjects and guards in times of war and conflict. Rodrigo picked several daggers and stilettos and started practicing with them. Within three weeks, he could hit a bull's eye at thirty paces.

Thereafter, he always carried a dagger under his belt and a stiletto tied to his right ankle. Before going to bed, he would tuck them under the mattress or pillow or under a pile of clothing on the floor next to the bed. Except when he was in the seminary, Rodrigo never gave up this practice and it served him well.

* * *

During those three weeks, Carolina, who had fallen in love with Rodrigo, trained him in all aspects of lovemaking. After all, she had been well trained in all facets of copulation before marrying Don Sebastian.

The first thing Carolina told Rodrigo was to always shave his pubic hair, for it allowed deeper penetration and the tiny stubbles could tickle and excite a female, especially if entry was done from behind. She did not shave herself, because her husband did not allow her to do so, but instead used a pair of gold scissors to cut her tufts of thick hair very short. She tutored him in the six positions of lovemaking. She educated him on how to exercise self-control to delay his orgasm and give more satisfaction to his partner. She showed him how to devour a woman's sexual organ, how to suck it, what parts to nibble on, and how to bring her to the height of passion. She showed him how a woman should suck on a man's organ without biting it to give him one of the ultimate pleasures of lovemaking. She told him how to restrain himself with unmarried girls and widows and pull out before orgasm to avoid making them pregnant.

Finally, she trained him in the forbidden art of anal intercourse, which can come in handy with young virgins, widows, and spinsters since it will never make them pregnant. In addition, it could be immensely enjoyable to both parties if done properly. Cleanliness was very important in this kind of sex. In Europe in those days, bathing was not something that people did every day. Carolina, being a very meticulous woman, washed her intimate parts before allowing Rodrigo near her.

Rodrigo, with his years of pent up sexual feelings, absorbed the information and indeed improved upon it. In the coming weeks and months, Rodrigo mastered lovemaking much better than most of his contemporaries did.

Eventually, Carolina received word that Don Sebastian and Pedro were on their way back. Now, Rodrigo was worried that despite all their precautions, Carolina may be pregnant.

A proud Don Sebastian and a joyful Pedro arrived back one afternoon after being gone for almost four weeks. There were parties and celebrations during the next few days. Rodrigo's father, Jofre, was hoping to announce the engagement of Rodrigo and Cristina, but Rodrigo managed to dissuade him for the time being.

As soon as Don Sebastian was back, Carolina slipped into his bedroom a few times to make sure that they were intimate. It was a wise move, because she was pregnant and in less than nine months, Don Sebastian, the count of La Rocha, was the proud father of Rodrigo's baby boy.

The relationship between Rodrigo and Carolina continued for two more years. Having been trained so expertly by Carolina and being able to put his own theories into practice, Rodrigo soon found other lovers to satisfy his intense sexual appetite. He was careful, however, not to approach the young girls of the rich and powerful families. He found a few young rich widows and the wives of several army and navy officers who were in need of male companionship while their husbands were away. He was so good at his craft that once they'd slept with him they would shower him with gifts and keep inviting him back.

Rodrigo and his half-sister, Isabella, were fond of each other to the point of obsession. By the time he was nearly eighteen years old, they were lovers in almost every sense of the word, yet he was careful not to ruin her chances of getting married. He truly wished that he could marry her himself but, of course, that was not possible.

Isabella eventually was betrothed to the son of a wealthy nobleman in Madrid. She received a big dowry with the help of Rodrigo and his lover, Carolina. Isabella came for a visit a few months after her betrothal. Since she was no longer a maiden and there was no fear of unwanted pregnancy, Rodrigo and Isabella were able to consummate their lifelong love.

Both families pressed Rodrigo to marry Cristina. Rodrigo liked Cristina but was not attracted to her and somehow could not bring himself to sleep with the mother and the daughter at the same time.

Eventually, the pressure proved too much for him. He gave up his worldly life to join a seminary and become a priest like his maternal uncle, Alfonso. Rodrigo spent two years at the seminary and impressed his teachers with his knowledge and intellect. Some predicted that he might even become a cardinal one day. However the seminary life bored him. He wrote to his uncle in Rome and asked him to send for him. His wish was granted and Rodrigo was called to Rome.

It was a crossroads. Rodrigo had to make a decision. Should he marry Cristina and get the noble title that his family truly deserved for its years of bravery in battles against the Moors? Or should he go to Rome as an apprentice priest?

One September night at the beach, he finally decided to go to Rome.

The news devastated his parents and Don Sebastian's family, and none more that Cristina, who had loved him longer than anyone else in the world. He stood by his decision and said his good-byes. He met Carolina for the last time and they spent a passionate afternoon in the abandoned shepherd's hut. No one, but Carolina knew how to drain him of all his energy. After three hours of passion, he could hardly get on his horse to go home.

* * *

Rodrigo left Valencia by ship and was in Rome via Naples within three weeks. The seat of Christendom amazed Rodrigo with its sophistication and opulence.

While in Rome, Rodrigo received news that Emili, who was one of the rich widows whom he used to frequent in Valencia, had died suddenly of unknown causes. She had left him a considerable fortune. It was then that Rodrigo decided to postpone his quest for priesthood and became one of the idle rich of Rome.

He enjoyed his new life of debauchery and decadence and in a very short period, he managed to offend many powerful Roman families. At first, the Romans being more sophisticated and tolerant than the Spaniards were, did not react violently to infidelity. In Rome, rumors abounded about who slept with whom and casual sex was not always taken seriously.

However, there were limitations to the Romans' broadmin-dedness. The Colonnas and the Contis were the two most pow-erful families of Rome, followed by the Orsinis. Rodrigo had seduced the wives and daughters of all three clans. He had devel-oped a death wish; his life was without purpose so he was not afraid of dying. He became a marked man. There was a price on his head.

The call of destiny came quite unexpectedly. One afternoon, a papal messenger accompanied by two Swiss Guards called on him to tell him that the pope, Nicholas V, wanted to see him right away.

CHAPTER SIX

PRINCESS AZIZA

On a balmy spring day Aziza was sitting on a bench in the lush greenhouse garden of the Royal Palace of Edirne, reading a beautifully hand-printed copy of Rumi's book of poetry. Aziza, a poet herself, found joy and happiness in reading the great poet's magical words. Beside her was her diary in which she wrote her own poetry. Aziza was a highly educated young woman who spoke several languages. In fact, like her compatriot Rumi, she wrote her poetry in the Persian language rather than in the guttural Turkish language of the Ottomans.

The Byzantine emperors who had ruled that part of the world for centuries had built a vast indoor greenhouse garden when Edirne was a Greek city called Adrianopolis. The garden was enclosed in glass and heated in the winter to keep the exotic plants alive. Vents in the roof kept the place cool in the hot summer months.

Aziza's mother had died when she was barely three years old. Her father, Sultan Murat, had assigned Katarina, an Albanian noble captive, who was barely eighteen, to be her nanny. Aziza had always lived a sheltered life. She never ventured outside the harem without a retinue of guards and eunuchs. She had no close friends or confidants except Katarina and a few carefully selected noble girls. Katarina herself was an attractive woman but since she was a captive, she did not have an opportunity to marry and live a normal life. This was the norm for the subjugated people under the Ottomans.

Even though the sultan and other male members of the court engaged in all kinds of sexual activity, the women were segregated and kept in isolation. Aziza was quite innocent of sexual relationships between men and women. In fact, she used to think that sleeping in the same bed with a man at night would make a woman pregnant. Like every other Muslim girl, she was taught the importance of keeping her hymen intact. Virginity was a girl's ultimate possession and should only be surrendered to her husband on her wedding night. The purpose of sex, she was taught, was procreation.

On that day, however, an incident occurred in the harem that shook Aziza's entire sets of values.

It was late in the afternoon. Aziza and Katarina were still enjoying the fine day, strolling through the gardens, when Katarina received instructions to report to the harem overseer's office. Aziza dismissed the other servants and walked into the harem building by herself. She had regularly been to the harem's bathhouse, which was in the basement at the north end of the palace. That section was sealed off from the rest of the basement, which was reserved for some of the concubines, the eunuchs, and the kitchens.

The nooks and crannies of the vast basement had always intrigued her and she decided to explore it that afternoon. A few servants worked busily in storerooms and kitchens. They did not even look up as she quietly passed the doors.

Aziza ventured further and came across empty bedrooms on both sides of the hallway. Near the end of the hallway, she heard whispers from one of the bedrooms. Curiosity got the better of her and she crept closer to listen. She heard the voices of two women gently, and yet passionately, talking to each other. She could not hear what they were saying but she could hear them kissing and moaning. She looked through the keyhole, and there on the bed, she could see Zeinab, one of her several stepmothers. Lying next to her was Aziza's favorite older stepsister, Ayesha. Zeinab was a dark Egyptian beauty about twenty-five years old. Ayesha's mother was a Serbian slave. The two were kissing passionately.

Suddenly, Aziza became aware of her own sexuality. It was so abrupt that it felt like she'd been hit by a bolt of lightning. One minute, she was a curious young maiden looking around a basement; the next minute, she was practically in heat.

Aziza had small but firm breasts the size of large lemons. Instinctively, she reached up and felt them as if to assure herself that they were still there. Her stepmother and stepsister, both fully clothed, were breathing so heavily that Aziza could hear them through the door. After a few minutes of kissing, Ayesha started to caress Zeinab's breasts.

Ayesha slid her hand underneath Zeinab's lace pantaloons and caressed her thighs. Zeinab quivered with excitement as Ayesha's hand reached her underpants and then gently pushed them aside. She was very gently massaging something there that Aziza could not see. After several minutes, Ayesha pulled her hand out and whispered, "Let's both get undressed." They took their clothes off very quickly and faced each other.

Ayesha, the younger girl, was about two inches taller than Zeinab. She was an attractive girl with brown hair, fair skin, and blue eyes. Her breasts were about twice the size of Zeinab's. Zeinab was sultry and had dark curly hair and intense black eyes. It seemed that in this relationship, Ayesha was the dominant partner. Ayesha started by caressing Zeinab all over her naked body with her long, tapered fingers. Every time she touched Zeinab's nipples, Zeinab would shudder with anticipation and moan in excitement.

Watching the scene, Aziza felt a weird and yet wonderful warmth under her belly button. After a few minutes, Ayesha picked Zeinab up and took her over to the bed. She put her flat on her back, gently pulled her legs apart and got in between her wide-open knees.

At that moment, Aziza heard a sound. Terrified that she might be discovered, she ran upstairs to her quarters. Aziza's long suppressed feelings were finally aroused. She was feverish and woozy. Katarina came back to their rooms shortly afterward and was concerned when she found Aziza so flushed and agitated. She gave her some quince sherbet to calm her down and put her to bed.

All through that night, Aziza had dreams and nightmares—dreams about what she had seen and nightmares about what would happen to those two women if they were caught. If a woman was suspected of cheating or adultery, the Ottoman rulers dealt with it quickly and quietly. The woman got the canvas sack treatment. An adulterous woman was sewn up in a canvas bag and dropped into a lake or the sea. Aziza woke up several times that night in a cold sweat, dreaming that she was being forced into a sack to drown horribly.

The dreams continued for weeks until, mercifully, Ayesha was married off to some vassal prince in Anatolia and moved away.

That sexual revelation between Ayesha and Zeinab had made Aziza aware of her own inborn sexuality. She was not comfortable with her newfound feelings and, being a princess, did not dare to discuss them with any of her former playmates, who were now her companions.

She broached the subject one day with Katarina by indirectly asking her what happens when a man and a woman are married. Katarina, who, in her thirties was an old virgin herself, could only answer some of Aziza's questions. For example, she knew that men had to enter the women and deposit their sperm in their wombs. However, she did not know the sensations that a woman would feel during the act of intercourse. Still curious, Aziza asked if it was possible for two women or two men to engage in sexual acts.

The question stymied and horrified Katarina. She knew the answer but she did not know why Aziza was asking the question. Like many women in the harems who were caged for long periods of time, she had indulged in lesbian relationships with other women. The sexual affairs were performed very discreetly, usually with a trusted eunuch acting as a lookout. In any case, in the Ottoman world, the penalty for such acts was death. Or, if the sultan was in a good mood, he would sell the transgressors into slavery. Therefore, Katarina thought, "Is Aziza asking the question because of something that she saw or, heaven forbid, was it because another woman, maybe a companion, had tried to interest her in a lesbian relationship?" Either way, Katarina could be in mortal danger if Aziza strayed from the strict Islamic path. Despite Katarina's entreaties, Aziza refused to provide any more details. She simply said she was just curious.

CHAPTER SEVEN

SEDUCTION OF AZIZA

A few months after Aziza saw her stepsister Ayesha with Zeinab, there was a new addition to the harem.

Charles Knutsson, the flamboyant king of Sweden who was deposed, sent into exile, and reinstated to the throne three times during a twenty-year period, wanted to maintain good ties with Mohammed. The men exchanged many valuable gifts, the sultan sending exotic slave girls from Africa, emeralds and rubies from Southeast Asia, and smooth silk imported from China. Charles sent Mohammed jewelry and fine wool from the British Isles and several striking looking maidens from the ranks of his nobles.

Anita was the jewel of this group. She was a goddess who stood at least five foot eight inches tall with golden, almost platinum blonde hair, and slightly tanned white skin. Despite her height, she had exquisite features. Her small nose was upturned and her eyes were as blue as the sky on a clear day. Her lips were full and gorgeous and she had a neck that put swans to shame. Her breasts were full and firm. She was physically big but well proportioned. The muscles of her arms and legs were strong and yet feminine.

The sultan, seeing a boyish attractiveness about Anita, immediately married her as a concubine and moved her to the harem.

Anita was not a feeble, wimpy girl. Soon, she dominated her section of the harem. The eunuchs admired her masculine traits and the other women were intimidated by her height and magnetic presence. She had the sultan's ear, and therefore, plenty of money. The eunuchs provided her with wine and forbidden food, such as pork products from the Christian quarters of the city.

From their first encounter, Aziza developed a liking for her. Being extremely feminine, she missed having a male father figure in the household and looked up to Anita. Anita, who was twenty-one years old, took a liking to Aziza, too, and they became very friendly.

Anita had demanded her own separate quarters. Usually, only the sultan's permanent wives were given their own wings of a building but Anita's request was granted and an isolated part of the harem became her own domain. Since there were extra rooms in her wing of the harem, Aziza and Katarina sometimes stayed overnight in her guest room. The eunuchs would warn them if Mohammed was on his way to visit his wife and they would clear out quickly through a back door.

The sultan did not object to Anita's drinking as long as it was not done openly. After all, she was a Christian and the sultan himself enjoyed drinking with her on occasion. Mohammed did not mind the friendship that was developing between Anita and his sister. In fact, he thought it would keep Anita out of mischief.

One afternoon as the sun was setting, painting the sky the coppery tone peculiar to that time of the year near the Black Sea, Aziza was visiting Anita. As usual, Katarina was chaperoning, and Anita's maids were at her beck and call. They were sitting gossiping about women and eunuchs and the books that they both had read.

Anita usually sent the maids away when they were gossiping since she did not want them to eavesdrop on her. The Nordic blonde offered Aziza a glass of wine, and Aziza, still curious about what she had seen in the basement between Ayesha and Zeinab, accepted it to give herself some courage. Then she cleared her throat and said, "I would like to ask you a personal question."

Anita smiled, thinking the question would be about periods or other women things. "Please, you can trust me. You know that I am very fond of you."

Aziza took another sip of wine. "I think we are very close to each other but even now I feel embarrassed to ask you this question. I am going to ask the question anyway, because it has been in the back of my mind for a long time. I did not even want to ask Katarina, who is as close to me as my mother would have been had she lived." Without waiting for Anita's answer, she went on, "Once, in the basement of this palace, I saw two women in bed together. They were not just being friendly. There was something else going on. I was interrupted before I could find out. I know men and women can have relations and even men and men sometimes sleep together. You may not know it, Anita, but, according to our Holy Book, sodomy is an immoral act and it is one of the ten cardinal sins that the Lord will never forgive. You will burn in hell for eternity for committing it. However, I do not understand this other relationship and I have always wanted to see if it was a dream or if I witnessed something sensual."

Anita was stunned. This young girl was so knowledgeable about religion and history and yet so naïve about human sexuality! She opened her mouth to say something and then closed it again.

Aziza, sensing the slight tension, blushed. "I am sorry if I offended you. Please forgive me. I better go back to my quarters." She got up to leave.

Anita put her hand on Aziza's shoulder. "Please sit down and let me explain. I was so amazed at your purity and yet your openness that I had to think for a few moments before responding. Obviously, you have learned a lot from reading the great books that you have in the palace library and observing the people around you. Unfortunately, since Katarina was enslaved at a young age, she does not have the worldly experiences that a mother or an older nanny would have had and, therefore, neglected to teach you certain facts of life. Even though you have lived in a harem, being the daughter of a sultan has made it impossible for other women or eunuchs to discuss the facts of life with you openly and honestly. I am older than you and I am used to living in an open society so I can fill in the gaps for you."

Both girls sat down. Aziza's face was still crimson. She cast her eyes down. Anita moved closer and with her left hand took hold of Aziza's right hand. "There has always been love between people of the same sex," she said. "I do not condone what people like Abdullah Hassan and your brother do, which is forcing young men and boys into lying with them. The love between men is called "Greek love" but it is supposed to be between two consenting male partners who are genuinely fond of each other and the sex act is the culmination of their affection for each other. This is a well-known fact and is practiced everywhere in the world.

"However, in the Orient, because women have been closeted for so many centuries, none of the prophets and seers was really aware or did not want to admit that sensual love between women could exist. There were no laws or taboos against the love and attraction between two women. That is because most of those great men, including our great savior, Jesus Christ, came from that part of the world.

"The Greeks were always more open. Men and women were more equal in ancient Greece than they are now. Therefore, it was a known fact that love between two women could exist. There were many female poets, who wrote great enchanting poetry about their love for other women. One of the greatest poets, Sappho, hailed from the great Isle of Lesbos, which is now in your brother's hands. Sappho had an academy exclusively for girls and she wrote many passionate love songs. Sappho was also attracted to men, which is common among many women who are attracted aesthetically and romantically to other women. The act that you saw between those two young women was something that happens everywhere, especially, in harems and places where girls and women are closeted together. But, of course, nobody in the Muslim world would ever admit that some of their wives were having sexual relationships with each other."

Aziza was absorbing Anita's every word.

After taking another sip of wine, Anita went on. "In my opinion, there are three forms of love and they can coexist. One is be the love between two men. It normally ends up with one or both men penetrating each other in the place where body excrements are supposed to exit. The next is between a man and a woman. That is a love that binds two souls together and it involves penetrating one body part into another. The third and the purest form of love is between two women. There is no real penetration. It is the ultimate bliss of caressing, touching, and holding of each other. It can lift you off the ground to highest levels of euphoria and there is no religion in the world that has ever banned this form of love."

As Anita was talking, Aziza moved closer and closer to her. She did not protest when Anita put her warm hand around her neck and rubbed it tenderly and gently pulled at her long hair. When Anita finished talking, Aziza felt her warm breath on her left ear as Anita softly nibbled and kissed her ear lobe. Aziza was enjoying it too much and did not want her to stop, but Anita heard one of the maids. She quickly got up, bent over Aziza's face, and kissed her lips before moving back to her seat.

That night, Anita asked Aziza to stay. Whenever Aziza stayed overnight, she slept in the guest bedroom, which was at the remote, secluded end of Anita's quarters. Katarina usually slept on the floor nearby her to protect her and to help her if she needed water during the night. On that particular night, Anita sent Katarina back to Aziza's quarters, which were in a different wing of the vast palace. Katarina objected strongly but, as a slave, she could not disobey the sultan's favorite concubine.

Later that night, Anita who was overcome with passion for this beautiful, young princess, took a hot bath and put on nice perfumes. She let her platinum blonde hair down and put on a gossamer nightgown. She covered herself with a long cotton cape, very quietly walked the short distance to the guest room, and let herself in.

A few candles burned gently in the room. Anita made her way to the large bed on which Aziza slept peacefully. Anita took a long look at her innocent beauty.

Then, she dropped her cape and disrobed completely. A sculptor would have seen her naked, Amazon-like body as a work of art. Anita gently lifted the blanket and slipped in beside the sleeping princess, who wore a short nightgown that left her naked from the waist down, as was the custom of her people. Anita slid close to her and very gently kissed her bare shoulder.

The essence of Aziza inflamed the gods of passion within her. She moved closer to Aziza and started kissing and caressing her body. Soon Aziza was responding, as if in a dream, to her skillful touch. Anita put a hand between Aziza's firm young thighs and tried to work her way toward her crotch. Aziza woke up, startled. "Don't worry," Anita whispered. "It is only me trying to finish what we talked about earlier. I am about to show you that lovemaking between two women is not sinful and does not diminish the love that you have for a man."

As Aziza turned, in confusion, to face Anita, Anita sealed her protesting lips with a fragrant kiss. Her red lips eagerly sought and clasped Aziza's and her warm tongue found its way inside her young maidenly mouth.

The carnal force of passion, helped by Bacchus, the god of wine, took over. Aziza melted in Anita's arms and she returned her kiss. Anita's hands expertly moved all over Aziza's body, from her long neck to her bare shoulders, to her nipples, to her navel, and to the soft skin of her firm, luscious thighs. In a few minutes, she had succeeded in building up a storm of passion inside the young girl's loins.

"Let me help you get out of this," Anita said, pulling at the nightshirt. Aziza arched her back and then lifted her shoulders to let Anita pull the garment over her head. She dropped it on the floor.

The two girls were now completely naked. Anita held Aziza tightly and whispered, "I will show you how a woman loves another woman." She turned Aziza gently on her back and while kissing her again on the mouth, she got on top of her. She put one hand on Aziza's right breast and massaged it before gently squeezing the now taut nipple between her thumb and forefinger. Aziza arched her back in pleasure.

"It is not over yet," Anita whispered. With that, she lowered her head and took Aziza's right nipple in her warm mouth and while sucking on it, she gently kneaded Aziza's left nipple with her left hand. Aziza moaned involuntarily. She thought the pleasure would never end.

Just then, Anita moved lower, licking Aziza's belly from just below her breasts to her navel. She dug her tongue at the tiny hole that was Aziza's navel and after pouting her lips sucked deeply, lifting it into her mouth. The pleasure was unimaginable.

While expertly caressing Aziza's sumptuous body with her long fingernails, Anita moved down between Aziza's legs. She lifted her small, firm buttocks gently with her hands and in the dim light, looked at the virgin's pleasure spot. It was a tiny crack with no hair, soft and smooth. She breathed deep to inhale the fragrance of Aziza's femininity before gently, very gently, licking her slit with the tip of her tongue.

Hearing Aziza's moans, she got bolder, making longer strokes with her tongue. Aziza, not used to the intense pleasure that she was experiencing, discharged copiously into Anita's mouth. Anita loved the taste and the aroma of this virgin who had never been touched by another human. She stopped for a moment to let Aziza relax and then started down her inner thighs, licking all the way to Aziza's pretty toes. She sucked on them lovingly and said, "This is the difference between men and women. We love the entire body of our lovers from their cute toes to the tips of their hairs. Each part gives us immense pleasure. You can still love a man and be in love with another woman at the same time. Now, it is your turn to show me if you have been a good student."

With that, Anita turned on her back and pulled Aziza on top of her in one swift motion.

Aziza instinctively buried her tongue into her lover's mouth and put her hands around Anita to hold her as tightly as possible. Anita murmured, "Remember, don't rush it. Take your time and go slowly, starting with my aching nipples."

Anita gave Aziza instructions on how to kiss, lick, and caress her body. When Aziza got down to the pubic area, she was bemused by the amount of curly hair. As she was licking between the hairs, she spread the lobes of Anita's organ with her tongue and took long licks from bottom to top. Anita wrapped her powerful legs around Aziza and pulled her closer. She said, "Please stick your tongue inside as deep as it goes and caress me there, right inside."

Aziza, her face drenched by the Northern goddess's profuse discharge, was so excited that she had another orgasm. The sun was breaking through the night sky when the women finally collapsed in each other's arms and went to sleep.

When Aziza woke up from her deep sleep, Anita was gone. The bed was a mess and she was sticky all over. She went back to her apartment to cleanse herself. She never mentioned anything about that night to Katarina. It was as if nothing had ever happened.

The next time they visited, Anita did not broach the subject until she had dismissed the maids and they'd had a glass of wine together. She asked Aziza if she had enjoyed their night of passion. Aziza blushed and said that she had enjoyed it tremendously and added, "Next time, I want you to stick your tongue inside of me like I did to you."

Anita replied, "That would not be a good idea. You are a maiden and even a strong tongue could rupture your membrane. I know how important virginity is to your people." Aziza asked if Anita was a virgin when she had married her brother, the sultan. To her surprise, Anita said, "Yes, I was. Most girls in Northern countries start relationships with men quite early in life. I was not interested in boys, so I did not respond to amorous overtures of boys or men. The fact that I was still a maiden was one of the reasons that they selected me to be sent to the sultan. They wanted a young girl of noble birth who had not been broken in and was untouched. It would have been an insult to send used merchandize to a king. Your brother actually had me checked by the royal mid-wife."

Then Anita chuckled loudly and continued, "Actually, your brother had a very difficult time breaking my membrane. It was so hard that it frustrated him the first night and eventually he used his finger to do the work for him. It was quite painful for me and I bled for days afterwards. Some women have very hard hymens and the sexual initiation is very painful for them."

The sexual relationship between the concubine and the princess was so discreet that people were saying that in Anita, Aziza had found the sister she'd never had. Little did they know of the passion that existed between the two women, one young and the other very young.

Anita was sometimes a tease and would make fun of Aziza. Sometimes, when they were both naked and Aziza was excited, Anita would refuse to go near her and would sulk. She would make Aziza run after her to try to catch her before she would make love to her. One night, Aziza wrote the following poem in her book about her relationship with Anita:

The Princess and the Viking Girl

She is tall and handsome
I am shorter and pretty
She fair and stunning
I am dark and feminine
We are standing in her dark bedroom
We are wary of outsiders
I only met her a month ago
I was innocent and unspoiled
I had never been with a man or a woman
I felt strange, in my groin, when our eyes met
I fell for her; head over heels
I gave myself to her freely even though I knew it was a sin

She hugs me and kisses me on my lips
I can feel the fresh scent of the North on her breath
I open my mouth and swallow her tongue
She is devouring my mouth
I whisper; I love you
She just holds me tighter
After a long moment, she lets go
She steps back
She unbuttons her shirt and it falls to the floor
My eager eyes feast on her strong muscles
Her breasts are firm upturned and soooo muscular
She is the most magnificent creature on Earth
With a smile, she slides her pants down
She is naked as Eve
I spy her magnificent red bush
Bulging proudly
Covering her intimate being
I am dying to touch her
She steps forward to undress me
First my tunic and then my pants
My breasts are but small
It embarrasses me
But, I am younger that she is
Firm and dark and sensuous
My essence is female
Only yesterday, it seems, she seduced me

I want her so badly
I look at the bed

It is her marriage bed
She is married to my brother
He makes passionate love to her
Yet I love her so
Do you love me? I plead with her
She smirks and kisses me again on the lips
She knows I cannot resist her
She knows all my weak points
I was an easy conquest
She rubs her lips against my breast
Oh my God! The feeling of her teeth on my bare nipples!
I am going to swoon with pleasure
She picks me up
She is strong
She carries me to the bed
She lays down next to me
I caress her sumptuous body
My hands are trembling with excitement
I whimper something
She guides my hand between her strong legs
I feel the heat of her womanhood
I love this woman
I caress her burning parts while she is touching me all over
I love to run my fingers through her fire red pubic hair
They are curly and twisted and snag around my fingers
Soon, I feel the dampness of her being
Shiny droplets of liquid are oozing from the center
I am dying to kiss it
I am still shy

I want her to ask me first
Maybe next time

She is breathing heavily
My hand is getting wet
I know it is time
She lies on her back
She pulls me on top of her
I bury my face into the red bush
I take a deep breath
My tongue finds her opening
I lick the flesh of my goddess
I enter her with my tongue
She moans crazily
Her legs wrap around me
My face is locked deep inside her
Her pelvis is riding the bed
Her buttocks lift me up and down
The bed joins in our pleasure
She has one final spasm
She passes out
My face still locked inside her vagina

She is awake
She smiles at me generously
Your turn now, she says
Without a word, she lifts me up
I am on my back and she is on top
She is strong

She can do what she wants with me
This Nordic princess
She devours my body
She kisses my virgin opening with care
Don't worry she says
I won't stick my tongue in
You will still be a virgin
She laughs loudly
She is a cruel lover
She is teasing me
She licks
My body is on fire
I coo amorously
She groans with pleasure
I push my groin into her face as hard as I can
She lifts my buttocks up with her strong hands
I'm suspended in midair
The bed creaks again as we consummate our love
I explode into her mouth
I drench the towel
My love tunnel contracts and expands
She screams with ecstasy

I am in seventh heaven
I enjoy her slow rhythm
I whimper adoringly
The rapture is too much
I swoon and collapse onto the bed
She falls down on top of me

I come to and hear her whisper into my ear
I love you
That's what I have been waiting for
I fall into a deep slumber and dream
I am lucky; I have my woman on top of me
Even though she is married to a man

CHAPTER EIGHT

RODRIGO'S TEAM

When Rodrigo finished reading the Chronicles of Arthur of Brittany, it was late and he fell asleep in his chair, as he did at times. For a man who led a dangerous life, it was more practical to sleep partially dressed in a chair, ready to wake up quickly to face potential attackers.

The following day, he met with Jean at the offices of his uncle, Cardinal Alfonso. The cardinal gave them additional information about their companions.

The Vatican had been planning the trip for some time. They had selected a few very trustworthy individuals who were each good at their professions to accompany Jean and Rodrigo on this trip. Although the selection had been done in secrecy, Cardinal Alfonso said, the French King Charles VII had spies everywhere and was probably aware that a mission was being sent to Constantinople. King Charles VII was not aware of its true assignment, so it was likely that either the French or the Venetians would try to sabotage this undertaking.

In addition, Charles had his eye on the papal states and he would do anything to weaken his holiness, the pope.

The cardinal then called the men one by one and introduced them to Rodrigo and Jean.

The first to arrive was the most senior of the lot. He was over fifty, tall, gray-haired, and walked with an air of assurance and authority. He was armed with a short broad sword. The cardinal introduced him as Renaldo Viviani from Florence. He explained that Renaldo was a learned man who had spent the better part of his adult life traveling in the Orient. Renaldo had traveled extensively in the Balkans and the Holy Lands and was fluent in Slavic and Greek. He also had learned Arabic and Turkish while in the services of Murat II, Mohammed's father. He had spent two years at the court of Murat as a translator and a liaison to foreign ambassadors. He had also undertaken several diplomatic missions for the sultan and had actually met Mohammed when he was a young boy. He had never personally met Emperor Constantine, but he had been to Constantinople and had visited the Cathedral of Hagia Sofia. He was a strategist and could help them plan ahead and avoid trouble spots on their trip. Rodrigo felt relieved when he met Renaldo. It was comforting to have a man of experience with them.

The next person to enter the room was Lorenzo Barbarino, a relatively short, swarthy man of about thirty. He looked very ordinary. Rodrigo could have walked by him a hundred times without noticing him. The cardinal explained that Lorenzo, from Sicily, was a linguist by nature. Rodrigo, himself, had had to learn foreign languages for his schooling. He knew that some people were able to learn other languages very quickly. Lorenzo had been a seafaring man and knew Arabic and Turkish. He was a tough man in hand-to-hand combat, especially with a dagger. He was a mapmaker, so with the aid of his maps and the stars, they could avoid being lost.

The next member of the team, Antonio Draghi, was not present. Antonio was from Pistoia, north of Florence, a city well known for its arms industry. In fact, the word "pistol" had originated in Pistoia. Antonio would meet them in Florence with more armament and ammunition. He was a professional gun maker and demolition expert.

The cardinal said Rodrigo and Jean would meet two more members of the team later. There was a genuine air of excitement about the team members. They were all sworn to secrecy. They knew that they had been chosen by the pope and Cardinal Alfonso personally because of their knowledge and their loyalty. They also knew that their secret mission would take them beyond the sea. They did not know where or why. Only Jean and Rodrigo knew the true purpose of the mission.

Later that afternoon, after sunset, they had another audience with the pope. Nicholas looked less stressed out and more upbeat this time. He received the team, the cardinal, and the ever-present Father Alfaro in his chambers He then sent for the other two team members.

The first to arrive was a young priest, probably in his early twenties, wearing the traditional dark gray garb of the men of his calling. The cardinal introduced him as Father Ricardo Parentucelli, the pope's nephew. As Father Ricardo kneeled to kiss the pope's hand, Nicholas put his right hand affectionately on Father Ricardo's head and said, "Ricardo will be your confessor and religious guide throughout this journey." Rodrigo was surprised at the choice of a young priest to accompany them on such a hazardous journey.

Before he could express an opinion, he was even more surprised by the appearance of the next man who entered the room. The man, who wore the customary clothing of the papal household servants, was black. He may have even been a slave at some point, but he was no longer a slave. He had thick, curly black hair. It was not frizzy like some blacks' hair, but curly nevertheless. He was broad shouldered and over six feet tall, towering above all others in the room. To his surprise, Rodrigo noticed that the man wore a dagger in his belt.

The pope addressed Rodrigo directly. "This is Giuseppe, but we call him by his old name of Zangi. He is one of my most trusted servants. You can trust him with your life, and his dagger is the most lethal weapon." The pope called Rodrigo forward and as Rodrigo kneeled in front of him, Nicholas took his staff and placed it on his right shoulder. He prayed quietly and then loudly proclaimed Rodrigo Borgia to be a new knight of the Roman Church.

With that, he dismissed the group with the exception of Cardinal Alfonso, Jean, and Rodrigo. Addressing Rodrigo, he said, "If you are wondering why I am sending Father Ricardo with you, I would like you to know that he is known and trusted by the emperor personally. He will be carrying a personal letter from me. He is the only other person who knows your true mission."

After receiving the pope's blessing, Rodrigo and Jean left the pope and Cardinal Alfonso. Following their departure, the pope asked Cardinal Alfonso, "Do you think we will see any one of those brave men alive again?" The cardinal did not respond.

Before leaving the Castle San Angelo, Rodrigo returned the chronicles of Arthur of Brittany to Father Alfaro.

~ CHAPTER NINE ~

THE SECRETS OF THE

VATICAN

The following day, Cardinal Alfonso sent for his nephew, Rodrigo. Rodrigo arrived at the Curia just after the noon hour. Cardinal Alfonso guided his nephew to one of the chapels on the north side of the old Vatican building. They crossed the empty chapel and walked through a small door behind the altar. They took a few steps up to a small wooden door, which was bolted and locked.

The cardinal pulled a key from a rope that was wrapped around his waist and opened the large padlock. He pulled the bolt back and the door opened with a gentle squeak. They stepped into a very large room and the cardinal closed the door quickly behind him and bolted it from inside. The room had several windows, all barred, facing the Vatican gardens. A huge wooden cross was hanging from the center of the ceiling. There were several bookcases around the room and half a dozen tables loaded with what looked like ancient scrolls of paper. Enough light came through the windows that they did not need to light the candles that were placed around the room.

Even though no one else was present, the cardinal, speaking in Spanish, addressed his nephew in a hushed tone. "These are the secrets of the Vatican, my son. Some of the books and artifacts date back centuries, maybe even thousands of years. These books and parchments were written in many languages and we can only read and understand some of them.

"Over there," he said, pointing to several scrolls inside a case, "is the complete Egyptian Book of the Dead. We have a partial translation of the book in Greek next to it, but unfortunately, we cannot read the entire book. That was the magical book that the pyramid builders used to create those structures. There is enough knowledge in that book to help us defeat the infidels, only if we could read it. There are many secrets that we do not know."

The cardinal took two parchments from the pile and spread them open on a large table directly under one of the windows. The two parchments showed identical drawings of Egyptian pharaohs, chariots, birds, and crops with hieroglyphic writings. Despite their great age, the drawings were still vividly clear. "You will notice that the pictures and the words are the same on both of these scrolls," the cardinal said.

"The Egyptians had a method of duplicating documents that we did not know until a Swiss man by the name of Gutenberg reinvented printing a few years ago. It takes a good scribe several months to produce a readable copy of the Bible. That is why only a few people can actually read the words of our Lord. I wonder how great it would be if we could produce many copies of the Bible quickly and then everyone could read it or at least have it read to them in their native tongues. My real wish is that, one day, the holy church will allow us to publish the Bible in local languages. As you know, hardly any of the peasants in our hometown of Valencia can understand Latin. The priests read the Bible to them in Latin anyway, since it is the only language that the holy church approves. The language of our Lord was Aramaic, not Latin or Greek. I think he would have wanted us to have the Bible available in all the languages of mankind."

The cardinal went on, "This much, we know. About six hundred years after the death of our Lord, the barbarians who originally came from the East, destroyed most of our civilization. To this day, many ancient cities still lay buried under overgrown forests. At one point, it was only the will of our Lord and the presence of holy fathers in Rome that kept the world from destroying itself. As God is my witness, I do not care for the Venetians and their greed for gold but they, because of their island location, were one of the few pockets of civilization left in this world, other than the Byzantines. The Church itself is partly to blame for the lack of knowledge. Over five hundred years ago, we had a female pope who was diabolically clever. She fooled everyone until the day she gave birth in the street just outside Castle of San Angelo. Even her bastard son became a cardinal. That was in the Dark Ages. Then the Dark Ages ended. We have never admitted that we had a female pope and have changed our records to obliterate her memory. It is all here in the books and records in this room. She was called Joan and she came from the British Isles. Even our holy father, Nicholas, who was the keeper of this room before me, does not discuss or mention her name.

"Then, about three hundred years ago, we had a revival of our Western civilization. We have been gathering old books, manuscripts, and artifacts from all over the world and are trying to understand our lost heritage."

He pointed to another pile of scrolls and books and explained, "The Romans and before them, the Greeks, had a tremendous appetite for fornication. We have detailed descriptions and drawings of their orgies. The Greek documents depict sexual acts between mature men and youngsters. The Romans were more interested in young girls. Caligula and Nero commissioned many of those drawing and stories, which we have found in the ruins of Rome. I am over seventy years of age and erotica do not affect me, but I do not believe in tempting the flesh with the designs of the devil. But, at the same time, I do not believe in destroying any kind of art work." Pointing to the big cross hanging from the ceiling, he said, "Just to be safe and be protected from any evil effects in this room, we have our savior's cross to guard over us."

Looking at his bewildered nephew, the cardinal smiled and added, "There is more. The cross that was used to crucify our Lord was lost for over three centuries. Many imitation crosses were sold to the churches and monasteries. As you heard from the holy father, Empress Elena, who was the mother of Constantine the Great, journeyed to the holy land to find it. Eventually, with the help of devout Christians, it was rediscovered. Thereafter, it was called the True Cross," he said, moving to a bookcase. "We know that because she brought back a fragment of the cross to her palace in Rome. We have discovered it in the rubble of her old dwelling."

Reaching into a corner of the bookcase, the cardinal carefully picked up an old, gold-covered box decorated with jewels. He reverently opened it and extracted a velvet pouch. After crossing himself, he untied the knot and handed it to Rodrigo. It contained a splinter of wood slightly bigger than a man's middle finger.

Rodrigo reached out to touch the splinter and felt a sudden jolt of indescribable warmth traveling from his fingers to his torso. He kneeled down next to his uncle to pray. After a few minutes, the cardinal said, "Now, my son, you know the power of the True Cross. You will know it again when and if you see the rest of it. The blood of our Lord has sanctified this piece of wood."

With that, he put the fragment back in the velvet pouch and carefully knotted the string. "Only his holiness the pope and his most trusted confidants know about this room. I am blessed to be his holiness's closest friend. The reason I am showing you this is that his holiness may be called to heaven soon. I am getting old and may not be around when you come back from your mission. Someone has to relay the knowledge in this room to the new pope."

Cardinal Alfonso put his hand on Rodrigo's shoulder and directed him to the far corner of the large room. There, Rodrigo observed several open caskets with human bodies wrapped in what seemed to be white linen bandages. "These are the mummies of Egypt," Cardinal Alfonso said. "In Rome, even in the middle of winter, you cannot leave a body unburied for more than a few days. In Egypt, they had discovered a method to embalm and preserve the flesh for thousands of years."

Cardinal Alfonso reverently touched the bandages on one of the mummies, as if to prove a point, and continued, "This art has been lost to us because we cannot read the ancient language of the Egyptians."

The cardinal led Rodrigo to another section of the room, where scores of jars and bottles of different colors were laid on a large table. "These are the remedies, the elixirs, and perhaps even the deadly poisons of ancient Egypt. In these jars and bottles, the secrets of a cure for leprosy or the hidden knowledge of eternal youth maybe stored. No one knows."

Pointing to some metal instruments next to the jars, he said, "When we first saw these strange knives and hooks, we thought that they were instruments of torture but we eventually discovered that they were used in surgery. There are mummies in this room with surgical holes in their skulls. Those ancient people could even operate on the brains of human beings.

"Julius Caesar and his conquering army burned the library of Alexandria half a century before the birth of our savior. Then, in the seventh century, the Muslim Arabs destroyed most of the other books and scrolls. The Muslim barbarians believe that any book or writing other than their holy book is blasphemous. They destroyed almost all of the ancient books and libraries of Egypt, Syria, and Persia, so many secrets were lost forever."

Moving slowly around the room as he spoke, Cardinal Alfonso pulled open a large, deep drawer. Inside were glass objects and metal instruments that Rodrigo had never seen before. Cardinal Alfonso explained, "Some of these are the tools of alchemists of the past. Holy Father Pope Sylvester II, who was the pope at the Millennium, over four hundred years ago, was the first to rediscover and understand alchemy. The rest we are not sure about."

He picked up a tiny metal arrow about two inches long. There was a hole in the middle of the arrow with a silk string looping through it. He held the string so that the arrow was hanging beneath it. "You see, my son, the tip of the arrow always points to the north and the tail of it points to the south. The ancient people used these instruments long before we learned how to navigate the seas with our compasses and sextants. Some intellectuals believe that the Egyptians and Greeks had devised a method of levitation and that was how the great pyramids of Egypt and the temples of Greece were built." He paused and looked at Rodrigo. "Some think that it is blasphemous even to think of such things. I have an open mind, my son. I believe in our Lord and his Son and the Holy Ghost. I think anything that men have done has been possible and blessed by the wisdom of our Lord. If the Lord did not wish it, it would not have been created or it would have been destroyed like Jericho was."

The cardinal, suddenly very serious and solemn, led Rodrigo to a large locked chest in a dark corner. Cardinal Alfonso did not open the chest. He just pointed to it and said, "In that chest are many different versions of our Bible. Some date back over a thousand years. By the time of Emperor Constantine in the fourth century, there were many versions of Christianity and numerous Bibles claiming to be the true Bible of the Lord. Some Christians believed in the trinity while others believed in Jesus as being the Son but not the Father and the Holy Ghost at the same time. Still some believed that he was married and had children. The emperor convened a council in Nicea, which is now in infidel hands, to unify the church and to create a version of the Bible that would be acceptable to all Christians. During that contentious council, many different versions of the Bible were banned and consequently burned. We have managed to collect most of those early books and save them for posterity. However, two books in that box are a source of concern to me. One is the Bible of Thomas, which is still used in Egypt by our Christian brothers, and the other is the amazing Bible of Johan. The latter Bible has foretold many occurrences that have so far proven correct."

The cardinal paused as if lost in thought. "Some Muslim scholars who have heard about this particular Bible claim that it prophesized the arrival of their prophet Mohammed and instructed all Christians to convert and follow in his footsteps. This is utter nonsense. It is, however, true that the Bible of Johan prophesizes a different version of the second coming of our Lord. This chest should never be opened and the contents should remain hidden from mankind for the rest of time. The Church cannot allow these Bibles to confuse the believers."

The cardinal gently took Rodrigo's elbow and guided him to another dark corner of the room behind a massive bookcase, where two large, locked chests sat side by side. The cardinal took another key from the rope that was wrapped around his waist and opened one chest, revealing gold coins. "Ever since before the first Crusade," he said, "many churches have been collecting a penny a head, from people who could afford it, for the liberation of the holy land. This has been known as the Peter's pence. That money is converted to gold and is kept here. The popes have used it to finance armies to battle the infidel. This is the pope's personal treasury and he spends it on the work of the Lord."

Noting Rodrigo's stunned expression, he continued. "Over the last few decades, we have been sending tremendous amounts of gold to the Persian kings in Tabriz. They hate the Ottoman Turks and are constantly harassing them from the East. Without our money, they would not be able to buy guns and ammunitions and the Ottomans would have conquered their territory and focused all their resources on us in the West. The pope cannot publicly acknowledge the fact that he is sending money to an infidel kingdom, even though they are on our side. So he is using this treasury."

With that, the cardinal locked the chest and guided his nephew to the door, which he carefully locked and bolted.

CHAPTER TEN

AMBUSH BY A MISTRESS

Over the next few days, the team members spent many hours getting to know each other and planning their trip. Rodrigo told them that they would go north toward Florence. To most of them, the next logical step would have been east to Ravenna or northeast to Venice for a sea journey.

During those days, they ordered and received food and ammunition from the Vatican stores. For the long trip to Florence, Rodrigo and Jean ordered prosciutto (dried ham), olives, dried fruit, and nuts. Since they were not sure about the water beyond Rome, they ordered caskets of wine and ale. On the morning of their departure, they would receive fresh bread, water, and parmesan cheese.

Several grooms and servants would accompany them on this trip. The pope had also assigned several of his Swiss Guards, mercenaries who had been in the service of popes for many years now, to protect them. They were his personal army.

A few nights before their departure, Rodrigo decided to visit his mistress, Teresa, who was the sister of Armando Colonna. Teresa's husband was away, looking after their estates in southern Italy. She had sent for Rodrigo several times but he had made excuses since he was busy arranging the trip. In addition, Rodrigo was more cautious now.

The holiest man alive had given him a mission that he intended to carry out and he did not want to take any unnecessary chances. Eventually, however, after refusing several invitations, he decided to visit Teresa, who was a nice looking woman of about twenty-three. She was of average height but her buttocks were slightly larger than normal. Rodrigo had known her for about six months and was gradually teaching her different forms of lovemaking that he had learned from Carolina.

For the sake of keeping up the appearance of Teresa's fidelity to her husband, they met in their usual place, at the home of Teresa's sister, Paola. Paola was a widow and anyone who saw Rodrigo visiting Paola's mansion would assume that he was courting a widow and think nothing of it. Paola, who was three years older than Teresa, had already betrayed her sister and was conducting an ongoing affair of her own with Rodrigo. She called him her shaved prince because unlike many Italians, Rodrigo shaved his pubic area.

That night, he arrived at Paola's mansion after dark. Despite Rodrigo's protests, Zangi had decided to follow him at a respectable distance. Both sisters were there. Before he could enter the main sitting room, Paola pulled him to a corner and whispered, "Don't be surprised or angry at what you are about to see in the other room. For my sake, please give it a chance." Then she gave him a wink and a kiss, took his hand, and guided him to their large sitting room.

Standing by the fireplace was Armando Colonna, one of Rodrigo's sworn enemies; a man who had promised to kill him.

Rodrigo's hand immediately went towards his dagger. However, he noticed that Armando was not armed. Still holding the dagger's handle but not pulling it out of its sheath, he looked around the room. No one else was present. He relaxed. Armando smiled and walked toward him, extending his hand. Rodrigo had no choice but to shake it.

Armando said, "Let us forget the past and be friends. I am sure that we can help each other."

Rodrigo was truly amazed by the turn of events. After exchanging some pleasantries, Armando said, "My sister, Paola, is very fond of you and wants to marry you. You know her husband was rich and did not have any other relatives. There will be a dowry of lands and buildings. I think that it would be a wonderful match."

Two weeks earlier, Rodrigo would have accepted the offer. For a minor Spanish nobleman to be accepted by the most powerful family of Rome was a great honor. To marry the beautiful Paola and be able to see Teresa freely sounded good. However, circumstances had changed and he could no longer accept the offer.

Rodrigo politely declined, trying not to be rude, saying that he had to leave town to attend to some personal matters. Armando was insistently curious about Rodrigo's trip and, in fact, offered to assign several of his own personal bodyguards to protect him. It was then that Rodrigo realized that despite all precautions, the Colonna family was aware that something was afoot. If the Colonnas knew, then who else did?

The two sisters joined them shortly. After about an hour of chitchat and a few drinks, Rodrigo excused himself. Armando, in a pleasant manner, saw him to the door.

Rodrigo had taken but a few steps away from the house when out of the shadows, an object forcibly hit him, throwing him to the ground. He almost lost consciousness, but he heard the unmistakable swoosh of an arrow flying through the air where he had stood a second ago. His hand went for his dagger, but then he heard Zangi's voice. Zangi, who lay on top of him, slapped his big hand over Rodrigo's mouth and whispered to him to be quiet.

Rodrigo quickly realized that the meeting had been a trap. If he did not divulge anything of value, he would be shot. He now remembered that before he left the room, Armando had pulled the drapes on the window shut, saying that it was getting cold. That must have been the signal. Obviously, Zangi, whose dark complexion allowed him to melt into the shadows, had seen the assassin prepare his crossbow.

While Rodrigo was thinking about how foolishly he had allowed himself to be trapped, the weight lifted from his shoulders and Zangi was gone. Rodrigo was surprised that Zangi, who had saved his life, had suddenly abandoned him. After a few minutes of waiting on the ground and listening for hostile action, Rodrigo walked back to his carriage, which was parked away from the premises on a side street, and went home.

Zangi arrived a few hours later with a look of glee on his face. He explained that he had followed the assassin and had managed to get a confession out of him. It was, as Rodrigo had suspected, Armando Colonna who had arranged for his murder and the signal had been pulling the curtains shut. He was glad that he was not part of that family. Only God knew what they would have done to him if they did not need him anymore.

Rodrigo thanked Zangi and went to his bedroom. This time, he was truly afraid. He prayed to the Lord again for his deliverance.

The following, day the pope sent for him. He had heard about the incident and was worried. Pope Nicholas shook Rodrigo's hand after he had kissed his ring. "My son, I heard of the attempt on your life last night. The Colonna and the Conti families feel that they own Rome and Italy. There are too many of them and they have deep alliances with the French and the Venetians. I cannot fight them and the infidels at the same time. The hope of the holy Church lies with you."

* * *

Later that afternoon, Rodrigo was astonished when an obviously distressed Paola turned up in his apartment. He was not too happy to see her. With tears in her eyes, she said, "All Rome knows about the attempt on your life last night. I want you to know that our family was not involved. I am in love with you and would never hurt you."

Two days later, Rodrigo said his confessions and his good-byes.

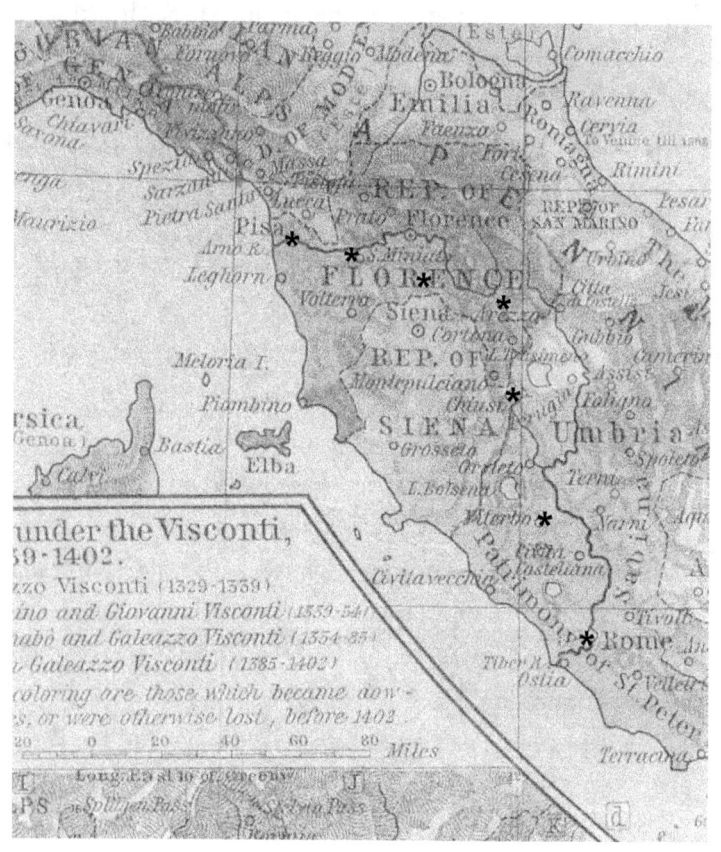

CHAPTER ELEVEN

THE ROAD TO PISA

At the time of Nicholas V, Rome was a thriving metropolis. However, it was a fraction of the size and had little of the vibrancy of the ancient Rome of eleven hundred years earlier when it was a city of over a million inhabitants.

In fact, since the first barbarian invasion in 350 AD, Rome had been steadily declining in population and importance for several reasons. One was the constant attacks from the savage Germanic tribes that repeatedly plundered the city, killing or carrying off many of its inhabitants into slavery. Arab Saracens attacked from the sea, plundering the city for booty and young girls they could sell in the Eastern markets. In response, the popes constructed a sixty-foot wall around the Vatican.

Additionally, there was the ever-present curse of the dreaded Black Death. The Plague, in its various forms, devastated what was left of Rome over a period of eight hundred years.

Most of the Roman nobility left Rome for Constantinople in the fourth century when Constantine the Great decided to abandon the Western seat of the Empire.

The people who went to Constantinople became Hellenized to such an extent that their descendants read and wrote in Greek instead of Latin. They also abandoned the Catholic religion in favor of the Greek Orthodox version of Christianity.

If it were not for the fact that Rome was home to the popes, who, over the centuries, steadfastly refused to desert the seat of Saint Peter, Rome would have become just another ancient ghost town.

The city that was home to more than a million people at the height of its glory had shrunk to a village of three thousand souls with hundreds of acres of ancient ruins. Those hardy residents were probably the last remnant of the true Romans and had all congregated in the Trastevere neighborhood near the Vatican. Their descendents still live there today.

Gradually, around the year 900, Rome's bad luck began to reverse. At the time of Nicholas, it boasted magnificent buildings and mansions built by the new Romans. However, most of the original city was in ruins. The crumbling buildings and empty dwellings offered an excellent haven for thieves, kidnappers, and ambushers. People were afraid to go out at night without an escort or even venture to the deserted parts of the city during daylight hours. A cautious pedestrian never simply turned a corner at a crossroad, lest an assassin be waiting around the bend. It was far safer to carry on walking to the middle of the crossroad so he could see what lay ahead before turning either left or right.

After swearing Lorenzo Barbarino to secrecy, the Vatican mapmakers worked with him on a detailed map of the route that Rodrigo's party would take to Pisa.

At Pisa, a friendly ship bought with Vatican gold would be waiting to take them around the boot of Italy to the town of Dubrovnik On the Adriatic Sea. Dubrovnik was one of the few towns in the Balkans that was still in Christian hands. Actually, the shortest route to Dubrovnik from Rome was north to Venice, followed by a short sea trip across the Adriatic. But Cardinal Alfonso had advised against this route. The Vatican did not trust the Venetians and their craving for wealth. Vatican spies were already reporting that Venetians were providing supplies and negotiating future commercial ties with the Ottomans.

The first part of the trip was considered quite perilous for unarmed travelers passing through the ruins and the abandoned buildings of ancient Rome. But Rodrigo did not anticipate any problems.

After leaving the ruins, they had planned to follow the old Roman road, Via Cassia, which cut through central Italy toward Florence.

The plan was to go north to Viterbo, which was still part of the Papal States. From Viterbo, the party would head north to the small town of Chiusi, then to Arezzo, and finally to Florence. In Florence, Antonio Draghi would be waiting for them with more supplies and they would make the two-day trip to Pisa. They estimated that the whole journey from Rome would take about ten days since the mules that would carry the provisions and gold would slow them down.

On the morning of February 15, 1453, Rodrigo and his party departed Rome. In addition to the members of the mission, the party included several Swiss mercenaries, servants, and mule handlers. Their first stop for the night would be the town of Monterosi. February 15 was a Sunday, which meant many Christians did not do any traveling or working. Due to the urgency of the mission, the pope granted them special absolution to start their journey on that Sunday. The day passed quietly as Rodrigo and his men went past the ruins of ancient Rome and made their way north. Rodrigo was not afraid of the highwaymen who lay in wait for pilgrims and merchants. His party was well armed and, except for the grooms who also served as cooks; they were all fighting men. Rodrigo sent Lorenzo Barbarino and Zangi to scout for potential danger.

By late afternoon, they arrived at Monterosi and camped close to, but not too near, the big volcanic lake there. Until early in the nineteenth century, people believed they would get malaria from the fumes of lakes or swamps if they slept too close to them. The Monterosi area is pockmarked with volcanic lakes, which gave rise to many diseases, including malaria. It was several centuries before most of the lakes were finally drained permanently.

Rodrigo implemented the nightly watch system that he had planned in Rome. He would take the first two-hour watch after dark, followed by Jean, Renaldo, Lorenzo, and Zangi.

Early on the morning of February 16, the party left Monterosi and headed for Viterbo via the ancient town of Sutri. Rodrigo was anxious to push his men hard but the mules stubbornly kept their normal pace. By nightfall, they camped several miles south of Vetralla. The following morning, February 17, they moved forward to Viterbo. The mule that was carrying the bulk of the munitions somehow had damaged his right front leg and started to limp. The mule handlers were not sure why. Maybe the mule had stepped into a hole, or had tripped and sprained his ankle.

They had to halt, unpack the animal, and distribute his load. They left the mule on the side of road to either recover or die.

Because of this delay, they did not get to Viterbo until late on February 18. Viterbo was, and still is, a picturesque town with many amenities. The party stayed in Viterbo for two nights and embarked for Chiusi early on Friday morning.

To get to Chiusi, the party had to pass through hostile lands that were not controlled by the pope. By two in the afternoon, Rodrigo was alarmed that his two scouts, Zangi and Lorenzo, had not reported to him. As the afternoon grew dark and cold, Rodrigo ordered a halt, ordering his men off the road. They camped in a little valley about half a mile from the main road. At dawn, they moved back to the road to wait for the scouts. By noon there was still no sign them.

Later that afternoon, Lorenzo and Zangi returned, exhausted and hungry. Rodrigo offered them wine, bread, and cheese. "Near Chiusi", Lorenzo said, "the road passes between two very high hills." He and Zangi had gone around the side of one of the hills instead of taking the road. On the north side of the hill, they had found evidence of a recent campfire and other human activity. Lorenzo, who was familiar with the notorious bandits of Sicily, believed that those were the signs of brigands planning an ambush.

Rodrigo and Jean called the other men to discuss their options. Since they had horses and mules laden with supplies and armaments, they could not climb behind the hills as Lorenzo and Zangi had done. Renaldo Viviani had experienced the savagery of bandits and argued for turning back. Bandits would have no qualms about slaying the travelers, he said.

Rodrigo and his party had only two options: turn back, as Renaldo recommended, or try to outsmart the bandits.

Rodrigo, who with Jean and Father Ricardo, were the only people who knew the true purpose of their trip, ruled out turning back to Rome. He told his team bluntly that any man who wanted to leave would have to deal with his sword first. Renaldo and Jean added their support.

Lorenzo stepped forward and offered his professional advice. He explained that when entering the ravine between the two hills, they should keep a sharp eye on any traveler approaching from the opposite direction. Bandits usually split into two groups, one riding towards and one following closely behind their target. An attacker usually would hold the reins of his horse with his left hand while concealing his right hand inside his jacket. He would get close to the lead horseman and, on a signal, pull his right hand out of his jacket and shoot him with a small but deadly crossbow or stab him with a stiletto dagger.

Then the bandits would fall upon the confused victims. The cutthroats trailing behind the travelers dealt with anybody who tried to retreat. Eight to twelve bandits could easily defeat a partially armed group of fifty. Because of the element of surprise, even an armed group of twenty would not stand a chance against them. As a rule, they took no prisoners. Children and men were killed first. Women, even nuns, were raped to death or sold to pirates who, in turn, would sell them in Egypt or Syria to the Muslims.

Rodrigo was eager to move on. But Father Ricardo insisted that they should not travel on Sundays. Rodrigo and his men stayed one more night in the hills near Via Cassia.

During the day on Sunday, Rodrigo and his companions formulated a plan to deal with the danger at hand. According to the information provided by Lorenzo and Zangi, the pass that lay north of them was about two miles long. In some places, the walls of the canyon were as high as a five-story building. About a mile inside the ravine, the road took a sharp turn to the right. Renaldo suggested a two-pronged attack.

First, he would dispatch Zangi and three of the Swiss mercenary guards on horseback to the north side of pass behind the bandits. They could leave on Sunday afternoon and travel very lightly, carrying only enough food and wine for one day. The Swiss soldiers, being professionals, could fire ten or more arrows in one minute using their crossbows. They could hit their targets within a range of 300 to 600 feet with accuracy. Their bolts could even penetrate the mail shirts that some knights wore.

This group was to go around the mountain, enter the mountain pass from the north, and then wait near the bandits' hideout. Renaldo had reasoned that the bandits would not be watching the north side of the mountain pass if they were planning to attack a party coming from the south. Zangi and the soldiers would then wait for the bandits to depart and follow closely behind them. This would close the bandits' escape route.

A second group of four Swiss mercenaries under the command of Jean would follow Rodrigo and the main body of the group, including the mules and servants, at a safe distance, looking for the bandits who would follow the party from the back. This would close the escape route of the second team of bandits once it entered the ravine.

Their predicament was that it was likely that some bandits with deadly crossbows would be hiding in the pass among the rocks. To avoid being caught in their crossfire, Renaldo recommended that they choose the site of the battle.

Lorenzo and Renaldo calculated that if Rodrigo's party maintained a rate of travel of three to five miles an hour, the bandits would be expecting them halfway through the pass where the road took a sharp turn to the right. Therefore, if they stopped just before reaching the bend in the road, the bandits would be forced to come to them. They could take care of the men hidden in the rocks later.

At three in the afternoon, before the first group led by Zangi departed, the sergeant of the Swiss mercenaries, Rudolf, approached Rodrigo anxiously and asked for a private word. The Swiss were an extremely disciplined and loyal group of men, which is why successive popes used them as Vatican guards.

Rudolf walked away from the camp and ducked behind some rocks. Rodrigo, somewhat baffled by Rudolf's nervousness. followed. "Sir," Rudolf said. "We do not have any usable gun powder for our guns!" Before Rodrigo could state his shock at the news, Rudolf went on, "Prior to leaving on any trip, especially in the winter, we pack our gun powder in small canvas sacks. We then cover the sacks with grease paper to protect them from moisture, which would make them useless. The gunpowder is then put in leather bags and tied tightly before being loaded on the mules. Someone has opened the bags and torn through the grease paper. The powder is now damp and in this weather it will never dry."

Rodrigo was beginning to feel troubled. First, the accident with the mule and now the useless gunpowder? He asked Rudolf if they could use their crossbows instead. Rudolf assured him that they could fire more bolts per minute from a crossbow than bullets from a rifle.

The rifles had to be filled from the end of the barrel with a combination of gunpowder and either a big steel ball or a bunch of small balls. The ammunition then had to be packed tightly by pushing a ramrod down the barrel and finally the fuse had to be lit by clicking a flint wheel. The rifle had a much better range than a crossbow and was much more destructive, but it was slower to reload. If the target was approaching and the first shot did not hit him, the rifleman had little chance of reloading a second shot. Rodrigo told Rudolf not to divulge any of this to anyone but simply to order his men to use crossbows in the pass, perhaps saying he was concerned that the bullets could ricochet in that narrow space.

Rodrigo had carried enough gunpowder in his own sash for a few shots only. They were stored in a small metal box. He was relieved to find that it was still dry.

The first group guided by Zangi took off just before dark. At first light on the morning of February 23, the main body, comprised of Rodrigo, Renaldo, Lorenzo, two Swiss soldiers, the mules, the grooms, and the servants, left camp. The last party, consisting of Jean and four Swiss soldiers, would follow half an hour later and travel slowly until they entered the pass. They would then speed up to catch up with the bandits whom they expected to fall in behind the main party.

Encounter at Chiusi Pass

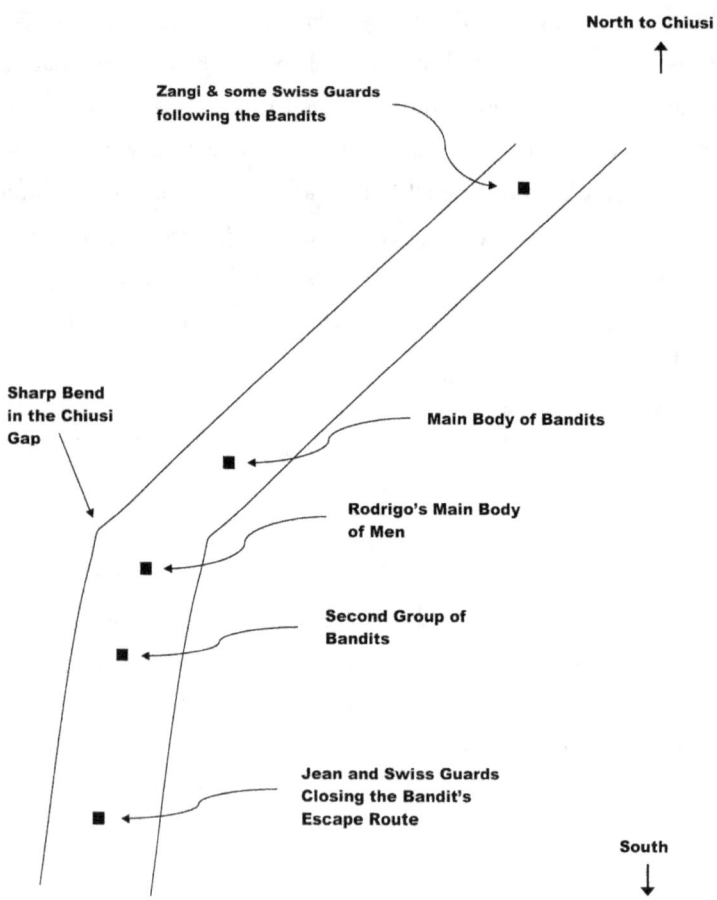

North to Chiusi

Zangi & some Swiss Guards
following the Bandits

Sharp Bend
in the Chiusi
Gap

Main Body of Bandits

Rodrigo's Main Body
of Men

Second Group of
Bandits

Jean and Swiss Guards
Closing the Bandit's
Escape Route

South

CHAPTER TWELVE

THE BANDITS OF CHIUSI PASS

Rodrigo's party entered the pass between the two hills two hours later. A lump grew in Rodrigo throat and his stomach muscles tightened as he led his men between the hills towering on either side of the road. What if he was wrong and the bandits attacked before they got to the middle of the pass?

As the hours went on, he became more and more apprehensive. But he could do precious little besides worry. He could not turn back because that would mean leaving Zangi and the Swiss soldiers at the mercy of the bandits. Near noon, they were within sight of the bend. Rodrigo and his men stopped and waited. While they were waiting, Rodrigo loaded his massive handgun and hung it within easy reach on the right side of his saddle. The handgun, a relatively new invention, was sixteen inches long. Rodrigo would need both hands to hold it steady.

The winter air was cold and misty. The wind howled through the canyon. Cold cut through their clothes, making them feel weak and miserable. About half an hour later, they heard movement up ahead. Rodrigo motioned to his men. The Swiss soldiers dismounted and moved out of sight.

Within minutes, four figures on horseback emerged around the corner. They were unkempt and dirty. The lead man, bearded and wearing a metal helmet that might have belonged to a soldier, smiled at Rodrigo "Signor, good morning to you." His missing front teeth caused him to lisp. His right hand was tucked inside an old brown woolen coat that smelled as though it had never been washed.

Rodrigo responded with the usual greetings and, as arranged, his men moved to the right side of the canyon as if to let the newcomers pass on their left. The lead man, realizing that Rodrigo was a foreigner by his accent, smiled broadly and urged his horse closer, his companions moving strategically towards Rodrigo's men. As Lorenzo had predicted, their right hands were inside their coat pockets; they held their reins in their left hands.

The man said, "Signor, you are pilgrims visiting our holy city?"

Timing was critical. Rodrigo's handgun was loosely hanging on the right side of his saddle, ready to cock and fire. Rodrigo jumped down to the right side of his horse, using the animal as a shield, he grabbed the gun, used the saddle to steady his aim, lit the fuse, and fired.

The gun went off with a loud bang as the man was pulling his crossbow from under his long coat. He had seen what Rodrigo was doing and hesitated for a fraction of a second, since his target was behind the horse.

The shot hit the man in the middle of his chest, throwing him from his horse. He fired his crossbow into the air as his body struck the wall of the canyon with a thud. The other bandits, who had never had to deal with a cunning enemy, tried to run. Two were cut down by multiple shots of crossbows. The last man managed to turn around and head back the way he had come, only to encounter the swords of the Swiss soldiers moving in from the north.

The bandits who had planned to close in on Rodrigo from behind tried to run away. They were decimated by the Swiss soldiers led by Jean.

Rodrigo and Zangi did not lose any time. They galloped to the bandit's main campsite. There, they found three men who had been left behind to tend the horses. The men were captured without a fight, their arrogance soon turning into miserable appeals for mercy. They knew that the townspeople would most likely skin them alive for all their acts of savagery. One of them was an older man who offered to show them the cave where they lived and hid their loot.

The guard at the cave tried to resist but before he could reach for his crossbow, Rodrigo dispatched him with his stiletto.

In the cave, they found chests of fine clothes, jewelry, gold, food, and wine. Much to their surprise, they found five young women, among them, two novice nuns who could not have been more than sixteen years old. They had been traveling with a chaperone sister to Rome to join a convent. The chaperone, who was over fifty, had been slain during the raid. Two girls of perhaps thirteen years of age, the daughters of rich merchants, had been on their way back to Sienna from Rome after visiting relatives. The fifth woman, who was in her early twenties, was the wife of a Florentine nobleman who had been kidnapped and held for ransom. The women were all very attractive. Four of them were brunettes and the older one was a blonde. Under their long brown overcoats, they were in rags and almost naked. Their captors had taken their shoes to prevent them from escaping, and their small feet were bruised and almost blue from the cold. That is, except for the older Florentine woman, who was better groomed and dressed reasonably well.

The bandits had held them for four weeks, waiting for the next slave trader to pick them up for shipment to the East. The slave traders paid top money, in gold, for white virgins, who were in great demand by the Arabs and the Turks. However, with the Ottomans in control of so much of Serbia and Croatia, a steady supply of slaves of all shades and colors was available to them. The market for slave girls had dried up and the bandits, tired of waiting for the slave trader, had ravished the girls. The novice nuns were in worst shape, since their faith had been shaken so badly. Rodrigo told the girls to open the chests, find suitable clothing, and clean themselves as best as they could.

The rest of the party arrived at the cave by nightfall. Since there was no danger any longer, the group decided to rest for the night at the cave.

Rodrigo, Jean, and Renaldo were drinking fine wine and talking when they heard a muffled cry. Rodrigo shot to his feet and followed the sound. Within seconds, he was astonished to find two of the stable hands on top of the two novice nuns trying to satisfy their carnal desires with these fallen symbols of purity. One of the nuns had passed out. The other was emitting incoherent whimpers of agony. Without hesitation, Rodrigo took his horsewhip and hit the men squarely on the backs of their necks. The men screamed in agony and fell back on their backsides, whimpering in pain.

"What kind of animals are you to desecrate the wards of the Lord?" Rodrigo fumed. "I should treat you the same way that I treated the bandits."

Deep down, Rodrigo knew that he still needed these men for a few more days. He ordered the Swiss soldiers to give each man five more lashes and tie them up to prevent them from fleeing during the night.

After dinner, Rodrigo and Father Ricardo spoke with the captive women. The two young girls were afraid that their families might reject them now that the bandits had used them sexually. The novice nuns likewise feared that the church would banish them. They were all concerned about pregnancy. Some nights they had been forced to submit to three or four men. Francesca, who had been married before being abducted, had instructed them to squat and try to get rid of the sperm after each intercourse to lessen the chance of pregnancy and wash their genitals in the water from a natural spring that bubbled from the back of the cave.

Francesca asked to speak to Rodrigo and Father Ricardo privately. She told them that she was from the rich and powerful Strozzi family of Florence. She was married to the son of another prominent family. Her husband, Alberto, had squandered the family fortune and her dowry gambling and was now almost penniless. That was when Francesca was abducted. While she was waiting for the ransom money, the leader of bandits, Franco, took a fancy to her and told her that there would be no ransom forthcoming. Alberto had arranged the kidnapping to extract a huge sum of money from Francesca's father and brothers. The instructions were to kill her and leave her body by the roadside after the husband had collected the ransom from her relatives.

Alberto already had his eyes on another heiress, whom he was planning to marry. Despite objections from his friends, Franco had decided to keep Francesca as a captive mistress. No one was allowed to touch her except Franco, whereas, the other girls were considered communal property.

Father Ricardo and Rodrigo were livid after hearing the story of evil Alberto. They had to find a way to punish the wicked husband and save Francesca's honor.

* * *

Rodrigo decided to leave the bodies of slain bandits where they had fallen. He did not have the time or interest in burying them. On Tuesday morning, February 24, the party headed to Chiusi. Somehow, the news of their triumph reached Chiusi before they did. A delegation of the townsfolk headed by the mayor greeted them as heroes and offered the hospitality of the town. Rodrigo did not want to draw any more attention to his group and their mission than was necessary. He thanked them and asked if they could provide lodging and provisions. Rodrigo was looking for a large house for the next few days to rest and tend to one of the Swiss soldiers who was slightly injured by a flying dagger during their battle with the bandits.

The grateful people of Chiusi and the mayor presented them with a large farmhouse just outside the main gate of the city. They provided a doctor to care for the wounded man and several maids to take care of the women. Rodrigo instructed the young captive women to keep their identities secret. As for the prisoners, Rodrigo was not sure what to do with them.

One of the prisoners was the older man who claimed to have been kidnapped by the bandits and had shown them the cave. His name was Petros and he maintained that he had been kept alive because of his knowledge of medicine and foreign languages. He claimed to be a Catholic from the town of Salonica in southern Greece, which had fallen to the Ottomans several years earlier. There were not many Catholics in Greece anyway, and the infidels were now running the country. He had decided to migrate to Rome to practice medicine there.

While he was in Chiusi, one of the bandit chiefs needed a doctor for a wounded comrade. He managed to lure Petros out of town. Petros claimed to have been kept a captive ever since.

Petros spoke some Italian and Turkish in addition to his native Greek and was very familiar with the Balkans. Rodrigo decided to take Petros with them. He turned the other bandits over to the local authorities in Chiusi who promptly garroted them publicly.

The women posed a dilemma. Father Ricardo wrote letters of absolution for the four women, releasing them from any sins, and signed them as the pope's emissary.

During the next two days, Rodrigo was struck by the compassion that Francesca showed for the injured soldier. She dressed his wounds meticulously and sat by his bedside when the doctor had to go away on other errands. Rodrigo had found her very desirable when they had first met. She dressed like the noble women of Valencia or Rome that he had courted at one time. Gradually, his attraction to her grew.

Two days later, on February 26, with the injured soldier still unwell, Rodrigo decided to leave him behind. He left two of the Swiss soldiers behind to look after their injured comrade and to escort the nuns back to Rome. He sent the other two girls back to their families in Sienna under the protection of two other Swiss soldiers.

The remainder of the group, with Francesca, embarked on the next leg of the trip to Florence. By now, Francesca and Rodrigo felt a strong attraction that was drawing them closer together.

The travelers stayed one night in Cortona, and arrived in the ancient city of Arezzo, famous for its jewelry, on the afternoon of February 28. In Arezzo, the resident papal representative arranged for them to stay in an inn far from the center of the city. Francesca also stayed in one of the rooms at the inn.

That night, Rodrigo had a bath and shaved for the first time since leaving Rome. He knew that it was his last chance to talk to Francesca privately and express his love and desire for her. He had a glass of wine and walked over to her room on the other side of the courtyard. He looked around. It was dark and there was nobody around to see him. Hesitantly, he knocked on her door. She opened the door and seeing him, immediately smiled. Huge candles and a roaring fire lit the room. She had just taken a bath and smelled fresh as a rose. Rodrigo decided to push his luck and asked if he could enter. To his utter surprise, she opened the door wider and he stepped into the room. She beckoned him to sit down.

Her blonde hair, still damp, hung in small curves around her face and neck and extended almost to her waist. Without makeup, she was even more striking. Everything on her face was perfect, from beautiful blue eyes to a perfectly upturned nose and full and sensuous red lips. She had a slightly pointed chin that complemented her face. Her skin was white and without blemishes or freckles.

Rodrigo could not control his feelings and suddenly blurted out, "How could anyone who is married to such a divine face plan to kill her?"

Tears welled up in Francesca's eyes. Rodrigo, realizing that he blundered, took a gamble. He took her warm, silky hands in his eager ones. Time was passing and he knew it. He said, "I am sorry, my love. I did not mean to upset you. Do you know that I have been in love with you ever since I first saw you inside that hideous cave?"

Through her tears, Francesca smiled back at him. "I was hoping to God that you would say that," she said shyly. Rodrigo got closer. He put his arms around her. She met his hot lips eagerly. Rodrigo felt the sweetness of her tongue and flashes of carnal desire traveled through his body to his loins. The kiss lasted for what seemed like a long moment. There was no further need for conversation or seduction.

Rodrigo's hand groped around and felt her body through her clothes. Awkwardly, he worked the knots and ties that held her bodice together. Women, regardless of their figures, wore those corset type dresses.

At that moment, Francesca's heart was filled with love and passion: She had met the love of her life and wanted to surrender herself body and soul to him. She decided neither to resist the temptation nor to pretend coyness. She smiled warmly and said,

"Amore, please don't be impatient. I have waited a long time for someone to really love me. Please let me change." With that, she glided away from Rodrigo's arms and slipped behind a screen that was used for changing.

Rodrigo took a deep breath and, throwing caution to wind, undressed and climbed under the thick eiderdown on the big, four-poster bed in the middle of the room. Francesca, emerging from behind the screen, laughed with pleasure like a little girl when she saw him in the bed. Wearing a robe taken from the bandits' booty, Francesca sat on the side of the bed next to him. Rodrigo took her hands, kissed them gently, and pulled her over to him.

They kissed passionately. "Why don't you remove your garment and join me, my dearest?" Francesca blushed, which made her even more desirable to him. Rodrigo moved over and invited her in. Without taking her robe off, she slid under the cover and lay on her back. Rodrigo gently undid the knot, opened the robe, and lifted the heavy eiderdown to look at her body. Francesca, still blushing, kept her eyes shut and her knees clenched tightly together.

Francesca's skin was satiny to the touch. Her firm breasts were shaped like lemons with pink nipples pointing up toward her face. She had a delicate navel. Rodrigo could see a hint of blonde hair jutting from between her tightly clenched thighs. She had perfectly shaped ankles and the prettiest small feet. With her long blonde hair and perfectly sculpted body, she looked like a Nordic goddess. Rodrigo thought, "No wonder the bandit Franco did not want to kill her or share her with anyone else." He massaged her feet, caressed and kissed her body all the way up from her ankles, to her thighs, her private parts, and finally her breasts. He took his time. Carolina, back in Valencia, had taught him well. "Take your time and go with the woman's tempo and you will be rewarded and remembered," Carolina had said.

The lovers embraced, kissed, and kissed again, each kiss more delicious than the last. Rodrigo gently massaged her right nipple with his thumb and forefinger. He then slid down a little and started sucking Francesca's left nipple without neglecting the right one. With his lips, he gently squeezed and pulled on the now hard nipple that was so proudly pointing upward. Her breasts were firm and voluptuous.

He kissed his way gently yet passionately to her navel before progressing to the center of her desire. Her legs were now open. He took a deep breath to inhale her essence before gently pressing his tongue into that forbidden zone. God, how he loved the scent of Italian women. With his tongue, he probed inside and worked his way around sucking and teasing her. He could tell by the way she writhed in pleasure that her husband had never done this to her. He kept on licking and probing and was soon richly rewarded with her first orgasm. He gently removed his tongue and started kissing and licking her body all the way up to her waiting lips.

She could feel his hard manhood, hot and pulsating, rubbing against her belly. Before long, he sensed by her rapid breathing that passion was welling up inside her belly.

Rodrigo had never taken a woman against her will. He looked into her eyes expectantly. In response, she reached down and lovingly squeezed his hard member. "Yes, my love," she whispered and opened her thighs even wider. He reached down and rubbed the tip of his manhood up and down against her small opening until she moaned before guiding it into her hot tunnel. It was warm, moist, and firm and it grasped him gently yet eagerly. Rodrigo consummated the act of love while looking at her eyes and uttering words of love and affection.

"Mio amore, mio amore" Francesca moaned. She seemed to have multiple orgasms before Rodrigo's seeds burst forth into her eager womb in one gigantic climax. The lovers lay exhausted next to each other.

After a few minutes, Francesca bashfully whispered, "My husband never kissed me down there. It felt so pleasant." Before Rodrigo could answer, Francesca suddenly got up and said, "Oh my God, the sheets are stained. What will the maids think of me in the morning?"

Rodrigo could not believe the innocence of this woman and burst out laughing. "Do not worry, my love," he said. "The maids are used to it and besides it is not over yet. By tomorrow morning, the sheets will be really wet." He pulled her over and kissed her fondly. Rodrigo stayed the night in Francesca's room and they repeated their passionate love scene several times. In the morning, they were both exhausted, yet full of the vigor generated by the act of love between a man and a woman.

CHAPTER THIRTEEN

FAREWELL TO FRANCESCA

The following morning, they packed their bags again and headed for the Republic of Florence.

From Arezzo, it took them two more days to reach Florence, a city that was new to Rodrigo and Jean. Rodrigo was eager to see the town that had nourished great artists and authors such as Dante and Giotto. He had read Dante's, *La Divina Commedia* several times. Coming from Spain, where inquisition was becoming the norm, he was amazed at the freedom of expression that existed in Florence.

Renaldo took it upon himself to show Rodrigo and Jean the famous Duomo and other structures, which were well preserved by the grateful citizens. Antonio Draghi, who had been waiting for them in Florence, joined the party.

Rodrigo sent for Francesca's father, Alfonso, who had given up any hope of seeing his daughter alive again. He was astonished to see her well. After some weeping and sobbing, Francesca told her story, which was corroborated by Petros, to a father who was getting angrier by the minute. When it was over, Signor Alfonso thanked Rodrigo for his gallantry and left to take care of matters his way.

That afternoon, Alfonso's men got hold of the servant who they felt was complicit in the kidnapping. After a night of torture, the servant admitted that he was the go-between who had arranged the kidnapping, which was supposed to end in murder.

The following day, Francesca's three brothers and her father invited Francesca's husband, Alberto, for a meeting. Alberto arrived, not knowing what lay in store for him. They asked him what had happened to the ransom money and his wife. Alberto responded that he had sent the money through his servant and there was no news of Francesca, as of yet. Tearfully, he said that he expected his wife was dead. It was then that the father called out for Francesca, who was waiting behind the door in an anteroom.

Alberto tried to talk his way out of the situation but then the battered servant walked in. Alberto ran from the house in mortal fear. That night, he was stabbed to death by an unknown assailant.

Francesca's family pretended that Francesca's ransom had been paid and she had returned safely, only to find that her husband had been murdered, possibly by the bandits. She returned to her house as a mourning wife. The servant who was involved in the kidnapping mysteriously disappeared.

* * *

Unfortunately, Rodrigo, who had found Francesca very attractive, had to move on. Early on the morning of March 2, they left Florence for Pisa, a two-day mule ride away. Rodrigo was very pleased that so far, no new attacks against his group of travelers had taken place. He continued sending his scouts forward and posting nighttime watches. He was now way outside the jurisdiction of the pope, so he was extra cautious.

That night, they neared the hill town of San Minato. Rodrigo decided to camp outside town in a hilly thicket away from the road. He was almost certain that no one had followed them from Florence, which was to his east. The road ahead to Pisa, which was to his west, was reported to be safe. To the south, lay the territory of the Republic of Florence.

He was only worried about being attacked from north of his location. On a hunch, he took the first watch himself and told Zangi to slip away north to another hill and maintain a lookout for any unusual activity. Rodrigo hated to do that to Zangi on a cold wintry night, since he could not light a fire while he was out there, alone, on scout duty.

After a supper of prosciutto, bread, cheese, vegetables, and dried fruit from Florence, washed down by Chianti, most of the party settled in for a deep sleep. Rodrigo usually ate after he finished his watch, otherwise he could not stay alert. Likewise, whenever he was not sure about his surroundings, he refrained from drinking. On this night, he did not eat much, since he was still brooding about Francesca. Their last farewell, in her bed-chamber, had been tearful.

Rodrigo turned over the watch to Jean and lay down to have a rest. He had just dropped off to sleep when Zangi shook him awake. Zangi quietly whispered that a party of about eight armed men was approaching from the northeast. Rodrigo looked around the camp. Everyone except Jean was fast sleep. By touching his lips with his index finger, he motioned for Jean to be quiet and they quietly followed Zangi into the darkness.

They climbed a little hill and in the moonlight, they could see movement and reflections on the armor of the men headed in the direction of their camp.

The intruders were not very careful; obviously, they did not expect to be noticed. Rodrigo hurried back to the camp. He had a problem waking up some of the men and when gentle measures did not succeed, he kicked them hard until they woke up. He managed to get Renaldo and three of the soldiers armed quickly, and they moved towards the hill. He did not extinguish their campfire, since doing so might tip the intruders that they had been noticed. Rodrigo, Zangi, and one of the soldiers went to the right. Jean, Renaldo, and two soldiers veered to the left. Rodrigo told Jean to try to get behind the prowlers and wait until Rodrigo had fired first, in order to catch them from behind.

They moved about three hundred feet and waited for the intruders. It did cross Rodrigo's mind that these people could be innocent wayfarers or local militia but he could not take any chances. He reasoned that if the intruders were innocent, they would not make directly for the camp.

They waited for the intruders behind a rock outcropping close to camp. The night was still. Soon they could hear the sounds of boots crunching gravel. Rodrigo held his breath as he aimed his big handgun, waiting for the sight of the first man.

The party approached. Some carried sabers; others, axes. There was no doubt then that they were hostile. Rodrigo fired his gun at the man nearest him. The man screamed and fell to the ground. They all fired their crossbows and muskets repeatedly. Before the intruders could see what hit them, Rodrigo shouted "Charge" and they all jumped into the melee. Rodrigo ploughed his sword into the nearest man, while Zangi stabbed each man that he could get close to with his deadly dagger. He inserted the blade into the right side of the body just below the rib cage and twisted one turn, pulled the blade out, and then moved on to the next man.

Jean was cutting into the crowd with his long sword and people were falling right, left and center. The Swiss guards had their broad, short swords out and were busy cutting the bandits down. Within a few minutes, it was all over. The intruders were dead or dying. A sharp sword blow to the throat by Renaldo killed the last one, who was kneeling and still alive.

Rodrigo gathered his men and they looked around to make sure that they'd left no enemy alive.

Jangly with adrenaline, they went back to the camp to wait for the first sunlight. Rodrigo fell asleep from exhaustion.

He was awakened by Jean way past sunrise. He was surprised that he had slept for so long. Jean smiled at him and said, "We have already checked the bodies. The leading man was a French knight and the others were probably local mercenaries hired to kill us. I actually think it was you that they were after because without you, we would have to turn back to Rome."

Rodrigo was mystified. First, the bandits near Chiusi seemed to have known about their movements and were following them. Now, these people, who were obviously French agents, had known where to find them. Someone was laying a trap for them.

Rodrigo decided to ignore Father Ricardo's pleas to bury the dead and they left as soon as they were able to move. Rodrigo pushed his men to make sure they would make Pisa that night, since he did not relish the thought of another night in the open.

* * *

They arrived at the beautiful city-state of Pisa after dark. The lights from the leaning tower helped them navigate the last few miles. Tired and exhausted, they stayed the night at an inn on the edge of town. In the morning, Rodrigo and Jean contacted Father Roberto, the pope's representative in Pisa. A fast messenger from the pope had informed Roberto about their visit.

Together, they found Signor Guardini, the master of the ship *Bella Pisa*, which was moored close by in the marina. Generally, Pisan ships were smaller than Genovese and Venetian ships. However, because of their shape and size, they could move faster and were more maneuverable.

Rodrigo was in a hurry to depart for two reasons. He was anxious to get to Constantinople and rescue the True Cross before the barbarians invaded the city. And he had a feeling that Italy was getting too dangerous for him. He was being betrayed and he did not know whether the traitor was a member of his entourage or another person following them discreetly.

Bella Pisa was loaded with horses, munitions, and supplies, and ready to move within two days. Rodrigo sent a report of his progress and his fears about a possible traitor to the Vatican by fast messenger through Father Roberto. He also sent a farewell letter to Francesca, declaring his love and expressing the wish that they might find each other again.

For the sea voyage, Rodrigo took Zangi, Jean, Renaldo, Lorenzo, Father Ricardo, Antonio, and Petros along with him. He told the Swiss soldiers, the grooms, and the servants to wait for him in Pisa for ninety days and then return to the Vatican. He was not sure whether they would ever come back alive.

After midnight on a clear, moonlit night, the Pisan ship slipped out of the harbor and into the sea. Rodrigo stood at the bridge looking at the lights in the harbor until they disappeared. He knew a traitor lurked in their midst, but who could that be? The dangers were just beginning. The day was Thursday, March 6, 1453.

* * *

During the first days of the trip, the sea was choppy and it kept the passengers indoors in the small cabins most of the time. There was plenty of food and as the captain had suggested, they kept their stomachs full to prevent seasickness. As they got closer to the port of Naples in southern Italy, the weather improved. The sun shone and the seas were crystal clear and indigo blue.

Rodrigo, Jean, and Renaldo spent a considerable amount of time together. Renaldo related stories about the court of the Ottomans. Being in his fifties, Renaldo seemed rather old to be in such an expedition and Rodrigo asked him why he had volunteered. Renaldo said that most of his friends were dead and after years of adventuring and wandering about the Mediterranean, he did not have a penny to his name. It was his last chance to be useful one more time before his time came.

Jean was the most enigmatic one in the whole party. Eventually, on a balmy night as they were sitting on the deck talking and drinking wine, he told them his life story.

* * *

"I was born near the town of Montpellier in southeastern France in the region of Languedoc," Jean began. "My father Roger, the count of Mont Claire, had extensive feudal land holdings. He was married twice. His first wife, my mother, died when I was only two years old. I have two older brothers and a younger stepsister.

"Our family was very close and we especially loved our sister, Monique, who was a beautiful and pure girl. We had a very happy childhood. My father was, for many years, a trusted advisor to Queen Yolanda of Aragon and managed her vast estates in southern France. He was well rewarded by the queen and respected by the clergy because he was known to have an open house for clerics who would come from afar on their way to Rome to visit the holy city and perhaps kiss the hand of the pope."

Jean stood and gathered his cloak more tightly against the sea wind. "After the death of Queen Yolanda, my father retired from public service and devoted the rest of his life to looking after his estate and hunting.

"Being the third son of a nobleman meant that I would get a good education and be trained in all the martial arts of the day. However, I would not inherit any of the property.

"That is in keeping with the feudal tradition, which discourages dividing the land and diluting the assets. In feudal states, the first son inherits almost everything. In the absence of any direct, male descendants, all assets go to other male blood relatives and ultimately, to the crown if no one is found. The women have to fend for themselves, which is not a very pleasant situation to be in. However, if one of the sons inherits the estate, then the remainder of the sons and daughters are allowed to stay on the family compound. This has always been the feudal custom.

"By the time, I was twelve years old, I had mastered Latin, Italian, and Greek. My military training progressed smoothly. I was trained in crossbow shooting, battling with the mace, and above all, fencing.

"One day, I was stricken with a high fever. My father called in the doctor but no amount of leeching or medication seemed to help me. They knew it was not the plague, since I was the only one who was affected. My sickness lasted several days. I was getting weaker, and my temperature was rising every day.

"After about a week, my father called in the priest to give me the last rites.

"The family held a vigil around my bed. I was too weak to speak properly, but somehow managed to ask them to leave. I knew that it was my last night on earth and I wanted to die alone. My little sister Monique refused to leave and sat there, on the floor, at the bottom of my bed crying and praying.

"Around midnight, I sensed a strange silence in the room. I opened my eyes. A very bright moon was shining through the window, casting its eerie light on objects around the room. The candles had gone out. I raised my head and I noticed that my sister, while still sitting on the floor, had fallen sleep with her head resting on the side of my bed. I assumed that I was dead and my soul had just left my body.

"Then I saw her, our Lady Joan, the maid of Orleans. She was an angelic young girl of about fourteen with very short brown hair. Her battle clothes were in tatters. In her right hand, she held a small cross that shone as bright as the sun, illuminating the room like a thousand candles. My little sister Monique woke up. She was stunned. She kneeled on the floor, transfixed, with both hands together as if trying to pray.

"Our lady got closer to me. I whispered, 'My blessed lady, I am suffering. Please take me away with you.' She put her left index finger to her lips as if to tell me to be quiet. As she came closer, I could sense her presence throughout my body. I felt warm and light, not feverish and miserable. She put her left hand on top of my head and said, 'Jean, it is not your time yet. The Lord has other plans for you.' With that, she gently closed my eyes with her hand.

"The next time I opened my eyes, it was daylight. My family was gathered around me. They were all smiling and I heard my sister repeatedly say, 'He is waking up.'

"The first words out of my mouth were, 'I am hungry.' My stepmother smiled and said, 'We will cook one of your favorite foods now. Meanwhile, Celeste, our cook, will get you some bread, wine, and cheese.'

"The fever was gone and within a day, I was out of my bed. It took me a few more days to recuperate. Meanwhile, most of my clothing had disappeared. I thought my clothing had been burned but then I heard the whole story.

"The vision that I had was also shared by Monique. As soon as I had closed my eyes, the room had gone dark and the image had disappeared. Monique had rushed downstairs to wake up my parents, my brothers, and the servants and tell them about witnessing the miracle. Everyone had rushed into the room to see me, expecting that I was dead, since that was what the doctor had expected to happen that night. Instead, they found me in a deep sleep. My temperature was back to normal. The whole family, including the servants, stayed up the rest of night, around my bed, to share in the miracle.

"When I woke up healthy and hungry, the miracle was proved right. Relatives, friends, and servants tore all my old clothes and bedding for their power of magic and gave the scraps to friends and family. Monique hid her clothes before miracle seekers could take them also. Even so, my stepmother practically shaved Monique's hair with her shears to send pieces of it to her relatives and close friends.

"After I was well, my education continued. However, ever since that day, my sister and I have been revered. My sister is especially sought after. People come from afar to ask her to pray for them or lay her hand on their heads to heal them. She had many suitors but she considered joining a convent. Then she had a vision that told her, 'Your brother has been selected to do the work of the Lord. You must marry and have children who will be messengers of Christ.' She was married to the son of a nobleman and lives near our estate. She is the purest being in this universe and her presence lights up any room.

"When I was eighteen years old, I was approached by the secret order of the Templar and asked if I had the calling to join. As you know, the order is extremely secret and only a few people know of it. I went to see my sister and together we prayed to the Lord.

"I joined the secret order of Templar when I was eighteen years old and here I am, four years later. His holiness sent for me several weeks ago. I went to see Monique, who seemed to know about my mission in advance. She has premonitions. My sister made me a little bracelet from the dress that she was wearing the night I almost died and I am wearing it around my wrist now."

* * *

Turning to Rodrigo, Jean said with a wry smile, "Holy Father must have seen something pious in you to send you on this perilous mission. I have heard about your scandalous life and it surprised me when I heard that he had selected you to lead this mission."

Before Rodrigo could answer, Jean said, "I implore you, Rodrigo. Our Lady Joan of Orleans has been in heaven for twenty-two years and I am a proof of her miracles. Yet the English have done all they can to stop her from being canonized and made a saint. Promise me, my friend, that if you are ever in a position to help her achieve her right place in the holy church, that you will do whatever it takes. You promise me that and I will die fighting for you."

Rodrigo was overcome with emotions that he did know existed. He clasped Jean's right hand in both of his hands and, looking into his tearful eyes, said, "I promise on my honor and the holy blood of our savior Jesus Christ that it will be the first thing that I do if I ever have the opportunity."

It was Renaldo's turn to speak. "To understand the Ottomans, you should know something about their heritage and religion. So, I am going to tell you what you will be facing."

CHAPTER FOURTEEN

THE INFIDEL KINGDOM

Renaldo took a sip from his glass of red Florentine wine, sat down, and told them the story of a kingdom of infidel barbarians who, in less than a century, had captured a third of the civilized part of Europe.

The Ottomans or Osmanli, as they call themselves, were a tribe of Asian nomads who lived in Central Asia alongside their Mongol cousins. The Mongols gradually pushed them out of Mongolia and the surrounding areas. They moved westward until they reached Anatolia, which is the Asian part of their current empire. First, they defeated the local Muslim rulers and emirs. Then, they gradually spread their kingdom south toward Syria. That was nearly two hundred years ago.

Slowly, the Christian Byzantines were also being pushed out of Asia Minor and confined to the southeastern part of Europe and their capital, Constantinople, which has remained impregnable for over ten centuries.

Eventually, the Ottomans crossed the Bosphorus for the European mainland. Their first target, Constantinople, proved impossible to conquer and they abandoned their siege after a few weeks.

Gradually, over the next decades, they kept pushing west and defeated the Serbs, the Greeks, the Croats, the Macedonians, and the Bulgarians, and thereby captured all of Greece and most of the Balkans.

The Ottomans, like other Mongols, have a streak of cruelty that has helped them conquer the civilized lands of southeastern Europe. However, they have not been able to make any inroads in the East, since there they are up against the Persians. The Persians are a Caucasian race and worship a different version of Islam and God. Their religion is called Shiite and they have been able to confine the Ottomans to Asia Minor.

The highest position in the Ottoman infrastructure is the sultan. For some reason, the Ottomans never established a proper practice for succession. In most countries of Europe and in the Orient, there is a tradition called primogeniture. Primogeniture means that the oldest son or, in some cases, daughter has the right to succeed the father.

In the Ottoman culture, once a sultan dies or is killed, the male children battle to the death to succeed him. The survivor is declared the next sultan. If you can be that cruel to your own flesh and blood what will you do to others? This custom has established a culture of family brutality and fratricide that continues to this day.

"I hear that they have a formidable army of zealots," Jean said.

Renaldo piped up, "It is not really an army in the sense that we know it in Italy or even France or England, for that matter. Their main fighting forces are the Janissaries. They are good fighting men because they have no other options. They cannot turn back or run away to their homes, since they do not have any homes."

"What else can you tell us," Rodrigo asked.

Renaldo poured more wine. "In the fourteenth century, after invading parts of the Balkans, the Ottomans started stealing young boys from Christian families, forcibly converting them to Islam, and developing them into a fighting army," he said.

"These young men are selected by Devshirme system. The ruthless officials of the Turkish Ottomans go from village to village and forcibly recruit young Christian boys from conquered lands for military service to the sultan. The boys are not allowed to marry or contact their families ever again. Naturally, there is a high incidence of homosexuality among those troops. The Janissaries are the main army of the Ottomans."

It was getting late, but Rodrigo said, "I have heard a lot about the harems of the Orient. Is it true that a man can have more than one wife legally?"

Renaldo smiled. "As a matter of fact, he can have up to four permanent wives and an unlimited number of temporary wives. They are kept in a harem and the bigger harems are managed by eunuchs."

Jean said, "I have heard about the eunuchs but I have never seen one. How do they make them into eunuchs?"

Renaldo picked up a piece of chalk from the yardarm casing and drew a diagram of a Muslim house on the wooden floor of the ship.

CHAPTER FIFTEEN

HAREMS AND EUNUCHS

"Harems are part of the Muslim tradition," Renaldo explained. "They are a technique used to keep the women inside a boundary and prevent outsiders from having any sexual contact with them."

Jean asked, "Are the women ever allowed to leave the harem?"

Renaldo grinned and said, "I will come to that soon. Muslim houses are divided into two parts. The anterior, or the rooms facing the street or alleyways, are the places into which visitors and tradesmen are allowed. There is usually a small garden between the anterior and the remainder of the house. One can only reach the interior of the house by first entering the anterior and then going through the garden and perhaps a corridor and yet another door. Only close family members are allowed to cross that threshold.

"A harem, which means a sanctuary, is a place for a man's wives, concubines, female servants, girls before they are married, boys under the age of ten, and eunuchs. A man is allowed to have up to four wives legally and they are supposed to be treated equally. The four wives and their children are eligible for inheritance. The Muslim laws are very explicit in these cases. A man could never completely disinherit this class of descendants from getting his money and land. Even with a will, he could only donate one-third of his belongings to others. His legal descendants, who are his sons, daughters, and wives, in that order, inherit at least two-thirds of his estate with or without his will.

"The concubines are temporary wives that a man can marry for a fixed period that is specified at the time of matrimony. It could be as little as half an hour or as lengthy as ninety-nine years. The concubines and their children are not eligible for inheritance.

"The slave women are treated as the property of the man of the house. He can do whatever he wants with them. Sleeping with the slave women or boys is not considered adultery or sodomy. The children of these slaves do not inherit anything, either. While the children born to concubines and slaves are not considered bastards, nevertheless there is a stigma attached to being such a child."

Renaldo continued, "When men speak of slaves, people visualize images of illiterate, but strong, men and women plucked away from their hamlets by Arab slave traders and sold to work in the fields. Zangi is a good example of this type of slave. While that is true, many of the slaves in the harem are highborn women who were captured by the Ottomans during their conquests in Asia Minor and the Balkans. Many know multiple languages and are trained in the arts of singing and playing musical instruments.

"The most important female in a harem is the mother of the man of the house, if she is still alive. Whenever a man enters a harem, unless it is late at night, he first visits his mother and kisses her hands. He usually sits at the foot of his mother's chair to show respect. Even the sultans do that.

"Next to his mother, come his favorite wives. In a large harem like that of an emir or a sultan, there are many, many women."

Renaldo looked at the faces around him. The men were hanging on his every word. "It is obvious that a man, even a sultan, especially when he gets older, cannot even meet, let alone satisfy, all his many wives and concubines. Usually, he has one or two favorites and socially and sexually ignores the rest. Becoming one of the sultan's favorites and getting pregnant is the sole ambition of these women. It is not uncommon for the wives and concubines to bribe the eunuchs to guide the sultan to their quarters whenever he enters the harem.

"So, how do those women satisfy their urges? For one thing, they give money to the eunuchs to smuggle in young men. They dress them as another eunuch or maybe as a woman. For example, supposing a woman sees a young gardener or a handsome soldier while looking through a window and she gets a hankering for that man. The eunuchs, for a fee, could arrange a meeting. The man would get money and the woman, satisfaction. That is fine for older women who cannot get pregnant but it is dangerous for the younger ones. Many of them are found out and receive the ultimate Ottoman punishment. The woman is placed in a canvas sack that is sewn shut and dropped into a river or a deep lake.

"The other method for obtaining satisfaction is the tongues of the eunuchs. It is thought that the eunuchs invented the cunnilingus or the intricate art of licking and sucking a female's genital parts. The coordination of mouth and tongue takes time to learn. The Muslim men would never do it, since they consider it below their dignity to lick or even kiss a woman's sexual organ.

"Then, there are candles. There is a saying that part of the job of a eunuch in a harem is disposing of used candles in the women's toilets. Most harem women, except the virgins, use candles to satisfy their urges.

"Finally, there is the girl next door. Many of the women and girls sleep in close quarters and even in the same beds. Of all the sexual aberrations, lesbianism is the only one that is generally tolerated by Muslims as long as it is not practiced openly.

"After a few months in the harem, the free women are allowed to see members of their immediate family. They are allowed to travel, under escort, to other towns and spend time with their own relatives. This does not apply to the slaves. However, some slaves manage to become concubines and wives. Some actually have become mothers of future heirs."

"What about the eunuchs?" Jean interjected.

Renaldo said, "Don't be impatient, Jean. That is my next topic."

Renaldo took a deep swallow of his wine and went on. "Eunuchs are the backbone of the harem. They are responsible for managing the servants and arranging ceremonies, such as weddings, funerals, and circumcisions. The chief eunuch is a very powerful man. He controls the harem's budget. He has his own quarters and is respected, and sometimes feared, by the men and women of the harem. He is at hand whenever the sultan visits the harem. As a sign of respect, he is called *agha*, which means 'sir' in Turkish. A good *agha* is esteemed at the court.

"The eunuchs are generally slaves who were castrated when they were young and assigned to serve in the harem. They are without testicles. Their testicles are either removed or crushed.

The eunuchs are considered equal to females and are thus allowed to associate freely with the women of the household. Sometimes a castration is not successfully carried out and a eunuch is able to enjoy himself with the slave girls or the wives.

"Castration is common among the Byzantine Christians, as well. If a king or an emperor wants to punish an enemy but does not want to kill him, he either blinds him or has him castrated. A merciful ruler might even let the enemy be blinded in one eye only.

"Ironically, some eunuchs, with the help of the sultan's mother or favorite wife, achieve positions of importance in the court and some become viziers to the crown. Some are quite capable men!"

Rodrigo and his men had forgotten their fatigue. They leaned forward, listening intently.

"A sultan's young sons are generally kept in the harem until they reach pre-puberty and then they are removed and assigned to male mentors who are usually men over fifty who can be trusted not to molest the boys.

"Young girls remain in the harem until they are married. Usually, neighbors and relatives hear when a girl has reached the age of marriage, which is around twelve. Then, women, usually the mothers or sisters of potential suitors, come to visit the harem to see and talk to the girl. Some families allow a male suitor to have a brief look at the girl before he makes his decision.

"Males are allowed in the harem to see their close relatives, such as daughters, sisters, aunts, and cousins. The cousins could fall in love and be married. The Muslim religion does not place any restriction on marriage between cousins.

"The sultan's harem is structured the same way as most Muslim houses, except it is a huge mansion and is surrounded by a large garden. In addition to having bedrooms and meeting rooms for the sultan and female visitors, the mansion contains several kitchens and has its own bathhouse. In the Turkish language, they call the bathhouse, *hamam*. The *hamam* is always in the basement. It consists of a cloakroom where the bathers undress and hang their clothes. After changing, the bathers cover the lower parts of the body with a thin loincloth and enter a very large room surrounded by three pools. Two of the pools contain hot water that is constantly being heated by wood or charcoal from underneath. There is also a cold-water pool. Upon entering the bathroom, the person initially goes to the first hot water pool to soak for a while. That is where women and their kids sit on platforms made of stone and tiles built inside the pool and chat. The kids play in the water and attempt to swim. The women sometimes bring in fruits and other food to eat and share. Water is constantly running in and out of these pools to keep them clean.

"After soaking in that pool, they go back to the large room. In that room, they soap themselves. The soap is washed off by pouring clean hot water from the second hot pool. They use small pails to scoop the water up and pour it over themselves. In the sultan's harem, there are slaves who are assigned to soaping, massaging, and cleaning the bathers.

"The next stop in purifying the body is dipping at least three times inside the second hot water pool. This is a very religious ceremony and they dip in until their head is under the water three times. Any excess soap is washed off and the body becomes squeaky clean. The cold pool is not always used. Mostly, it is used in summer just before leaving the bath.

"Men and eunuchs are only allowed to use the bathroom very early in the morning or very late at night. The Muslims are usually bodily clean, even if their souls are false. They cannot say their daily prayers if certain parts of their bodies are dirty. After a man has had sexual intercourse or even a wet dream, he has to take a bath to cleanse himself before he can pray to God again. Hence, the reason for early morning bathing. Women cannot enter a bath during their menstrual cycle.

"Usually, no one uses the bath alone late at night. Many Muslims believe that fairies and genies occupy the bath after midnight. The genies and the fairies look like human beings except that they have hoofs instead of feet. The fairies are either benign or good. The genies are supposed to be bad and could possess a person's body, similar to the Christian belief that demons can take over a person's soul. These creatures are supposed to exist in a different dimension and materialize in certain places or upon certain circumstances."

Rodrigo and Jean were mesmerized by these revelations. They were beginning to see the face of the foe that had been such a constant threat to Christianity for hundreds of years. Jean addressed Renaldo, "You seem to have a very detailed understanding of the Muslim world. How did you acquire such a depth of knowledge?"

Renaldo shrugged his shoulder and simply said, "I kept my eyes and ears open!"

* * *

During the next few days, the *Bella Pisa* sailed around the boot of Italy and up the Adriatic Sea. Soon, the travelers were within two days of their destination, the port city of Dubrovnik.

On the last night at sea, Jean asked Renaldo to tell them more about Mohammed II, whom the pope had said was an evil person.

Renaldo paused for several minutes before answering. Then he said, "You must look at these historical figures in the context of their time and location. During my time at the Ottoman court, I was employed by Murat several times to do his biddings. I also met Mohammed, who was a young boy then. Even as a boy, he was mischievous and cruel.

"Murat, the father, was nothing like him or any other Ottoman ruler. He even spared the life of Mustafa, his brother, who later rose up against him. Unlike his son, Murat was a benevolent ruler."

CHAPTER SIXTEEN

THE HOUSE OF EVIL

"As I mentioned previously," Renaldo said, "Murat was not a wicked or a malevolent man. As a king, he was actually a compassionate ruler. In fact, if he were a Christian, he would have made a better king than some of our European royalty. Nevertheless, unfortunately, in that savage kingdom, he ended up with evil relatives.

"Murat II became a sultan in 1421. Unfortunately for him, he neglected to kill one of his younger brothers, Mustafa, who staged an uprising against him. Eventually, Murat managed to defeat and kill Mustafa.

"Like many Ottoman sultans before him, Murat tried to conquer Constantinople but was defeated and had to withdraw. Nevertheless, he consolidated his power in all the territories in the Balkans and made further inroads against the Serbs and the Venetians.

"Murat had many children. His favorites were his son and daughter, Mohammed and Aziza, by his fair-skinned Albanian wife. Aziza was about five years younger than Mohammed.

"In 1444, Murat decided to abdicate and spend the rest of his life in prayer and solitude to atone for the murders committed during his reign. To avoid family bloodshed, he made his twelve-year-old son, Mohammed, the new sultan and retired to Eastern Anatolia.

"Mohammed proved to be incompetent and lost several battles against the Bulgarians. Murat had to come back to save the empire from total collapse at the hand of the Bulgarians."

Renaldo continued, "If he had failed, he would have been defeated by the Bulgarians and that would have been the end of the Ottomans."

"What do you know about Mohammed?" Rodrigo asked.

"From what I have heard and read in letters from my friends, he is one of the cruelest sultans that the Ottomans have ever had. However, thanks to pillaging the Serbian and other Balkan cities, monasteries, and churches, he has a lot of money at his disposal. He spends this money freely to hire European mercenaries and even painters and poets to accompany him in his marauding ways."

After a long pause, Renaldo went on. "Murat died two years ago in 1451 and Mohammed took over again, this time as Mohammed II. Mohammed was older and wiser this time around. As his father was on his deathbed, Mohammed dispatched agents to kill all of his brothers, including an infant who was barely one year old, even though his mother pleaded at his feet to save her son.

"Later, he issued a decree to require the slaughter of all potential heirs to the throne on succession of a new sultan."

Rodrigo and Jean exchanged glances. This is the man they would be facing!

"When Mohammed was growing up, his schooling was handled by teachers who were proficient in history, languages, and military techniques. In addition to Turkish, which was the language of the common Ottomans, he could speak Persian, which was the language of the Ottoman poets and writers, such as Rumi. He also spoke Albanian, which was his mother's tongue, and could understand some Greek. He could read the Koran, which was written in Arabic, but like so many non-Arabs, he did not understand it," Renaldo continued.

"Mohammed's sister, Aziza, was educated in Latin in addition to other languages. She did not need any military training and had more free time to pursue literary interests before getting married.

"After ascending to the throne, Mohammed's first priority was to consolidate his power base in the Balkans.

"During his childhood, Mohammed had developed a deep friendship with one of the boys assigned to be his playmates. The Ottoman royalty does not allow the male members of their ruling classes to get too close to the sultans or the potential sultans, for fear that the sultan would be usurped and replaced by another emir or lord. Instead, they search for and elevate intelligent sons of lowborn parents, such as bakers, cooks, and tailors, and assign them to sensitive ministerial posts. One such child was Abdullah Hassan, whose father was a barber. He was selected to be a childhood playmate and he stayed on as a close friend of Mohammed after they grew up. Eventually, he was appointed governor of the Balkan province. His mission was to deal with the unruly Serbs, who were pining for independence and would battle the Ottomans every thirty or forty years. He was made a *bey*, which is equivalent to an overlord.

"Abdullah Hassan Bey is as cruel if not more cruel than the sultan. He is fond of heinous reprisal techniques. For every

Ottoman soldier killed, he rounds up and kills ten civilians. The Serbs, being obstinate and obdurate, do not seem to flinch at his methods, but they have nicknamed him Abdullah the Butcher."

The gentle-hearted Jean was offended by the atrocities that Mohammed had performed to keep his throne. He asked Renaldo, "What do we know about his sister?"

Renaldo replied, "When I saw Aziza last, she was but a small child. From what I hear through my Ottoman friends at the court, she is now of the age of marriage. There have been many suitors. Even the Christian king of Bulgaria has asked for her hand in marriage to his son and heir."

CHAPTER SEVENTEEN

IN THE CLUTCHES OF EVIL

After ten days at sea, they spotted the old lighthouse near the coast of Croatia. The voyage was over. Within a few hours, they were disembarking at Dubrovnik, an ancient commercial port with proud citizens. Dubrovnik reminded Rodrigo of Venice, a few hundred miles northwest.

Dubrovnik was neither as big nor as powerful as Venice, but it was a prosperous republic. The city had strong-walled defenses. To keep the infidels away, they sent regular tributes to the sultan in his capital city of Edirne. There was even an Ottoman legation in Dubrovnik.

Many commercial ships came and went from Dubrovnik, so their small Pisan ship did not attract any attention. Fortunately for Rodrigo and his companions, Dubrovnik was a Catholic city inhabited by Croatians. Orthodox and Muslim interlopers inhabited the Serbian heartland surrounding the city. At times, the Serbian and Greek Orthodox populace detested the Catholics almost as much as they hated the Muslims. This animosity had allowed the Muslims to drive a wedge that had split Christianity into two hostile camps.

The first thing that Rodrigo and Jean wanted to know was the status of Constantinople. The news reaching Dubrovnik was becoming gloomier by the day. The sultan was gathering a great army of Muslim fanatics and East European mercenaries for his final assault on Constantinople

Renaldo volunteered to visit the Ottoman legation to obtain some firsthand news. He thought he might even come across some old acquaintances there.

The first night in port, Rodrigo told everyone to go out and enjoy themselves. They were exhausted from their battles with the French mercenaries near Pisa and the long sea voyage. He told them to stay in groups of two to avoid being drugged or kidnapped. Ottoman spies were everywhere.

The members of the group went different ways. Renaldo left for the Ottoman legation. Rodrigo and Jean decided to rest at the inn with the ever-present Zangi, who stayed within sight of Rodrigo. He had his orders from the pope and would not let Rodrigo get hurt.

Rodrigo and Jean had a merry time feeling the solid ground beneath their feet, drinking, and talking about their experiences. After a few drinks, the topic turned to the attacks they had survived so far. Rodrigo said that he was sure that the attack by the bandits near Chiusi was not a coincidence. He definitely had no doubt about the ambush near Pisa by the French mercenaries. "How many people would have known our route?" he asked.

Jean shook his head. "Do you suspect anyone?"

Rodrigo said he was not sure. They went to bed late.

The following day, they had a late breakfast of boiled eggs, goat cheese, and bread washed down with some fortifying honey-sweetened warm milk. The other members of the group turned up by mid-day. Meanwhile, Jean was busy managing the logistics of their transportation to the Macedonian city of Skopje.

All the members of the team were anxious to find out where they were going next. Only Rodrigo, Jean, and Father Ricardo knew the true mission. Renaldo was told that the destination was Constantinople before they had left Rome, since he was supposed to help them arrive there safely, but he was not told why they were going.

While onboard the Pisan ship, Rodrigo had told the others that their next destination would be Dubrovnik on the eastern side of the Adriatic Sea. He had told them that under orders from his holiness, Pope Nicholas, he was not permitted to give them any more information about the trip until later.

Later that afternoon, he asked all his team members to meet him in the small church of Santa Carla. He had Zangi and Jean search the church before the meeting and positioned Jean outside the church to prevent intruders and spies from coming in.

He addressed them all. "My dear friends, you have proved your devotion to our holy church and the true successor to Saint Peter by being here today. You could have abandoned the holy father and me in Florence and in Pisa, but you stayed the course. Last night, or even this morning, you could have taken one of the several ships bound for Venice and be back in Italy in a few days. You stayed and I am eternally indebted to all of you. I am now allowed to explain to you the rest of our mission. We are going to Constantinople to deliver an important message from his holiness to the emperor there.

"The day after tomorrow, we will be leaving Dubrovnik and will first cross into Serbian Orthodox territory and then into the

Muslim lands. The Serbian Orthodox have no great love for us and the Muslims hate us. As far as we know, the sultan is not, as of yet, aware of our mission."

Rodrigo then said, "We will need everyone in this room for this trip. I wish I had ten more people like you for this perilous journey. However, I am willing to release you from the oath that you took when you agreed to undertake this journey. The next Venetian ship will be sailing at first light tomorrow morning. You can be there with letters from Father Ricardo absolving you of any blame. Come and see me afterward if you want to leave."

With that, Rodrigo left the podium of the church. Before he was out of the door, he was besieged by his team. The swarthy Sicilian, Lorenzo, was the first to speak. "*Signor*," he said, "We have suffered the bandits of Chiusi, the French mercenaries near Pisa, and the long sea trip, and we are not turning back now that the journey is getting really interesting. We will follow you wherever you go." The rest of the group nodded in agreement.

Rodrigo had never realized the depth of these men's loyalty. Obviously, his uncle, Cardinal Alfonso, and the pope had done a great job selecting this devoted group.

Later that afternoon, Renaldo returned with disturbing news. Apparently, the sultan was indeed gathering a huge army of Muslims and renegade Christians. He was waiting for the weather to improve before marching to Constantinople. The good news was that the roads from Salonica and Edirne to Constantinople were still open to travelers.

According to Renaldo, the Ottomans were so sure of victory that their courtiers were already addressing Mohammed as *Padeshah*, a Persian word meaning "king of kings" or "emperor" in anticipation of the conquest of Constantinople. As Renaldo had said, the Turks had borrowed many words from their arch-enemies, the Persians. In the tribal Ottoman life, there was no Turkish word for king of kings or emperor.

"The worst news is that Mohammed is apparently developing a secret weapon somewhere near Constantinople and it is said to be able to destroy the impregnable walls of the city," Renaldo said.

A cold shiver ran down Rodrigo's spine when he heard about the secret weapon. The pope had told Rodrigo that Constantinople's fall was near and he was about to witness the permanent end of a glorious civilization. A civilization that had lasted more than a thousand years was about to be destroyed at the hands of nomadic barbarians who did not even have a complete language of their own.

Renaldo also had some other news about Abdullah Hassan. Aziza, the sultan's sister, was to be married to Abdullah the Butcher in late March in Skopje, Macedonia. Abdullah was on his way to Skopje already and they were planning fireworks and a big celebration for the wedding.

Renaldo sounded surprised that Aziza would deign to marry Abdullah the Butcher. Based on what he knew, the man was a maniacal murderer and, was more interested in boys than girls. "As you know," Renaldo said, "in many Muslim countries, the girl has no say in who she will marry even if she is a princess."

Rodrigo replied, "Even in Europe, marriages are arranged against the will of both men and women. I was being forced into one, myself. That was one of the reasons why I left Spain."

The following day, Renaldo and Lorenzo went searching for mules and supplies. Antonio went around town searching for dry black powder.

In the marketplace, Dubrovnik was more like an Oriental city than like Venice. The travelers had to do some bargaining and posturing to purchase supplies. They had plenty of gold but since they were acting as merchants, they had to play the game according to the rules. If they did not haggle about prices, like every other merchant, people might become suspicious of the true nature of their trip. By late afternoon, however, they had their mules and food supplies for the long trip to Skopje.

Lorenzo and Renaldo had decided on a particular route that would take them through Skopje, Sofia, Edirne, the capital of Ottomans, and finally to Constantinople. Their reason was twofold. First, since it was a route well traveled by the sultan's army, it would be relatively free of the bandits who plagued this part of the world. The other reason was that many European merchants wishing to trade with the Ottomans would have chosen that route. Ostensibly, they were merchants carrying fine European wool and jewelry, which were in high demand in the Orient, to barter for Oriental silk and spices, which were in high demand in Western Europe. Their chosen route would first take them through Serbian territory, then the Ottoman protectorate of Macedonia, and finally through Muslim territory to the outskirts of the great city itself.

From this point on, Rodrigo did not expect any help from the Templar knights or the Catholic clergy, for that matter. They would encounter few Catholics after Dubrovnik and no Templar knights to help guide their way. They hired a well-recommended

Croat guide by the name of Stepan Polancec to help them get to Skopje.

That night, the group had a final meal together before venturing into the unknown territory. Father Ricardo led the group in the Lord's Prayer. The men were tense, since they were now entering a territory that was alien to them. Apart from Petros, Renaldo, and to a lesser degree, Lorenzo, they did not know the languages or the customs of these people. They could trust no one and would have to be suspicious of all. What made the trip more difficult was that because of their unfamiliarity with the territory, they could only travel during daylight hours.

Even though Rodrigo was not an early riser, he woke up very early on the day of departure to inspect the cargo. After his fateful journey from Rome to Pisa, he did not trust anyone with munitions and food. After he made sure that the supplies had not been tampered with and the mules looked healthy enough, he sat by the courtyard, in a hidden corner, on an ice-cold stone bench and kept an eye on the mules and the valuable freight that they would be carrying. Rodrigo was a night person. He disliked getting up early in the morning; being up at dawn always made his stomach feel queasy. The rest of the crew woke up soon afterward and they were ready to depart by the first sunlight.

The morning was chilly and a cold mist was descending on the city from the interior mountains. The road between Dubrovnik and Skopje consisted mostly of mountain passes.

Lorenzo and Renaldo estimated that the travelers could cover the distance between Dubrovnik and Skopje in six to nine days. From Skopje, it would take them eight to ten days to get to Edirne, and then another two to four days to get to

Constantinople. So, the entire trip was expected to take around three weeks. They were hoping to travel as fast as possible to get to Constantinople before the infidels completed their tight ring around the city. What Rodrigo had not told anyone was that he was planning to make a detour when they neared the city to search for Mohammed's secret weapon.

CHAPTER EIGHTEEN

THE ROAD TO SKOPJE

The sun rose in the East as Rodrigo and his friends left Dubrovnik. They were now entering a territory that was just superficially friendly. Each man was thinking about his life and how he had served God. Rodrigo was still thinking about Francesca, who seemed to be a million miles away. He felt that he had a better chance of getting to the moon than of ever seeing her or his elderly uncle again. He was sure that he would die in foreign lands and yet somehow he did not mind it. A cold wind was blowing from the East, but it was not a strong wind. As the sun rose, the day got warmer and the men felt better in their bellies. The road leading to the little town of Cavtat, which was their first stop on the way to Skopje, was well traveled and therefore easy for the mules and the men.

As the day wore on, they started climbing hills that led them higher into the mountainous territory.

* * *

Mules are created from the forced copulation of a mare with a male donkey. The mare is held in place in a tight stall while a donkey with his huge member erect is placed behind her. The donkey mounts her from behind. There is no room for the mare to move and there is only pain and suffering for the female horse from this act of rape by a lesser creature. The mule is, therefore, a strange, obstinate, and even nasty creature that seems to enjoy antagonizing men. Rodrigo noticed that as they started climbing up steep hills with deep gorges to the sides, the mules chose to tread close to the edge of the narrow roads, as if hoping to discard their human tormentors and their cargo over the edge in the deep valleys below.

Many travelers kept their eyes shut while riding mules across mountain passes with deep gorges. Some disembarked and walked with the mules. However, it was dangerous to walk too close behind a mule because it was apt to kick with its powerful hind legs. The mules were generally surefooted but occasionally the ground slipped from beneath their feet and they fell to their deaths taking with them their riders and cargo.

In some places, the steep sides of the valleys were littered with carcasses and skeletons of animals and men who had perished making the trip across the mountains. It was an unwritten custom of travelers in those parts that if an animal slipped and fell into a gorge and its cargo or rider could not be recovered easily, they would be left to perish and rot away by themselves. This was the Balkans and compassion, then as it is now, was a rare commodity.

* * *

On the first day, they managed to cover the distance to Cavtat with ample time to spare. They spent the night there. Rodrigo was cheerful and felt relieved that no accidents had befallen them. Maybe, he thought, what had happened before was just bad luck.

They got up very early the next morning to start their journey to the next milestone in their expedition. The trip progressed uneventfully and around noon, as they were climbing another steep mountain with an almost vertical chasm on the right side, the saddle on one of the mules carrying food loosened up and tilted to the right. The heavy load pulled the unfortunate mule over the edge. With a cry of agony, the mule disappeared into the abyss. While this event was a disaster, there was no point in stopping and they pushed on.

About two hours later, real disaster struck. The saddle on Father Ricardo's mule loosened up and before he noticed what was happening, Father Ricardo slid off the mule and down the sloping side of the hill. He grasped at the grass and the bushes to no avail, sliding several hundred feet to a precarious clearing just above another vertical drop to the valley floor. The travelers gathered at the edge of the road, trying to see what had happened. Rodrigo shouted to Father Ricardo but he could not hear any response.

Their experienced guide, Stepan from Dubrovnik, being a practical man and a survivor, suggested that they should not waste any time trying to rescue Father Ricardo. It would delay their schedule and they would have to spend the night in the cold, dangerous mountains. Rodrigo was so enraged by the remark that he hit Stepan across the face with the back of his gloved left hand and simultaneously pulled his sword out with his right. He pointed it at the throat of the bewildered guide. "We are not leaving our brother down there, dead or alive," he said. "You are coming down with me to rescue him and if you return alone or try to escape, that man over there, pointing to a grinning Zangi, who already had his dagger out, will cut your throat in an instant. Do you understand me?"

The guide, who was scared to death, nodded his head vigorously. Rodrigo sheathed his sword and called on Antonio and Lorenzo to get some rope.

They tied a length of rope together and tethered it around a huge boulder at the side of the road, and dropped the rope down the slope. It came close to where Father Ricardo lay motionless. Rodrigo motioned to the terrified guide to go first.

Stepan grabbed the rope and started gently down the hill, holding the rope tightly with both gloved hands and using his feet against the side of the hill to ease himself downward. Rodrigo told everyone that if something happened to him, they should continue their journey with Jean at the helm. He added that he would follow the guide down and Lorenzo should follow them next.

The climb down the hill was not easy for a person who had never climbed mountains. However, Rodrigo's youth and determination carried him through as he slowly inched his way toward the priest. A few times, he lost his footing and dangled over the deep valley below, but his grip held and he eventually made it to where the shivering guide was standing, about twenty feet above the ledge where Father Ricardo lay motionless.

The evening wind was picking up and Rodrigo's ears and nose were getting numb from the cold. Rodrigo called out to Father Ricardo. There was no response. It was a desperate situation. Here they were in the middle of a steep valley in the dead of winter in hostile land with no one to call for help. If Rodrigo fell, there would not be enough time to save him and the father before nightfall, and they would both freeze to death. Oh, what he would give for the warm fireplace of his home in Rome and the warm comfort of one of his mistresses, even the treacherous Paola Colonna. At least he knew how to handle the Colonnas. But this?

Soon, Lorenzo arrived with some pieces of bedding material and trouser legs that the others had scrounged and tied together, creating a short, makeshift rope. Even though Rodrigo wanted to go down, Lorenzo begged him to allow him, a smaller man, to slide down to the priest. Rodrigo reluctantly agreed. Lorenzo tied the makeshift rope around his waist and while Rodrigo and Stepan held one end of the precarious rope, he lowered himself. "Remember," Rodrigo told the guide, "if the rope slips, you will be killed by me or by my servant above." There is sometimes nothing more powerful than fear. The guide held to the rope for dear life.

Lorenzo reached the ledge that had stopped Father Ricardo's fall. He listened to the priest's heart and felt him breathing. He shouted, "He is all right, he is still alive."

Rodrigo was relieved. Lorenzo continued checking Father Ricardo's body for evidence of fractures and not finding any, he shouted, "I think he will live. We will need to get him up to you. I will wrap the end of this rope around him and push him while you pull him up to you."

The cold wind was picking up now and it took nearly an hour to pull the unconscious Father Ricardo up from the ledge. Stepan and Rodrigo untied him and dropped the rope for Lorenzo.

Eventually, all four men were on the slippery slope above the ledge. Rodrigo got his flask out and poured some brandy wine down Father Ricardo's throat. Father Ricardo spluttered, coughed, and opened his eyes. Rodrigo was afraid of that the shock might drive the priest berserk, so he forced some more of the fiery liquid down his throat. Father Ricardo was now coherent and remembered what had happened to him. Rodrigo said, "The light will be getting dim soon and we cannot stay down here much longer. We are going to tie the rope around your waist and shoulders and they are going to pull you up. You can help by pushing your feet against the walls of the hill to lessen the load. Do you think you can do that?" Father Ricardo nodded.

They tied the young priest up and motioned to Jean and the others above to start pulling. The poor father was almost dangling from the rope with cold winter wind of the Balkans blowing through his clothes.

At first, the cold was painful but then the young priest felt numbness in his limbs. A sense of abandonment and delirium overtook him, and as he looked up, he saw a glorious light from heaven beckoning him to come home. This must be rapture, he thought, and then he passed out. It was getting dark, rapidly, but eventually a comatose Father Ricardo made it to the top.

Renaldo and Jean wasted no time in undoing the knots from the rope and throwing it back down to the three remaining people. They then covered Father Ricardo with all the heavy clothing and blankets that they had at hand.

Petros, who knew the symptoms of severe shock and cold exposure, took over the priest's care. He tore Father Ricardo's pants down, exposing his almost frozen genital organ. He took his own pants down and let out a stream of hot liquid onto the frozen man's private parts. Father Ricardo's body convulsed. Suddenly, a thin shaft of frozen urine shot out of his penis and he started urinating uncontrollably. Petros smiled happily for, as a doctor, he knew that once a man's genital area is frozen he is almost dead unless hot water is applied to it immediately. In the absence of hot water, urine was the best treatment that Petros could think of. He was pleased that it had worked. He quickly covered the priest with warm clothing.

Down on the slope, at Lorenzo's suggestion, Rodrigo climbed out first, followed by Lorenzo, and finally their guide, Stepan. By that time, it was almost dark. Stepan, who was now more terrified of dying from exposure than at the point of Zangi's dagger, said, "There is a blizzard coming and we have to move back to a sheltered grove about a mile up the road." They had no choice but to follow him. The snowflakes had already started falling. The wind was getting stronger and colder. The journey to the sheltered area was miserable.

By the time they arrived, they could hardly see more than a few feet in front of them. They were cold and hungry. They set up their tents and grabbed whatever was available to eat and drink. Stepan and Zangi tied down the mules and gave them some hay. Father Ricardo was badly bruised but no bones were broken. He could hardly move his right arm but Petros suggested that the pain would go away within a few days. Before Zangi settled down for the night, he tied up Stepan to make sure that he would not escape with the mules. They were so tired that they did not wake up until the sun was already shinning on a blanket of snow.

The bitter wind had stopped and the sun felt warm and wonderful. They had some bread, cheese, and wine, which made them feel good to be alive after the ordeal of last night. They were short on food supplies but they could restock at their next stop.

Before they set out, Renaldo approached Rodrigo with some grim news. "While you and the others were down in the ravine yesterday trying to pull Father Ricardo up, I checked the mules' saddle belts. Some of them were a notch or two looser than they should have been."

Rodrigo knew that the saddle belt was usually tightened slightly more than the animal could bear since throughout the journey, due to sweating and other bodily activities, the beast would lose fluid and the stomach would shrink. A loose saddle belt would cause the payload of humans or cargo to slip and fall to the side. Rodrigo thanked Renaldo for his diligence and asked him to check the loading personally this time. After Renaldo left, Rodrigo sat back on a nearby stone and thought about their bad luck so far. Everything was pointing to a traitor in the camp. It could be anyone. What if it was Lorenzo, the Sicilian? Last evening, he could have pushed him down the deep gorge and blamed it on the Croatian guide. Rodrigo tried to remember the events of last evening. Did he ever turn his back on Lorenzo? Maybe he did not and that is why he was still alive.

Rodrigo tried to remember what everyone was doing yesterday. He felt dizzy and faint until he felt a hand on his shoulder. It shook him out of his morbid state. He looked around. It was Jean and the guide Stepan telling him that they were ready to move on. Stepan suggested that because of the snow and the slippery conditions of the road, they should walk the mules rather than ride them until the snow melted. Rodrigo agreed. In fact, he was happy that he did not have to mount one of those wretched beasts again. He sent Lorenzo and Petros to scout ahead and followed with the rest of the group.

Normally, Rodrigo would be happy to lead his men. However, he had become very apprehensive since yesterday, as he was constantly worried about turning his back on a group that included a traitor or assassin.

Late that afternoon, they arrived at their next rest stop, which was really a hamlet of just a few shacks and a feed store for the animals. They would have been there last night if it was not for the unfortunate accident with the mules. They had to stay the night since the next stop was a day's ride away.

Another caravan traveling from the East was already there. Those men had left Skopje a few days earlier and were on their way to Dubrovnik. They reported that the road was passable but the big news was the impending attack on Constantinople. As usual, there was a fair amount of exaggeration. Some were saying that Mohammed had a million soldiers while others believed that he had huge battering rams made of steel that would break through any gate. There was also talk of a secret weapon. The Muslims believed that angels had descended from heaven to help him create a fiery engine that would engulf the city in flames and burn all the non-believers.

All of this talk worried Rodrigo, but he was more worried about the morale of his men, who had been battered by accidents and bad news since leaving Rome. He kept his anxieties to himself.

The following morning, they left early. The road to Skopje wound through several small towns and villages on high plains and low mountains. Although they encountered snow and sleet several times, the snow did not last long on the ground. Before long, they were in the fabulous Vardar Valley and getting close to Skopje.

CHAPTER NINETEEN

SKOPJE

Skopje was a medium sized city by medieval standards. At the time of Rodrigo's visit, it had a population of around 50,000. The city was bisected by the magnificent river Vardar flowing from the north and it was a major trade crossroad from north to south and east to west. The city had been under Ottoman protection for many years. The Ottomans had renamed the city Üsküb and had built several magnificent mosques and big public bathhouses or *hamams* in the city. There was already a growing population of Muslims, converted Muslims, and Spanish Jews in the city proper, although the countryside remained overwhelmingly Serbian Orthodox.

Rodrigo and his group arrived in the city late in the afternoon. They were hungry, exhausted, and filthy. At Renaldo's suggestion, they decided to visit a bathhouse to get themselves cleaned up. Rodrigo's niggling worry that he had a traitor in his midst had eroded his trust in his men and, what's more, he did not want to be ambushed while the entire group was naked in the bathhouse. Therefore, he divided the men into two groups. He sent Jean and half of the men in first while he and the other half maintained a vigil outside the bathhouse. When they emerged, Rodrigo and the others went in to bathe. Renaldo decided to wait, saying he would bathe alone. He wanted to take a nap inside the hot steamy bathhouse and rejuvenate his old bones.

Rodrigo discovered that the bathhouse was even better than Renaldo had described. It was very warm and there were attendants who washed them with coarse cloth followed by soap and water. There was even a barber to shave them. They noticed that Muslim men were defoliated with the use of a special paste that was applied to all of the hairy parts of the body, especially the genital organs. After about fifteen minutes, the men washed themselves and lost all the hairs on their bodies. However, they did not shave their beards, only trimmed them!

After bathing, they felt fresh and lively. They went back to the rooms they had rented at the inn, leaving their dirty clothes to be washed, and went out for food and drink. The city was in a jovial mood for the upcoming marriage ceremony of the sultan's sister to the viceroy and governor of the Balkans, Abdullah Hassan. Banners, signs, and multicolored lanterns festooned the thoroughfares in preparations for a brilliant fireworks display.

The group had a dinner of rice topped with tender skewered lamb kebabs marinated with basil vinaigrette and washed down with good local wine. They went back to the inn very tired and ready for sleep. Even though Rodrigo hated to deprive his party of a well-deserved sleep in comfortable beds, he insisted on posting the regular watch outside their living quarters. Rodrigo took the first watch.

After breakfast the next morning, Rodrigo sent for Stepan. He paid him off and asked if he wanted to continue with them to Edirne and then to Constantinople. Stepan, who had started to respect Rodrigo after observing his courage and determination on the trip, said that he would be happy to continue the journey with them. If his services were not satisfactory, he could recommend a Macedonian guide from Skopje. Rodrigo decided to keep him on.

After Rodrigo dismissed Stepan, Zangi approached him to report that Jean had left the inn that morning near dawn and was gone for approximately two hours. Rodrigo wondered if Zangi ever slept. Rodrigo had already decided not to share any of his thoughts with his fellow travelers for fear of being betrayed. Therefore, he decided not to challenge Jean about his unusual absence.

That day, for the first time, they saw the dreaded Ottoman Janissaries. They were tall, handsome men in colorful uniforms. However, they looked very stern as they patrolled the palace of the viceroy.

Interestingly enough, they did not have the Asian features— the almond-shaped eyes, straight hair, and high cheekbones— that the Mongolians usually have. As Renaldo had explained, most of these Janissaries were white Christians. In addition, during their rapid conquest of Eastern Europe, the Ottomans took many women prisoners. At times, a man had ten or more white slaves and the babies of those women were brought up as Muslims. Therefore, the Ottoman race in Europe was gradually becoming a mixture of Asians and Caucasians but the culture remained strictly Muslim.

Later that day, Rodrigo sent for Stepan, Renaldo, Petros, and Jean and asked them to provision them for the trip to Edirne. They needed food, water, wine, and dry gunpowder. They also needed to buy a few more mules to replace the ones they had lost and those that had become too weak to travel during the trip from Dubrovnik. Since the road to their next stop, Sofia, was not very mountainous, Rodrigo decided to buy some horses to ride instead of the dreaded mules that he disliked so much.

Rodrigo knew that he had to give his people time to rest, so they spent the next two days recuperating and buying supplies. Rodrigo, Renaldo, Lorenzo, and Jean conferred to decide which road they should follow to Constantinople. They knew that the shortest route was through Sofia in Bulgaria to Edirne and then on to Constantinople. However, they could take the longer road south to Salonica and then make a detour to Edirne from there.

The shorter road was busy with Ottoman soldiers and couriers and it would drive them deeper into Muslim-held territory. The longer road passed through mostly mountainous, Greek-populated country, which was less traveled and friendlier. Jean and Lorenzo suggested the longer and safer road. Renaldo advocated taking the shortest possible route since Constantinople could be besieged soon. If they took the longer road, he argued, they might not be able to get in, let alone get out of the city after completing their mission. Rodrigo sided with Renaldo and on the third day, they departed Skopje fully rested and ready to face the next leg of their journey to Sofia.

CHAPTER TWENTY

FROM SKOPJE TO DISASTER

The first two days of their journey east were uneventful. The horses and mules were fresh. The roads were not so steep and mountainous now, but they were still hilly and the ride got a little more precarious as they left the relatively flat Vardar Valley.

Stepan and Renaldo, who knew the roads well, had estimated it would take six to eight days to complete the trip. However, each day they were delayed by late starts and sick animals that they had to leave behind. On the fourth day out of Skopje, they camped at night in a shallow valley just off the road. Rodrigo favored leafy places, which were not too far from the road, to camp for the night. As was usual, he set up a rotating watch shift, starting with Zangi at ten, followed by Jean at one in the morning, and Renaldo at four. Renaldo was supposed to wake everyone up at daybreak.

Just before dawn, Renaldo curtly awakened Rodrigo, who was dreaming of happier times in Valencia. Renaldo was in bad shape. He said he had been hit on the head from behind and knocked unconscious. When he came to, he discovered that most of the supply mules and the horses had disappeared. Poor Renaldo was almost in tears for having been ambushed.

Rodrigo woke the others and they surveyed their losses. All their food was gone; however, their guns and swords were mostly intact since they had taken them to bed with them. In addition, Antonio had learned from previous disasters and every night, he unloaded the gunpowder and slept next to the bags. They also had the gold that they were carrying on their persons. The worst news was that their guide, Stepan had been murdered, his throat slit, ear to ear, in the Ottoman fashion, while he slept.

With only two horses left, they started the journey toward Sofia on foot. Rodrigo sent Lorenzo forward on one of the horses to scout ahead for another caravan or some other source of food. Later that afternoon, Lorenzo rode back excited. He reported that a very lightly guarded caravan of about twenty people was heading their way. It looked as though they were carrying plenty of supplies, based on the number of supply mules they had. He had approached them to offer them gold for food but they had not let him get anywhere near the caravan and, in fact, the armed guards had chased him away with their swords drawn.

Rodrigo decided to stop the caravan and try to bargain for mules and supplies. However, how would six men stop a caravan that is guarded by probably ten to twelve armed men? Antonio proposed that since the area was hilly, they should try to find a location with overhanging rocks or loose gravel and use explosives to block the pass as soon as half of the caravan had passed through. In the ensuing confusion, they could overcome the guards and then try to bargain for horses and mules with the gold they were carrying. Rodrigo did not like the plan, which seemed like highway robbery similar to what the bandits at Chiusi Pass had tried to do to them. But there was little choice. The alternatives were raiding the caravan, expiring of starvation, or being captured by the sultan's men.

Antonio borrowed Lorenzo's horse and went forward to reconnoiter for a suitable ambush area. He was back soon with the news of a perfect location. They walked another half an hour before they arrived at a narrow gorge with high, rocky walls. Antonio and Rodrigo went up to inspect the rocky hill. They soon found several perfect spots to plant explosives. Time was of essence since the westbound caravan would be arriving soon. They shouted down to Zangi and Jean, who brought the explosives up to them. Antonio, the munitions expert, soon set up the charges and the fuses. He told Rodrigo, Zangi, and Jean to go down the hill since he did not need any help in lighting the fuses.

On the floor of the ravine, Renaldo suggested that he, Father Ricardo, and Petros should stay on the Skopje side of the road before the explosion. If members of the caravan got away, they could deal with them. Rodrigo and the remainder of the crew would hide on the east side of the road and wait for the caravan. As soon as the vanguard of the caravan crossed the point where Antonio had set up the charges, he would ignite the fuses. The avalanche of rocks, pebbles, and stones would separate the caravan in two and cause confusion. Rodrigo and his men would deal with the dazed guards on the east side of the gorge while Renaldo would deal with anybody who made it to the other side of the pass.

They had just a few minutes to hide behind bushes and rocks before the advance guard of the slow-moving caravan appeared about a mile away. As they came closer, Rodrigo noted that there were only ten guards with the caravan. What alarmed him, however, was that Lorenzo had neglected to mention that these men were not just ordinary guards. They were wearing the uniforms of the Ottoman soldiers! There were at least ten mules in the caravan, several of which were loaded with special litters called *houdahs*—small living quarters. Two sides of the *houdahs* were covered with curtains. The travelers, usually women, sat cross-legged inside, although they could stretch a little and even sleep in a fetal position. The passengers could peek through the curtains and communicate with the caravan's leaders by calling out.

What worried Rodrigo and Jean was the fact that the mules with the litters bore the green colors and the insignia of the Royal House of Ottoman. There was no turning back now, however, since Antonio was out of reach and the caravan was almost upon them.

They waited as the slow-moving mules ambled past their hiding place. Then, there was a series of explosions and a blanket of dust rose up in the sky and rained upon them for a few seconds. Maybe Antonio had used too much explosives! They jumped out and charged the startled soldiers, who, not knowing what had hit them, mostly ran away. Rodrigo was hoping there would be no bloodshed since he did not want to bring the entire Ottoman army upon his head. However, several soldiers were killed by the falling rocks and a few put up a valiant fight and had to be killed.

When the cloud of dust had settled, they surveyed the aftermath. None of the soldiers were still standing, but several eunuchs ran about or tried to hide for dear life. Rodrigo and Jean approached the middle *houdah* but were stopped by a tall, black eunuch who blocked their way, speaking in Turkish. They pushed him aside and pulled back the curtains.

Rodrigo and Jean were amazed at what they saw. Inside was probably the prettiest girl Rodrigo had ever seen and yet she did not have a speck of makeup on her face. She wore an exquisite red cashmere jacket with long, soft, blue pantaloons tied at her pretty ankles. Her long brown hair was tied back with a wide green ribbon. On her head she wore a small, flat hat with a lace veil. The veil had fallen to one side of her face, exposing her loveliness. She had the smallest nose that Rodrigo had ever seen on a woman. Her mouth was small with full, red, pouting lips. Her skin, as much as could be seen, was young and slightly tanned. Her deep brown eyes burned with anger.

Realizing that they did not speak Turkish, she lashed out at them first in Greek and then in Latin, asking if they were Christian infidels. Without waiting for their answer, she demanded to see the leader of the bandits.

Rodrigo was dazzled by the perfect beauty of this young woman and actually stammered for a long moment. Jean stepped in and answered in Latin that they were merchants on their way to Sofia.

"I demand that you clean up the road and arrange for our passage right away," she said in the tone of someone who is used to giving commands and expects them to be obeyed.

While Rodrigo stood open-mouthed, watching the scene unfold, two other things happened. First, another woman jumped out of a second *houdah* and ran towards the first, screaming loudly, asking if the younger woman was all right. At least that is what Rodrigo thought she was doing, since she was shouting in Turkish and seemed to be cursing and growling at them.

She grabbed the young girl's hands and started kissing them. It seemed that she was praying to God that her lady was safe. This woman was white and about thirty with dirty blonde hair and green eyes.

Almost at that precise moment, Renaldo, who had made his way over the rubble to join them, reached the top of the pile of rocks that covered the road. He took one look at the insignia on the mules and sank to his knees. He just sat there, murmuring to himself and cursing himself. After a moment, he got up in a daze and walked towards his companions. He seemed to have lost all of his self-assurance. He looked at the mule train again, shook his head in disbelief, and with his index finger summoned Rodrigo and Jean out of earshot of everyone else.

Looking at the ground to control his anger, he said, "You fools! Do you realize what you have done? This is a royal caravan and is probably carrying one of the sultan's concubines or relatives to visit her kinfolk. You have doomed us all to a horrible death."

Rodrigo was not accustomed to being called a fool. But before he could answer, an excited Lorenzo came running over, and said, "Signor Rodrigo, I must talk with you now! It cannot wait."

Rodrigo left the other two and moved away with Lorenzo. "What is the matter?" he asked impatiently. "You are as pale as Renaldo. Have you seen a ghost? What is going on now?"

"Signor Rodrigo, the young woman in that *houdah* is Princess Aziza, the sister of Mohammed," he said. Now it was Rodrigo who felt the color drain from his face and got a sinking feeling at the pit of his stomach. He thought, "God, what are you doing to me? Why all of this? Out of the fire and into the frying pan?"

Lorenzo continued, "But that is not all, sir. There was another, much bigger caravan behind them and it should be arriving at this location by nightfall. We will have to move, signor."

By then, Father Ricardo and Petros had made their way over the rubble and joined them.

Rodrigo told the men to guard the prisoners and rushed back to join Jean and Renaldo. Addressing Renaldo, who was squatting on the ground staring into nothingness, he said, "It is actually worse than you thought. The lady is not a concubine but the sultan's sister, Aziza."

Tears rolled down Renaldo's cheeks. "I have failed and this is the end of us," he said. He placed his face on his knees, and just went quiet.

Rodrigo had not seen a grown nobleman cry before, but he knew that he had to make a decision fast before they were trapped by the next caravans. He motioned to Jean to watch over Renaldo and went back to survey the scene. There were ten mules in the caravan. The first mule was carrying the woman who was obviously the nanny. The second mule was carrying the princess and the third one was carrying two women who were apparently handmaidens. Four of the other mules carried supplies. The last three were ridden by eunuchs, who had dismounted and now stood anxiously next to their animals. The soldiers were dead or dying; some had run away on horseback.

Rodrigo was annoyed with Lorenzo for not noticing the royal emblem and for getting them into this mess. However, there was no time for recrimination.

He decided to keep the princess as a hostage, since he was in very hostile territory and now had offended the sultan. He needed a bargaining tool. He told his men to gather up the eunuchs and the women in the third *houdah* and send them back towards the other caravan. He inspected the mules with supplies and decided to keep the food and the ammunition that he needed. He discarded the many chests of jewelry and clothes.

He told the nanny, whose name was Katarina, to ride with her mistress in the second *houdah*. Then, with his men, the supplies, and the hostages, they headed off the road. They knew that they could not continue on the same road east towards Sofia. Rodrigo decided to head south, away from the main road, and then perhaps circle back east toward Constantinople. They rode south for about two hours, and then they turned east. Rodrigo's plan was to stay off the main road but to continue on a parallel path until he went past the big caravan that was following the royal caravan. Then he would rejoin the road to Sofia again.

That night, they camped in a clearing in a small valley using tents carried by the supply mules. They set up three camps, one for the princess and Katarina and two for Rodrigo's men. Renaldo insisted that the women be treated respectfully, even though he did not think that they would get away with what they had done. The moment he saw the green colors of the Ottoman royalty, he assumed they would all be put to death, but maybe it would be a death with dignity if they did not mistreat the women.

Later that night, Rodrigo and Jean paid a visit to the tent of Aziza and her nanny, Katarina. The two women were sitting on a thin mattress. Aziza was busy scribbling something in a notebook that she had in front of her. They assumed it was her diary, since it was common for educated women of nobility to keep a journal of their lives. Rodrigo cleared his throat to announce his presence and respectfully said, "I am sorry, Princess Aziza, about what happened today."

Aziza glanced up from the book and looked at them. The defiant gaze of that morning was gone. Instead, she wore a puzzled look of bewilderment and denial. She could not yet accept the fact that she was a captive. "Why did you abduct us? Are you brigands and plan to hold me for ransom?" she asked. "If that is the case, you are playing with fire and will burn yourselves. I demand that you release us immediately before my brother destroys you and your families."

Rodrigo was surprised at her tone, which implied great self-assurance. This woman was not just a harem resident, she was a woman of inner strength; yet she somehow reminded him of his true love, the tender Isabella.

Aziza turned to Jean and with a note of sarcasm asked, "Is this man, who seems to be in a daze most of the time, your commander?" That shook Rodrigo out of his daydreams. He smiled and said, "I am sorry, princess, but somehow you reminded me of an old friend and I have been trying to remember who. We are not bandits or brigands; we are on a holy pilgrimage. Unfortunately, we were robbed by bandits two nights ago and were looking for food and water. It is unfortunate that we had to fight your soldiers. We assumed that they would run away at the sound of the explosion."

Aziza snapped back, "Then why do you not release us immediately?"

Rodrigo hesitated. Then he said, "Regretfully, under the circumstances, I cannot release you until we are safely out of the area. Now, if there is anything else that I can do, please let me know. Meanwhile, your nanny can pick up your food anytime you feel hungry. I do not advise you to leave this tent without informing one of my men." With that, Rodrigo followed by Jean, was gone.

After a few minutes, Aziza lifted her head up and said to Katarina, "I think our life is in real danger. I know these infidels will do us harm. I am going to escape tonight." A horrified Katarina pleaded, "Please, my princess, don't be foolish. I was born and raised in this land. It gets very cold at night at this time of the year, and there are many hungry wolves and brown bears around that will attack and slay men. Bears are bad enough. Sometimes a man can outrun a bear, but the wolves hunt in packs and you can never outrun them. They can tear you apart in minutes."

Aziza was visibly shaken. She had kept track of their trip since they had gone off the main road, however, and she thought she could make it back on a mule in two or three hours. She told Katarina of her plan to slip out of the tent after midnight and get hold of one of the mules.

A patient Katarina tried to dissuade her from this petulant foolishness. She reminded Aziza that she had never saddled a horse, a mule, or even a donkey. "Have you ever picked up a saddle to know how heavy it is? You are good with horses but they are fully tamed horses that are saddled for you by a team of stable hands. You are but a young girl and have never ridden an animal bareback."

Aziza was dismayed and sat pouting, looking at her diary.

Rodrigo's men were happy for the food that they had found in the caravan. There was plenty of rice, salted beef, fresh bread, and dried fruit. They sent some food to the women. Katarina was hungry and ate her share. Aziza did not feel hungry and sent hers back. Rodrigo assigned the watch rotation and, after supper, one by one, the men went to sleep. Rodrigo did not. He sat there looking at the dwindling flames of their fire.

It was about ten at night when Aziza and Katarina heard a shuffling noise outside their tent. It sounded like someone was moving about. A minute later, a piece of paper was pushed through a gap in the tent wall. Katarina snatched it up and gave it to Aziza. It was scribbled in Latin and obviously written in great haste since it was almost unreadable. The note simply said, "Be ready to leave after midnight. There will be a mule ready for you inside the corral area. Head north towards the big star and ride as fast as you can and please destroy this note after you have read it."

Aziza was very pleased and prayed to God for being so merciful. Katarina was more cautious and voiced her concerns. They did not know who had written this note and why any Christian bandit would want to help the sister of the sultan. Aziza, like her brother, was a brave soul. She decided to go it alone. It would be faster to travel by herself and the bandits would probably run away, as fast as they could, once they had discovered that she was gone. Katarina implored her not to go but to no avail. Aziza burnt the paper and doused the candle.

They waited and waited on that cold night. Aziza dressed herself in the warmest clothing that she could find and peeked out of the flap that served as the tent's door. There were no guards around. She and Katarina made their way cautiously to the mule pen. There was a mule, already saddled, just inside the corral.

Katarina helped Aziza mount the animal and gave her the reins. The untied beast started moving almost immediately. There was hardly any time for good-byes. Aziza promised to send help as soon as she got to the main road and pulled on the reins to guide the animal to the north. The mule did not need any prodding, since that was the direction from which it had come earlier that day. Aziza was soon out of sight of the weeping Katarina, who went back to her dark tent and kneeled on the ground to pray for her young princess.

The fire had gone out and Rodrigo had fallen sleep. It was almost five hours later that he was shaken awake by Renaldo, who had discovered the missing princess and the missing mule.

Rodrigo Borgia in his later years as Pope Alexander VI

Pope Nicholas V (Tomasso Parentucelli)

who was pope at the time of the fall of Constantinople

No paintings of young Rodrigo have survived,
but he probably looked like his son, Cesare Borgia.

Lucrezia Borgia, Rodrigo's daughter

Depiction of an Ottoman (Turkish) princess

Houdahs on a camel train. *Houdahs* also were mounted on mules.

Constantine XI, the last emperor of Byzantine (Constantinople)

Europe in mid 1400s

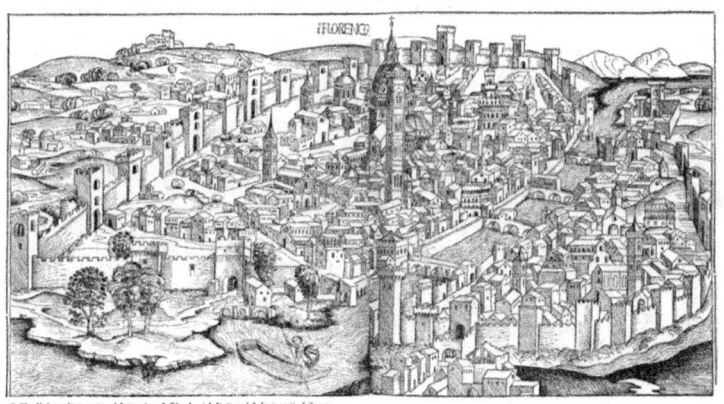

© The Hebrew University of Jerusalem & The Jewish National & University Library

Florence in medieval times

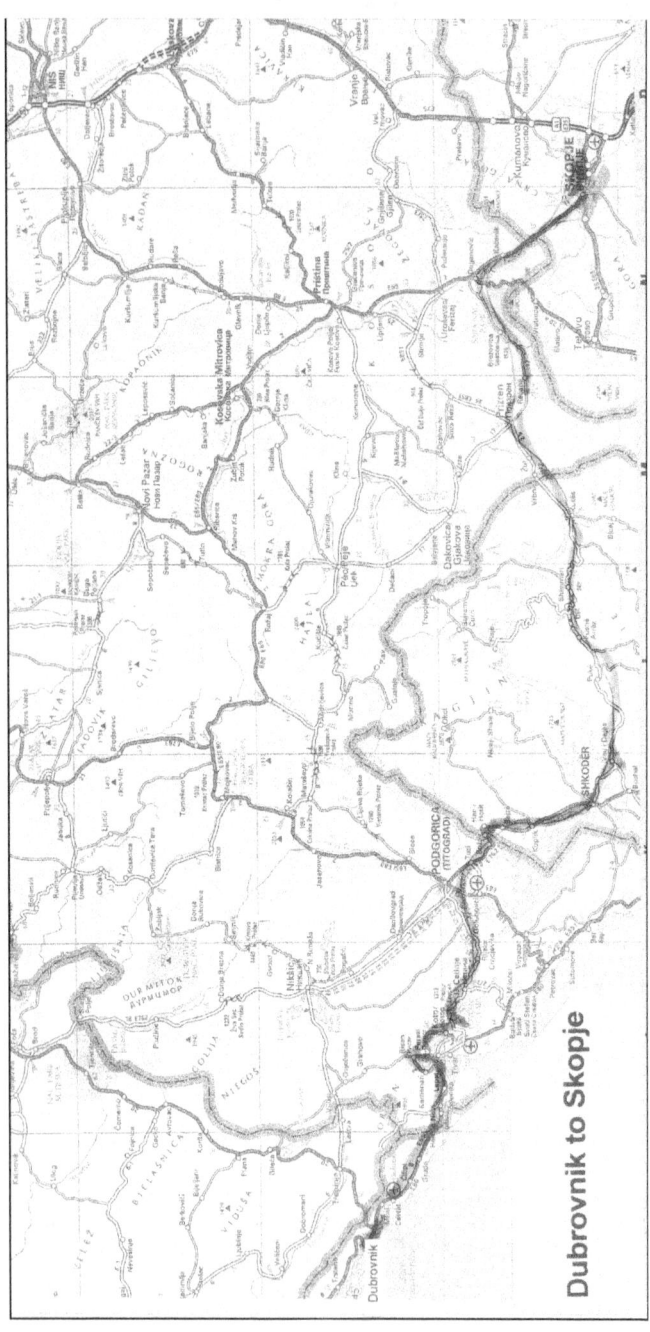

Rodrigo's journey from Dubrovnik to Skopje

Dubrovnik to Skopje

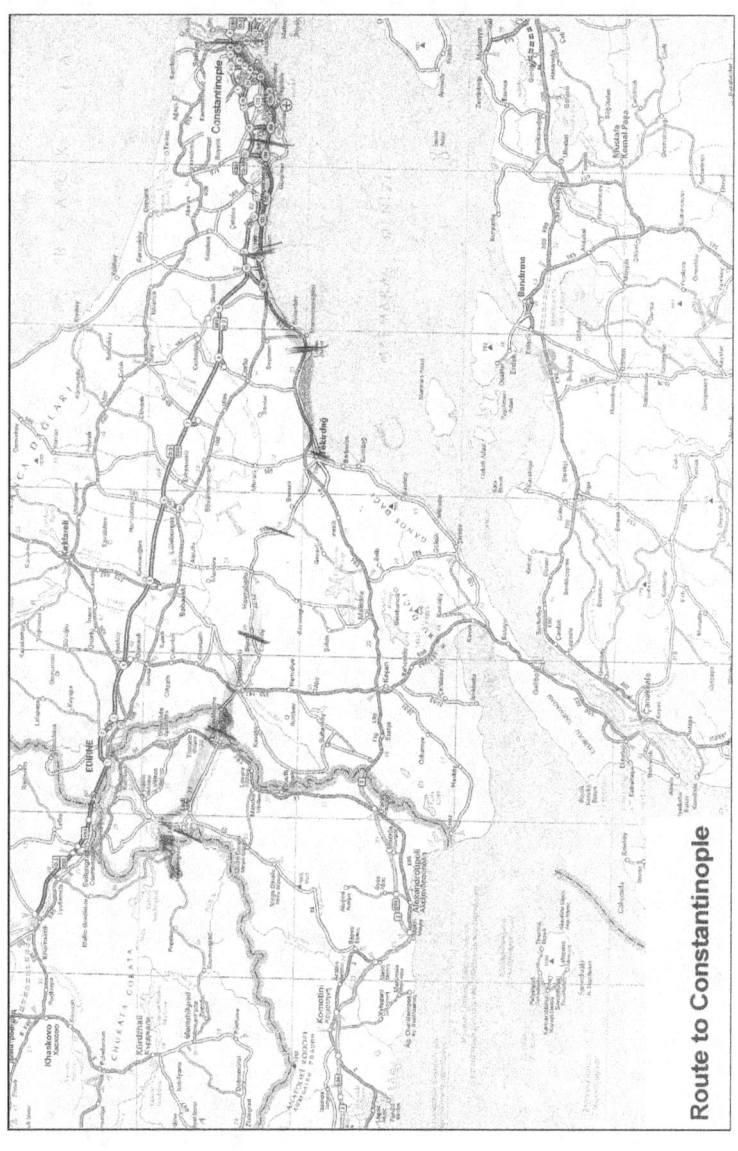

Rodrigo's final flight from the Ottomans to Constantinople

~ CHAPTER TWENTY-ONE ~

THE PRINCESS AND THE
WOLVES

Rodrigo woke up with a jolt. He had been having a night-mare that they had been captured and tortured by the Ottomans. When Renaldo shook him awake, he almost went for his dagger before recognizing Renaldo's calm, modulated voice. Renaldo kept repeating, "She is gone and so is the mule." Eventually Rodrigo came to his senses and asked, "How long has she been gone?" Renaldo was not sure, nor did he know in which direction she had ridden.

Rodrigo felt cold and miserable. He needed to drink something warm to rejuvenate his system. His legs were stiff from the night cold. Nevertheless, he jumped up and headed for the princess's tent. In the dark, he saw Katarina, who was curled up under two blankets. He rudely pulled the blankets away and asked the startled nanny what had happened to the princess. Frightened, she claimed ignorance. "She was over in that corner last night. I told him that already," she said, pointing at Renaldo. Rodrigo knew that she was lying but there was not much that he could do about it. He had not posted a guard on the tent since he did not believe that Aziza would be foolhardy enough to try to escape in the middle of the night in such hostile territory.

Miserably, he left the tent, telling Renaldo to wake up the others and tell them to join him by the dead fire. He called for Zangi and told him to start a proper fire again. It was cold but not as cold as the days they had spent in the desolate mountains of Montenegro, near Dubrovnik. Still, his teeth were chattering. Was it the fear of discovery and death? Aziza's caravan being Muslim, there was no liquor in the supply train; no wine he could drink to warm himself.

The rest of the crew hurriedly assembled. They had already heard the story and he could see terror and gloom in their faces. Without waiting for anyone to offer advice or an opinion, Rodrigo said, "We will need to find the princess and bring her back. You have heard the howling of the hungry wolves all night. This is wolf country and they are so ferocious that the local people have built legendary stories about men who turn into wolves at night. There are also plenty of vicious brown bears around. There is also a remote possibility that she could make it back to an Ottoman outpost and that would be disastrous for us. No matter what happens, we are in mortal danger. If the beasts kill her, we will be responsible. If she makes it back, we will be hunted down. Therefore, we need to find her alive and in one piece."

There was no time to waste. Rodrigo and Zangi headed north, back toward the main Skopje-to-Sofia road. He sent Antonio and Jean to the west and Lorenzo and Renaldo to the south of the camp. He reckoned that the princess would not have gone toward the wilderness in the east. They grabbed some food and left immediately.

* * *

Aziza had second thoughts almost as soon as she lost sight of the camp. The darkness surrounded her quickly and she could hear the sounds of nocturnal animals scurrying around her. They had camped on a plain with very few trees but soon she entered a heavily wooded area, which became denser as the mule moved further north. In the harsh moonlight, the trees cast frightening shadows around them. Aziza was holding the harness very tightly and praying every step of the way. She avoided looking around for fear of seeing something scary jump out of the shadows at her. After nearly an hour, the ground rose and she came across a small lake that they had crossed the previous day. That made her a little less gloomy, for at least the mule was on the right track back to the main road.

No sooner had she relaxed than she sensed the mule acting differently, as though it was nervous about something. After a few minutes, she could sense the presence of other beings around her. Her courage was draining fast and she closed her eyes, but then she realized that she could be knocked off the mule by a branch if she did not see it in time to duck. Something or someone was following them and the mule seemed to know it, too, since it had started to trot faster. Aziza was scared to look behind her, but eventually she glanced back and let out a muffled scream of fear when she saw a pair of ferocious yellow eyes shining in the darkness. The creature was following them closely.

Surely, this must be a nightmare, she thought. She bit her lower lip hard to wake up but the wolf was still there and God, holy merciful God, she was petrified!

Another wolf joined the first one. Aziza egged the mule to move faster with her stick, not that the mule needed any encouragement. It started galloping and in the process nearly knocked her off the saddle. Aziza leaned forward with her head close to the neck of the animal to make sure that the branches did not hit her. The icy cold air rushed through her hair. Her hands were numb from the cold and her eyes were watery.

In a few minutes, another hungry wolf joined the chase. The mule was getting tired and the predators were getting closer. Then, one of the wolves made the big mistake of trying to bite the mule's left hind leg. The mule jacked its hind legs up, striking the wolf so hard on its jaws that it was thrown into the air and collapsed on the hard ground, yelping in pain. The jolt was too powerful for Aziza. Her grip gave way and she flew up and landed on top one of the wolves. The beast, more surprised than hurt, ran away in shock from the impact. The mule, now lighter, galloped away with one lone wolf hot on its trail.

It took a few seconds for Aziza to come to her senses and realize what had happened. Fortunately, the body of the wolf had absorbed the impact and she was only slightly bruised. Her primeval instincts, dating back tens of thousands of years to when humans lived in the forests with wild beasts, returned to her in an instant. Without thinking, she looked for the nearest tree and ran toward it. She was in a daze and did not realize that the wolf that she had crashed on had recovered and was running after her. She grabbed the tree trunk and started climbing as fast as she could. Fortunately, it was a skill she had honed as a child playing at the summer palace with her brother.

Aziza was several feet off the ground when the wolf lunged for her legs. Her left shoe came off in its mouth and it nearly bit off her big toe but she continued climbing before it could pounce again. The tree was not very thick but she climbed until she was about ten feet from the ground. Then she managed to wedge herself between two stout branches. She knew that wolves could not climb trees but how long could she last up there?

The lone wolf circled and snarled. Aziza could see its ice-cold yellow eyes. Every now and then, the wolf leaped at the tree and Aziza let out an involuntary scream, even though she knew the wolf could not jump high enough to reach her. She was bruised and scratched and having lost her shawl, she felt the freezing dampness of the forest. Her bare left foot bled from the bite for a while before a scab formed on the toe. However, the smell of fresh blood made the wolf even more enraged and drew two other wolves into a circling pack beneath the tree. She wanted to scream for help but thought better of it since it might bring more creatures to hunt her.

Just when she thought that things could not get worse, they did. Aziza had not slept for nearly two days and she was exhausted from the rough journey after being abducted, the tension of her escape, and the chase. After about an hour, she felt drowsy and despite herself, fell sleep for what was perhaps a second. It was long enough that she lost her balance and slipped from the branch. But she woke up just in time to grab another branch with both hands and pull herself up before the wolves could lunge at her dangling figure. Now she pinched herself every few minutes to keep herself awake.

After three more hours of hellish terror, it was almost dawn. The distant horizon changed from black to dullish red and gradually became light. She could now see where she was more clearly. She was half way up an evergreen tree. It was not a very big tree but it seemed sturdy enough. She moved to a bigger branch that would hold her weight rather than balancing herself between smaller branches. She was even colder now and could not stop shivering. She was hungry, thirsty, and the wolves were still under the tree waiting for her to fall down.

* * *

Rodrigo and Zangi were traveling lightly. They carried very little food and no water, since there was plenty of water and snow around. Rodrigo was armed with a broad sword and his dagger, plus his hidden stiletto. Rodrigo chose the broad sword instead of a thin, long sword because he knew that when fighting with big animals such as bears and wolves, the long sword could bend if it hit a bone, causing very little damage. The broad sword would cut through any bone. All he had to do was tease the animal so it would jump into the sword; its own weight would do the rest. Zangi was carrying two daggers. They walked as fast as they could without tiring themselves too much. After a while, they picked up the tracks of a mule, which infused them with hope and energy.

After almost two hours of walking, they stopped for a ten-minute rest. Before long, they picked up the trail of wolves following the mule. Rodrigo's heart sank when he saw the new tracks. He was hoping that the princess would be alive, but now with these tracks, the possibility seemed remote. They walked even faster. They did not want to call for her lest they attract the attention of an Ottoman search party.

* * *

It was now nearly nine in the morning. The sun was shining but clouds were gathering in the south. Aziza knew that sudden thunderstorms were not unusual at this time of year. The wolves suddenly looked south and started sniffing. They seemed puzzled and curious, as if they could sense something approaching. Aziza looked but could see nothing other than the trees around her. The wolves were more restless now. Maybe help was coming, thought Aziza; maybe soldiers had been sent to rescue her. She started yelling, hoping for a friendly response.

Rodrigo and Zangi, following the trail, soon heard the sound of her voice. Rodrigo could not believe it. Adrenaline flooded their systems and they started running toward the sound, shouting loudly at the same time to let her know that help was coming her way. In a couple of minutes, they were almost upon her. But they also found three hungry wolves snarling at them.

Wolves, like dogs, can read humans better than any other animal. They know when a human is frightened and when he is not. When they saw Rodrigo and Zangi running towards them with their blades drawn and heard their screams, two of wolves simply ran away. One decided to attack, lunging towards Rodrigo, right into his sharp blade. The blade cut through the animal's chest and came out of its back.

Rodrigo let go of the blade and ran to the tree. A tearful Aziza started climbing down and as she neared the ground, lost her foothold, slipping and falling into Rodrigo's outstretched arms. They both fell backwards with Rodrigo on his back and Aziza snuggly in his arms. Their faces touched and they looked into each other's eyes. At that moment, a bolt from cupid's arrow glued them together, even though they did not know it at the time.

They got up and brushed themselves off. Aziza's flesh was showing through tears in her clothes. Zangi retrieved the sword from the wolf's body and said, "We better get out of here before the wolves come back." Rodrigo picked Aziza up, slung her over his shoulder, and started walking back toward the camp. Aziza did not protest. They stopped by the lake, where Rodrigo put her down tenderly and washed the blood from her left ankle and bare foot. "It is badly scratched," he commented. "You have such small feet."

Aziza blushed. No man had ever touched or even seen her bare body before. Rodrigo's hands were warm and gentle and as he held her ankle and cleaned her foot, he asked, "Did the wolf break any bones in your foot?"

Aziza shook her head. She was happy to be alive and somehow, deep down in her heart, she was comfortable with this magnificent bandit.

Rodrigo dried her foot with his shirt and said, "I am going to carry you over my back since you are in no condition to walk." He called on Zangi, who picked Aziza up and put her on Rodrigo's back. Rather tersely, Rodrigo said, "You will have to put your arms around my neck or else you will fall down." There was little defiance left in Aziza. She did as she was told. Rodrigo clasped his own arms around her knees to hold her to his back and resumed walking back to camp.

The route was not difficult since it was slightly downhill. An exhausted Aziza soon felt the warmth from Rodrigo's body and after a few minutes of being rocked by the rhythm of his gait, she fell asleep. They stopped for rest one time. It was an hour past noon when they arrived at the campsite, tired but exhilarated by their success.

Rodrigo took Aziza to her tent, where a tearful Katarina welcomed her back and put her down on the mattress to rest. The other two search parties had returned empty handed a few hours earlier, after failing to find tracks of a mule or a human being. Rodrigo was dog-tired but knew that they could not wait any longer. The sultan's army would have new tracks to follow and they had to get out of there fast. He ordered the men to break camp. In twenty minutes, the group was moving east.

* * *

Later in the day, a thunderstorm forced them to seek shelter under the trees. It did not last very long and Rodrigo was actually grateful for the rain, since it washed away their trail. Eventually, they found a well-hidden clearing surrounded by dense trees on all sides. They were all tired, none more than Rodrigo. Before going to bed, he told Lorenzo and Petros to estimate their current location by the position of the stars and their knowledge of the area. He assigned the first watch to Zangi, followed by Antonio, Lorenzo, Jean, and Renaldo. He was asleep before his head hit the rough saddle he was using as a pillow. When he woke up, it was dawn.

Rodrigo had something to eat and soon every member of the group was up and moving about. He called everyone over to discuss their next move. According to Petros and Lorenzo, they were about two days southwest of Sofia. The sultan army's main camp, as best as Renaldo had been able to estimate, was about one day to the east of Sofia, closer to Constantinople.

Obviously, they could not go to Sofia, especially with the two captive women. Renaldo suggested that since the rain had washed away their trail, they could stay for another day to recuperate and reconnoiter the areas around them before making their next move.

Everyone but Jean agreed with the plan. Jean, who seemed to have had one of his visions, wanted to move on as fast as possible and try to bypass the sultan's camp and push on to Constantinople. Rodrigo decided to wait for a day.

Rodrigo had lost what little trust he had in his men. He did not know who had betrayed them all along and had arranged for Aziza's escape. He decided that in the future, he would send people on joint scouting missions. That day, he sent Lorenzo and Zangi together to look around and see if there were any friendly villages nearby or shepherds around.

Before Rodrigo could venture to Aziza's tent to check on her, she emerged with Katarina. She looked much healthier than she had the previous day. The women walked a short distance to a large stone and they sat on it, facing the warming sun of early spring. It was a nice day. Rodrigo approached the two women and asked Aziza how she was doing. Aziza, who had regained some of her self-assurance, responded by thanking him for saving her from the wolves.

Rodrigo asked if she would walk with him; he wanted to talk to her about certain things. Aziza got up and the two slowly strolled away from the center of the camp. Rodrigo said, "You are such a cultured young woman. I did not expect women from the Orient to be able to read and write and yet you speak several languages."

Aziza, still a little wobbly from her ordeal, responded, "What you just said is actually true in many cases, but the sultan and I have the same mother. All the other sisters are from different mothers. I was educated from an early age to become an authority in arts, history, and languages. I was to be the one advisor that my brother could always trust if he ever needed to seek counsel outside his immediate courtiers. You should not malign my religion, either. During the first century of Islam, women were almost as important as men were. For example, Ayesha, the wife of our Prophet, raised an army and fought against her adversaries. After the first century, the women were shut out and relegated to the harems. Even now, however, our women have more financial rights than your women do. Any property that we own or inherit belongs to us and not to our husbands." Aziza's voice turned defiant. "In any case, as a princess I am better off than most other women. Or at least I was until you and your bandits kidnapped me." Then she fell silent.

Rodrigo said, "I will tell you the absolute truth." He crossed himself as he said those words to show his candor. "But, please listen and try to understand my position as I will try to understand yours." Without waiting for an answer, he went on, "We were sent by His Holiness Pope Nicholas to deliver a message of support and friendship to the emperor in Constantinople. Ever since we left Rome, which is the center or our Christian world, we have run into one trouble after another. We were starving before we approached your caravan and actually wanted to stop it and bargain for some food but things got out of hand and then we discovered that we had stumbled upon the sister of the greatest enemy of Christendom. On my honor, as a Christian knight, we never meant to harm or kill any of your companions. We took you and your maid with us as a bargaining tool in case we were captured by the infidel—I mean, The Muslim army. Then you foolishly ran away and were almost eaten alive by the wolves."

Aziza's suppressed memories of that horrifying night returned to her and she almost keeled over. Rodrigo caught her, putting his arm around her to steady her. "I am very sorry," he said. "I did not want to frighten you. I am glad that we got there on time. I just wanted you to know that I did not mean any harm to you or to your companions and I will release you as soon as we are out of harm's way."

After a pause he continued. "However, a nagging question bothers me. I noticed that you mounted a mule to ride out of the camp and I also noticed that one of the saddles was missing. How did you saddle that mule? It takes a strong man to lift that saddle up and place it on a mule that is taller than you are."

Aziza, still leaning on Rodrigo's arm, smiled faintly and said, "I actually thought it might have been you but then I am not always right."

Rodrigo looked even more puzzled. "Why did you think that I would have helped you to escape?"

"Well," Aziza said, "I had a feeling that you did not really want to hold me captive and were trying to find a way to release me. I do not think it matters anymore since I was almost killed anyway, but someone in your camp sent me a note, in Latin, which said that he had a mule ready for me to escape from your clutches. I burned the note, as I was told to do, so there would be no trace of why or how I had left the camp and who had helped me. I wanted so badly to return home that I took a chance. I did not realize the risk that I was taking when I fled. It was actually while I was in that tree, fighting for my life, that it occurred to me that the person who had sent me that message and saddled that mule actually wanted me dead!"

The information did not really surprise Rodrigo. Since Chiusi Pass, he had suspected that there was a traitor among his associates. Now, he had no doubt about it. Rodrigo, still holding her against his side, said, "I really do not know why, but I am going to trust you. I have had a suspicion about this for some time. Please do not tell anybody what you have told me just now. I will try to find out who tried to kill you and implicate the rest of us for your murder. As we speak now, I feel that Zangi is the only one that I can trust. He is a true servant of the pope and he does not know Latin. Zangi and I will keep an eye on you and will protect you. One of us will always be around, even if you cannot see us." He reached into his right pant leg, retrieved his favorite stiletto, and surreptitiously passed it to her. "Please carry this with you at all times. It saved my life many times in Rome. Do not hesitate to use it if you have to. If anyone but Zangi or I comes near you, be wary."

They continued walking and talking for a while longer. The depth of Aziza's knowledge of arts and philosophy surprised

Rodrigo. Aziza was amazed that this barbarian was not a brute at all but an educated loyal knight trying to fulfill a promise he had made to his uncle and the pope.

After almost two hours of talking and walking in the woods, they returned to the camp.

Later that afternoon, after consulting with Lorenzo and Renaldo, Rodrigo decided to move out the next morning and continue east toward their goal. They spent the rest of the day cleaning their weapons and grooming their mules and themselves. Rodrigo washed his face and hair in cold water and shaved his beard off. As he walked by Aziza's tent, he heard her singing a beautiful melody in a foreign language. It was not as melodic as Italian, but it did not have the harsh, guttural sound of Turkish, either. It seemed like a very sad song. Her gentle voice carried over the camp and made them feel deeply nostalgic for their homes, the good times of their lives, and their loved ones, even though they did not understand any of the words.

~ CHAPTER TWENTY-TWO ~

THE SEDUCTION OF

INNOCENCE

Later that day, Lorenzo and Zangi reported that they had seen several ruins nearby but no signs of human activity.

At dawn the next morning, they broke camp and moved east. First, they came across the ruins of an uninhabited village. They kept going and soon they arrived at the ruins of an abandoned small town. The roofs had long since collapsed and many of the walls had disintegrated into piles of dried mud. They could see the remnants of the stone walls of several churches, still standing as a testament to the ruinous passage of time. Renaldo explained that many villages and towns had disappeared thanks to attacks by hordes of Asian barbarians. People who were not killed by the marauders or sold into slavery had died in the plagues. In those villages and towns, the grapes dried on the vine and the wheat withered since no one was left alive to pick the grapes or harvest the wheat. The arable farms soon died and grass and new forests replaced the crops and vines. What had taken men a thousand years of hard work to create had disappeared in a few decades.

As they moved through the ghost town, they noticed that even the cemeteries had been taken over by tall bushes and trees.

They could barely see the headstones and stone crosses that had fallen onto the ground. Tree roots had lifted other gravestones up. Rodrigo shivered at the thought of what the roots must have done to the bodies of the people underneath.

This area, which was roughly to the south of Sofia, must have been a prosperous farming community at one time, he thought.

They came across the ruins of several other villages that day, deciding to camp inside one of them early in the afternoon to give Lorenzo and Zangi a chance to scout ahead before nightfall. They found an old church, part of its roof still standing, and built their campfire there.

Rodrigo, feeling lonely and unable to have confidence in any of his associates, sought out Aziza. She was in her tent writing in a book. She smiled at Rodrigo and put her book away. Rodrigo asked what she was doing. Aziza explained that that was her diary and book of poetry. She loved to write poetry and record important events in her life in her book. Rodrigo asked her if she wanted to walk with him and she readily accepted the offer.

The two of them walked side by side and talked. Rodrigo told Aziza about his life and how he had lost his mother early in his childhood and about his half-sister Isabella and how much he loved her, omitting their intimate relationship. He said that somehow, Aziza reminded him of her, especially her deep brown eyes.

He also talked about his maternal uncle, Cardinal Alfonso Borgia, who was quite old by the standards of the day, and how he had adopted Rodrigo and given him his name so that he would be eligible to be a knight of the Catholic Church. He even told her about his battles with the Colonnas, the leading family of Rome. Rodrigo was amazed at his own frankness.

The princess was an avid listener. She was glued to his every word and every now and then would ask him to repeat something.

Rodrigo asked about the sad song that she had sung the previous day. Aziza blushed and said that she had not realized that they had been listening. He asked her to sing the song again.

Aziza had a soft, gentle voice and yet the sadness of the song penetrated every fiber of the listener. When she was finished singing, he asked what the words meant. Aziza said it was a love story about a girl and a boy. The girl was rich and the boy was poor. They had grown up together and they had been in love since they were children. Then one day, the parents of the girl decided to marry her off to a rich prince. Aziza paused and asked if Rodrigo really wanted to hear the rest of the story, since the ending was tragic. Rodrigo insisted. Aziza translated each line of the poem as she sang it again.

The tale of Shireen and Farhad
The Star-Crossed Lovers

Many moons ago
In the land beyond the lake
In the town of fifty minarets
There lived a beautiful girl named Shireen
Shireen meant fairy and she was as beautiful as one
She had tresses of golden sand

She had the sweet voice of an angel
She had the fiery dark eyes of Eve
She was tall and striking
She had a rich father

There was a boy named Farhad
He was tall and handsome
He was kind and selfless
He was a sculptor
He was the son of a stonemason
He had a poor father

They were in love since young
Farhad made little carvings for her
Shireen would sing of love to him

One day Shireen was promised as wife to a prince
Farhad was brokenhearted
He went to the mountain nearby
He started carving the statue of Shireen for eternity
In the quiet of night he could be heard from her house
His axe hitting the stones second by second
Then one night Shireen could not hear the mallet sound
She thought maybe he is asleep dreaming sweet dreams
of Shireen

In the morning, they found him
Farhad was dead
In the dark, he had hit his head with the axe

Some said he killed himself
Heartbroken, Shireen leaped from the mountain
To join her lover in eternity
They buried them side by side
Beneath the statue
To this day, you can see their stone monument
If you listen, at night, you can hear the sound of his mallet
The enchanting voice of Shireen

Pilgrims go to the site
They all weep
Lovers pray for their loved ones
Childless women pray for a baby
Mothers pray for their lost sons
Shed a drop of tear for this poet
Even though long, I may be gone

* * *

When the song ended, Rodrigo had tears in his eyes. It sounded all too familiar. One hundred and fifty years later, Christopher Marlowe would relate the same poem to his friend, William Shakespeare, who would rewrite it as *Romeo and Juliet*.

They walked some more and Rodrigo admitted his failure to determine the identity of the traitor in the camp. He said, "I actually try not to sleep in a comfortable position, because I am afraid that I will be stabbed to death in my sleep."

Aziza grabbed his hand, held it tight with both hands, and tearfully said, "I do not want to lose you. It would be too devastating to me." Suddenly, she realized what she had done and pulled her hands away and apologized.

Rodrigo was both astonished and pleased, since he had developed very strong feelings toward her, too. He took her small hands in his, kissed them gently, and said, "I think it may be the wrong time to admit it and it may not sound sincere but I think I have loved you since the day you were born."

He kissed her hands again and she melted into his arms, sobbing on his manly chest. She knew that she had fallen in love with the wrong man at the wrong time and in the wrong place. One way or the other, they would be separated soon and even now, one of her brother's henchmen could be aiming a deadly arrow at his back. The realization made her hold him closer. They looked into each other's eyes and their lips met. It was the first time she had been kissed on the lips by a man. It felt hot and moist and reawakened her quiescent sensuality. Their kiss lingered on. There was no need to say it, but Rodrigo uttered the words, "I love you." And that was enough for Aziza.

It was still light when they walked back to the tent, holding hands. Aziza took one last look at her loved one before she disappeared inside.

* * *

Zangi and Lorenzo approached Rodrigo nervously. They looked around apprehensively as they made their reports. "Signor, the road ahead is quite clear for at least the next five miles," Lorenzo said. "However, when we returned from scouting, we decided to circle back to make sure that no one was following us. This is when we found some evidence that is worrying us."

Rodrigo was half listening to their findings, his mind drifting to Aziza. The word "evidence" shook him back to reality. "What kind of evidence, man? What are you talking about?" he snapped.

Lorenzo, who was still nervous, said, "Well, it seemed that someone has been marking our progress. We found branches placed strategically and then little, tiny carvings on the ground made with the side of the boot, like someone had dug his toe in and pulled it in the damp ground, drawing an arrow, pointing in the direction of our travel. If there was only one sign, we would not have been concerned. But we found several such markers."

Rodrigo felt the bottom fall out of his stomach. He felt like someone had dumped him in a vat of ice-cold water. He told them not to repeat what they had told him and asked them to find the others and bring them to him at once.

It was already getting dark when his crew gathered around him. Rodrigo was too scared to camp there for the rest of the night. He told everyone to pack up and be ready to move in fifteen minutes. Some protested but he would have none of it.

The men were ready in fifteen minutes. Rodrigo reckoned that if the sultan's men were following them, they would assume that they would go east as they had done the last few days. Therefore, if they suddenly turned north and then doubled back to the west, the stalkers would be confused and may even lose their trail completely. Consequently, he ordered his men to turn north. It was a strange order, but no one dared to ask him the reason since he seemed extremely irritated. He told Zangi and Lorenzo to remain behind for fifteen minutes and then, with branches, to clear the ground of any signs that might have been left on their trail by the traitor in their midst.

After half an hour of going north, Rodrigo turned left, toward the west. He was trying to double back and fool his pursuers. They traveled for almost another hour before it was too dark to move. Then they set up camp for the night.

Rodrigo called everyone, including Aziza and Katarina, for a meeting and told them, "Some of you may know what I am about to say. We have an extremely clever traitor in our camp. This person has been trying to sabotage our mission before we left Rome. I now realize that the reason I was nearly assassinated in Rome was not the anger of the brother of my married mistress. I was targeted because I had been selected for this mission. Since I do not trust any one of you, we will have two sentries in each shift instead of one. Before you protest, remember that the alternative is being captured by the sultan's troops. He drew up the sentry duties for the night and dismissed them all except Aziza, who stayed and held his hand while he was thinking.

He turned to her and said, "Let me tell you about all the problems that we have had since leaving Rome. Maybe talking about it will help." He explained all the misadventures of the past few weeks and then added, "I have been trying to figure out the identity of the culprit, but he is too clever for me. After a few minutes of silence, Rodrigo said "I need fresh air to think, let's get up and walk for a while." They both started walking, arm in arm, away from the main camp.

Rodrigo continued, "Let us start with Zangi. He was a Muslim slave captured by Christians. How do we know that his heart is not still with your people? I am not even sure that he really saved my life that night in Rome. Perhaps it was all a masquerade. I noticed that the big cross that he always wears around his neck has been missing for the past few days and when I asked him about it, he said that he had lost it.

"Then there is Lorenzo. To start with, he is a Sicilian and they do not generally like the Northern Italians. They think of them as uppity and snobbish. In fact, they do not think of themselves as Italian at all. Lorenzo has spent a good portion of his life in the Orient and he does not have much money to show for all his years of adventuring around the Mediterranean. Maybe he was tempted by gold. Aziza held his hand ever tighter and had her eyes fastened on him as he continued talking.

"Then there is Antonio, the master gun maker. We do not know much about him. It is true that he joined us after the Chiusi Pass incident in Florence, but he could have been in contact with spies in Rome by horseback messengers. We were traveling by mule. A messenger on horseback could travel from Rome to Florence in a couple of days.

"As for Renaldo, he is the most aristocratic of the lot. He is an older man and well respected by my uncle and the pope. However, he has also traveled to the Orient and he was even at your father's court when you and your brother were small children.

"Jean seems to be living in a different universe. He is an eccentric character who is more religious than the pope is. He is almost fanatical in his beliefs. However, his piety could be a charade. We do not know much about him. He is French and the French king is one of pope's bitterest enemies. They sat down on a clump of stones. Aziza snuggled close to him as he continued.

"Finally, we found Petros at the Chiusi Pass. He claimed that he was a Catholic Greek doctor. That was what the captive girls told us, too. The remaining bandits were executed by the towns-people very quickly. Maybe he was actually the slave trader whom the bandits had been expecting. Perhaps, they did not want to reveal his identity to the captives until he was ready to take them back East.

"Father Ricardo is actually the pope's nephew and I would trust him more than I would trust myself.

"Someone is trying to sabotage the mission, yet he knows that if we fall into the hands of your brother or Abdullah Hassan, he may be killed along with the rest of us. That is what makes it so frustrating for me to understand. Why would anyone want to commit suicide?"

Aziza looked at him with her lovely tear-filled brown eyes and said, "I know I cannot help you much but I have my jewelry box, which is worth a tremendous amount of money. We can go south to the Greek ports. No one is looking for us there. I will go with you anywhere that you want to go. We can go back to your native land if you want. I only know that we cannot stay here and be together. If my brother does not kill you on the spot, he will put you on one of his ships as a galley slave. In any case, we will never see each other again and I think I will kill myself if that happens."

Rodrigo put his arms around her and held her close to him. Soon, she fell asleep on his shoulder. He gently picked her up and carried her to her tent. Katarina was fast sleep. He laid her down and covered her body. Aziza, who was half sleep, opened her eyes and seeing Rodrigo, reached out for him with both arms.

Rodrigo bent down and kissed her passionately on the lips. The lovers' lips interlocked and for a long moment, they forgot about the rest of the world and their own miseries.

In the heat of passion, Rodrigo removed the cover and joined her in the bed. The lovers' bodies soon intertwined like two snakes in the act of lovemaking. They were oblivious to the dangers surrounding them. Rodrigo moved his right hand to Aziza's firm belly and worked it under her outer garment to stroke her satiny skin in a circular motion. His hand gradually moved up towards her firm bosoms and hardened nipples.

Unconsciously, she helped him remove her clothing one piece at a time until they were both stark naked. He made sure that his lower body did not touch her yet since he did not want her to feel his hardness and be embarrassed or frightened by it. His hand gradually crept down below her navel and for the first time felt the tiny, smooth crack between her thighs. She trembled at his touch. Passion was roaring inside her and she arched her back and lifted her buttocks up to meet the burning fingers that gently probed the outer lips of her untouched, hairless organ.

With his middle fingers, he rubbed up and down against the peach fuzz entrance to her womanhood.

He turned sideways, took her small hand, and guided it to his hot member. The heat of passion sparked from the tip of his hardened pole all the way to her loins. She fondled him gently, as a baby strokes a doll. She was breathing heavily and he felt the wetness of her response on his fingers. Without removing his fingers, he managed to get on top of her and, while nibbling at her ears and kissing her tender lips, gently pried open her legs. He rubbed his eager member against the opening of her hot, dripping vagina and prepared to enter the forbidden snatch of the princess.

At that moment, Katarina, who was suddenly woken by the noise of the lovers, interrupted them. She half rose from her bed and pleadingly half-shouted, "Sir, please do not spoil her virtue! She is a maiden and has never been touched by a man. She is betrothed to be married. Please sir, have mercy. Just be satisfied to caress her and cuddle her."

Rodrigo respected and loved Aziza too much to despoil her. He stopped dead in his tracks and responded gently that he understood. They continued kissing and holding each other. Soon, Aziza could not contain herself any longer. Her loins were inflamed with desire. "Please," she whispered, "enter me now for I am dying from fever and I need you inside to quench my desire."

Rodrigo whispered back, "But you are a virgin, girl, I do not want to take away your virtue."

An irritated Aziza, intoxicated by passion, snapped back, "I am telling you now to make love to me." She opened her legs wide for him. She stuffed her right wrist in her mouth and bit hard to stop herself from screaming from the pain of the rupture, which, she had heard, accompanied the first intercourse. Rodrigo positioned himself between her young thighs and once more rubbed the fiery head of his member against her outer lips.

Aziza was on fire with desire for his manhood. Rodrigo quietly lubricated his shaft with his spittle to ease the entry and with his right hand guided the head of his member against her young, tight orifice. In her passion, her body had lubricated her entrance but, even so, it was a hard entry. He pushed the head in and soon felt the maidenhead blocking his way. He took a deep breath and lunged forward, breaking the membrane and burying his shaft deep inside the young virgin's belly. The pain was excruciating and Aziza passed out for a minute. When she came to, she could feel the pole all the way inside her belly.

The nanny who was awakened by Aziza's muffled scream, piped up, "You did your dirty deed, you scoundrel! You ruined this young, innocent girl forever. May gods have no mercy on you and may you be burnt alive!" With that, she stormed out of the tent.

Aziza's tight love tunnel seized his member in a vice grip. The tightness and the gentle throbbing of her vagina caused Rodrigo to spend almost immediately. The copious sperms of his manhood soothed the searing pain of rupture. Rodrigo kissed Aziza's tearful eyes and whispered his love. Soon, the pain subsided and Rodrigo started a gentle rhythmic motion inside her body. Her first orgasm caused by a man was very profound. She had to bite her wrist again to keep herself from screaming in pleasure and waking up the countryside. Soon, Rodrigo emptied his seed one more time inside her eager womb.

That night, they made passionate love until the morning hours and until she was so sore that the pleasure was becoming painful. He left her just before dawn.

Katarina, who was keeping a vigil, soon returned with a pail of water to clean up her mistress. Aziza was sore and her thighs were covered with their crusted love seeds mixed with dried blood. They hugged and both women wept. But the deed was done. The dam was broken and there was no going back.

Aziza slept for a while. When she woke up, she took her book out and wrote a poem about her night of passionate desire.

* * *

Seduction of a Princess
The Virgin and the Knight

I am the daughter of a sultan
I am the sister of a sultan
I am a princess of the blood
I was on my way to get married
A bandit knight kidnapped me
He kept me at a forest full of thieves

I ran away
I was hunted by the wolves
They nearly killed me
The knight came after me
He slew the wolves
He rescued me

I fell in love with the bandit
I did not want to
He came to my tent one night
He undressed me
He lay on top of me
His heart beating against mine
I opened my legs for him
I could feel the heat of his manhood
I was blind with desire
Make me a woman, I whispered

But, my nanny woke up
She beseeched him
Aziza's a maiden
She is a princess
Have mercy sire
Don't ruin her forever
Just fondle her and be satisfied

Surprisingly, the knight obeyed
All that night I spent in his arms naked
Fading of passion and lust
My loins burning with desire
Then I could take it no more
Pray enter, I said
You are a maiden, he rejoined
Do it now for I am dying

I put my hand in my mouth
I bit it hard lest I'd scream
I felt him enter
He hit the barrier, it shattered
The flesh tore
I felt searing pain
I passed out
I came to
The rod was lodged in my belly
I had lost my honor to a Christian knave

The nanny awoke
She cursed
You ruined her, you fiend
We will all be killed now
She left the tent in disgust
With tearful eyes, I begged him to go on
The pain soon subsided
The ecstasy took over
It felt I was in the promised paradise of the Holy Book
That night he loved me thirteen times, I counted
He was gone by the morning light

My nanny brought me water
I washed away his seeds and my virgin blood
From my thighs and within
But the stain is not gone
I am ruined, I know

You brute
You saved me from the wolves
But you slaughtered my virtue

I kept the bloody sheet, as a token
I know we will die
I love you my brute knight
You slayer of my maidenhood

They will find us soon
My brother will burn you alive
And, I will be sold in the slave markets of Zanzibar
But, I love you and always will
With all my being, body, and soul

~ CHAPTER TWENTY-THREE ~

THE FACE OF A TRAITOR

Rodrigo slept for almost two hours. When he woke up, he was rejuvenated and for the first time in days had a smile upon his face. He called for Renaldo and Petros and sent them out to scout the immediate area. He then walked back towards the village that they had left last night. After about half an hour, he climbed a tall tree to survey the landscape. In the distance, he could see the abandoned village and, to his horror, the reflections of sunlight off the armor of the sultan's soldiers.

He rushed back to the camp to warn the others. He had been gone for over an hour and everyone, especially Aziza, was worried about him. She rushed into his open arms, weeping with joy to see him back again. She said, "I thought that my brother's spies had kidnapped you." He hugged her tightly. This young girl was so innocent and so full of love. He felt happy and sad at the same time. Happy for having found the love of his life, depressed knowing that they were reaching the end of the trail and soon they would be separated forever.

Renaldo and Petros reported that the passage to the north seemed clear. Jean and Renaldo asked Rodrigo if he had seen anything. Rodrigo lied, saying that he had not.

Jean insisted on talking to Rodrigo privately. He suggested that under the circumstances, it would be best if they left Aziza behind. The soldiers would discover her and treat her royally, and they might even abandon their search for the rest of them. Rodrigo did not want to leave the women alone. What if the soldiers did not find them for several days and the wolves or the bears attacked them first? Jean volunteered to stay behind to protect them and watch for the soldiers. He would follow the rest of the men as soon as he saw a sign of troops closing in on the camp. Rodrigo thought hard about the proposition and asked Aziza's opinion. She did not want to leave Rodrigo and neither of them trusted Jean's motives.

They moved north toward the main road that connected Skopje to Sofia. Rodrigo's plan was to do a zigzag. He planned to rejoin the road that connected Skopje to Sofia so the soldiers would lose their tracks. If the soldiers still followed them to the road, they would not be able to distinguish their tracks from those of other travelers and, in any case, they would assume that they were going east toward Sofia and not going back west. Rodrigo planned to go west toward Skopje for a few miles and then double back behind the soldiers, following the same route that they had taken earlier when they left the road after capturing Aziza. No one would expect the prey to follow the hunters. If he managed to fool their pursuers, they would be in the clear for the rest of the trip, Rodrigo reasoned.

He sent Renaldo and Petros to scout ahead and followed them with the remainder of his group half an hour later. After about three hours, he called a halt to wait for the two scouts. But there was no sign of them. Soon they heard rustling noises in the brush and Petros appeared. He was out of breath and worn out. He fell to the ground, exhausted, and stammered that Renaldo had been captured by the Ottomans.

When Petros caught his breath, he explained that they had run into scouts of the sultan who were searching the territory from the north. Renaldo managed to fight them off and shouted at Petros to get away and warn the others.

Rodrigo had no cards left to play. He was surrounded on all sides. If he had been alone, he could probably try to slip away through the bushes and the trees. But he was not alone.

Rodrigo reasoned that if the Ottomans had captured Renaldo alive, they might torture him to find out where they were going. Renaldo would endure the pain for at least one or two hours before telling the soldiers of their whereabouts. Rodrigo's last chance was to try to go east through the rough countryside and perhaps put some distance between his party and the soldiers. The dispirited group started moving, this time heading east.

They had traveled for less than two hours when he heard the sounds of galloping horses and before he knew it, Mohammed's cavalry surrounded them.

The soldiers pointed long lances at them as they advanced slowly. Rodrigo and his friends took their swords out and formed a semi-circle away from the women so they would not be hurt in the skirmish. For the last time, Rodrigo glanced at Aziza and whispered his love.

The soldiers halted once they were close enough to prevent them from escaping.

Rodrigo hoped to die fighting, but first he wanted to know who the traitor was. Yet none of the men in his group made a move to join the Ottoman soldiers. After about half an hour, another group of horsemen arrived from the north, led by an evil looking man whom Rodrigo guessed must be Abdullah Hassan Bey. He motioned to the horsemen, who suddenly lunged at them.

Rodrigo shouted to his comrades, "I wish I knew who the coward traitor was and I do apologize to the rest of you. Good-bye!"

They tried to fight and die valiantly. However, the soldiers apparently had been ordered to take them alive. A few soldiers were wounded but Rodrigo and his men were soon overwhelmed and disarmed. Abdullah Hassan Bey approached them with a sick grin on his face and with his long whip, lashed at them. He only stopped when Aziza started screaming.

Suddenly, Zangi began shouting in a foreign language, which Rodrigo assumed was Turkish. He seemed to be begging for mercy. To Rodrigo it sounded like Zangi was claiming that he was a Muslim captive. Zangi, still screaming and yelling, walked to Rodrigo and spat on his face. He took his hidden dagger from above his ankle and lunged at Rodrigo. But he missed and fell, burying the dagger to the hilt in the soft ground. Abdullah Hassan Bey and the rest of the soldiers laughed heartily and before Zangi could make another attempt, two soldiers jumped down and restrained him.

Abdullah Hassan Bey rode towards Aziza and Katarina and dismounted to greet her. The rest of them, except Zangi, were bound and tied with ropes behind horses and pulled away by the soldiers. Rodrigo had one more look at Aziza before she disappeared from his view.

The soldiers obviously had orders not to kill them, as they did not gallop away very fast, just fast enough to drag them on the rough ground every now and then, to tear their clothes to shreds, and to make them bleed. The pain was excruciating and Rodrigo wondered how Petros and Antonio, who were older, were taking it. After a while, the soldiers stopped dragging them and walked them to the main Ottoman camp, which was not far away.

When they arrived at the camp, soldiers who had lined up to see the bandit Christians who had abducted the sultan's sister greeted them with catcalls, pebbles, and spit. They were slapped and kicked as they were led to a big tent that apparently was a meeting area.

It took a few minutes for their eyes to adjust to the darkness inside the tent. There were many people around. They were forced to kneel down and their faces were pushed to the ground. Then the soldiers let go of them and Rodrigo looked up. Abdullah Hassan Bey was sitting on a raised platform. Zangi stood respectfully, his arms folded across his chest, to his left.

What Rodrigo saw next made him want to throw up with rage. A grinning Renaldo, dressed like an Ottoman, was standing next to Abdullah Hassan Bey. "*Benvenuto, i miei amici stupidi* (Welcome my stupid friends)," Renaldo said in Italian, with a self-satisfied smile. Rodrigo tried to get up but strong hands pushed him down again. He looked up and saw Zangi standing near Renaldo with a sick smirk upon his thick lips.

"So, our luck has run out Rodrigo, hasn't it?" Renaldo said. "You and that Templar friend of yours thought that you could outsmart the great sultan. You were so wrong! I warned you not to attack the caravan and you did not listen. You had the audacity to kidnap a member of the royal family in her own country. I told you to let the princess go, but you did not listen. You are a Christian pig."

Jean responded first, in a very calm voice, "I had a vision that you were the traitor and I should have run my sword through your body days ago. I am only sorry that I did not slaughter you like the animal that you are. I may be a pig but you are a snake and will get your just rewards soon. In my vision, I saw you rotting alive with worms eating you from inside out."

Abdullah Hassan Bey, who had been listening to the conversation with a bemused smile, said, "Enough! Take the prisoners away. His imperial majesty, the great sultan, will decide how to punish them."

They were taken away and put in chains in a stockade at the edge of the camp. There was just one guard on sentry duty but there was no way to get out of the chains to attempt an escape. They sat there forlorn and dejected, hoping for a quick death.

* * *

Earlier that day, after the Christians had been captured, Abdullah Hassan Bey, the butcher of Balkans, had paid his respects to his future wife and sent for a *houdah* to transport Aziza and Katarina back to the camp.

On her arrival at the camp, Aziza was treated like a returning heroine by the courtiers. Mohammed himself came to her tent to hug her and thank Allah for her safe deliverance.

The sultan had access to a portable bath comprised of several huge tubs of water that were heated for him and his immediate family. Bathing was very important in the Muslim culture. They could not pray after sex unless they took a bath to clean their bodies. There were some exceptions to the rule, such as when an army was engaged in battle. However, the sultan made sure that he had bathing facilities at all times. Soon they arranged a hot bath for Aziza to cleanse herself. Aziza was used to taking communal baths with other members of the harem. However, this time she did not want them to see her condition since she was still sore and there was still a small amount of bleeding. Nevertheless, with Katarina's help, she managed to get herself cleaned very quickly.

When she heard that Rodrigo and his friends were still alive, she decided to seek an audience with her brother and plead for their lives.

Mohammed was astonished that his sister would ask mercy for the Christian bandits who had captured her and held her prisoner. He sent her away angrily.

Fatima, who was one of his favorite concubines and had ambitions to become his permanent wife, overheard the conversation and suggested to the sultan that he should have Aziza examined to make sure that she had not been sexually assaulted.

According to Muslim tradition, a virgin who is raped is not considered pure anymore. This worried the sultan because if Aziza was not a virgin on her wedding night, Abdullah Hassan Bey would have every right under the Islamic law to send her back and the scandal would be unacceptable.

The suspicious sultan sent one of the harem midwives to check Aziza's condition. Aziza was furious but no amount of bluster could stop the examination. The midwife, noticing the slight blood spots and the freshly torn hymen, reported back to the sultan, who went into one of his rages. He sent for Aziza and Katarina and asked if she had been raped. Aziza, for the first time in her life, faced her brother defiantly. She told him that she was in love and had had consensual relations with Rodrigo. This made the young sultan even angrier.

He turned to Aziza and said, "If you had told me that you were raped, I would have forgiven you. Now that you tell me that you had that Christian dog inside you and allowed him willingly to desecrate your Muslim body, you are no longer my sister and will be considered a whore." Selim Pasha, his confidant and grand vizier, who was the only other person in the room, fell down on his face groveling and asked for mercy for Aziza. He asked that the princess be sent to Anatolia and be allowed to spend the rest of her life in meditation and prayer. The enraged sultan kicked him in the face with his boot and said, "This is my final decision: She will be made into a whore and sent to Zanzibar to be sold at the slave market to the savage blacks." With that, he stormed out of the room.

A weeping Aziza returned to her tent. Selim Pasha, a wizened old man of Egyptian descent, still bleeding from the nose, followed Aziza and begged her to reconsider her statement. He asked her to say that she had been angry and exhausted from her long ordeal and she had made up the story about being in love and ask for her brother's mercy. Aziza, still rebelliously angry, refused.

The sultan decided to torture Rodrigo and the others before killing them. He wanted to demonstrate that he was a man of principle. He ordered Rodrigo separated from the other prisoners so he could be singularly tortured publicly.

CHAPTER TWENTY-FOUR

CONFESSIONS OF A TRAITOR

Later that night, Renaldo paid a visit to Rodrigo, who was tied up with strong hemp rope in a stockade all by himself. He sat down near his former traveling companion and asked, "Do you know why you are still alive?"

Rodrigo, in his agony, ignored him and looked away. He tried to dissociate his mind from his present physical condition by concentrating on other things.

Glancing at the silhouettes of the distant mountains, which were dimly visible in the moonlight far in the horizon, he envied the peasants and shepherds who led simple lives in those mountains. They had their daily toil, but they lived safely with their families and loved ones. They did not have any money but they were almost independent and free, far away from any danger of capture or torture. Yet, here he was, in this stockade tied to a pole. He was the son of a nobleman who, until yesterday, was in charge of a major mission. Too late, he had realized that Renaldo and Zangi had fooled and betrayed him from the start. Rodrigo was resigned to being killed. He would be joining his ancestors in heaven or hell soon. Death could come tomorrow or at most, within the next few days. But would anyone ever find out what had happened to him and his friends?

Renaldo disregarded Rodrigo's silence. "I was a spent force believing in a false god ten years ago. My friends and associates had achieved fame and fortune and lived in nice villas, whereas I was reduced to carrying messages and acting as a translator for petty rulers and princes," Renaldo said. "Then I arrived in Edirne. The great Sultan Murat, peace be upon him, gave me a job at his court. There, I met the brilliant scholar Abu Hamzah of Egypt. He had memorized the Bible as well as the holy Koran. He sat with me and we read every major passage of the Bible and the Koran. Like Abraham and Moses, Jesus was a prophet of God and no more. Nowhere in the Bible is he mentioned as the son of God. Greedy priests, to fool the ignorant masses, created this fallacy centuries later. Abu Hamzah made me see the light of the true prophet. I realized the hoax of Christianity. The popes sitting on their mighty thrones are nothing but creatures that came out of the anus of the Lucifer. Nicholas is a fool to believe in a bogus god. He is despised by the true God and will burn in hell for eternity for his denial of Allah."

Rodrigo could not believe his ears—the stream of obscenities against Nicholas and blasphemy against the almighty. It was too much.

Undaunted, Renaldo continued, "After I saw the light, it was so easy and inspirational to become a Muslim. I had to utter just two sentences. The first was, "Allah is great." The second was, "Mohammed is the messenger of Allah." I was suddenly reborn as a new person and, like the true Muslim that I had become, I was circumcised and learned how to pray toward Mecca and the one true Lord.

"The sultan was so gracious to me that he visited me while I was in bed after the surgery. He even let me marry his niece. I now have a young, virtuous wife, not like Aziza, who surrendered her virtue to the first man that she met. My wife was a virgin like the day she was born. Unlike your Christian wives, she does not commit adultery with other men no matter how handsome they may be, or how long I may have been away. She is devoted to me and I do not need a chastity belt to keep her from committing sin. We have several children and live on a great estate near Edirne.

"Sultan Mohammed graciously asked me to be his ears and eyes at the court of the pope. I tried to stop your trip by paying the bandits to ambush you at the Chiusi Pass. I had also informed the French cardinals about your trip so they could get their mercenaries to stop you if you made it past the bandits. You were lucky and you also happened to have those dogs, Jean and Zangi, with you to spoil my plans. I wish Zangi was not a Muslim so I could kill him myself.

"I was in constant contact with the Ottoman agents from the day we arrived in Dubrovnik until we were captured. The sultan's men were always a half a day behind us, following us every step of the way. I loosened the belts on the mules after we left Dubrovnik to slow you down and perhaps kill you. The mule that threw that stupid priest, Father Ricardo, off the road into the chasm below was supposed to be your mule, but Father Ricardo managed to mount it first. We nearly ran into the sultan's men that night when we had to turn back and seek shelter from the blizzard. Then, we managed to steal your supplies to slow you down. But, lunatic that you are, you attacked the caravan that was carrying the sultan's sister. That was not enough for you. You had to sign the death warrant of all your companions by seducing the princess. It took only a few days for the sultan to find out what had happened and send a rescue party. Nevertheless, you managed to do your dirty deed with her before they arrived to rescue her. The sultan was even angry with me for not preventing the dishonor of his sister.

"At first, the great sultan was merciful to her because he thought you had forced yourself upon her. Then, when she pleaded for your life, the truth came out. She is a bad seed, anyway. No Muslim woman would allow an uncircumcised man inside her body, only whores and Christian women do. You, Rodrigo, are a boor and an idiot who has been very lucky so far. Now your luck has run out and you will soon join the other heathens in everlasting hell."

Rodrigo was livid with anger but helpless, since he was bound securely.

Without a pause, Renaldo went on, "The reason that you were not killed when you were captured is that the sultan does not believe you were just carrying money and messages of support for that Christian dog emperor in Constantinople. Throughout the trip, I tried to find out the true purpose of your mission. Now, I think you were a stupid decoy because you are such an arrogant bastard that you would have been boasting about your true mission before we got to Florence. However, the sultan thinks otherwise, and so you and Jean are going to be tortured until you tell him the truth or die denying it.

"Do you know what they have planned for you tomorrow? Of course not. After sunrise, you will be taken to the center of the camp and raised on a cross with your hands and feet tied down with heavy ropes. The master of ceremonies, that is what they jokingly call him, will pick a long pole that has a razor sharp knife attached to its end. He is honing it now because it has to be sharp. He will make a long, shallow cut across your body from left to right, from shoulder blade to shoulder blade, making sure that he does not go too deep. You will cry with agony but that is just the beginning. Next, he will pick up a rake. The prongs are as sharp as razor blades. He will very gently pull your skin away from your body inch by inch. You will die a thousand horrible deaths and still be alive by sundown when mosquitoes will start feeding on you. The master is very skillful. He is attached to the court in Edirne and the sultan sent for him specially. He can keep you alive for several days while flies and maggots feed on your body and you beg for a quick death over and over again. However, it is not over yet. At night, they bring you down and lay you flat on your back. Dogs and cats will start licking and feeding on your defenseless bare flesh. Do you know the feeling of hot coal against bare flesh? Of course you don't. That is the next treatment for the next several days. You will still have your balls, which will be plucked from your body with his pliers. Next, your stomach will be cut open and your intestines will be taken out and displayed against your eyes while you are still alive. All this time, the soldiers, some of them Christians, too, will be laughing and enjoying the spectacle.

"Eventually, you will die a wretched death and will be fed to the dogs. I know you are not a very religious man. If you were, I would not tell you any of this, since I know you would be glad to endure all those torments and feel that the more severe the torture, the more likely that you would achieve salvation with God. But you do not really believe that garbage, do you? The idea of the trinity and all that nonsense! They sound absurd. Jesus Christ was a prophet of God like our great Prophet Mohammed. The God almighty in the holy book, Koran, ordered Christians and the Jews to follow Mohammed. There is only one God and that is Allah and I am his follower."

Rodrigo was nauseated. He had great difficulty trying to control himself and not show any signs of weakness. He bit his tongue hard and dug his fingernails into his palms to steady himself.

Renaldo was surprised by Rodrigo's resilience. He said, "I was saving the best part for last. Do you want to know what will happen to your lover, Aziza? She was a princess, the daughter of a sultan and the sister of one, and yet she betrayed her religion and her family and fornicated with a Christian dog. You made her a harlot. The sultan has disowned her and tomorrow, she will be made to watch you being skinned alive.

"According to Islamic Sharia laws, Aziza should be stoned to death for committing adultery, but the sultan was merciful and did not want to kill her. According to our Muslim traditions, if a woman has fornicated with fifty or more men for money, she is considered a harlot and is not subject to stoning. It is assumed that she needed to do it out of a need for money to look after herself or her family and not for carnal desires. You see, our religious laws are very fair.

"Therefore, our grand imam has decreed that tomorrow night, she will be given to the troops for a fee of one silver coin each. She will have many circumcised and uncircumcised penises in her tight vagina before the night is over. Even her virgin ass will be deflowered. They are already drawing lots for the fifty lucky soldiers who will be penetrating her from each orifice. By the time it is over, every orifice of her body will be oozing with seeds of Christian and Muslim soldiers and she will be truly a whore. In the morning, she will be given the money and will be sent to Salonica to board a ship to Alexandria in Egypt and then to Zanzibar, where she will be sold as a slave to the black heathens that inhabit that continent. She will end up bearing many half-breeds in some unknown part in Africa and will die wretchedly for falling in love with a knave like you.

"You can change what will happen to you and Jean by telling us the truth now. The sultan has promised to grant you a quick death by the axe if he is satisfied by your answers."

"And what about Aziza?" asked Rodrigo.

Renaldo's response was quick. "There is nothing that you can do for her. Her fate is sealed." After a moment or two, Renaldo said, "Well, there may be a way out yet. If you tell the truth and the Sultan is satisfied, he may be merciful and allow both of you to be stoned for adultery. It is far better than being skinned alive. You may even be lucky and the first stone may hit your head and knock you out. Let me find out. First, you will have to swear allegiance to the Muslim religion and then they will have to circumcise you to make you a true Muslim. I know that Christian fathers have forcefully baptized the Kaffirs and heathens to save their souls before condemning them to fire to destroy their bodies. Sounds stupid, doesn't it?" Before Rodrigo could say anything, Renaldo, with a satisfied grin on his hideous face, got up and walked away.

Rodrigo wondered about the conversation. It was so unreal that he thought he was having a nightmare. If he did not reveal his true mission, he would be skinned alive. If he did tell the truth and they liked what he said, they may cut off his head with an axe or stone him to death. What about Lorenzo, Father Ricardo, Antonio, Petros, and that murderous traitor Zangi, who turned tail and changed his religion at the last minute to ingratiate himself with the sultan?

Rodrigo sat there in the stockade with his hands and legs roped tightly together and no hope of an easy end. He wondered if he could commit suicide. Would it be acceptable to the Church since the alternatives were far worse? But how could he commit suicide? He did not have a sharp instrument to cut his veins. A rope and a tree from which to hang himself would be great! And, what about Aziza, Jean, and the others? What if he told the truth? Would the sultan really believe him?

CHAPTER TWENTY-FIVE

ESCAPE FROM EVIL

INCARNATE

Those morbid thoughts raced and roiled in Rodrigo's feverish mind. Eventually, exhaustion took its toil and Rodrigo fell into a fretful, nightmarish sleep. He dreamed of being skinned alive, screaming for mercy, and seeing his parents and all of his former lovers and friends watch in agony as dogs and other animals decimated him. He woke up several times that night. Then, around two in the morning, he heard some voices.

He looked sideways, and there he saw Zangi, laughing and talking to the guard outside the stockade. That treacherous ex-slave Zangi never seemed to need sleep. He was always around, day or night. How Rodrigo wished to get his hands around his neck. However, Zangi would be second on his list after Renaldo. Rodrigo could not hear the conversation. Anyway, it was in a foreign language and he soon lost interest. After ten or fifteen minutes, the conversation stopped.

Rodrigo looked again. The guard had apparently collapsed and Zangi was pulling him to one side, away from his view. Then Rodrigo saw Zangi again. He was smiling and held a large key in his hand. He unlocked the gate of the stockade. Without a word, he rushed over and cut Rodrigo's ropes with a bloody dagger. Rodrigo knew better than to make a sound or ask questions. Zangi went out again, brought back the motionless body of the guard, and sat him on the floor where Rodrigo had been sitting earlier. The guard was still alive, his eyes wide open in amazement and his throat slashed deep, with blood still oozing out of it. Quietly, Zangi and Rodrigo left the stockade, closing the door behind them. Zangi whispered, "Jean and the others are all together near here." Before Rodrigo could ask, Zangi added, "Aziza and Katarina are further in the middle of that camp. She is not guarded, since they know she cannot escape. There are some horses in the corral and we should have no problem getting rid of the guards. I have stashed away some daggers and swords."

Zangi handed Rodrigo a sharp dagger and together they approached the second stockade. Rodrigo's men were all asleep. Two bored guards were dozing while sitting on the ground. Rodrigo and Zangi had no problem dispatching the two guards with their blades. Zangi used his favorite method while Rodrigo stabbed his man on the back of his neck above the spine. They dragged the bleeding men inside.

Jean and Lorenzo had already heard the quiet commotion and were awake. They woke up the rest of the men and quietly followed Zangi to the corral, which was near a stand of trees. About half a dozen horses were there; no sentry was on duty.

Rodrigo faced his men. "I will have to go back and try to save Aziza. Please leave me a couple of horses. You are free to make your way back to Rome as fast as you can." By now, he knew that Zangi would never leave his side but the rest of the men insisted that they would wait for him. Lorenzo said, "Let me and Zangi come with you. In the dark, they will mistake me for one of their own. The others can wait here." Rodrigo nodded his approval but added that if the men heard any turmoil in the camp, indicating that the escape had been discovered, they should take off without waiting for them.

They each holstered a dagger and a short, curved scimitar that Zangi had taken from the bodies of the dead guards and followed Zangi to the center of the camp.

The camp was quiet but as they got closer to the center, their anxiety level increased. Here, tens of thousands of hostile troops surrounded them. Even a loud sneeze could cause a stampede. Rodrigo recognized the huge tent of the sultan. They could almost see the whites of the eyes of the ferocious soldiers guarding the sultan's tent. Zangi pointed to a tent nearby. To reach Aziza's tent, Rodrigo realized, they would have to circle around to the south of sultan's heavily guarded tent and then work their way back to Aziza's tent on the other side. The next few minutes, as they stealthily made their way between tents, seemed like an eternity.

As Zangi had said, there were no guards outside Aziza's tent. A dim light was shining inside. Rodrigo motioned to the others to wait and gently crept to the entrance of the tent. He peered inside. Aziza was sitting cross-legged on the floor with her diary and poetry book in front of her. Rodrigo whispered to her through the opening. She looked up. Recognition came to her face and she almost fainted. Rodrigo put his index finger to his mouth to ask her to be quiet. He undid the knots holding the flaps of the entrance together and entered the tent. She ran and collapsed into his arms as soon as he stepped inside. He whispered, "I will explain later. Wake up Katarina. We need to leave now."

Aziza rushed over to Katarina and shook her awake. She could not believe her eyes either. Seconds counted. Any minute now, one of the dead bodies could be discovered. Each woman grabbed a long cloak and followed Rodrigo quietly out of the tent. At the last moment, Aziza rushed back to pick up her diary and her box of jewelry. The trio joined Zangi and Lorenzo, who were hiding in the shadows, and made the trip back to the grove where the horses were corralled. Rodrigo's men had saddled the horses while they were gone. They mounted the horses and drove quietly out of the camp, heading west toward Skopje. Katarina, who did not know how to ride a horse, sat behind Zangi with her arms circled tightly around his waist, holding for dear life. Once they were clear of the camp, they galloped as fast they could for the next half hour. Eventually, near another wooded area, Rodrigo called a halt. They moved off the road into the woods and dismounted. They were still worried that they could be captured again and tortured to death.

Rodrigo addressed the men, "Thanks to the turncoat Renaldo, our mission seems to be over. We are in the heart of the enemy territory. They have been following every step of our movement. Does anyone have any ideas as to which direction we should take next? We could continue going west until we reach Skopje but we do not have any food, ammunition, or money. We could try to make it to Constantinople, which is still ten days or more away to our east, but in that case, we will be facing the same problems of shortage of food and ammunition and will also be hounded by the sultan and Abdullah Hassan."

"Signor Rodrigo, I would like to make a suggestion," Petros said. "We are just south of Sofia. Over those mountains," he pointed south, "is Salonica, which is a hard drive over rugged, arid mountain roads. However, just a two-day ride from here, going south, we can reach an abandoned Roman military road, which will lead directly to Constantinople. We will have to cross a few high hills and go down into the valley south of here to find the road. We will have to follow it until we get near Edirne and then follow it to the big city. Being Greek, I know the roads better than the sultan's scouts do. But we will have to hurry before we are discovered."

Rodrigo and his men had no other choice. This was a welcome chance for escape. With Lorenzo's help, they followed the stars in a southerly direction. By dawn, they were climbing one wooded hill after another. Fortunately, the tall trees camouflaged them, making them invisible from the main road. By noon, they had put a good distance between themselves and the main Sofia-to-Skopje road.

* * *

Rodrigo was fatigued and above all, hungry. He ordered a halt. They all dismounted and sat in a clearing, letting the horses feed on the branches and bushes, they discussed their next course of action. According to Petros, if they kept going south they should meet the old road by nightfall or maybe early the following day. However, they were all hungry and thirsty. The horses could survive by foraging amongst the branches but the men and the two women badly needed water and food.

Rodrigo dispatched Zangi and Lorenzo to see if they could find any nutrients, one going east, and the other going west. He told the others to try to nap. After about an hour, Lorenzo came back to tell them that he had found a stream very close by but no food. They waited for Zangi, who eventually arrived empty handed.

They headed southeast to the stream and drank as much as they could and watered the horses. They did not have any water containers, so they soaked all the absorbent material that they had and continued their journey up and down the hills. The trees began to get sparser as they moved further south. By nightfall, they camped in another grove. Rodrigo hoped that they would find some food soon.

CHAPTER TWENTY-SIX

THE RAGE OF THE SULTAN

An officer of the guard making his normal rounds discovered the escape of the Christians before dawn. The officers and the courtiers were too afraid to inform Mohammed about the break out. They did not know about the loss of horses yet. Abdullah Hassan Bey sent scouts to scour the countryside and when they returned empty-handed, he had the unpleasant task of waking Mohammed, who had celebrated the night before with wine and several concubines.

Mohammed was furious and ordered a full search in all directions. No one noticed that Princess Aziza was also missing. The search parties fanned out in all directions and came back empty-handed. In their zeal, they had gone far beyond the place where Rodrigo's group had turned into the forest and headed south, thereby obliterated their tracks.

Meanwhile, Renaldo, being the wizened old diplomat, kept out of everyone's way. He had noticed that Aziza was also missing but did not say a word. It was not a good time to bring more bad news to the sultan.

It was later that afternoon that Mohammed, remorseful for his wrath against Aziza, sent for her. He was about to write the whole thing off. He could marry his non-virgin sister to a captain or some other officer and send them to Anatolia in Eastern Turkey to rule a small province. His master plan was to conquer Constantinople and he did not want to divert resources to find a few foreign spies. However, when his page returned to announce that Aziza and her nanny were not in their tent, Mohammed was truly enraged. His sister suddenly became a martyr in his eyes. He assumed that the infidels had kidnapped her again.

Mohammed ordered a high-priority search. He promised one hundred gold coins to every member of the troop that brought his sister back safely. No quarter was to be given to the infidels. However, he wanted the eyes of Rodrigo at his feet. The Muslim armies were not known for their expertise in intelligence-gathering and mental acuity. They usually relied on huge numbers of brutal soldiers, fanatically motivated, blundering, and busting their way to victory or total defeat. They were not expert at tracking horses' hooves. Instead, they ran pell-mell in circles, trying to outdo one another.

It took a renegade Christian tracker from Bulgaria to finally sort out all of the horse tracks and establish where Rodrigo and his associates, along with Princess Aziza and her nanny, had left the road to head south. It was three days after the escape.

Mohammed was a little calmer now. It was then that Renaldo approached him for the first time. He suggested that it would be futile to try to catch the runaways; instead, his men should try to head them off before they got to their destination, which he still believed to be Constantinople. All the roads to Constantinople merged into two major highways. It was easy to send soldiers, in disguise, to monitor the arrivals and departures on each highway near the city.

Abdullah Hassan Bey was so eager to exact revenge that he immediately volunteered to take a group of men to where the roads intersected and lay an ambush.

The sultan dispatched another group of soldiers with the Bulgarian tracker to try to catch Rodrigo and his friends from behind.

CHAPTER TWENTY-SEVEN

THE HARD TREK EAST

The weary travelers had no shortage of water. At that time of the year, pockets of snow lingered and little streams of melted snow ran down hills and into gullies between the hills. They had a few swords and daggers and one rifle, but no ammunition. The horses had plenty to eat and drink and were in good shape. The major problem for Rodrigo was the lack of food.

On the second night, Lorenzo and Antonio set makeshift traps near holes in the ground and managed to capture a rabbit. They were so hungry that they did not wait for it to be fully cooked and almost ate the bones, as well. Rodrigo considered slaughtering one of the horses, which could provide food for a week or so.

The next day, they rode south for two hours or so until they came across what looked like a wash between two hills. On closer examination, they discovered that it was actually part of the old abandoned military road, overgrown with vegetation and cluttered with debris. Petros was pleased to have been proven right. Rodrigo asked Lorenzo to stay behind for a few hours and see if they were being followed.

Without further delay, they followed the road east. It was easy to follow this old road. In some places, it was almost covered with stones that had tumbled from the surrounding hills but it was still passable on horseback and they made good time. They camped and waited for Lorenzo, who showed up after about two hours to report that all was quiet behind them. They set out again and rode until it was quite dark. The moon shone brightly, casting eerie shadows on the hills around them. In the Middle Ages, people did not travel at night, mainly because they were afraid of wild animals and bandits, but also because they were superstitious. They feared they would encounter ghouls, gnomes, and goblins.

Rodrigo addressed his friends, "I do not think ghosts and phantoms can do more to us than Mohammed and his men. Let's ride on for a few more miles." The ride was actually easy, since there was enough moonlight to see around them and the horses instinctively followed the road ahead. After two more hours, they dismounted and lit a fire. It was their first opportunity to sit down and speak about the events of the last few days. Aziza and Katarina huddled together close to Rodrigo.

Rodrigo asked Zangi what had tipped him off that Renaldo was the traitor. "Signor Rodrigo," Zangi said, "when we were in the mountains about two weeks ago, I happened to see Renaldo relieve himself and noticed that he was, like me, circumcised. I was circumcised by force when I was only a young lad and it was painful. No grown man would willfully go through that experience unless he really believes that it will save his soul like the Muslims and Jews do. Therefore, I started watching him closely but I did not want to alarm you. Then, when we got close to Sofia, I noticed him disappearing one night and lost him in the dense forest. That is when I decided to take off my cross to be prepared to claim my allegiance to the Muslim god, since that was the only way that I could help you. Finally, after we were captured, they decided that I was a real Muslim in captivity. Renaldo was so busy with the sultan that he left me with the soldiers and since I had freedom of the camp, I managed to help you escape."

Rodrigo said, "They were going to skin me alive the following day."

Aziza started weeping quietly and said, "My love, I am sorry that I did this to you."

Rodrigo replied, "Actually, it was I who ruined your reputation with your brother, but I am glad, since it saved you from marrying that horrible butcher."

"If I ever get hold of that murdering renegade Renaldo, I will tie him to the muzzle of a cannon and fire the cannon with a slow-burning fuse," Antonio said.

The following day, they got up early to continue their journey. Rodrigo suggested that they scour the countryside first to see if they could find any food. Antonio and Zangi went north and Petros went south with Lorenzo.

After a few hours, Petros and Lorenzo came back with a slaughtered goat. Lorenzo explained that they found and killed the goat several miles to the south and had tried to cover their tracks. Rodrigo decided to move on immediately. He posted Antonio to keep up the rear and told him to wait for two hours and watch for any human activity before following them.

That night, they camped at dusk. The men dug a pit in the sandy ground, gathered brushes and twigs, skinned and cleaned the animal as best as they could and wrapped the carcass inside its pelt. They lit a fire in the pit, placed the animal inside, covered it with sand and stones to hide the smell and smoke, and cooked it overnight. By morning, the goat was fully cooked. They had their first hearty meal in almost a week. They cut the leftovers neatly to take with them and buried the bones and the skin.

They continued heading south and around noon, they noticed smoke on the horizon. Soon they saw the rooflines of a town.

Petros volunteered to go and visit the town. Aziza gave him her emerald earrings and a necklace that she was wearing to trade for food and supplies. Petros was gone almost until dusk. He came back loaded with food and supplies. He reported that this was the Greek town of Smolyan and he had not seen any Ottoman Turks. He estimated that they were within four days of Edirne and five or six days of Constantinople. Additionally, he suggested that they change their clothes to pose as Greek merchants, move to the main road, which passed through the town, and continue east.

The next morning, Lorenzo and Petros went back to town and came back with clothing and some ammunition for their single rifle. Antonio made sure that the rifle worked. They crossed over to the main road to Edirne and for the next few days, they passed several small towns. Thanks to Aziza's jewelry, they had enough money to buy food and wine.

The number of people who were traveling west, away from Constantinople, surprised them. In talking to them, it became obvious that these were families with young children who were hoping to get away from the conflict to avoid capture and enslavement by the Ottomans. The refugees were safe in the Ottoman territory as long as they entered it voluntarily and paid the non-Muslim tax known as *jazia* to the authorities. However, if they stayed in Constantinople and were captured within the city after the conquest, they would be enslaved instantly.

Rodrigo's exhausted group of six men and two women arrived at the town of Zoni within two days. Just outside Zoni, there was a fork in the road. To the north, lay the Ottoman capital of Edirne. To the south, the road led to the Ottoman port of Tekirdag and from there to the coastal road to Constantinople. They took the road south. This was all Ottoman territory now, but they were safe since the local people did not suspect them. The journey to Tekirdag took only two days. Just before arriving in Tekirdag, they stopped at Banarli, which was about fifteen miles outside the town, and at Lorenzo's suggestion, they changed their outfits to look like Muslim merchants from the Balkans. The women wore veils to hide their faces.

There were breathtaking views on the coastal road to Constantinople. However, there were many mosques and most people looked Turkic. The Muslim influence was too great here. In his heart, Rodrigo knew that the Christians would never again rule these parts.

Aziza and Rodrigo occasionally got a chance to hold hands or even steal a kiss. There had never been a time for intimacy since they escaped from the camp. Katarina, who always rode with Zangi, was getting very comfortable with him and the two had become friends. They spent what was supposed to be their last night in Ottoman territory about twenty miles from the famed city and by the afternoon of the following day, they could see the outline of the great metropolis in the distant east. The coastal road led to the Golden Gate, which was the royal entrance to the city.

Rodrigo ordered a halt for the day. That afternoon, he called a gathering and told everyone of his plans to search for Mohammed's secret weapon. Lorenzo drew a rough map of Constantinople on the ground. He explained that Constantinople was a peninsula surrounded by water on three sides. It was just over two miles wide at its widest point, facing the mainland, which was occupied mostly by Ottoman Turks. Therefore, if the Ottomans were building a secret weapon it must be very near the city itself. Most, but not all, of the area surrounding the city had been in Ottoman hands for a long time now and the Ottomans could have hidden the weapon in the woods near the walls of Constantinople. If it were a huge siege engine, as Rodrigo suspected, it would be easy to find.

Even though the Ottomans controlled most of the countryside adjoining the city, the majority of the people in that area were white European Greeks. The following morning, they divided into three groups and fanned out from their base near the Golden Gate at the southern end of the city. They agreed to meet again at dusk. They left Zangi to look after Aziza and Katarina.

Petros was the first to return. He was excited and could not wait for the others to come back. When a dejected Rodrigo and others returned by dusk, Petros told them that he had found the secret weapon. He had spoken with the Greek inhabitants and had managed to locate it. They were all excited, but Petros refused to tell them what it was until they could see it with their own eyes.

Early the following morning, Rodrigo, Antonio, and Jean led by a proud Petros, went northwest across rugged terrain.

After about a mile or so, they came to a hilly, heavily wooded area guarded by Janissaries. Petros said, "The Janissaries do not know it, but there is another way around to the gully below the hill." They went around the hill through a narrow gorge. Then they saw it down below in the clearing: the secret weapon.

It was a huge monster; the biggest cannon in the world. Antonio, in awe, said "I have never seen or heard of a cannon this big. The longest I have seen measured fifteen feet. This must be fifty feet long!" Their jaws dropped in amazement. Rodrigo had to sit down to steady himself. "With a cannon that size, you could destroy the world," he whispered. Antonio, the master gunsmith was out of his depth. Said he, "We were dead before we started this journey and now I know that we will all perish in Constantinople. I cannot even imagine the power of this gun."

Down below, the Ottoman workers were busy working on the monstrous gun. A man in European dress led them. Petros pointed at him. "The local Greeks know this man as Urban. He is a Hungarian Christian and stops by the village sometimes for a drink at the local *taverna*. He is a mercenary doing this for the money."

Rodrigo got up and looked down into the valley again. The enormity of the gun still amazed him. "It can probably fire projectiles of one thousand pounds or more," he said.

Antonio, with his keen professional eye, said, "This gun will probably work, but it is so huge that it will need to cool down for several hours between each shot. I wish we had some gunpowder. I could try to destroy it now."

"Let's go back," Rodrigo said. "After we get to the city, we will have to come back with enough manpower and ammunition to destroy this gun." With that, they left the site, retracing their steps to the clearing. Rodrigo let Antonio explain their findings to the others.

~ CHAPTER TWENTY-EIGHT ~

CONSTANTINOPLE AT LAST

The following morning, they entered the city through the fabulous Golden Gate. Mohammed's spies were in the crowd watching for them, but they did not expect them to be dressed as Muslim merchants. Rodrigo was impressed with the huge, twin walls of the city, which, he knew, had been built by Theodosius, a Roman emperor, over one thousand years earlier. They had stood proudly, defending the city, through ten centuries, against invaders from Attila the Hun to the Arabs to the Ottomans.

The travelers were awed by the city's magnificent splendor and its size. Next to Rome, it was larger than any city that Rodrigo had ever seen. There were many abandoned buildings and mansions along the thoroughfares of the city, but the city retained its grandeur with its magnificent churches and castles. Rodrigo said aloud, "No wonder they call it the greatest and longest-lasting empire that has ever existed. To think that a state has lasted over one thousand years..." He shook his head, his voice trailing off.

They were even more surprised when they came across the splendor of Hagia Sofia. None of Rodrigo's band of travelers was Greek Orthodox, but they were dazzled by the spectacle of the glorious church. Even Aziza, a Muslim by birth, was amazed by this Christian city.

Still, they saw Christian, Muslim, and Jewish residents alike streaming out with whatever possessions they could carry or load unto their beasts of burden. All of the city gates remained open, they were told.

They found an inn and Father Ricardo immediately left to arrange for meetings with the emperor and the court dignitaries. Jean sent for the Genovese banker who lived with many other Europeans in Galata, across the water from Constantinople, but conducted business in the city. His name was Paolo Monteverdi.

Signor Monteverdi was a fifty-year-old man of medium height with a gray beard. He arrived with two bodyguards and a clerk who carried a large satchel bulging with papers and coins. Jean showed him the letter of recommendation from the Vatican Curia. The man advanced him some gold coins and had Jean sign a receipt. Every week, Signor Monteverdi explained, the receipts were put aboard a Genovese ship and sent to Genoa. There, the banker's correspondent would collect the money from the Vatican's banker with interest.

Jean looked askance. "Interest?" he asked.

"In three months time, the banker in Genoa will collect two hundred gold coins for the one hundred that I have advanced to you today," Signor Monteverdi said.

"But the Vatican does not condone usury. It is not legal," Jean persisted.

Signor Monteverdi smiled. "It is actually a rental fee or facilitation fee. It simply covers the risk that we take in lending money in a foreign land. After all, some of the ships carrying the receipts never make it to Genoa."

* * *

After lunch, Rodrigo left Zangi to look after Aziza and Katarina. Zangi did not protest. Rodrigo had noticed that a bond was developing between him and Katarina. Rodrigo and the rest of the men hired one of the inn's employees to help them reconnoiter the city.

Constantinople was built on a peninsula. To the north, a wide river estuary, known as the Golden Horn, separated Constantinople proper from Galata. Galata, they learned, was a small, thriving community of European merchant colonies. The Genovese and the Venetian colonies were the largest. To the northeast lay the strait of Bosphorus, which connected the Black Sea to the Sea of Marmara in the south. The Bosphorus also separated Europe from Asia. Rodrigo stood there, looking across the narrow strait to the other side. He said to Jean, "Do you realize that once upon a time, they were all Christians over there? The Turkic tribes, first the Seljuks and then the Ottomans, depopulated the Christian cities and replaced them with hordes of Asian Muslims."

Jean remained quiet. They went inside the main forecourt of the splendid cathedral of Hagia Sofia and like many other visitors, were awed by its vastness and magnificence.

They then went to the western side of the city to look at the defensive walls. Their guide, an old Greek named Leo, told them that the walls were named after Theodosius. They dismounted and walked along the side of structure, which actually was a double wall with a gap between two. The outer wall was the shorter one and yet it was twenty-six feet high and over six feet wide. The inner wall was about forty feet high and sixteen feet wide. Beyond the outer wall, there was a moat sixty feet wide and thirty feet deep. The walls were reinforced every hundred feet or so with strong towers.

They counted eleven gates from south to north. Rodrigo noticed that the northern portion of the Wall around the Imperial Palace of Blachernae consisted of just a single wall. In addition, the last two northern gates, the Kerkoporta and the Blachernae, were not as solid as the other nine. Looking at those gates, Antonio said, "I am relieved to see these walls. For the most part, even that giant cannon of Urban cannot really damage them that much. However, if I were the enemy, I would not waste my ammunition on trying to destroy the two walls at all. I would concentrate my firepower on those two weaker northern gates."

After seeing the fortifications, they returned to their inn, feeling somewhat more secure. Father Ricardo arrived soon with some news. The emperor was out of the city inspecting the outer defenses beyond the moat. He would be back next day and they would probably be granted an audience soon.

Rodrigo decided to have dinner with Aziza that night. However, he made sure that Katarina was included. After what had happened in the past few days, he did not want to give the appearance of taking advantage of the young girl. She was not his ward, nor was she war booty, and he did not want to do anything to sully her reputation further.

The following morning, John Justiniani arrived to seek a meeting with Rodrigo. John was the head of the volunteer Latin Christian soldiers from Europe. The pope and some other princes had contributed to this force. However, it was mostly a volunteer effort by a few hundred knights who did not want to see a Christian state fall to the Muslims of the Orient.

John explained that, according to his intelligence, Mohammed's army of Muslims and renegade Christians outnumbered the Christians in the city by at least ten to one. Officially, there were supposed to be ten thousand soldiers defending Constantinople, but John thought it was more like five thousand against the two hundred thousand soldiers in Mohammed's army. As John explained, there were two things in the defenders' favor. One was the quality of the Ottoman army, whose ranks were filled with peasants conscripted to fight without much training or weapons. The other was the Theodosius Wall.

Mohammed, Murat, and his father before him had tried to storm the city, but the Wall had stopped them. John added that a few hundred years before the Ottomans, the Arabs lost 150,000 men trying to storm the city. The only time that the city was invaded was by the Christian knights of the Fourth Crusade, who had used trickery to scale the seaside walls two hundred and fifty years ago. The cruelty of those medieval Catholic occupiers had driven a permanent wedge between the Greek Orthodox and the Roman Catholic churches since then.

It seemed that, by now, everyone knew that Rodrigo Borgia was the envoy of the pope and Father Ricardo was the pope's nephew. John, like everyone else they encountered, were eager to solicit help from them and to find out when the shiploads of

European soldiers would arrive to help defend the city. Rodrigo was non-committal. He knew that the pope did not have any more resources to commit to the defense of the city and without the help of other European powers, it was not going to happen. Nevertheless, he responded diplomatically that his holiness was working hard to resolve the shortages of material and manpower.

After John left, Father Ricardo arrived with the news that the emperor would see them now in his palace. Blachernae Palace was located at the northern end of the Theodosius Wall almost next to the Golden Horn estuary. It was within spitting distance of the weakest point of the Wall.

CHAPTER TWENTY-NINE

THE EMPEROR'S PROPHECY

Even though the Byzantine Empire was at war and it was reduced to a city-state, Rodrigo, Father Ricardo, and Jean were forced to go through many bureaucratic courtiers and officials before they were allowed to gain access to the throne room. There, in his faded splendor, sat Constantine XI on a gilded throne. He was a man with a very dark complexion and a short black beard. Rodrigo thought that the emperor could be very easily mistaken for a Saracen Arab. Emperor Constantine, obviously preoccupied with the war at hand, received them rather curtly.

By that time, Rodrigo had had enough. It was too much for him to take this official stupidity from a decaying court. Despite his diplomatic upbringing, he spoke up. "Your majesty," he said, "we do not really have time for this. My companions and I have risked a long treacherous journey and I was nearly skinned alive to be here and be of service to you. Instead, I find a group of courtiers and eunuchs who are so embedded in the old traditions of an ancient empire that they do not realize the empire is close to coming to an abrupt end. His Holiness Nicholas has sent me and my companions to try to help. We have endured great hardship to get here. If you are dissatisfied with us, we will go back. Otherwise, please treat us like the friends that we are."

There was a sudden hush in the great hall. No one had ever talked to an emperor like that before. Constantine's tired face broke into a smile as he got up from his throne and walked toward Rodrigo. "You are," he said, "the most honest man that I have ever met in my life. It is difficult to be an emperor and hear the truth. My courtiers and eunuchs still think that they are living at the court of Justinian or Heracles. Alas, that is all gone. Frankly, right now, I am the ruler of just this city and no more.

"However, we still have a good spy network. We knew when you arrived in Dubrovnik but lost track of you after your miraculous escape from Mohammed's camp. We knew that you took his sister with you when you made your escape and that has actually made that mad man even crazier than he normally is. I think he may even be willing to trade the freedom of Constantinople for your capture and delivery."

Constantine dismissed his courtiers and guided his visitors to his private quarters. He said, "I know His Holiness Nicholas has sent you to help us. I have an army of less than ten thousand Greek and Latin Christians. The only way that this city can be saved is with additional troops from Europe. I know no more help is coming so we will have to rely on our twin walls and our Greek fire. So why are you here?"

Father Ricardo said, "You majesty, we are here to fight alongside your troops and also find the True Cross of our savior. It was rescued from the infidels by the Templar knight Arthur of Brittany and his fellow knights two hundred years ago and was left for safekeeping at the court of Emperor Alexius III. We would like to save it from falling into the hand of the infidels."

Constantine replied that he did not know anything about the current location of the True Cross, but he had heard that it was in the city. He was too pre-occupied with defending the city that he did not mind who and how they looked for the cross. He gave Father Ricardo his blessings and permission to search for it, wherever the search might take him.

Constantine put his right hand on Rodrigo's shoulder and said, "Why don't you and your group have supper with me tonight?" Rodrigo gratefully accepted the invitation.

Constantine continued, "Now, to more serious matters. As you know, the vanguard of the sultan's army is close to our northern gates. In fact, I think we will be able to see them from one of these windows soon. The rest of his army is marching steadily toward the city. Today is April 4. We estimate that by April 6 or 7, he will have completely surrounded the city from the land side. This has happened many times before but the intruders have always given up and gone back to their own lands. Mohammed's father tried it on a big scale and so did Mohammed, a few years back. The problem this time is that we do not have enough soldiers. Then, there is talk of a secret weapon, which is scaring the citizens." Turning to the visitors he asked, "What is your opinion?"

Rodrigo motioned Jean to answer. Jean explained about the cannon and how dangerous it could be. Constantine called a senior courtier and instructed him to allocate plenty of powder and ammunition to Rodrigo and Jean for their use against the big gun. Then he turned to Rodrigo with a smile and said, "Father

Ricardo is my friend and he knows that even if I am an Orthodox, not a Roman Catholic, I do not misstate the truth." His comment elicited a chuckle from everyone.

Constantine called for his secretary, who arrived so quickly that it seemed as if he had been eavesdropping on every word. Turning to Rodrigo, the emperor said, "You are already a knight of the papal state. I have a new mission for you for which you will need a Byzantine title." Constantine took his sword out its scabbard and in a solemn tone, he told Rodrigo to kneel. He then placed the sword on Rodrigo's right shoulder and after uttering a few words in Greek, he said, "Arise, Rodrigo Borgia, the count of Blachernae. You are now a knight of this realm." As was the custom, he extended his hand to Rodrigo, who kissed it as a symbol of his allegiance to the emperor.

Abruptly, he turned and walked to a table on which a parchment map was spread. Rodrigo and Jean exchanged puzzled looks, and then followed him.

"I have divided the defense of the city into several segments," the emperor said. "First, there is the northern section, which includes this palace and the two gates of Blachernae and Kerkoporta. I have assigned that task to our Chancellor Loukas and his son Christopher."

He pointed to the map on the table. "Two more groups of soldiers and knights are protecting the narrow estuary of the Golden Horn and the straits of Bosphorus.

"Then there is the navy that is protecting us from attacks from the Mediterranean and the Sea of Marmara.

"I am going to command the force that is defending the Theodosius Wall in the middle," he said, drawing an imaginary circle with his index finger.

"I will need a commander that I can trust to defend the southern end of the Wall from Selybmria Gate down to the Golden Gate and the sea walls next to it." His finger traced a line from one gate to the other. "I am going to assign the defense of that sector to the Latin troops and I want you to be their commander. Those troops are loyal and strong but most of them do not trust each other. I would think that putting a papal knight like you, who has managed to make a fool of Mohammed, at the helm, would boost their morale."

Rodrigo thanked the emperor for his trust and the honor that he was bestowing upon him. He had already reckoned that the Byzantine knighthood that Constantine had granted him would make it easier for him to move freely around the city to complete his mission.

They followed the emperor to the dining hall to have some supper. As they ate from silver plates, Constantine said, "Do you know that in the old days, all of these plates would have been made of solid gold and visiting foreign royalty were requested to take the plates with them every time they dined with the emperor? Now, thanks to our high debts to the Venetians, we do not even have one set of gold plates for our own internal use!"

The rest of the time was spent talking about hunting, traveling, and other items of trivial interest to Rodrigo. He was wondering how to find the cross and save Aziza from the ominous disaster that they were facing inside this soon to be besieged city.

Toward the end of their meal, two tall handsome men arrived in the chamber. The older one was a distinguished looking man of about fifty-five with gray hair and a short beard. He wore the traditional robe of aristocratic Byzantines with flowing, white tunic that came down to his knees and white pants with calfskin sandals. Bejeweled rings adorned his fingers and a large golden pendant, which looked like a symbol of authority, was hanging from his neck. His companion, a taller man with exquisite features that to Rodrigo resembled those of the Greek statues he'd seen in the city, was in his mid-twenties. He wore a military uniform with short pants. Both men bowed down and kissed the emperor's hand, as was the tradition of the Byzantine court. The emperor introduced the older man as Grand Duke Loukas Notaras, his chief of staff, the treasurer and the commander of the garrison defending the northern walls and northern gates of the city. The younger man was his son Christopher.

The younger Notaras crossed over to where Rodrigo was standing and with a broad smile shook his hand warmly. "The whole city has been talking about how you escaped the clutches of the sultan and killed hundreds of his troops. You are already a hero," he said. Rodrigo was surprised that word had gotten out so quickly. He was pleased but meekly said, "There is a lot of exaggeration in that story, commander; maybe we killed a few sentries."

They all sat at the table and Constantine outlined his plans for the protection of the city and the commanders that he was putting in charge. Grand Duke Loukas Notaras reported that the latest intelligence suggested that the bulk of Mohammed's army, with its siege towers, heavy guns, and catapults, was still far away. However, his cavalry and some units of infantry should be arriving at the Wall by the day after tomorrow, on April 6. They would effectively seal the city from the land side to the west from that day on. The Ottoman navy was not as good as the Ottoman army and, therefore, they would not be able to block the sea routes completely.

The emperor called for his aide and told him that, in future, Count Rodrigo should be allowed to see him without waiting for an appointment. Additionally, he ordered him to have Rodrigo and his party installed in one of the royal mansions on the south side of the city, near his command center. Turning to Rodrigo, he said, "Princess Aziza is a member of the Royal House of the Ottoman and as such it would be best if she stayed in this palace with my family. You can visit her and she can visit you anytime but she must always be chaperoned."

Rodrigo, feeling more comfortable with the jovial young emperor, impulsively put a question to him that had been on his mind since he stepped foot in Dubrovnik. "Your majesty, during the past few weeks, my friends and I have seen and felt a great amount of mistrust and hostility between the Muslims and the Christians. I am not sure if this hatred will ever end. What is your opinion, sire?"

Constantine was quiet for a few moments as if he had not heard the question. They all felt embarrassed and uncomfortable by the long silence. Eventually, Constantine lifted his chin up and said, "The West, and by that I mean Italy, Central and Western Europe, used to be civilized more than a thousand years ago. Then the barbarians came and destroyed Rome and nearly all of Europe. The Byzantine Empire, thanks to the fortress city of Constantinople, survived, expanded and prospered. Above all, it preserved the Western civilization. Then the Arabs came, from deserts of Arabia, hungry for booty and with a fanatical belief in paradise and afterlife pleasures. They conquered the Asian part of our domain and even destroyed the mighty Persian Empire. We managed to survive and gradually won some of our lands back from them. In the end, the Arabs learned from us and became civilized. In time, other Muslims even surpassed our knowledge in medicine, mathematics, and philosophy while Western Europe entered into a deep, cold, dark age.

"It was because Constantinople survived and was at the crossroads of the two civilizations that the forgotten civilizations of the Greeks and the Romans were transferred back to Rome and a rebirth of culture, which you call the Renaissance, took place in Western Europe. If the Muslims ever conquer this great city, they will be the real losers. The Ottoman Turks, being who they are, will stifle the flow of ideas from either direction. The West will prosper and succeed and the Orient will go backward. Therefore, even five hundred years from now, the Muslims will still be clinging to their present-day ideas and will be living in the past. That is something that we hope will not happen."

Constantine asked Father Ricardo to stay for a while to discuss some religious issues with him. Rodrigo and Jean went back to the inn, where to their surprise, a crowd of curious people had gathered to see the heroes who had defeated the sultan. By now, thanks to Antonio and Lorenzo, the story had them reaching new heights of heroism. Rodrigo knew that once those stories reached the sultan's court, the sultan would be even more infuriated at him and at his sister. Many years later, Greek historians were still writing of Rodrigo and his band of men breaking fearlessly into the sultan's camp to rescue Princess Aziza from the clutches of Abdullah the Butcher and her mad brother.

That afternoon, Rodrigo spent some time with Aziza and Katarina before he moved to his new quarters in the mansion, a solid old building that was part of the emperor's treasury, where two servants were assigned to serve him. Like everything else in Constantinople, the mansion had seen better days. But it was still quite comfortable. Aziza and Katarina packed up their meager possessions and were taken to the Imperial Palace of Blachernae at the northern end of the city.

CHAPTER THIRTY

COUNT RODRIGO BORGIA

The following morning, Rodrigo called all the commanders of the Latin forces to his room for a meeting. Even though most of them were older than he was, they had heard of his exploits and showed him great respect. Together, they reviewed the defenses of the city's southern end.

In addition to the great dual Wall of Theodosius, the city also had a sea wall that would be difficult to scale since the Ottomans did not have much of a navy. There was also a chain link across the Golden Horn estuary to stop the Ottoman ships from using that narrow passageway. In addition, as one of the Greek officers explained, they could use the Greek fire as a means of defense. Rodrigo wanted to know more about Greek fire and how it worked.

The officer explained that it was a secret formula created a thousand years ago. In its finished form, it was a gel-like liquid that was easily ignitable and could not be put out with water, which made it particularly useful in sea battles. When sailors splashed it on enemy ships or even on the waters surrounding the ships, they could ignite it easily. Since it could not be extinguished by water, it would burn the enemy ships very quickly. If a sailor got a few drops of the burning liquid on his body, it would burn through his flesh quite deeply.

The officer then explained, "In the old days, we used flaming arrows to light it from a distance but now guns are used to ignite it remotely after the liquid is pumped into the sea around the ships. On land," he said, "we use a catapult to hurl a container of the liquid at the enemy and try to ignite it before it hits the ground. It works like burning oil on the troops trying to scale the walls. However, there is an added advantage. Within a few yards of where it is ignited, all living things die of asphyxiation. They used to think that it was some kind of poison in the liquid. But actually, we have discovered that the combustion eats up the air around it so rapidly that there is no air to breath for a few minutes."

Rodrigo was impressed. He made it clear that he did not know the defenses of the city and was going to find out for himself. He dismissed the officers and after lunch, he and his friends, along with John Justiniani, toured the defenses. They went through the Golden Gate to inspect the moat and the areas beyond it. The area to the west of the moat had been clear-cut for approximately a mile to prevent the enemy from hiding behind the trees and firing at the city. The defenders had set subtle booby traps such as covered pits with sharp spikes and traps to ensnare and impale the invading soldiers. Beyond the one-mile perimeter was a no-man's land dotted with Greek villages.

The Ottoman Turks had moved into position very close to the northern part of the Wall near the palace of Blachernae, so the main road to Edirne was already closed. However, non-combatants could travel to and from the city using the road. The

Ottomans would let them pass without molesting them since the siege had not yet begun. Rodrigo and his entourage went deeper west for a few miles until they reached a hill overlooking the wooded plains to the west. There, in the far distance, they could see the great army approaching and could faintly hear the sound of pots and pans and metal implements clanging together as the soldiers and the supply mules moved closer. It was a chilling spectacle. As far they could see in every direction, soldiers marched up and down the hilly terrain like rolling waves of water in the ocean.

As they returned to the city, Rodrigo realized that he had neglected to do anything about the monster cannon. He asked Antonio if he would go with Petros and a detachment of Greek soldiers and try to destroy it.

Later that night, Antonio reported that the monster cannon was being moved under heavy protection of Ottoman troops, so they could not get close to it.

CHAPTER THIRTY-ONE

THE EMPEROR'S HAREM

Aziza was very reluctant to leave Rodrigo and the others. They had been through so much together that it seemed like she was leaving her own family. She had never been so close to so many men. She had been brought up to mistrust all men except her blood relatives and her husband, after she was married. Even then, she was brought up to believe that women had less intelligence than men did and, based on Islamic laws, she was forced to submit to their wills. Therefore, Aziza like so many other women of her station, felt inferior to men.

Now she was in the company of men who treated her with respect and friendship. She had been eating with them and sleeping in the wilderness near them. They had become like her family and she was attached to them. She did not want to go back to a harem where her movements would be restricted. Rodrigo had promised that he would come and visit her regularly and would be looking out for her in case of trouble.

The Blachernae Palace looked familiar to her since it was built by the Byzantines, just like the palace of her brother in Edirne, which was also a Byzantine city before the Ottomans conquered it. A eunuch led her to her apartment. After a few minutes, the emperor's sister Elena, with two of her maids, arrived to greet her. A woman in her early twenties with jet-black hair, black eyes, and dark complexion, Elena smiled sweetly at Aziza and said, "Welcome, my sister," and hugged her, as was the custom. She told Aziza that her maids would show Katarina around the palace so she could find whatever she needed. After their long travels, Aziza needed a bath badly. They arranged a bath for her and she slept soundly that night after a light supper of vegetarian Greek food.

The next morning, Aziza and Katarina took a walk around the extensive palace grounds and buildings. She saw many good-looking women and some handsome men. What surprised her was that the women did not wear veils in presence of men and they co-mingled and talked without chaperones. What's more, it was remarkable to note that the women did not look down when they encountered men in the gardens or hallways. In the Muslim world, one did not look directly at any man unless that man was a close relative. Katarina, sensing Aziza's surprise, chuckled and said, "This is the way it is in all Christian countries. Women do not have to cover their faces. The two of us can even go to the city and look at the sights by ourselves without having to hide in a litter. The only things this palace has in common with your brother's are the eunuchs."

Aziza was very pleased with her newfound freedom. She sat in the garden and let the gentle Mediterranean Sea breeze gently caress her tender skin. She asked Katarina to get her notebook and some writing instruments, and for the first time in many days, she felt so good that she started to write poetry again. She thought that she would rather live one year as a free woman than another fifty years as the indentured wife of the likes of Abdullah the Butcher.

Later that evening, Elena invited Aziza to her quarters. Elena had ordered a dish of roast lamb and rice. The lamb had been butchered in the Muslim quarter of the city and prepared by her chef. It was delicately cooked and very enjoyable. Aziza remarked that Elena's chef was as good, if not better, than their cook in Edirne was.

After dinner, the two women sat and talked about their lives and their dreams. Aziza wished that she had a sister like Elena, who was so genuinely lovely and friendly and without the pretensions of the Ottoman wives and concubines. However, every now and then, a terrible thought occurred to her. What if her brother and that fiend, Abdullah Hassan, conquered the city? She knew what would happen to her. But what would happen to Elena and to the many innocent young maidens of this great city? For the first time in her life, she realized the injustice that was done to slaves, such as Katarina. Slavery was such a vile practice, she thought to herself. There was at least one thing that she could do about it and she was determined to do it that night.

It was way past midnight when the two young princesses said their good-byes. Aziza retired to her apartment with Katarina. As soon as they were inside, Aziza tore a piece of paper from her book and in writing freed Katarina from slavery. She handed the paper to Katarina and said, "I now realize how horrible slavery is. As Allah is my witness, you are no longer a slave. You are free to go. I have put my mother's maiden name as a code in this letter. Not even Abdullah Hassan knows that. Only my brother does and he knows my handwriting. So, if you are ever caught, present this note and it will set you free."

Katarina could not believe her eyes. After all these years, she was free. She had always thought that she would die an old spinster, unfulfilled and craving a man's attention. Now she was free and for a moment, she thought of Zangi. She was quite fond of him but had not allowed herself to fall in love since it seemed such a futile hope. She cried with joy. The two women embraced and wept together.

When she was a mere child, Aziza had often run to Katarina's arms for protection and safety. Now the two women needed each other, as they were both in mortal danger and both in love. Katarina was the first one to speak. She said, "I am more than indebted for this freedom. I was a free girl before the dreaded Janissaries took me as a prisoner. I was very lucky to be selected to be your nanny. Many other girls were sold in the slave markets from Baghdad to Zanzibar and only our Lord Jesus Christ knows what happened to them. I have loved you since I started caring for you and I have always stayed by you. As a free woman, I will stay with you until the end and I am praying that the end will be happy for all of us."

Aziza, with teary eyes, hugged and held her. After a moment, she said, "Of course, you know what my brother had planned for me. He was going to have me ravished by fifty of his men and then sell me in Zanzibar to black tribesmen, just to satisfy his false religious principles. I am beginning to doubt my religious beliefs already."

* * *

That night, in his new rooms, Rodrigo could sense that he was not the only one who was missing Aziza and Katarina. The two women had brought so much joy and vibrancy to their dull lives. The men were gloomy and listless. Zangi sat in a corner staring into the sky. Jean was drawing invisible circles with a stick on the marble floor. Antonio and Lorenzo were unusually quiet.

Finally, Rodrigo announced, "All right you people, stop being so melancholy. I will send for them tomorrow." The change in attitude was instantaneous. Zangi jumped up and volunteered to go now and tell the princess of the invitation. But the hour was late. "You can go tomorrow," Rodrigo said. "And don't rush back. Spend some time with Katarina." Rodrigo thought he saw Zangi blush.

CHAPTER THIRTY-TWO

THE SIEGE OF

CONSTANTINOPLE

The following day was April 6. Rodrigo and Jean were up very early and went to the Wall to check the readiness of the troops. They climbed the outer wall and there it was, right in front of their eyes, the huge spectacle of the Ottoman army on the other side of the moat. The Ottoman soldiers had arrived the night before and were completing their encirclement of the city.

"This is it, then," said Jean.

Rodrigo nodded.

That afternoon, there was a war council meeting at the emperor's palace. There were many commanders there. The emperor asked for the latest news.

The young Christopher Notaras brought everyone up to date, stating that the Turks had formed an arc around the land side of the city. However, the line was still weak in places, such as the extreme north of the Wall near the palace. He added, "We could easily penetrate the line if we wanted to, but more troops and ammunition are arriving by the hour. The sultan, himself, is probably still looking for Count Rodrigo somewhere in Bulgaria!" Everyone laughed.

As for the city, Christopher Notaras went on, many people with young children had fled. Other than the soldiers, there were probably 20,000 to 50,000 people left in the city. Many buildings were abandoned and stood empty and there was enough water in the cisterns to last for a year or more but the food supply would not last beyond a month or two, at the most. There was enough ammunition at hand to last for a siege of several months and cannons were being mounted at strategic locations on top of the Wall.

Christopher continued with his depressing report. "We estimate that we have less than 10,000 Western European and Greek soldiers, volunteers and mercenaries, in total. Our spies and scouts report that the enemy has at least 150,000 to 200,000 soldiers. They also have many more cannons than we have, plus the monster gun that Count Rodrigo and Jean have already seen. With those odds, the best that any defending army could do would be to cut and run, but we have the Theodosius Wall." Christopher concluded by apologizing for being so gloomy but he said that the commanders should know the truth.

The emperor, who had been carefully listening to the proceedings, spoke next. He opened a scroll of paper and held it up for the assembly to see. "This," he said, "is the design that Urban presented to us for the gun. We refused him for two reasons. One was that we did not have the money that he was demanding for his invention. The second reason was more practical. This is a field gun, useful in pitched battles of armies in the field or for storming castles and walls. This gun was at least twice as long as the width of our two walls, so there was no way we could mount it on the Wall. Many rulers would have blinded Urban or at least imprisoned him to stop him from selling his ideas to the enemy. Unfortunately, we were merciful and let him leave the city unharmed. What we will need to do now is to find the gun and try to destroy it, and there is no need to show mercy to Urban this time."

After the meeting was over, Christopher approached Rodrigo and the two talked about defenses of the city. There was something likable and genuinely friendly about Christopher that made people like him and Rodrigo was no exception. Christopher asked if Rodrigo and his friends could join him for supper that night. Rodrigo welcomed the invitation but explained that that very night, Princess Aziza was coming over to visit her old friends. Christopher then suggested that perhaps they could get together another night that week and he said that he would also ask Princess Elena and Princess Aziza to the gathering.

Soon after sunset, Aziza and Katarina arrived from the palace of Blachernae at Rodrigo's temporary mansion. Aziza had to borrow a dress from Princess Elena, since her modest outfit that had lasted throughout their tortuous escape was no longer useable. The dark blue robe covered her almost to her ankles. She wore leather sandals and, for the first time in her life, she had painted her fingernails and the toenails of her dainty feet a subdued rose color. Katarina also wore new clothes. No longer was she dressed as a slave girl. She looked quite attractive.

The men welcomed them heartily, lining up to kiss their hands. Zangi, who had awakened one of the servants at dawn to take him to the palace so he could deliver the invitation in person, was standing in the semi-dark entrance of the mansion beaming happily, his white teeth glistening in the dark.

Petros and one of the servants had gone to the market and purchased fresh lamb, rice, vegetables, apples, and oranges. There were many hot houses in the city that produced plentiful supplies of out-of-season fruits and vegetables. Petros knew that because of her religion, Aziza would not eat pork and was reluctant to eat meat slaughtered by Christians; therefore, they bought their meat from a Muslim butcher. There were many Muslims and Jews in Constantinople, Petros said. "Even Ottoman Turks are allowed to live peacefully in the city."

In fact, the only discrimination and enmity was against the Catholics. This hatred dated back over two centuries. The Fourth Crusaders had invaded the city under the guise of friendship and massacred many of its inhabitants. They then crowned their own puppet as emperor and ruled the city for about sixty years before the Greeks overthrew them. A few years ago, Constantine, being a realist, had decided to accept Catholicism as the official religion of the empire instead of Orthodox Christianity, hoping to elicit help from European Catholic kingdoms. This was a savvy political move. However, the local populace, led by nobles such as the Grand Duke Loukas Notaras, rebelled against Constantine and forced him to repeal his decision.

The two lovely guests and the men all sat in the main hall around an enormous oval-shaped banquet table that had seen better days. Rodrigo and Aziza sat next to each other. Zangi, at first, hesitated to sit with the others, fearing the rest of the men would not welcome him at their table. Rodrigo stood up, walked over to Zangi, put his arm around his shoulder, and said, "You are a free man and have always been since you entered the service of his holiness and I am speaking for everyone in this room. We all owe our lives to your quick thinking and courage. Why don't you sit next to Katarina?"

This made Katarina smile and blush deeply. Aziza smiled knowingly at Rodrigo.

They all relaxed, talked, drank Greek wine, and enjoyed each other's company. Even Katarina, who was now a free woman, had a drink for the first time in twenty years or more. The wine and the company made them all feel relaxed and soon started conversing about themselves and their adventures during the last few weeks. Lorenzo, being a sailor, had many interesting tales to tell about his trips to the Eastern Mediterranean and the Muslim lands.

Zangi was urged to tell the story of his boyhood and his village, which Arab slave traders attacked and burned in the middle of the night. They slaughtered many people and carried him off to slavery. He told them about the years he spent as a slave to a brutish master who whipped his slaves and servants to prove his manhood.

Next, the topic turned to the trek from Dubrovnik to Constantinople. Rodrigo apologized to Lorenzo and Jean for thinking that they were traitors. Lorenzo recalled how when he picked up Father Ricardo on the ledge below the road to Skopje, he nearly dropped him into the deep valley. "My hands were frozen and the father suddenly felt so heavy that my knees buckled under me. Only by the grace of God, I managed to get up and push him up to Rodrigo and Stepan, the Croatian guide," he said.

Soon the dinner arrived. Greeks had never been great cooks like the Italians. However, they were all hungry and the cook had done an excellent job with the leg of lamb smothered with spices and slow roasted to perfection. The rice was steam cooked and then mixed with ground basil and a dash of the drippings from the roast lamb. It was then tossed in a large skillet until it was just right. The vegetables were steamed in water, strained, and then covered with salt, vinegar, olive oil, and spices and left to marinate for several hours. There was also bread made with crushed garlic and grated cheese. It was truly a wonderful dinner.

During the meal, Rodrigo suggested that Aziza and Katarina should come and visit them every day. Aziza said that she and Katarina were planning to come and visit their friends regularly and they might even bring along Princess Elena, who was practically living alone in the palace with them. Everyone was happy to hear her announcement. Zangi who was sitting very close to Katarina was so absorbed in her that he heard little of the conversation. Zangi and Katarina were happily talking and laughing to the exclusion of the others.

Later that night when the dinner was over, Rodrigo took Aziza's hand and they went up to the balcony overlooking the ancient city, which had withstood attacks for over a thousand years. It was dotted with light from many lamps, but there were pockets of darkness. Those were the homes of the residents who had abandoned the city in fear for their lives or the lives of their loved ones. Turning to the south, they could see the Sea of Marmara and the glistening light of the moon gently caressing the small waves on that small sea. It was such a romantic moment that at any other time in his life, Rodrigo would have used the moon, the sea, and the lights as a tool of seduction. This time, it was different, for he knew that he had never loved anyone so deeply since falling in love with his half-sister, Isabella.

Of all the women he had known intimately, three before Aziza stood out. There was Carolina, who was his first love and who had taught him the secrets of Spanish and Moorish lovemaking. Then, there was Isabella, his half-sister, who had always been the love of his life by blood and carnal attraction. He always felt at one with her as she did with him. Then there was Francesca, the abandoned noblewoman of Florence. Everyone else was a passing fancy. Now, he knew that Aziza was going to be his only true love for the rest of his life.

Rodrigo, while still holding Aziza's hand, turned to face her and said, "I want to talk to you about my past, and how I feel about you."

Aziza put her dainty fingers on his quivering lips and said, "My only love, you do not have to explain. I think I have loved you since the moment we met, if not before in my dreams."

Rodrigo, somewhat chastised, said, "You should know, there were others before you. But you are the only one for me now and forever. Somehow, I feel it in my inner being."

They embraced and kissed innocently. For Rodrigo, it was probably the first childlike and yet fulfilling kiss of his life. The kiss sealed their destiny together.

After a few minutes, Rodrigo and Aziza joined the rest of the party. A couple of the men were slumbering in the great hall. Some had gone to bed. Only Zangi and Katarina were still fully awake, sitting next to each other on a sofa and talking like two lovebirds. Rodrigo pointed to them and said, "Let's hope we will all have happy endings. I personally hope that we all end up in

Valencia in two villas, one for our children and us and one for Zangi and Katarina. Jean could stay with us or with them permanently. I think Antonio would like to go back to his family in Pistoia. Lorenzo may go back to Sicily or stay with us, and we should not forget about Petros. So we may need three villas after all."

They giggled and were happy, for the moment oblivious to the great army of Muslims camped within a few hundred yards of them. It was time for the women to go. Much to Zangi's delight, Rodrigo asked him to accompany the ladies' coach to the palace and come back in the morning. He was sure the palace guards would find a place for him to sleep. They said good-byes and Rodrigo, not wanting to compromise his lover publicly, simply kissed Aziza's hand as he helped her into the coach.

The next day, Rodrigo met Christopher at Christopher's headquarters near the Gate of Kerkoporta to discuss security issues. At the end of the meeting, Christopher told Rodrigo that he wanted to show him something that could save his life and maybe the lives of his loved ones.

They rode the short distance from Kerkoporta to the old Hippodrome site and stopped in a leafy square between the Hippodrome and the Hagia Sofia. There was no one around. Christopher guided Rodrigo to an alley on the south corner of the square where several abandoned villas stood. They walked past the first two and stopped at the third villa on their right. Christopher opened the door and said, "This villa belonged to my cousin and his family. They were among the first to leave the city and head for Venice." They entered a large garden, which led to a two-story house.

There was no one home and no intruders had touched the contents. Christopher took him into the kitchen; he lit two lanterns and handed one to Rodrigo. He opened a door at the north side of the kitchen and, with the help of the light from the lanterns, they walked down a few steps to a large basement. At the far corner of the basement, Christopher carefully removed some old furniture to reveal a round trap door about three feet in diameter. He pulled it open and Rodrigo sensed the cool dampness of water rising from the pitch-dark area below the opening. Rodrigo lowered his lantern into the cavity to take a better look. He could see the reflection of the lantern in the immense black body of water below and dim shadows of huge columns holding up the roof of the cavern. A cold shiver went through his body, old fears came rushing back, and he nearly dropped the lantern.

Christopher turned to Rodrigo and said, "There are several large cisterns under the city of Constantinople. This one is called the Basilica Cistern. It is about a thousand years old and was built at the time of Emperor Justinian exclusively for his great palace that is now abandoned. This is actually one of the largest cisterns. Most people, except the residents who live on top of it, have forgotten about its existence. These cisterns are filled with rainwater and can supply the city for long periods. You can even catch fish in some of them. In case of a successful invasion, you could live off the water and the fish in this cistern for quite some time, even longer if you bring some supplies with you. Before you ask me why I am telling you all this, let us say that I am mistrustful and scared about our state of preparedness. If the Ottomans had any brains instead of brute force, they could have conquered this city long ago. So, if by a fluke of chance they enter the city, this is where I would recommend bringing your friends to hide. You would be quite safe down here for a while. Once the blood bath is over, you could emerge and blend back into the city and perhaps get out of harm's way. I am sure you will bring Aziza with you, but please do not leave Elena behind."

Rodrigo started to protest, but Christopher stopped him short. "I am still hoping that it will not come to that, but even if one of your men survives, he should be able to save the women from the fate that would await them if they were captured. So, for the sake of them, let us say no more."

Rodrigo nodded in agreement and asked, "But, the columns holding the ceiling must be at least twenty-five feet high. How are we going to get down there?"

Christopher said, "I just wanted you to see one of the very few trap doors on top of the cistern. Now I will show you the only known remaining entrance to the cistern." They replaced the trap door and covered the manhole with the old furniture. Still carrying the lanterns, they went back through the villa to the back garden. In one corner of the garden, there were two solid ornamental stones, each about five feet high and partially covered by vines.

Christopher, followed by Rodrigo, circled around to the back of the larger stone. He put his lantern down, reached for the side of the stone slab, and pushed a stone knob into the slab. Then, with both hands, he pressed hard against the stone, which, surprisingly, rotated on its axis to reveal a small opening with a spiral staircase leading to the dark void below. Christopher explained that the large stone sat atop stone rollers and the knob locked it in place. Once one pushed the knob, it was relatively easy to move the stone away from the stairwell opening. When one pushed the stone back, the knob would reconnect and lock in place. There was another release knob at the bottom of the stone for coming up and out into the garden but it require two people to open it from below.

They descended the narrow staircase to an antechamber and looked around. Rodrigo was amazed at the size of this truly giant manmade cave. There were huge columns as far as he could see in every direction. The water was several feet deep. Christopher pointed the lantern to their left and they could see walkways going all over the place. Christopher said, "You can go all the way around without getting wet. In addition, several large chambers were meant for storage and are currently empty. They even have doors that have not been closed for centuries." Christopher proceeded to show him around the cavern.

Ever since he was a child, Rodrigo had a strange fear of large bodies of dark water at night. It was a strange phobia, since he loved swimming and enjoyed looking at the sea in the moonlight. However, he would sometimes break out in a cold sweat at the site of a black stagnant pool of water at night.

There was a very large pool of water not more than three feet from his boots. He did not want to show weakness so he had no choice but to follow Christopher around and look at all the possible hiding places. As they moved into the cavern, it got darker and he hated the ominous shadows that the columns cast on the black water. What if the lanterns went out?

Christopher was leading him around the nooks and crannies of the place and chattering away about the history and the purpose of the rooms and other things. Rodrigo could hear nothing but his inner fears, making him sicker by the minute. His palms were sweating and his hands were shaking uncontrollably. He felt the black mass was sensing his fears and reaching out to grab him. He was terrified of slipping and falling in that black hole and being lost forever under tons of water. He tried to close his eyes or just focus on the light of the lanterns. It was nearly an hour later before they emerged into the warm sunny day in the garden. By then, Rodrigo was a total wreck. He fell face down on the ground, throwing up and shivering violently. Christopher put his arms around him to steady him and said, "You must have a cold or something. I am sorry; it was probably too cold down there."

Christopher ran into the house and came back with a sealed bottle of liqueur and a cup. Apologizing profusely, he smashed the neck of the bottle against a rock, poured some liquid into the cup, and handed it to Rodrigo. The cup was shaking in Rodrigo's hand and the liquid was spilling out. Christopher held both of his ice-cold hands in his warm hands and helped him drink the fiery liquid. It took a few moments for Rodrigo to regain some of his composure. The sun and the alcohol helped him recover somewhat and he apologized and thanked Christopher for his help. Christopher was truly worried and suggested that they should see his family doctor. Rodrigo declined, saying that he was fine and he would consult with Petros if he had another attack. It was difficult for him to ride a horse the few blocks to his place of residence. By leaning on Christopher for support, Rodrigo eventually made it home.

Rodrigo was still rather wobbly when he entered the mansion. Christopher called Petros and explained Rodrigo's symptoms to him. Petros made a liquid elixir and sent him to bed. He also brought a pillow and some blankets and slept on the floor next to Rodrigo's bed to keep an eye on him during the night. Eventually, Rodrigo fell asleep. He woke up the next day feeling much better.

Rodrigo spent the rest of the next day with Jean to supervise the defenses of the city. Antonio and Lorenzo were assigned to make a tally of guns and ammunition in their sector of the city. The Ottomans had sent word that anybody who wanted to leave should depart the city now. Many people took advantage of the offer and left the city, passing through the partially opened gate of Charisios and headed west on the road to Edirne and an uncertain future.

Later that day, when Rodrigo got home, he expected Aziza to be there but she was not. She had sent word that she was spending time with Elena at her request. He felt sad and melancholy. He was already missing her and now that he had committed himself to her, he could not wait to tell her about his life, his joys, and his fears. He did not want to keep things to himself any longer.

That night, Petros, who had been to the market, came to see him and said, "Signor, I have been a doctor for many years and can diagnose a disease by looking at the eyes or the tongue of a patient. I also use my nose to smell some sicknesses. I know that you are a very courageous man but I smelled fear on you yesterday. I do not know the cause of it but I have made you some capsules to take if you ever again come down with the same symptoms." He handed a small packet to Rodrigo and left without waiting for a response.

~ CHAPTER THIRTY-THREE ~

THE TWO PRINCESSES

Aziza and Elena had a nice time that evening. First, they went for a walk in the beautiful gardens of the palace. Then, they sat on a balcony in Elena's apartment overlooking the Golden Horn estuary. Across the estuary was another town, which was well lit. Aziza asked what that place was and if it were also under attack.

Elena said, "That is Galata. It was assigned to Genovese, Venetians, and other Italians as their base of commercial operations in the Orient. They have several colonies there and they have made it look like their hometowns as much as possible. They are not under attack. There are no real defensive walls there and they also trade with your brother, Mohammed. He could just walk in any time he wanted to. Galata is a fun place to visit. You take a boat there in less than fifteen minutes. The Venetians are the most intriguing of the lot. They do not have a king, a prince, or even a republic. They have a doge, who is like an arbitrator. They claim that they are free but they are enslaved to gold. That is what they seek all the time. My brother says he has never seen greedier people than the Venetians."

The maids brought in some wine mixed with sherbet. Elena asked, "Is it because your religion forbids it that you do not drink wine? I have lots of time on my hands to read books and study things. My understanding is that certain foods, such as pork, are expressly forbidden but wine is not anywhere expressly forbidden in the Muslim world."

Aziza replied, "You are right. In fact, eating pork is in the same class as cannibalism. However, the holy book only says that one should not say prayers when one is drunk but since we have to pray so many times a day, it basically rules out drinking completely. My brother and most of his courtiers drink and then wash their mouths and gargle with water seven times before praying. That is supposed to purge their mouths of alcohol."

"That is really hypocrisy," she said. "I will have a glass of wine and I will tell you a story that will make you laugh." The two women relaxed and each had a few sips of the delicious Greek wine expertly mixed with sweetened sour cherry juice.

"Do you know what some of our imams do?" Aziza continued. "In the summer when the grapes are in season, they eat large quantities of grapes and then sit in the sun. Apparently, in the heat of the sun, the grapes ferment very quickly and the imams get an elevated feeling." Both women laughed.

"Maybe we should try it tomorrow. I think we have some grapes in cold storage in our cistern." Elena refilled their glasses.

"There is another practice that is expressly forbidden by our religion and yet it is practiced widely and openly. It is written that lying with men or boys is an unforgivable sin. It is called *lavat* in Arabic and Turkish. We know only a few words of Arabic and yet are required to learn and recite the Koran without knowing what it means," Aziza said, the wine eroding her inhibitions. "Anyway, it is an open secret that many Muslim men practice *lavat* almost openly. It is rampant among the Janissaries, since they are not allowed to marry. I have heard that there are houses in Edirne that men visit to fornicate with men. They call their acts of disgrace 'Greek love' instead of *lavat,* which is an act of abomination. It must be the climate in this part of Europe that makes men different."

Elena smiled faintly and replied, "Actually, Greek love has been practiced by men all over the world since time immemorial. It is even in the Bible. In ancient Greece, it was an acceptable activity and many older men would take younger lads under their wings to teach them arts and sciences and to sleep with them. It became a great sin under Christianity, and yet it is still practiced here as well."

Elena changed the subject, saying, "We have all heard how Rodrigo risked his life by charging into the camp to rescue you from the clutches of that evil Abdullah Hassan. Are you two in love?"

Aziza took another sip of the delicious wine and chuckled. "The story gets better every time I hear it. It is true that he risked his life to save me but he did not exactly charge into the camp. That is a different story, though. I do love Rodrigo more than anyone else. I think I fell in love with him when I first saw his handsome, dirty, unshaven, and gaunt face."

Aziza looked around to see if anyone else was within earshot. Seeing that the maids were not nearby, she said, "The fact is that I had never been with a man before Rodrigo. That is the Muslim custom. So, when my brother found out that I was…well…not pure anymore, he got mad and wanted to sell me as a slave to prove that he was a man of principle. He is such a fool and a vicious one at that. I am a few year younger than he is and I used to adore him. Then I found out about his cruel disposition. When we were small children, I once saw him capturing flies and sticking them inside spider webs and watching the spiders slowly attack and cocoon the helpless flies as they tried to free themselves from the web. I even saw him pulling the wings of flies off and then putting them next to anthills to watch them tear the poor things apart while they were still alive. That was when he was only ten years old. I threw up when I saw what he did.

"Abdullah Hassan was always his playmate and was always at his beck and call," she continued. "Now that I look back from here, I see things so differently. We all knew that my brother kept young boys to satisfy his sexual desires but he also liked women. However, I have heard that Abdullah Hassan has a harem of young lads only. I suppose I would have been his trophy bride and maybe he would not have even bothered with me, but I doubt that. I am so glad that I met Rodrigo and his friends. They are so real and unpretentious. That is, except Renaldo, who turned out to be a real snake and a true back-stabber. We had a rough time getting to Constantinople, but I am so pleased over the turn of events. I am sitting here with you now instead of being in the harem of a brute and I consider that being lucky." Suddenly, Aziza blushed. "I have been talking about myself all this time. What about you, Elena?"

Elena sighed gently and said, "My sweet Aziza, until yesterday, I was the only princess in this household. I am so thankful that you are staying with us. I find it so easy to tell you things that I cannot tell anyone else. My brother Constantine is probably the bravest man in the world and perhaps the most stupid, in a sense.

The sultan has been offering him the kingship of any island that he chooses if he would just give up this city. Constantinople is just a city. This is what is left of an empire that once stretched from the borders of Persia to the isles of Britain. But my brother is stubborn. He is so devoted to being an emperor that he does not really know how minuscule his empire really is. He is so committed to preserving the Western civilization against those barbarians who came from the bowels of Central Asia that he is willing to sacrifice his own life. If the Ottomans take this city, they will treat us as your brother treated those flies. And since we are talking about our lives so openly, I will tell you about mine.

"I am twenty-two years old and not married yet. Several people wanted to marry me. Even your brother, the sultan, wanted to marry me to unite the two kingdoms, but neither of us was willing to change our religion. It is interesting to think that if I were captured in a war, he could have had me without thinking about religious differences, since I would have been his war booty. But he could not marry me as a free woman unless I changed my religion. Just like Muslims, it is also a Greek custom for a girl to remain a virgin and keep her hymen intact until she is married. I am still a virgin."

Aziza blushed so deeply that even in the dusk, Elena noticed it. She remembered with a sense of shame that she was no longer a maiden and had willingly let a man inside her not once but several times during that heady night in the forest of Bulgaria. Elena paused for a moment and then went on. "We are the real Christians, not like the women of Britain and Northern Europe who sleep and fornicate with any man whenever they feel an itch below their navels. I have loved Christopher Notaras since we were kids playing in those gardens below. Everyone wants us to be married except Christopher. If my brother does not have any children, which is likely, since he is married to his empire, then Christopher would eventually become the co-emperor with me but still he is not interested. I know his father is in favor of this marriage but Christopher treats me like a sister. He has never kissed me passionately on my lips but he is here regularly, worrying and fussing about my well being."

Elena drained her glass. "While we are talking about Christopher's father, Loukas Notaras, I do not trust that man at all. My brother signed an act to unify the Orthodox Church of the East with the Roman Catholic Church of Rome. This was a formality to obligate the Latin countries of Western Europe to come to our aid against the infidels, but our Grand Duke Loukas Notaras was one of the first to entice a citywide rebellion whose slogan was 'Better under the turban of the Turk than the miter of the Vatican.' My brother rescinded the order to satisfy the mob. I wish he had resisted. Either my brother would have been thrown out of office and Loukas would have been the next emperor and he would have had to deal with your brother, or my brother would have prevailed. I distrust Loukas because he has such a complex character. Christopher, who is much wiser and more compassionate, once said that we are all Christians believing in Christ our Lord. The rest of it is embellishments and misunderstandings. But no one listened."

The two women talked some more. Elena summoned her maids and told them to serve the food on the balcony. There was the usual selection of meats, vegetables, and rice. Aziza said,

"As of tonight, I am never going to ask if a piece of meat was slaughtered by a Christian or a Muslim." The two women giggled happily at that remark and dug into the meal.

Suddenly, Elena sobered. With tear-filled eyes, she turned to Aziza and said, "I just thought of something dreadful. Here we are, the sisters of two warring kings, happily chatting with each other. I know we will be safe as long as the Wall survives. But if they capture the town, what will happen to us?"

Aziza, in a matter-of-fact manner, responded, "It is simple. I will be killed and you will be sold into slavery. So, it is best to enjoy the time that we have now."

With all that wine and good food, Aziza soon felt sleepy. They hugged and Aziza, with the help of Katarina, went to her quarters, where she slept soundly.

* * *

Observant Muslims pray five times a day, starting at dawn and ending at sunset, on their hands and knees. They are required to pray every day except when it is not possible for some reason. For example, a woman must not pray during her menstrual period because her blood is impure and it is sacrilegious to the Lord. But a married or unmarried woman with a broken hymen is not excused from praying just because she is bleeding, since that blood is supposed to be the blood of purity.

Aziza had not prayed often since being captured by Rodrigo. This morning, however, she got up early to pray. She just wanted to plead for Rodrigo, Elena, Christopher, and herself. Still in her nightgown and bare feet, she walked to the balcony outside her bedroom, and facing east toward Mecca, she kneeled on the hard marble floor. She raised both hands to the heavens with her palms up and quietly prayed:

In the name of the God merciful and kind

Dear Creator, we thank thee and are grateful for your kindness and forgiveness so far

We beg thee to keep your shadow of kindness over us and show us your forgiveness

Dear Creator, I beg thee to keep your kind shadow over our heads and protect us in the future as you have done in the past

Dear Creator, I am specially beseeching you to be kind and merciful to Rodrigo and his friends and Elena and Christopher

I beg of thee

Amen in the name of Lord of the worlds

Amen in the name of God

* * *

Those were the exact words as she later recorded them in her diary and book of poetry.

~ CHAPTER THIRTY-FOUR ~

KING OF KINGS

After Rodrigo and his friends' escape with Aziza, the young sultan, who had never genuinely faced defeat before, was furious. At first, he could not believe that they could have escaped from the middle of his mighty camp without inside help. Then, the soldiers sent to capture them returned empty-handed. To the sultan, it was a loss of face and he had to blame someone other than himself. He executed several sentries for negligence but that did not help matters much. He also sent Abdullah Hassan to the gates of Constantinople to try to capture the fugitives before they made it to the city. That mission failed also. Finally, he received the news that the renegade infidels had arrived in Constantinople and had become the toast of the town for having made a monkey of him and his army.

This enraged him so much that he screamed in anger and stabbed the sides of his royal tent with his dagger until they were shredded to little pieces.

Mohammed was given to sudden bursts of anger when he was extremely agitated. He would foam at the mouth and attack anything and anybody who came near him. His courtiers and soldiers had learned to avoid being near him during those episodes. The few who did paid for it with their lives when his dagger tore their bodies apart during his fits of madness. Usually, after several hours of rage, he would suddenly calm down and become quiet and pliant as a child.

After he had calmed down, Selim Pasha and a few trusted eunuchs carried the sultan to his large harem tent while workmen rushed to remove and replace the royal tent.

Later that day, Abdullah Hassan suggested that they send an emissary to Constantinople to demand the return of the criminal Rodrigo and his friends as well as the abducted Princess Aziza.

Renaldo objected strongly. He said, "You are at war with Constantine. There is no way you could dictate terms to him. You will need some bargaining chips here that you do not have. That dog, Rodrigo Borgia, is now a hero to those people and they will never let him go. However, you may be able to offer your sister safe conduct and promise her that if she comes out she will be treated respectfully and sent to one of your palaces in the far east of Anatolia to live the rest of her life. However, my humble suggestion is to forget offering any terms. After you conquer Constantinople, you will have all of those dogs in your hands, dead or alive."

Abdullah Hassan, who was still smarting from humiliation, disagreed. He said, "Constantine will not refuse the order of the great sultan. Those dogs are fugitives and they have had the audacity to abduct the princess twice. We should demand their return and certainly the release of our princess, who is the ward of our sultan."

Despite objections by Selim Pasha and many others, the sultan decided to follow Abdullah Hassan's suggestion. He appointed Abdullah Hassan to head the mission, which also included the usual coterie of scribes and translators. Renaldo declined the honor of going as the sultan's ambassador. He did not want to be associated with failure. He had already seen Zangi's handiwork, and knew that diplomatic immunity meant nothing to Zangi, who would kill him as soon as he laid eyes upon him.

* * *

The entourage arrived in Constantinople on April 9 and was granted an audience with Constantine on the tenth. Abdullah Hassan, who was a pure-blooded Turk, could only speak Turkish. He was a brazen man who was accustomed to having his wishes obeyed by everyone. Through an interpreter, he read the long and confusing letter from the sultan demanding that Rodrigo and Aziza, along with all the others, be handed over to him. At Constantine's request, Rodrigo and Jean were listening to the conversation from an unseen alcove in the great hall. They did not know whether to laugh or be angry at the nerve of this man.

Constantine had to control his temper at the arrogance of the Ottoman. After a few minutes of silence, he said, "You have not told us what crimes these people have committed. We have the oldest law court in the world in this city. If you have any evidence, they will be tried fairly. If the court so decides, they will be handed over to you. That, of course, will happen after the war is over. As for Princess Aziza, I would need to investigate the circumstances before taking any action."

Abdullah Hassan was clearly rankled by his reception. He was accustomed to dealing with conquered tribes and lords who had to kiss his boots to save their lives. He was not a diplomat, but before he could say a word, the audience was over and the emperor bid them good day.

After the Ottomans had gone to their quarters, Rodrigo and Jean approached the emperor to ask if he was really considering sending Aziza back with this bloodthirsty savage.

Constantine said, "In your hearts and minds, you and Jean know the answer better than I do. They are claiming that Princess Aziza was abducted against her will. On the face of it, that argument makes sense. You, Rodrigo, ambushed a royal caravan in the heart of their kingdom and then proceeded to kill several members of the royal household who were guarding a royal princess. You then kept the princess captive until she was released by force. Then you had the audacity to abduct her again, this time from the middle of an armed camp. So, in any court of law, you would all be condemned as highwaymen. The Turks also claim that the princess is a ward of her brother, the sultan, because she is under age. I am assuming that none of you had any physical relations with her, because that would make matters even worse."

Neither Rodrigo nor Jean had a ready answer for that. They were crestfallen. Rodrigo felt the color drain from his face for fear of losing Aziza once again.

Constantine continued, "On the other hand, you were papal envoys on your way through hostile territory and had already been attacked several times. So one could say that you took pre-emptive action to avoid another ambush and that the girl fell in love with you and you thought you were rescuing her from marrying someone whom she detested. Even that does not excuse what happened. However, we are at war with the Ottomans and

I do not see why I should honor the sultan's request. But I am not sure that as a Christian I can keep Princess Aziza in captivity."

Constantine walked away toward his chambers, followed by Loukas Notaras. The thought of abducting Aziza for a third time and taking her away in a Genovese ship occurred to Rodrigo, but Jean, who could usually read his friend's mind, said, "I know what you are thinking. Don't even consider it. Just trust in the Lord."

Brokenhearted, Rodrigo and the others went back to the mansion. Rodrigo gathered his friends around and after making sure that the servants were not within earshot, told them what had happened that day. Father Ricardo, who was at the meeting, urged caution and prayers. Lorenzo, the hot-headed Sicilian, suggested storming the palace and bringing the princess to their mansion, which could then be protected by the Western European soldiers under Rodrigo's command. Jean suggested waiting for events to take their course. Father Ricardo led them in a prayer.

Rodrigo added, "The other reason that we are gathered here is to discuss our future. I will let Antonio speak first."

Antonio nodded. "I have been examining the Wall and the gates carefully. None of the cannons in existence today can destroy them easily. Any minor breach can be repaired quickly and the defenders are quite apt at doing that job. I do not know about the monster gun of Urban, since I have not seen it in action yet. The two northern gates are the weakest. But, looking at the way the Ottomans have positioned their artillery, I would think that they are going to concentrate their fire on the middle of the Wall. What I am not sure of, since I am not a general, is what happens if one of the gates is breached or a portion of the Wall collapses. At Rodrigo's order, Lorenzo, Petros, and I have been estimating the number of hostile troops independently. In terms of troops, they probably have a twenty to one advantage over us."

Rodrigo then told them about the hiding place in the Basilica Cistern. He said that he would take Antonio and Lorenzo with him to show them the place and make sure that they know how to open the door to the secret stairwell. Next, he said, the others should go in groups of two or three and take some food and ammunition with them to store in the cistern in case they have to hide there for a long period of time.

Later that afternoon, he took the two men to the villa. After showing them how to release the catch on the stone cover, he left them to search the cistern for themselves.

Lorenzo and Antonio came back around dusk to report that they had made a tour of the cistern and had determined where they could live temporarily if they were forced to move down there. They had made a list of provisions that would be needed.

Antonio and Lorenzo had managed to open a little spy hole on top of the staircase so they could actually see the garden and the villa from below while standing on the staircase. Lorenzo said that he had also uncovered a long passageway in the middle of the cistern but they did not have enough light to see where it led. He planned to continue his search the following day with Zangi.

CHAPTER THIRTY-FIVE

THE EMPEROR AND THE PRINCESSES

After he returned to his chambers, Constantine dismissed his advisers and sat down to think. After an hour or so, he sent for Elena and Aziza and asked them to meet with him in his chambers. Both ladies arrived dressed in brown and obviously unhappy, since they had already heard the news about Abdullah Hassan's mission.

Constantine dismissed their maids and his personal servants and said, "We live in a civil society. At least, we try to be better than those barbarians and their primitive laws that originated from the harsh, deep, deserts of Arabia. They are asking me to hand over Count Rodrigo and his associates to them and send Princess Aziza back to her brother. They say that you are under age and were abducted against your wishes."

Aziza, her head bowed, remained silent.

He then explained the legality of the situation to them as he had to Rodrigo and Jean. Elena immediately protested, saying that he could not send Aziza back to certain torture and death. Constantine calmly continued, "There are two issues here. First, whether or not Princess Aziza was abducted, and secondly, the age of consent for girls. I understand that in the Muslim world, it varies from nine years old to fourteen. I assume that you are over fourteen and can make your own decision as to whom you want to marry. But the sticking point is that you were abducted against your will in the first place. They may even claim that you were sexually abused, which I hope is not true."

Looking Aziza squarely in the eyes, he asked, "Do you want to stay here or would you rather go back to your brother?"

Aziza replied fervently "I would never go back to that brute of a man. I would rather die first."

Constantine said, "For now, you should go back to your chambers and let me think more about this."

The two depressed girls walked away hand-in-hand to Elena's apartment and sat there waiting for a decision.

Constantine sent for Christopher Notaras and spent some time with him. Next, he called Abdullah Hassan to a private meeting with just the two interpreters present. He asked Abdullah Hassan what they would do if they recaptured Count Rodrigo and his group. Abdullah flinched at the mention of Rodrigo's name but replied that that was a decision for the sultan to make. Constantine persisted, stating that if Abdullah Hassan was an envoy with full credentials as he claimed to be, he should be able to give a direct answer and be willing to negotiate.

Abdullah Hassan, who was a rash individual, was caught off guard. He knew that if Renaldo had been there he could have come up with a satisfactory answer. He mumbled something about severe penalties for abduction under the Muslim laws.

Constantine replied, "Does that include skinning them alive and taking their intestines out while they are still alive and feeding them to dogs? Is that what the benevolent Muslim laws are about?"

Abdullah Hassan's hand subconsciously went for the dagger that was not there, since all visitors were disarmed before entering the emperor's presence. Constantine actually stationed two sharp shooters behind the curtains who were ready to shoot in case of treachery.

Feeling out maneuvered, Abdullah Hassan begrudgingly admitted, "I can promise them a very quick death with a sword or an axe." Constantine called for his guards and told them to go to Abdullah Hassan's quarters and fetch one of his aides with a copy of the holy Koran. Soon, the aide arrived, reverently holding the holy book with both hands in front of him.

Constantine said, "Abdullah Hassan, repeat what you just promised me by swearing it on the holy book." Abdullah Hassan, who was sweating profusely, hesitated for a moment. Swearing to a falsehood on the Koran was a grave offense and God would not forgive him. However, he could not go back empty-handed and face the wrath of Mohammed.

Reluctantly, he put his right hand on the Koran and swore.

Constantine then said, "And what about Princess Aziza? What will happen to her?"

For a moment, Abdullah Hassan was his old belligerent self again. He replied, "She is the daughter of a sultan and the sister of a great sultan. I cannot discuss that with you."

Constantine dismissed them all.

Later that day, he sent for the senior Muslim clerics of the city and spent some time with them. During the meeting, he also asked Princess Aziza to join them for a few minutes. The following morning, he sent for Count Rodrigo and his associates. The messengers came back empty-handed. He sent another messenger to search the Wall, but he could find no sign of them.

Constantine then called Abdullah Hassan to his court and said, "As to your first request, we cannot find Count Rodrigo and his friends to hear their side of the story. It is wartime, as you know. You are welcome to stay a few more days as our guest while we look for them."

Then he turned to the senior Muslim clerics of the city who were standing with the Christian clerics and asked them if they had talked to Princess Aziza. They replied that they had. He asked if, in their opinions as arbitrators of Muslim law, she had reached the age of consent. They all replied that she had.

Constantine turned to Abdullah Hassan and said, "Princess Aziza is a guest in my palace and she has expressly told me and these Muslim dignitaries that she does not wish to return to her family. I am honor-bound to grant her request for asylum."

Before Abdullah Hassan could say another word, Constantine dismissed the court and walked out. The imperial guards then escorted the Ottomans to their quarters. They were gone by the afternoon to face an angry sultan.

* * *

The next morning, Constantine sent for Christopher Notaras, who told him that he had managed to keep Rodrigo and his men at a friend's house all night. Their wine was drugged so they slept well into the day and went back to their posts after Abdullah Hassan had left town in disgust.

The two princesses were overjoyed and invited everyone to a party at the palace. However, Christopher said that it was his turn to host a dinner, so they all agreed to meet at his father's mansion, which was where Christopher also lived.

That night, Elena decided to make Aziza even more attractive. She put a very tiny amount of rouge on Aziza's cheeks and had her hair set in nice curls by her maids.

Rodrigo and his friends, including Zangi and Petros, were invited. They arrived at Loukas Notaras's mansion after sunset and were amazed at the opulence of the rooms and the beauty of statues and mosaic work done by the famous artisans of the era. Grand Duke Loukas himself welcomed the party and led his guests into a big banqueting hall, where finger foods were laid out. There was plenty of wine, which had been cooled in the cisterns. A Greek band played joyful music. They met Theo, the younger brother of Christopher, who was just fourteen years old, and his cousin, Tomas.

Rodrigo noticed that those boys were even more handsome than Christopher was. The boys were so nice looking that they could easily pass as girls, if they put on women's clothes. The hostess was Grand Duke's wife, Alexandra, a very gracious woman in her thirties with manners that reflected high breeding. She was a very attractive woman. Obviously, her sons had inherited their looks from her.

The night went very well. In a short while, Rodrigo forgot about the war and the Turkish soldiers who were camped just a few hundred yards away. There was some Greek dancing and they even managed to get Rodrigo, Christopher, and the two princesses on the floor.

Since it was a semi-formal occasion, Rodrigo and Aziza discreetly exchanged glances and touched each other with their eyes more than their hands. However, Zangi managed to get close to Katarina and the two of them seemed to be unaware of anyone else. Jean, gesturing toward the couple, remarked to Rodrigo and Antonio, who were sitting close by, "This must be true love. These two seem to be like one soul in two bodies."

Father Ricardo, who overheard Jean, responded, "The Lord truly moves in mysterious ways. To think that these two creatures of God were born in different lands and also what they went through to find each other amazes me."

The festivities were over before midnight. Before leaving, they agreed that they should dine together once a week while the hostilities lasted. Next week it would be at Blachernae Palace, hosted by Elena, and the following week at Rodrigo's mansion, hosted by Princess Aziza, and then back to Christopher's mansion.

The next few days were quiet as the Ottoman army swelled in size outside the Wall, aiming more cannons at the Wall and the gates. Aziza came to visit Rodrigo two days later. She was excited about her new role as the hostess of the mansion. She brought some food and table coverings and cushions from the Blachernae Palace and redecorated parts of the mansion with the help of her maid and the servants.

When Rodrigo and his men returned that night, the mansion looked homey and comfortable. Lorenzo remarked that it would be nice if they could live there forever as they were. They all knew what he meant. They were all in love with Aziza and Katarina and the way that these two women were keeping them together as a happy family in this foreign land surrounded by savages on all sides.

After dinner, Aziza and Rodrigo went to the balcony to look at the sea and the lights. Rodrigo held Aziza's hand while they talked. Aziza said, "There is something I want to tell you that I am not sure you have noticed yet. Did you notice the way that Elena was looking at Christopher?"

Rodrigo smiled knowingly, and said, "It was difficult to miss. She is in love with him. Is that what you wanted to tell me?"

Aziza said, "Men can sometimes be so self-assured of their opinions. I am glad that you noticed that she is in love. Now, this is the hard part for you. Who was Christopher looking at most of the night?"

"Elena, of course," replied Rodrigo almost condescendingly.

"Well, that is where you were wrong," said Aziza with a slight smile.

"Then who?" demanded Rodrigo impatiently.

"Now, do not get upset with me," Aziza said, stealing a glance at him. "He was looking at you. I think he is in love with you."

Her words hit Rodrigo like a bolt of lightning. His immediate response was, "No, it is not possible. He is such a handsome man. Why would he be interested in me?"

As the words left his mouth, however, his mind went back to his encounters with Christopher and how he had stood close, holding Rodrigo's hand every now and then, and how, on that awful day in the cistern, Christopher had been worried sick that Rodrigo was ill. He did not want to admit it to Aziza or even to himself. Then he wondered how many other people knew. This could be embarrassing.

Aziza, holding his hands in both of her small, warm ones, said, "My love, do not worry. It is called Greek love here like it is in my own country and no one seems to mind. In any case, if you are not attracted to him, there is no reason for you to be concerned or ashamed."

Rodrigo said, "I assume it is alright. I think of you as being part of me and I promise to tell you the truth always, even if it hurts. The fact is that I do not have any sexual attraction toward Christopher. When I was a young boy, I used to swim naked with my friend, Pedro, and I never felt a twinge of excitement but I did if I saw the naked ankle of a woman. What I am trying to say is that Christopher is my friend and I will love and respect him as one. I am very glad you told me this because at least I can try not to give him the wrong impression in the future. But I will continue to love and honor him."

"You are a wonderful man, Rodrigo. You always try to be honest and sincere and I love you for that." Then she added playfully, "I will always love you anyway, with or without that."

The lovers exchanged a brief kiss and Rodrigo led Aziza back to the main sitting room. Soon after, she took her carriage back to the palace.

CHAPTER THIRTY-SIX

THE OTTOMAN'S PLANS

The sultan arrived at the siege site soon after Abdullah Hassan had returned miserably from his failed diplomatic mission. First, Mohammed sent for the interpreter who had accompanied Abdullah on his mission. The man told Mohammed of Abdullah Hassan's belligerency and the blunder he had made by reaching for his non-existent dagger when he was talking to the emperor.

Mohammed then called Abdullah Hassan to his presence and gave him a public tongue-lashing for his failure. Unfortunately for Abdullah Hassan, the sultan had found the perfect scapegoat. He forgot Abdullah Hassan's past services and banished him to the army of the East to fight the Persians. That was almost like a death sentence to Abdullah Hassan, who was the viceroy and the master of Serbia. He left that very night before the volatile sultan could ask for his head and was never heard of again.

* * *

The sultan called his counselor, Selim Pasha; his vizier; the army commanders; and the navy admirals to a war council. The purpose was to determine how to conquer a city that had never been conquered. Admiral Baltoglu, who was commander of the fleet in the eastern Mediterranean, reported that his sailors were ready to attack. However, there were strong chains across the Golden Horn estuary. He suggested that they build a pontoon bridge by linking boats and barges, stern to bow, across the water from Galata, which was an open city across the estuary, to the mainland in Constantinople and try to get the soldiers across it. Then they could breach the seawall, which was not as strong or as wide as the Theodosius Wall was.

The Ottomans were already building war boats further north, near the source of the Golden Horn, and were planning to carry them overland to launch them in the estuary for an assault on the city's northern seawall. The sultan agreed and gave orders to commandeer all boats that could be found on the Asiatic side and build new ones necessary to create a pontoon bridge between Galata and the seawalls of Constantinople.

The army commanders spoke next. In their opinion, their existing cannons would not make much of a dent in the Wall. It had been tried in Sultan Murat's time and it had not worked. However, they had many more guns than before and the constant firing could weaken the inhabitants' will to fight.

Mohammed sent for Urban, a forty-year-old Hungarian engineer who had spent years trying to build the perfect gun. Urban's father was an architect and, as was the custom, he had taught his son his engineering skills. Urban had always wanted to build a gun big enough to fire a projectile that would reach the moon. He had drawn many plans and had submitted them to the princes, the royalty, and the money men, all of whom had laughed at him. Then, he had hit upon the idea of modifying his space gun for land battles and had tried to sell the idea to

Constantine's court. He was ridiculed there, as well, when they saw his plan for a monstrous cannon that they said could never be built.

Heartbroken and dejected, Urban had stopped at Edirne on his way home to Hungary and sought an audience with the sultan. Strangely enough, Sultan Mohammed liked Urban's idea for a super gun that could destroy the walls of a city like Constantinople and gave him money and resources to build the gun. Urban set up his foundry near Constantinople and built his gun under the protection of the sultan's troops. When they discovered that their location had been exposed, they moved the gun farther inland and finally completed its construction under heavy guard.

Urban arrived nervously with his hat in his hand. He bowed down and kissed the ground, as was the custom for this sultan's subjects. The sultan asked, "You are a Hungarian, are you not?"

Urban, with a quivering voice, answered, "Yes, my lord, I am."

The Sultan said, "Do you know that Hungarians are Huns from Central Asia, like my ancestors?" Whether he knew it or not, Urban replied that he did. Mohammed continued, "You should realize that we are here trying to fight those white skinned devils who are trying to destroy us. They are all around us. In the West, there are the Austrians and the Italians. In the North, there are the Rus people and in the East, there are the white races of Persians who have always hated us and have made a mockery of my ancestors' religion by creating their own brand of Islam. In the South, there are the fleets of European ships that sail from Venice and Genoa and vandalize our ships. Do you want to help us, Urban?"

A petrified Urban was about to defecate in his pants and kept looking at the ground but he said nothing because he knew that to contradict the sultan meant death. The sultan went on, "I want that gun ready and aimed at the Wall by the end of the week. Selim Pasha will give you all the help that you need to move the cannon. Can you do it, Urban?"

Urban weakly replied in the affirmative and was dismissed immediately.

Mohammed turned to his commanders and asked them if they had anything to contribute to the discussion. They were too intimidated to say anything. He dismissed them with orders to start the attack on the dawn of April 14.

CHAPTER THIRTY-SEVEN

AND SO IT BEGINS

It was dawn on the eighth day of the siege when the fireworks began. First one cannon fired, and then another. Finally, what sounded like hundreds of cannons, joining into a disharmony of death, started pummeling the Wall that had stood proudly against intruders for a thousand years. The sultan's engineers had suggested that he concentrate his cannons on two locations a few hundred yards from the very center of the Wall[2]. One cluster of cannons would be on the south side of the Wall and the other cluster to the north side. The guns were pointed at a sixty-degree angle from the Wall so that their combined firepower was focused at the middle of the Wall, close to the Gate of Charisios. The idea was to concentrate the destructive power of all of the guns at one point in the Wall.

This was the first time cannons had been used in a siege. Prior to that, they were used as field guns. The sultan's engineers estimated—guessed, actually—that with continuous pounding, the walls would start shaking like they would in a severe earthquake and finally collapse in the center. Since all of the engineers were European Christians, they apparently thought that if Joshua

---

2 The famous Constantinople Wall was actually two walls, one behind the other.

could bring the Walls of Jericho down with a few horns, then Mohammed should be able to do the same to Constantinople with hundreds of cannons. The bombing and shelling continued for a few days.

To Rodrigo and other people inside the city, the shelling sounded more like rumbling of distant thunders than volleys of cannonballs. The city architects examined the Wall every day and reported the extent of damage to the emperor directly. After ten days of bombardment, the Wall had not collapsed.

Urban was late with his big cannon and the sultan was furious. But he could not kill or punish Urban yet, since he was the only one who knew how to operate the monster gun.

On the tenth day, a very proud Urban reported that the gun was ready. The gun needed a stable solid platform to rest upon to fire the twelve-hundred-pound cannonballs that were specially manufactured for it. Even for a great army such as the sultan's, it had been difficult to move the mammoth gun to within range of the city Wall. The soldiers also had to transport the heavy cannonballs.

While soldiers were constructing the platform for the gun emplacement, others had used ox-driven carts to move the gun and the cannonballs over the uneven terrain.

Overnight, they had placed the cannon on its base and worked hard to load it for the first volley. First, they poured the gunpowder into the long muzzle and then, even though they used pulleys and winches, they had the almost impossible task of lifting a cannonball and inserting it into the gun barrel. They tamped it down tightly against the gunpowder.

Finally, at seven o'clock, Urban, with shaky hands, lit the first fuse. The gun went off with a roar. Twelve hundred pounds of mass arced into the air aimed at the center of the outer wall. The supersonic roar of the massive ball cutting through the air astounded the citizens. The ball hit the Wall half way from the top, near the gate of Charisios. The impact was horrendous. Mohammed, who was watching the first firing, had his troop ready to charge in as soon as the Wall collapsed.

The ball shattered and fell. The Wall vibrated heavily and a few of the soldiers on the top lost their footings and fell to their deaths. The vibration gradually died down and then...nothing!

Meanwhile, the force of the firing had lifted the gun off its platform. It arced into the air backwards and landed on its side, next to its base, crushing two of the soldiers to death.

The Ottoman commanders ordered the full scale shelling by the smaller cannons to start again.

* * *

Inside the city, the emperor's architects hastily conducted their evaluations and reported that the venerable Wall was shaken but not damaged. This was great news to the emperor and the people. That night, people celebrated and danced in the streets.

The sultan was angry at Urban. He lashed the quivering man with his whip several times. Obviously, Urban had not estimated the full recoil power of the gun. All through the next night, they worked to raise the gun and remount it on its base. The enormous task of hoisting and loading another cannonball took hours. They were ready to fire around ten o'clock the following morning.

At Urban's command, the gun fired again. It made a tremendous roar and hit the wall, and shaking it strongly. The gun itself jumped off its emplacement and fell on the ground again.

There was no need to beat Urban anymore. It was obvious that this gun could only be fired once a day and the sultan had to live with that. He spared Urban's life because he was the expert and he knew how to load the gun correctly. Urban organized his gun crewmen so that they worked all night and completed the loading by daylight. The gun would be fired whenever the sultan or one of the commanders issued the order. Then they would wait for the gun to cool down before starting to re-load it for the following day.

* * *

Life in the city had not changed much. By now, all of Rodrigo's friends knew how to get to the hiding place inside the Basilica Cistern. Lorenzo had discovered that the old passageway inside the cistern led to the ruins of an abandoned palace. It was unlikely that any invading soldier would look for loot in that part of the town. Zangi, Lorenzo, and Petros had taken loads of supplies to the cistern. They had food, torches, and bedding material. They had carpeted one of the storerooms so that they could move in and live there for a week or maybe even longer. Aziza and Elena knew they would have to be ready to flee the palace at a moment's notice. Everyone hoped that day would never arrive.

About two weeks into the battle, Rodrigo pulled Jean to one side and said, "I have been looking at this Wall for some time now and I have been thinking that there is something missing. I could not put my finger on it until now."

Jean looked at Rodrigo eagerly hoping he would finish his statement. Rodrigo, who was enjoying the suspense, said, "We have been lucky that they have so far been shelling the Wall to frighten us into submission. They have not started shooting with the rifles, bows, and arrows yet. When they start shooting with those weapons, the first targets will be the soldiers on top of the Wall. Once they get the range right, the Ottoman bowmen could shoot into the air at the precise angle for the arrows to come down on top of the Wall to kill anybody who is unlucky to be around."

Jean's eyes lit up. He said, "You mean, we will need a hoarding?"

"Yes, and we will need to complete it before they start shooting at us," Rodrigo said. A hoarding was a temporary wooden structure, like a long shed with a roof, built on top of the walls or rampart of a castle during a siege to protect the soldiers from flying arrows and bullets coming in from above.

Rodrigo's troops started constructing the hoarding on top of the Wall that day. With all the abandoned houses in the city, there was no shortage of wood.

The bombardment of the Wall was soon followed by the bombardment of the city. Archers were brought in to shoot into the air and try to hit the soldiers who were not protected by hoardings. They also tried to shoot into the city, hoping to strike people on the other side of the Wall. Soldiers with rifles followed suit.

On the sea, Baltoglu, the admiral of the Ottoman fleet, was trying to get closer to the city but was held back by the defensive boom that protected the Golden Horn Estuary and the city's naval defenses. The battle raged on. The sultan repeatedly ordered his soldiers to rush the Wall but the deep ditch along its face prevented them from getting close. The dead soldiers became feed for the stray dogs that abounded around Constantinople, as they did in all Muslim territories, where dogs—except the sheepdogs needed to protect the herds—were considered unclean.

Then on the morning of April 28, Antonio approached Rodrigo with some news. Antonio was always checking the status of the Wall and its defenses. He had found that in several places near the gates, secret passageways had been dug into the surface and opened just under the ground on the outside of the Wall. Those passageways were well camouflaged. The Genovese and Greeks had used them to raid the sultan's supply lines and harass the troops.

Rodrigo had been thinking about how to reach the monster cannon to destroy it. He had been considering using rope ladders to drop down outside the Wall at night. Antonio's discovery of the passageways was great news.

Rodrigo sent for John Justiniani, and after reprimanding him for failing to inform him about the secret passageways, told him to bring ten strong volunteers to Rodrigo's mansion later that afternoon.

They met in the banquet hall to form a plan. It was obvious that killing the cannon crew or even Urban would not permanently stop it from firing. They needed to find a way to permanently damage or even destroy the gun. The gun was solid and even if they could hit it point blank with another cannon, they would simply dislodge it from its platform.

Antonio, who was listening intently, came forward with a suggestion. "Why not let the gun destroy itself?"

There were some snickers and laughs from the Genovese Soldiers. Rodrigo looked sternly at them, causing the laughter to stop, and said, "Please go on."

"The weakest point of any gun, whether it is a musket or cannon, is at the bottom of the barrel where the firing mechanism and the flint are located," Antonio said. "Unlike the rest of the gun that is round and strong without any imperfections, gun makers have to make slits and holes to allow for the fuse, the wick, and the trigger." He looked at the faces of those around him for signs that they understood the implication.

"Several years ago, in Tuscany, there were two rivals for the hand of a rich girl," Antonio continued. "The rivals were friends who hunted together. One day, one of them filled the barrel of his rival's loaded gun with mud while he was sleeping. The next time the man tried to fire, the gun exploded in his face and killed him. Many months later, after the killer had married his sweetheart, I was asked to look at the gun for defects. They had assumed that the gun had exploded because of bad workmanship. That is when I discovered the truth."

Rodrigo asked, "How do we duplicate that result with the big gun?"

"Well, it takes that crew virtually all night to load the gun and have it ready for firing," Antonio said. "We want to let them do the hard work and then arrive after the gun has been loaded. We will need sacks of quick-setting cement or mortar, gypsum plaster, and water. There is plenty of water near the gun, but we will have to carry the other stuff with us. We will need at least twenty sacks of the mixed material to seal the inside of the barrel tight. Even then, there is no guarantee, but that is the only way I can think of to permanently destroy that monster."

They all looked at each other. John Justiniani was the first to speak. "I think it's our only chance. That gun may yet find its true mark and damage one of the weaker spots in the Wall. I would suggest that we get at least fifty sacks of mortar and other materials and store them near the secret passageway to the outside. We will take no fewer than twenty sacks with us to the gun emplacement, and if needed, we could use relay teams to get more." Since nobody else had a better suggestion, John explained that there was an abundance of the type of supplies that Antonio needed for demolishing the cannon near the inner wall, as they were used to repair the two walls after each attack. He promised to round up the necessary material by the following night.

Rodrigo decided to lead the operation personally. He would leave Lorenzo, Petros, and Jean behind to take care of Aziza and to carry out their real mission, the papal mission, in case he did not make it back alive.

The next day, they cordoned off the area near the secret passageway and stacked big sacks of cement, mortar, gypsum, and plaster near the exit. They dressed as Turkish soldiers and waited until after midnight before a few of the men entered the tunnel leading under the moat. The lead man opened the manhole on the far side of the moat near the Ottomans' camp. The exit was disguised to look like a pile of stones. One by one, they passed the sacks of material through the tunnel and stacked them outside.

Then the rest of the men entered the tunnel and exited at the other end.

They sent a Greek scout who was familiar with the terrain to reconnoiter. After about twenty minutes, which seemed like hours to them, the guide came back ready to lead them to the gun site. They crept out of the ditch, picked up their heavy loads, and followed the guide through the no-man's land between the outer wall and the Turkish camp. Rodrigo was once again in the middle of the Ottoman army. He knew what would happen to him if he were caught. If that happened, he was determined to die fighting. He would not let himself be captured alive. The sacks were heavy, but the men were determined.

The scout and two of the soldiers acting as guards did not carry any sacks. Everyone else, including Rodrigo and John Justiniani, carried two loads each. When they reached the Turkish lines, the scout made a turn to the right through a forest and after a few minutes, they came to the clearing where the big gun rested on its platform. It was an awesome sight! The area around the giant cannon had been cleared to make it easier to load and fire the gun. About fifteen Ottoman soldiers worked on the gun, packing the powder down with a huge ramrod and preparing to lift the heavy cannonball using hand winches. Urban impatiently directed their activities. An array of tents at the back of the clearing appeared to be their living quarters.

Rodrigo's men moved back behind the trees and waited. He sent some of the men back to the tunnel to retrieve more sacks.

It took another three hours before the lazy crew supervised by Urban completed loading the cannon. Urban and most of the men moved back towards their tents, leaving a few sentries behind. Rodrigo sent Zangi to reconnoiter and find out where Urban was staying. By now, the Genovese volunteers had pinpointed the exact location of each sentry. They remained quiet for another twenty minutes to give the tired workers a chance to fall sleep and then they moved noiselessly forward, each man assigned a sentry. Genovese archers shot the sentries who were facing them. Rodrigo's men strangled or knifed the rest from behind.

The sacks of mortar, gypsum, and other materials were moved to the cannon. They used the ladders that the crew had used for servicing the gun to get close to its muzzle. Antonio orchestrated the effort of lifting and emptying the sacks, adding water and mixing the contents using the cannon's large ramrod.

Rodrigo turned to Zangi and said, "You know where Urban's tent is located. Go finish him off but make it quick. No need to torture him. He has not done us any wrong." Zangi was gone before Rodrigo could finish his sentence and returned in less than ten minutes with a satisfied look on his face.

It took less than half an hour to fill the cannon with the material they had brought with them. At Antonio's direction, they filled the rest of the barrel with mud from the surrounding ground. Antonio told all of them to go back.

As was planned, the majority of the men, led by John, started the trek back to the moat. Rodrigo, Zangi, Antonio, and two Genovese soldiers remained behind. Antonio motioned them to stay back and then lit the fuse. Then they ran back about fifty yards to crouch down and watch the results.

At that moment, one of the gun crew emerged from his tent and saw the fuse. He screamed something in Turkish and rushed towards the cannon but was cut down with an arrow from one of the archers before he could get close. His scream brought the workers out and they rushed towards the fallen man.

The wick seemed to fizzle out as it reached the barrel. Rodrigo's heart almost stopped and he stood up, involuntarily. All that effort and now a total failure? They would never have another chance to destroy the gun. Antonio grabbed Rodrigo and tried to pull him down.

Suddenly, there was a giant blast. The massive gun was lifted off its base and thrown twelve feet into the air. It danced briefly against the night sky, rotating like a wheel, and then dropped with a broken back. Showers of shrapnel and high-speed projectiles hit the workers. The lucky ones were killed on the spot. A razor sharp piece of shrapnel hit Rodrigo on his left shoulder and knocked him out cold.

When he came to, he was stretched out inside the city next to the secret passageway. He tried to get up but Zangi put a heavy hand on his chest to hold him down. "The doctor says you should rest until we get you back to the mansion."

Rodrigo could hear cannon fire and see flames in the dark sky but it seemed too early for the sultan to be letting loose another barrage of deadly fire against the city. Rodrigo tried to ask about the monster cannon but soon was engulfed in darkness as he passed out again.

It was morning before he awakened in his own bed. He looked around and things seemed normal. He called out and Zangi stepped in, smiled broadly, and said, "You had a bad cut. The doctor fixed it before sending you home." Rodrigo felt well enough to get up to resume his regular duties. He called for Antonio, who told him that the operation had been a success and apparently, it had maddened the sultan so much that he had ordered his troops to start bombarding the Wall and the city in the dark without being able to see what they were shooting at!

That night, Rodrigo, feeling a little feverish and lethargic, asked Petros to check his temperature. Petros seemed somewhat troubled after taking Rodrigo's pulse and examining the wound on his shoulder. Rodrigo went to bed early but by midnight, he was awake with a high fever. He weakly called for help and Zangi, who usually slept outside Rodrigo's door, was at his side immediately. Zangi fetched Petros, who examined Rodrigo thoroughly and gave him some medicine to help him sleep. In the morning, Petros set out to the Oriental quarter of the city to purchase some powerful pain-killing medication. By that afternoon, the fever had worsened. Jean sent for Aziza, who arrived distressed and worried out of her mind. She kissed Rodrigo and tried to talk to him but Rodrigo was unconscious.

* * *

Rodrigo was spiraling deeper and deeper into blackness. He was being pulled down. From above, he could hear the voices of his mother, Carolina, Pedro, Isabella, Aziza, and his men calling him and reaching out to him, trying to pull him out. Then he was in a giant room. It was as big as a stadium. The furniture and the windows and the doors were huge. They were so big and he was so small. Everything was out of proportion. He felt like a trapped mouse. The fever was eating his mind.

* * *

Petros arrived with some medication. Aziza, with tears running down her face, asked what was going on. Petros replied, "I think it is blood poisoning. The imbecile Italian doctor who treated him at the gate must have used contaminated bandages that poisoned his blood. There is not much that we can do. The body has to fight off the poison or..." His voice trailed off. Aziza and Zangi sat by Rodrigo's bedside all night.

* * *

Rodrigo came to around midnight, only to feel the chills. Now he was feeling cold, incredibly chilly. He murmured and asked for blankets. They put layers of blankets upon him, yet his teeth kept chattering from the cold. He was dreaming he was back in that cold damp cistern. It was very dark. He was suspended above the water and could see the ghostly columns. He did not want to look down but he had to. He had a mortal fear of looking at that ice-cold black water, which was waiting to engulf him. He could hear cries of agony rising from beneath the black surface. That must have been what the river Styx sounded to the ancient Greeks. No wonder no one wanted to fall into it. He was delirious, calling for his mother and Aziza at the same time. He felt the chill of death.

* * *

Petros looked at Aziza and said, "In cases like this, it is best for one of the family members to get into the bed and hold the patient tight to warm him with body heat." Without hesitation, Aziza lifted the blankets and joined Rodrigo. She held him tightly in her slender arms. Petros gave Rodrigo some Oriental painkillers. They were actually opium-based Chinese knockout drugs.

Rodrigo eventually went to sleep and woke up sweating profusely. He was dying of heat and kicked everything off. He asked for water, drank the whole jar, and then wanted more. The wound was getting worse and his fever was getting higher. Aziza told Petros that if Rodrigo died, she would not want to be alive anymore.

At Jean's suggestion, Father Ricardo administered the last rites and gave him the blessings. The fever and the dreaded chills went on for another day. Sometimes, Rodrigo could hear the gentle voice of Aziza calling him from a distance and begging him not to leave her alone; to come back to them. He started talking about his life and his loves to Aziza as if she was his confessor. At other times, he was unconscious or shivering too much to hear anything.

In desperation, Aziza approached Petros and begged him to try anything possible to save Rodrigo. After a few moments, Petros said, "There is one way left, but those Italian Catholics will not like it since they do not understand it."

Aziza said, "Please do whatever is necessary. I am no Catholic!"

Petros called Zangi over and said, "I will need to burn the wound to get rid of the poison. I will need to get a rod and heat it up until it is red hot. The two of you will have to hold him down and keep him quiet. The others might kill me for practicing black magic, but I am willing to try."

They all agreed. Aziza gently removed the bandages to reveal the wound and was appalled by what she saw. Already, maggots were eating away at the dead flesh. The wound was leaking and she could almost see the white of the bone. She kissed Rodrigo's lifeless hands.

Soon, Petros arrived with the red-hot poker. Zangi sat on Rodrigo's chest and stuffed a small towel into Rodrigo's mouth to stifle any cries. He grabbed his left arm and held it down. Aziza held the other arm with all her might. Petros did not waste any time. He brought the poker to the wound and gently pressed it against the raw flesh for a few seconds. The flesh sizzled. Smoke rose from the wound. Rodrigo squirmed, tried to scream, but to no avail. Soon he passed out. Petros made sure that he had cauterized the entire area before lifting the hot iron away from Rodrigo's arm. He applied some ointment to the wound and announced, "The rest is up to the Lord Almighty."

By morning, the fever was miraculously gone. Rodrigo opened his eyes. His left arm was throbbing, but he was not hot nor did he feel the harrowing chills. Instead, he saw the smiling faces of Aziza and Zangi. He tried to say something but he was still weak. Aziza caressed his face with her soft hands and said, "You are back. I prayed all night for you and you are back to us."

* * *

He drifted back to a pleasant sleep. He was a child in Valencia again, running barefoot on the sandy beach. He could hear his parents in the distance talking and laughing. Then he heard his mother's voice, "Don't go so close to the water. Watch out for the waves." He drifted in and out. Next, he was riding a horse with Carolina at his side, galloping up the hills. Then he was with Aziza, walking in a green forest hand in hand. He looked behind and Zangi was following at a short distance.

* * *

He woke up again in the afternoon, hungry and thirsty. Aziza was still there, smiling at him with her eyes. He mumbled that he was hungry and thirsty. Aziza shouted for Petros, who ran up the stairs. "Signor, you gave us a big scare. We thought you were gone. I will get you something to eat and will bring you something to drink right away," he said, smiling broadly.

It was difficult for Rodrigo to speak. They propped him up and Aziza and Zangi helped him to eat some soup. That night, he stayed up late talking with Aziza and his friends. They told him that Christopher and Elena had been over to see him every day and that the emperor had been worried about him, too. The good news was that the big cannon had been destroyed, but the Ottomans were continuing their bombardments.

Rodrigo was back to take charge of his duties after two more days.

CHAPTER THIRTY-EIGHT

THE SECRET CHAMBERS
OF HAGIA SOFIA

They had been in the city for three weeks. During that time, Father Ricardo had been frantically searching for the location of the True Cross. He had been reading old documents and talking to priests and historians. They knew that the relic had been given to Emperor Alexius III and his patriarch, John Camaterus, for safekeeping but very shortly thereafter, the Fourth Crusaders invaded the city. They ruled it for about sixty years until the Greeks drove them out. All of that had happened over two hundred years ago and so there was no living memory of the fate of the True Cross.

One day, as Father Ricardo was comparing old building plans of Hagia Sofia, he noticed a discrepancy between a plan dated 1150, which was fifty years before the rescue of the True Cross in Damascus and its delivery to the emperor in Constantinople, and a plan made after a fire had damaged parts of the church in 1250, approximately fifty years after the True Cross had been given to the Byzantines for safekeeping. By now, Father Ricardo knew the church inside out, having visited it so many times.

In the old plan, there seemed to be a doorway and a small room, possibly used for solitude, at the north corner of the main building near the Northern Gallery. In later drawings, starting in the mid thirteenth century, that room did not seem to exist. He went to the church to look for himself and sure enough, just below the Northern Gallery, there was a passageway leading to a locked door. In the middle of this hallway, he noticed the outline of what could have been a doorway but was now plastered over.

He rushed to find Rodrigo and Jean to tell them the news. Since they did not want to attract undue attention from the sultan's spies or even the Greeks, they announced to their friends that they were going to pay their respects by praying at the Church of Hagia Sofia. Upon entering, Rodrigo was again astonished at the size and magnificence of the church. He had seen it many times from outside and had been in the courtyard several times. In fact, the Basilica Cistern, which was their hiding place, was next door.

They worked their way to the deserted hallway and examined the plastered spot. Rodrigo took his dagger out and, with its hilt, gently tapped the center of the plastered area. It sounded hollow. They looked around to see if there was another doorway leading into that area. The walls on the other sides were solid. They studied the arrangement of interior walls and then made their way back to the main garden, where they sat on stone benches.

"Even assuming that the True Cross is there behind that plastered door, how are we going to get it out? We cannot just go in there and start knocking down the wall," Rodrigo said, his voice low. "The emperor and the priests will roast us alive. If we wait and the Ottomans win, they will turn this place into a mosque and we will not be able to get near it anymore."

Jean, who had not said much until now, said, "We will need a diversion so we can break the wall and see what is inside."

Rodrigo half mockingly said, "Great! And what is the diversion? We dress up like a bunch of Ottomans and attack the place?"

Jean said, "That may not be a bad idea but let's think some more about it." They left the second-greatest church in the Christian world and walked back to their residence, thinking and arguing about the best way to get inside that hidden room.

By now, Rodrigo knew that the end was near. Time was running out for them one way or the other. Either they would get the True Cross or it would be lost forever. Additionally, they had to get out of the city or be prepared to stay and be killed in combat. More important than his life was Aziza's life. He had to find a way to send her out of the city to a safe place out of the reach of her brother.

* * *

That night, Rodrigo paced up and down the great banquet room and thought about his options. They could still get out of the city and escape back to Rome. He knew that if he stayed on, his reward would be death, either in battle or in captivity. He did not want to sign his friends' death warrants. It was all right to face the fury of elements and the ambushers while they had a clear goal in mind. Now that the goal was within their reach, what should he tell his friends? Should he tell them why he had risked their lives? And what about Aziza? He loved her and could not leave her behind.

While he was wrestling with his thoughts, a messenger arrived to summon him to the court of Constantine. He arrived to find the court in deep mourning. A lucky shot by a Turkish soldier had mortally wounded Christopher. They had brought his almost lifeless body to the palace and he had asked to see Elena and Rodrigo. When Rodrigo arrived, a tearful Elena was already at Christopher's bedside, trying to keep her composure. Rodrigo kneeled down and called to Christopher, who half opened his eyes. There was a faint smile on his lips. He tried to raise his right arm but it fell down.

Elena and Rodrigo each took one of his hands in their hands, trying to comfort him. He muttered his love for them before his hands went limp and he passed away peacefully.

Elena could not stop sobbing. Rodrigo held her hands tightly and called for Aziza, who arrived promptly and hugged Elena before leading her away to her apartment.

That night, the whole city mourned the loss of their champion. The emperor was never the same again. Loukas Notaras was speechless and in a daze. Funeral services were held the following day, but because of heavy shelling by the Ottomans, the viewing period was short. Nevertheless, thousands of citizens paid their last respects to their idol at the great church before he was interred with family members in a church near their mansion.

CHAPTER THIRTY-NINE

AZIZA AND THE

FACTS OF LIFE

The morning following the death of Christopher, Aziza got up before dawn because she could not rest. She was feeling sickly and wanted to throw up. Katarina helped her and cleaned up after her as she had done for many years before. The sickness did not stop, and she was sick the following morning. Katarina informed Princess Elena, who inquired if she'd ever had similar symptoms before. Katarina did not remember Aziza throwing up like that before.

On a hunch, Elena decided not send for a doctor and went to Aziza's apartment herself. She dismissed all of the maids, including Katarina, and asked Aziza if she could examine her body. Aziza did not resist. She just relaxed. Elena put her right hand on Aziza's belly and gently pressed down on the area just above Aziza's genitals, about four inches below her navel. Then she removed her hand and smiled mysteriously. She asked Aziza to do the same thing to her. Aziza felt the same area on Elena's stomach and then felt herself. Elena's stomach was tight but not as rigid and hard as hers was. She looked at Elena anxiously. "Am I going to die?" she asked.

Elena gave a short laugh and said, "I don't think so. If I am not mistaken, you are pregnant!" To Aziza, the shock was like falling off a cliff and having a castle crash down on her head at the same time. She covered her face in her hands and burst into tears.

Elena said, "It is not the end of the world, you know. It is the beginning for that little creature. When are you going to tell Rodrigo about it?"

Aziza blushed. Still sobbing, she said, "I am not going to tell him. I do not want him to feel obligated."

"Then you are going to have a bastard child?" inquired Elena.

Aziza was at a loss for an answer and started to cry again. Elena held her tightly. After a few minutes, she said, "I could send a midwife to look at you but that will create rumors and I think we could do without that."

Aziza nodded. "I feel lucky to have you as a friend. What would I have done without your wisdom?"

Elena left Aziza in bed and told Katarina that it was a sickness that most strangers got when they first arrived in the ancient city.

Aziza stayed in bed that day, sobbing and crying most of the time. Rodrigo found out about it from Zangi, who visited Katarina at every opportunity. The palace guards were so used to him that they simply waved him in. Aziza was happy to see Zangi's familiar smile, but seemed very melancholy and could not be cheered easily.

The following day, Aziza was out of bed but still had her morning sickness. She did not want to make a fuss so she went to see her friends at the mansion.

Rodrigo was very pleased to see her. He asked Zangi to find everyone else and bring them to the banquet hall for an important meeting.

He took Aziza's left hand and led her to the balcony overlooking the Sea of Marmara, the same sea that they had viewed many nights while holding hands. This time, the sun was shining and the sea was calm. In the distance, they could see the Ottoman fleet trying to maintain a blockade of the city.

While holding Aziza's hand, he said, "I have been a foolish man most of my life. In our world, most men do not last beyond their fiftieth birthdays and I am almost halfway there now. I am going to tell you everything about me. I have been with many women. Most of them married women. By Christian law, and even your Muslim law, I should have been stoned to death many times. Maybe my soul belongs in hell and maybe not. I have seen so many strange things in the past few weeks that I am not that sure about my faith anymore.

I believe in Nicholas, who is the messenger of our Lord and the symbol of purity and godliness. That is why I think to myself that there must be a truth to all of this. If Nicholas believes in it, then it must be true. I do not want to go off the subject, for we have very little time left. I feel it in my bones that the end is near. Will you, for the love of God Almighty or Allah the Great, marry me and give me your everlasting love before I die?"

With that, he stopped talking and kneeled in front of her expectantly.

Astonished, Aziza said, "Yes," without a second thought.

Rodrigo jumped up and kissed her gently on the lips. "I am the happiest man in the world," he declared.

Aziza, laughing like a child, said, "And that is not all. You are already a father."

That was too much happiness for Rodrigo. He jumped up and grabbed the curtain rod between the balcony and the banquet room behind it and swung from it wildly and yelling with pleasure. Soon, the rod gave way and he landed unceremoniously on his back in the banquet room. Fortunately, no one was around to see his foolish display of pleasure.

"I will ask the emperor for permission to get married in the Hagia Sofia and we will have a big ceremony," he said. Then he paused. "Or maybe not, since we do not want your brother to be jealous of our happiness."

Aziza could not stop giggling at her foolish lover and his antics.

Soon the group gathered in the hall. Rodrigo made sure that the servants were not within earshot and said, "For several weeks now, we have been together fighting the forces of evil and battling tremendous odds to get here to perform our duty. Two of you, Princess Aziza and our doctor, Petros, are new to our group and we are very lucky to have them. We are very fortunate that we are rid of that snake, Renaldo. Renaldo and the sultan were going to torture Jean and me to find out the real reason for our journey. I am going to tell you what that reason is now."

Rodrigo cleared his throat. "The dark period for Europe is over and we are at the dawn of a great civilization that is blossoming all over Europe, while the Turks and other Muslims will regress back to their fanatical ways. His holiness, Pope Nicholas, asked Jean and me to try to locate the True Cross of our Lord, which was left here in safe keeping for the Church of Rome over two hundred and fifty years ago."

As soon as Rodrigo mentioned the True Cross, there was a sudden quietness in the room and the men crossed themselves.

Rodrigo gave them a brief history of how the True Cross was found by Constantine the Great's mother, Saint Elena, then captured by Saladin, and eventually rescued by Arthur of Brittany, who delivered it to the Byzantine Emperor Alexius. Rodrigo continued, "Unfortunately, soon afterward, the city was invaded by Latin marauders who called themselves the Fourth Crusaders. Priests hid the True Cross before they could get their hands on it.

"Our dear brother, Father Ricardo, has been working day and night to find the hiding place of the cross of our savior. He now tells me that he thinks that he has found its location. Unfortunately, we are running out of time. We will need to locate the True Cross and take it out of the city under the watchful eyes of both the Greeks and the Ottomans. It is not going to be easy. However, the most difficult part is getting to the True Cross, since we think it is sealed in a room inside the great church of Hagia Sofia."

That was the bombshell that Rodrigo knew would make them sit up and take notice.

After a long silence, Antonio said, "Could we blast our way in?"

Rodrigo said, "The Greeks are our friends and our allies. I do not think his holiness would approve of that. Nevertheless, if there is a chance that it would fall into the hands of Ottomans, we should do whatever we can to extricate the True Cross and take it with us.

"This is my plan. I would like Antonio and Lorenzo to visit the location and come back with some idea of how we could knock down the wall in the shortest amount time, without making too much noise. I would like Jean to contact his fellow knights and arrange for transportation for the True Cross and the rest of us out of here, if the need arises."

* * *

The following day, Rodrigo sought an audience with the emperor. Constantine was an extremely tired man. His eyes were red and his eyeballs shifted erratically. Nevertheless, he graciously agreed to see Rodrigo. Rodrigo explained that he wanted to marry Aziza and as a knight of the court, he requested Constantine's permission. For a brief moment, Constantine seemed happy. He smiled faintly and said, "Not only do you have my blessings, but I would like to be at your wedding. Aziza is a princess and must be given away by a king. I will do the honors. Let us have the ceremony in Hagia Sofia. It may yet help to unite the Catholics and the Orthodox. I will talk to the bishop."

As Rodrigo prepared to leave, Constantine, with a gentle wink, added, "And let us do it very soon. We do not want to wait too long."

Rodrigo went directly to Aziza's apartment to give her the good news. Elena and her maids, dressed in black in mourning for Christopher, soon arrived. Elena promised to take care of the ceremony in the church.

For the next few days, Rodrigo and his friends were oblivious to the cannon fire and the mortar shots falling into the city. They were getting ready for the marriage ceremony.

The festivities were small and intimate. Elena gave Aziza her own wedding gown, which she had prepared in the hopes of marrying Christopher. The gown of cream-colored satin had a long train of hand-woven lace. Aziza's hair was carefully styled and tied back with wide purple ribbon, the color of Imperial Byzantine royalty. Her face was covered with a very fine veil.

As was the Greek custom, her face was made up with powders, her lips painted light red, and her beautiful eyes made up discreetly with kohl. Rodrigo's friends and the entire Notaras family attended the wedding.

Elena was the bridesmaid, the emperor gave Aziza away, and Katarina wept throughout the ceremony. Rodrigo thought about the irony of the situation. A Muslim princess was given away by an Orthodox emperor to a Spanish Catholic while cannons of her brother's army pounded the city

There were three ceremonies in all. First there was a private Muslim ceremony officiated by the imam of Constantinople. Aziza insisted on it because she wanted her brother to know that she was legally married, according to Muslim law, and he did not have any more rights over her. Then, there was the Catholic one conducted by Father Ricardo. The first two were private. The bride, the groom, Katarina, and two Muslim witnesses who signed the marriage document attended the first ceremony. All of their friends, including Elena, attended the second one. Finally, a public ceremony led by the acting archbishop of Constantinople, took place. So, Aziza became one of the few women to say "yes" three times on the same day.

They all decided that it would be best for Aziza to stay in the palace with Princess Elena for the time being. She and Rodrigo would spend their wedding night together in Aziza's apartment and Rodrigo would go back to his mansion and duties the following day.

When Rodrigo first lifted the veil to kiss his bride, he was astounded at her beauty, always innocent but now rather provocative with the makeup. Their wedding night was a blissfully happy night for both of them. They managed to forget about their enemies, Mohammed, Abdullah the Butcher, and Renaldo. For them, the guns were briefly silent.

~ CHAPTER FORTY ~

BREAKING INTO THE HOUSE OF GOD

The wedding ceremony had given Rodrigo an idea. He had noticed that during the periods of bombardment, all of the priests disappeared, fleeing to the basements. He told Jean and others that the best thing to do was to be ready for a period of intense bombardment and try to break through the wall in the church then. Antonio had already visited the site and had said that he could drill a few holes in the blocked off doorway and blow it inward with carefully placed explosives.

The battle was getting more intense. The sultan's commanders wanted to call it quits, since they were not getting anywhere and they were suffering huge casualties. However, Mohammed kept urging them on.

The food supply in the city was dwindling fast. Rodrigo knew that the end might come any day now, so he decided to put his plan into action.

Jean had already made contact and a ship, controlled by the Christian Knights Hospitaller, also known as the Knights of St. John or the Knights of Rhodes, was ready to take them to the Isle of Rhodes, which was the knights' command center.

Rodrigo went to the palace to discuss an escape plan with Aziza. Initially, Aziza did not want to leave. Rodrigo begged her to go for the sake of their child.

Finally, she agreed but she wanted to take Elena along with them since if the city fell, Elena, being the sister of the emperor, would be badly abused. Rodrigo reluctantly agreed to send Elena and her maid with Aziza and Katarina; however, he did not want Elena to know that they were planning to take the True Cross back with them.

That afternoon, Aziza asked Elena to walk with her in the garden of the palace, as she did not want to be overheard by anybody. She broached the subject to Elena. She was surprised that Elena welcomed the suggestion and said that her brother had been asking her to leave for a long time and she had refused. But now that Christopher was dead, she was willing to leave with her brother's permission.

On May 26, there was another heavy bombardment. The daily bombardments were meant to harass the population and destroy property. The heavier bombardments were usually done before a major assault by the Ottoman troops, who would try to capture the Wall or, at least, one of the towers. They were usually followed by the sounds of large horns, drums, and the rattling of pots and pans to instill fear in the hearts of the defenders. Then, the invaders would scream profanities in Turkish, sounding like banshees out of hell clamoring for blood while they charged the Wall carrying ladders and climbing hooks. So far, they had made it only as far as the moat and, each time, were forced to retreat with heavy casualties

The defenders had learned that during those bombardments, they only needed to post a few lookouts on the Wall. They would hide in dugouts and wait for the music to start.

That day was no different. Rodrigo and his friends met at the safe house above the cistern. They put on monk robes and headed for the church. The courtyard and the inner sanctums were empty; they did not see a soul. They headed for the hidden door.

With a piece of charcoal, Antonio marked several locations around and in the center of the plastered-over doorway and with Lorenzo's help, drilled holes in the marked areas. Each hole had to be angled approximately forty-five degrees to force the exploding charge inward, which would force the doorway to implode. As soon as they were finished, Antonio planted charges in each hole. Lorenzo pushed them in with a wooden mallet.

The shelling was continuing, but any moment now, it could stop. Rodrigo nervously pleaded, "Please hurry up, we don't have much time."

Antonio ignored him and continued methodically planting the charges. Then he announced, "Everybody back."

And before they had moved back, he started lighting the fuses. He jumped back just in time before the doorway imploded with a muffled thump, raising a great cloud of dust.

They did not wait for the dust to settle before rushing into the room, coughing, and sneezing. Zangi had already lit two candles that he had borrowed from the church. As the air cleared a little, they realized they were in a small room that had obviously been abandoned very quickly. There were half-burnt candles and open books on the table. A rather large object, about four feet long and covered with a dusty, gray linen cloth, leaned in one corner.

Rodrigo went forward to inspect the object. He gently pulled the cloth back and put his right hand inside to touch it. He immediately felt the same strange sensation that he had felt back in the Vatican when he had visited the secret room with his uncle. He kneeled down on both knees and with his head bowed, he simply whispered, "Thank you, Lord."

Zangi interrupted to say that the bombardment was tapering off and he could hear people approaching. Rodrigo hastily got up and said, "Zangi, you and Lorenzo go ahead and get rid of them. But, no killing this time. I do not want any blood to be shed over this." Zangi and Lorenzo disappeared through the door.

Rodrigo covered the True Cross. Jean and Antonio picked it up after crossing themselves and followed him out. Two priests, whom Zangi and Lorenzo had knocked out, lay face down on the floor. They were breathing normally and there was no blood. Rodrigo and the men moved out of the building as fast as they could and made their way to the safe house above the Basilica Cistern, and hid the relic there.

Jean went to arrange for the boat and Rodrigo hurried back to his post. The shelling had stopped. He could hear the music and the clatter of pots and pans and the screams of the soldiers and the camp followers. The human wave started coming toward the Wall and as it got closer, the soldiers picked up speed. The defenders' big cannons started firing into the human throng and with each volley, scores would fall, but they kept coming.

As soon as the Ottomans were within shooting distance, the defenders let fly their arrows and fired their rifles. Hundreds fell, but the unruly, frenzied mob of warriors continued its onslaught. A few invaders managed to bridge the moat with long planks of wood and the rest rushed across bearing ladders and hooks.

The defenders poured hot oil and stones on top of them. The screams of burned and maimed soldiers merged with the music and the drums. There was dust and smell of burning flesh and gunpowder and blood everywhere. Surely, hell was not any worse than this. The defenders could not use Greek fire on the Wall because of the fear that it might ignite the wooden gates. They relied instead on old-fashioned hot oil and boiling water. Then, after several hours of slaughter and mayhem, as the sun was going down, they sounded the retreat. The killing continued until the last live soldier was out of the gunshot range.

Seemingly from nowhere, flies and vultures appeared to feast on the bodies of people who had been alive only a few hours earlier. As the two sides had agreed, there was a cease-fire for the rest of the day to allow the opposing armies to collect and bury their dead.

Rodrigo hurried back to the safe house, where his men were waiting. Jean said a boat would pick them up near the ruins of the old palace and carry them past the chain that blocked the Golden Horn. Just north of Galata, a Genovese ship would be waiting to take them to Rhodes.

Rodrigo told them that he had to stay because of his promise to the emperor and because he was hoping to find Renaldo and pay him back for his treachery. The others wanted to stay with Rodrigo, but he refused, saying they must protect the True Cross and get it safely to the Vatican, where it belonged for eternity. Zangi and Jean refused to leave Rodrigo alone. Reluctantly, he capitulated. He told Antonio, Lorenzo, Petros, and Father Ricardo to board the boat with Aziza, Katarina, Elena, and her maid.

When they arrived in Rhodes, he said, they should take the first available ship to Italy, preferably to Venice, which was the nearest safe port. Rodrigo, Jean, and Zangi would meet them there as soon as it was possible or at least they would try to send word to them through the papal office in Venice.

They all returned to the mansion except Lorenzo, who was left to guard the True Cross. Rodrigo sent Father Ricardo to the palace to see if news of the explosion in the church had made any ripples in the court. Oddly enough, they were so busy with the war that a little attempted robbery had not even been reported! Father Ricardo then visited Princess Aziza and Princess Elena to give them the location and the time of their departure.

An hour before midnight, they met at their safe house. Rodrigo took the cover off the True Cross to take one last look at the object that so many people had sought for so many centuries. The bottom piece of the cross was gone, chipped away by souvenir hunters and miracle-seekers. The cross stood less than four feet tall. As Arthur of Brittany had written over two centuries earlier, the headboard was missing and the cross looked like a capital "T." They all kneeled and prayed silently. Rodrigo respectfully covered it again.

In the dark, they departed for the waterfront. Lorenzo insisted on carrying the cross on his shoulder. Father Ricardo, Elena, Aziza, and their maids were waiting for them. The small boat was ready to depart. Rodrigo addressed Antonio, "I leave you in command for the safety of these passengers and the precious cargo until we meet again." The men shook hands.

Rodrigo hugged his sobbing wife tightly and murmured his everlasting love to her. Father Ricardo said a prayer. The boat departed and soon disappeared into the darkness of the night.

the
Borgia Seed

BOOK II: THE RAPE OF THE

MILLENNIUM

~ CHAPTER FORTY-ONE ~

BETRAYED BY A FRIEND

The crestfallen men went back to the mansion. They knew it would be only a few days until the end. There was no food and hardly any ammunition to go around. With Christopher dead, the morale of the Greek army was at its lowest point. Many of Constantine's friends urged the emperor to leave the city like Emperor Theodore I had done two hundred and fifty years ago when the Latin armies took over Constantinople. The Greeks eventually came back because they still had an emperor.

Even the Persian envoy to the court, KayKavous, the arch-enemy of the Turks, kneeled in front of the emperor and begged him to depart. He had a small boat ready to leave but he insisted that Constantine should take his place with his family. The boat would go north into the Black Sea, away from the Ottoman blockade, and land in Georgia. From there, the emperor could go to Tabriz where the shah of Persia had promised to put an army at his command to battle the Ottomans.

The envoy and most of the courtiers beseeched the emperor to go, assuring him that an army of Persians and Greeks, who would join him in exile, could defeat the Turks. The emperor refused.

It was then that Rodrigo began to realize that Constantine had a death wish and was determined to die with his city and take everyone with him to the other world.

* * *

Meanwhile, in his palace, Loukas Notaras was debating his next course of action. As the second in command, he knew that the city was doomed. Even if the Wall did not collapse, the citizens would die of starvation. For some time now, he had been in contact with Mohammed through the sultan's spies in the city. Mohammed had offered him and his family safe passage in exchange for his help in capturing the city. He knew that if he did not cooperate with the Ottomans, his family would be massacred along with most of the other residents of the city when the Ottomans eventually prevailed. Mohammed's spy was anxiously awaiting his final answer. Loukas decided to save his only surviving relatives—his son Theo, his wife, Alexandra, and his nephew Tomas.

Loukas, like many other defenders, knew that the Kerkoporta Gate was one of the weakest gates of the city. Although heavy bars spanned the two gate doors to keep them shut, they were not strong enough to hold the doors against a concentrated cannon attack. Therefore, four massive wooden beams had been propped against the doors to buttress them. Loukas knew that if those props failed, the gate would spring open after a few well-placed cannon shots. In addition, the secondary defense wall that started at the Golden Gate in the south abruptly ended at Kerkoporta, so if the gate was opened, the Ottomans could pour in. With their superior numbers, the city would fall in a matter of hours.

Loukas walked to his ornate study and called on his servant to admit Photeus Skouzas, a Greek Christian by birth, who, like Renaldo, had converted to Islam. Traitors come in different shapes and forms. Renaldo had become a traitor to his country and friends because the Muslim Imam had played to his intellectual vanity and his anger that after so many years, he was still a poor second-class citizen with no wife or family. Photeus was a shrewd businessman who had decided that being a Muslim would make him rich and powerful. He did not believe in the Muslim or the Christian religions. Photeus was an opportunist. He was probably descended from the Greeks who built the Trojan horse and destroyed Troy by treachery. He had kept his conversion to Islam secret and the sultan had appointed him as his chief of spies in Constantinople.

Photeus was ushered into Loukas's study. After the servant had left, he asked Loukas if he had made up his mind. Loukas Notaras looked exhausted and irritable. He was about to sell his city and his emperor to the savages. He snapped back that, yes, he had made up his mind, and he outlined his plan.

Sometime during the early hours of morning, on the day after tomorrow, Loukas said, he would have the props holding the Kerkoporta doors loosened. His excuse would be that the Greeks were planning to launch a surprise attack through that gate.

Photeus or his spies should wait near the gate at that time to send a signal to the sultan to concentrate his cannon power on that gate. The Ottoman infantry should be ready to charge as soon as it was forced open.

Photeus, who communicated with the sultan by means of carrier pigeon, bowed to the grand duke and left without another word.

* * *

The following day was Monday May 28, 1453. Rodrigo and his friends were waiting for the sounds of bombardment, expecting the final assault to occur at any time. However, the morning was eerily quiet. It was so deathly quiet that they thought they could even hear the waves of the Sea of Marmara lapping against the shores of the city. Rodrigo inspected the Italian army one more time. The Genovese were still in good spirits, with John Justiniani bragging that no Turk would ever break through their ranks.

Rodrigo paid a visit to the emperor. After a few minutes of discussion about the defenses of the city, Constantine, who had not slept for several nights, actually relaxed and fell asleep while sitting in his favorite chair. Rodrigo left the room quietly and told the servants not to disturb the emperor. He tried not to think about Aziza and his unborn child but he could not keep his thoughts concentrated on anything else for long. With luck, they were at sea, getting farther away from the areas controlled by the Ottomans.

When the emperor finally woke up it was dark. He called his servants and had some food. He called for Loukas Notaras and others to join him for a briefing. The attack that they had expected that day had not materialized; therefore, he gave the soldiers time off to rest and visit their families.

It was around ten that night that Rodrigo, who was sitting in the banquet room of his mansion thinking about the battle to come, heard strange noises in the streets outside. It sounded like a mass funeral, with mourners wailing in unison.

Then, a very disturbed and frightened Zangi rushed in and said, "Signor Rodrigo, Signor Rodrigo, you must come and see this." Zangi, the man who was never scared of anything, was terrified of what he had seen. He pointed to the balcony facing northeast towards the Golden Horn and the Church of Hagia Sofia. Rodrigo stepped out onto the balcony to look. An eerie, opaque blue light surrounded the church. Zangi said, "The light appeared a minute or two ago."

The light shrouding the church was intense enough that the soldiers in Mohammed's camp saw it, too. Rodrigo could hear the commotion in the Ottoman camp as soldiers tried to understand the phenomenon. The ghostly light flickered around Hagia Sofia for another five minutes or so and then it rose up and disappeared into the dark sky above.

Rodrigo felt the intense pain of despair in his bones as the entire city howled in agony and wept in harmony. All was lost. They had been forsaken. Whatever force had protected them was gone.

Great shouts of joy erupted from the Turkish camp, as the Ottomans perceived that God was on their side.

* * *

Back in Rome, at that very moment, Nicholas woke up screaming from a nightmarish vision. His frightened servants sent for his old friend Cardinal Alfonso Borgia. He found the weeping pope kneeling in front of a cross, shivering, and praying for forgiveness. He kept repeating the same sentence, "Father, forgive me for I have failed you."

Cardinal Alfonso embraced his comrade of many years to calm him down. After Nicholas was still, he told Alfonso that he had seen Constantinople burning the great Church of Hagia Sofia soaking in blood. He had seen the fiery figure of a grinning Lucifer standing atop of the great church, his hands dripping with the fiery blood of the innocents. After that night, the great pope was never the same.

* * *

Back in Constantinople, the hapless emperor immediately called for a service to be held at the great church. It was late, but who could sleep now? Most of the population of the city attended. The Orthodox and the Catholic bishops and priests jointly conducted the service.

Old enmities were forgotten. They asked for forgiveness from their sins. Husbands kissed their wives and small children. The men shook hands and hugged. The younger children laughed and played. The older children were frightened and clung to their parents or whomever they had left in this world. Tears ran down Rodrigo's face. Zangi, standing next to him, wept bitterly. Looking at him, Rodrigo promised himself that if they ever got out alive, he would send Zangi back to Africa to find his family. Only Jean was quiet and sober, kneeling next to them with his head lowered and his right hand at his forehead.

The adults knew that barring a divine intervention, they would be dead or enslaved by the next night. To Rodrigo, it seemed that even the walls of the great church were weeping with them.

When they had returned home, Rodrigo and Zangi sat quietly in the banquet room sharing some wine. Jean disappeared onto the balcony facing the Sea of Marmara. After half an hour, he came back teary eyed, sat down, and said, "Rodrigo, do you remember that you promised me you would clear the name of our lady, the maid of Orleans?" Rodrigo responded that he did. Jean continued, "I was praying to our lady to intercede on our behalf and save the city. I then had a revelation. The city is doomed and the last Christian empire of the East will be gone forever. By tomorrow night, the infidels will be sitting where the emperor is sitting now. I will die tomorrow, I know. Just remember your promise."

Rodrigo and Zangi had been through so many strange experiences in the last few weeks that they thought nothing would shock them anymore. Still, they were stunned by the finality in Jean's voice. They stood up and tried to say something appropriate, but they realized that there was nothing to say. They just wept.

But Jean had a smile on his face. "Brothers, do not weep for me," he said. "I am going where I should have gone many years ago. I was saved for this mission and now that we have found the True Cross and it is out of the hands of the infidels, my job is done and I must depart this world. Believe me that after the True Cross gets to Rome, the Christian world will thrive and expand all over the world, while the Muslims will regress back in time, just as the emperor predicted a few weeks ago."

It was getting very late. There was no point in going to bed. They simply fell asleep in their chairs. The men slept soundly. They had come to accept their fates and since death seemed inevitable now, there was nothing to do but to welcome it as an opportunity to join their brethren in heaven.

CHAPTER FORTY-TWO

THE SAVAGE HORDE.

Several hours later, they woke up to the sounds of the sultan's army screaming obscenities at the defenders. Strains of Turkish military music, played by a band of hundreds, followed. Then, what seemed like hundreds of drums started their rhythmic, ominous, nightmarish sound. The barrage of cannon fire soon followed. The first waves of soldiers, the Bashibazouks, who had been recruited from the peasantry and had little training, were sent forward to attack the Wall in several places, including the Golden Gate. The Bashibazouks had no choice but to go forward and die. Behind them, the well-armed Janissaries stood ready to shoot anyone who tried to turn back.

The first assault lasted for more than an hour before the big guns fell silent, but the music and the drums continued, irritating and upsetting the soldiers on the Wall and in the towers. Then, at about ten in the morning, a white dove was released over the city. That was the signal from Photeus. The cannons started firing again and the soldiers charged toward the Wall. The sultan did not neglect the other part of the Wall, but he concentrated his cannon fire on the Kerkoporta Gate and soon it flew wide open. Wave after wave of the Bashibazouks stormed toward the opening.

Further to the south, the Janissaries attacked the Golden Gate and managed to climb the Wall. Some of them entered the city. The soldiers at the Golden Gate did not know about the breach at Kerkoporta Gate further north and they fought on bravely. Then, a stray shot hit John Justiniani in the shoulder and wounded him slightly.

At the site of his own blood, the coward nearly fainted! His legs buckled beneath him and when he got up, he started running away from the battlefield. Rodrigo and the emperor, who were fighting alongside the soldiers, tried to stop him but he brushed past both of them. This created a panic among the Genovese soldiers and they broke rank and followed their coward of a leader to the town. The remaining Italians and the Greeks continued fighting but the Janissaries soon outnumbered them greatly.

Then, Constantine received news of the breach at Kerkoporta. The emperor rushed to help the defenders close that gate. Rodrigo and Zangi followed him, leaving the valiant Jean in command. At that time, there was still a standoff between the two forces.

Arriving at Kerkoporta, Constantine was appalled to see the Bashibazouks pouring through the gate. The bloodthirsty peasant soldiers were massacring the defenders caught in the gap between the inner wall and outer wall. Other defenders tried to hold their ground. The emperor yelled to his men to hold the line and, with Rodrigo and Zangi by his side, jumped into the fray. With super-human strength, he slaughtered many of the invaders and eventually his men managed to drive the intruders back towards the gate.

But then, a Muslim lance pierced the valiant emperor from behind. He fell to his knees.

Rodrigo and Zangi pulled him to the side, away from the fighting. The bleeding emperor smiled weakly at Rodrigo and said, "This is the way that I wanted to die. With my city." Rodrigo and Zangi picked him up and carried him all the way to their secret hideout. They lowered him down the staircase into the cistern. The black waters surrounding them did not bother Rodrigo anymore.

The emperor was still alive. He said, "After I die, please take the purple cloak off me and throw it away. I do not want to give that savage the satisfaction of seeing me dead. Nicholas is a holy man. Tell him to pray for my soul and please look after my sister as your own." They gave him some wine and soon he was gone.

Rodrigo and Zangi, their bodies covered with blood from fighting, went in search of Jean and the other defenders. It was nearly noon. The Greek soldiers were running in all directions and the Italians were either dead or dying. Most of the Genovese had managed to cross the Golden Horn and head for Galata and the safety of their boats. Rodrigo and Zangi found Jean, who had been wounded, but had almost made his way back to the safe house before passing out. They carried him down to the cistern and sat there waiting. Jean came to one more time to remind Rodrigo of his promise and said, "You may now think that you are nobody, but you will survive this and one day you will be the most important person in Christendom." By midnight, Jean was also dead. Rodrigo wept bitterly.

* * *

Once the Ottomans entered the city, the defenders were so outnumbered that those who survived fled back to their homes to try to defend their families and die with them, if necessary.

CHAPTER FORTY-THREE

AZIZA'S ESCAPE

The night was cold. Aziza's teeth were chattering from the breeze from the east that lifted the freezing dampness from the seawater and pushing it into the boat. The icy mist penetrated her garments, permeating every fiber of her slender body. Being a young expectant mother, she was afraid that the cold might damage the tiny baby in her womb. The boat was purposely small and shallow to avoid detection by the Ottoman blockaders. In pitch darkness, the oarsman gently and silently dipped the oars into the water. Before long, they could see the dark, menacing outlines of the Ottoman fleet. Being late at night, there were hardly any lights on board and little activity. The monstrous ships looked gloomy and even more ominous. They came very close to two great warships that were blocking their way. The coxswain steering the boat whispered to them to be extremely quiet and hunker down in the boat. He covered them with a dark cloth.

Aziza could see faintly through the holes in the fabric. When they were about forty yards from the two ships, the oarsman stopped rowing and let the boat drift gently towards the narrow gap between them. The prevailing current would gradually take them in a southerly direction and if the coxswain were not careful, they would run smack against the side of one of the ships. He maneuvered the boat expertly while sweating profusely in that cold night. The little boat glided within inches of the two ships.

The oarsman let the boat drift another hundred yards before removing the cloth and starting to row again. Everybody breathed a sigh of relief. They had broken the blockade.

Lorenzo volunteered to help with rowing, and even so, it took another two hours before they spotted the dark but welcome outline of the Genovese ship waiting for them. The coxswain used a covered lantern to signal their presence and soon they were on board.

The captain, Signor Manfredo Campi, did not waste any time. As soon as the boat was hauled up, he lifted anchor and let his ship drift south. They unfurled the sails and the ship started to pick up speed, heading away from Constantinople and towards the Sea of Marmara.

To reach the Isle of Rhodes, the ship had to cross the very narrow Straits of Bosphorus and enter the Sea of Marmara. Then it had to cross another narrow but longer channel, the Straits of Dardanelles, to enter the Aegean Sea. The problem that Signor Campi, like other blockade-runners, faced was that most of the lands surrounding those bodies of water were in Ottoman hands. To avoid being spotted, he had planned to do most of his traveling at night and hide in little coves, which his Greek pilot knew well, during the daylight hours. Fortunately, due to the difference in the salinity of the Black Sea to the north and the Mediterranean Sea to the south, the surface current usually runs from north to south, so even without any wind, the ship would drift southward.

The scariest part of the trip, Signor Campi knew, was at the narrowest point of the Dardanelles. There, on the eastern shore of the Straits, only a few hundred yards away on the port side, stood the Turkish-held Castle of Canakkale with its big guns. Many a ship had been sunk or was boarded there by the Ottomans.

After three days of hiding during the day and sailing at night, Signor Campi folded the sails and relied on the current to carry him quietly past the fort in the dead of the night. Fortunately, the Ottomans were so happy with the news from Constantinople that they had neglected to post a lookout that night.

Once Signor Campi entered the Aegean Sea, he stayed close to the land on the Asian side of the sea. He knew that Ottoman ships avoided getting close to land because of the treacherous rock formations close to the surface.

They hugged the coast for the next several days until they eventually reached the city of Rhodes, which is located on the northern shore of the Island of Rhodes.

The Knights Hospitaller had captured Rhodes after the Muslims pushed them out of the holy lands. The knights fortified the island by building almost impregnable castles. The northern tip of the island is less than twenty miles from the Turkish mainland but the strong fortifications kept the invaders away and in fact, the knights even controlled the tiny peninsula on the Asian mainland.

They were welcomed by Jean de Lastic, the grand master of the knights. The Genovese captain, Signor Campi, was immediately paid off and the knights provided accommodation for their guests inside the castle. The grand master assigned one of his junior knights, Fabrizio de Ponte, who had not yet taken the vows of the order, to be their protector and chaperone during their stay. Fabrizio was a young man of about twenty-five from Aosta in northern Italy, close to the French border.

The knights were a religious order, so the quarters given to Elena and Aziza were very Spartan, but they were happy to be standing on solid ground and out of reach of Mohammed and his henchmen. Aziza had been sick throughout the journey and was scared of losing her baby. Father Ricardo and Antonio took the True Cross to the castle vault and left it there for safekeeping.

Merchant ships plied the waters of the Mediterranean, sailing from port to port and deciding where to go depending on their cargo. Rhodes, because of its location, was out of the way of most major sea traffic. The grand master said they simply would have to wait for a ship bound for Italy.

While they waited, Aziza was examined by a Christian midwife and was assured that her baby was in perfect shape.

About a week after their arrival, they heard the news of the fall of the great city. The sailors who brought the news reported that the emperor and most of his senior officers had been slain. The two princesses were grief-stricken, one having lost a loved one and then a brother, and the other having lost her husband of one week and the father of her unborn, orphaned child. Ricardo tried to assure Elena that the pope would take care of her and Aziza. Aziza's child was heir to the Borgia family and Cardinal Alfonso Borgia, who had adopted Rodrigo, would provide for her and her baby.

The two princesses had reached the point of no return in their lives. There was nothing to go back to and the future looked very bleak. The news got even worse as stories of murder and atrocities arrived daily.

While most of the knights had expected the city to fall without massive help from Europe, they were not prepared for the news of the rape and enslavement of the nuns and the innocents. That news so traumatized the knights and the Greek population that the island went into total shock.

The grand master ordered a black flag flown on top of the castle and they had seven days of mourning and prayers.

Fabrizio de Ponte was a handsome man. By the time he was twenty-four, he was bored with his life and had decided to seek adventure by joining the order of the Knights Hospitaller. A pleasant man and well liked man, Fabrizio was quickly charmed by Elena. There was something magical about the way Elena looked and carried herself that made him fall for her. After many days of close contact, a bond of friendship and affection developed between Elena and Fabrizio. Fabrizio made up his mind that he wanted to marry Elena and spend the rest of his life with her.

For Elena, who had lost everything and had nowhere to go, it was easy to succumb to the affections of a person who genuinely was in love with her. This shift did not go unnoticed by Aziza and the maids. They asked her if she was finding love again, but Elena was hesitant to commit herself to another man.

Grand Master Jean de Lastic also noticed the attraction developing between the two. He called Fabrizio to his quarters one day and said, "My son, you have not yet taken your vows, so I am going to release you from your obligations. I do not think that you were meant to be a monk. From this moment on, I will appoint you as the protector of your charges and the True Cross until they safely reach Rome."

* * *

The next few ships that arrived were destined for Alexandria or Salonica. They could take a ship to Salonica and from there sail to Venice. But since Salonica was in Turkish hands, they did not want to jeopardize the True Cross by taking it back to a land under Ottoman control. After two months of waiting, a small inter-island boat arrived that was heading to Crete. The Island of Crete, which was about one hundred and fifty miles away, had been occupied by Venice for several hundred years and was considered a safe location. Because of its position, Candia, the main port on the island, was a major transshipment harbor in the Mediterranean. From Crete, they could easily find ships traveling to Venice.

The grand master sent four of his knights, in addition to Fabrizio, to accompany the group and to make sure that the master of the ship did not change his mind on the way. Eventually, in mid-September, they arrived in the Port of Candia. By now, they had heard news of the horrors at Constantinople and never expected to see Rodrigo, Jean, and Zangi alive again. In Candia, they waited for a ship that would not make calls on Ottoman ports, and after two weeks, they boarded a ship bound directly for Venice.

The sea journey to Venice was uneventful since the seas were calm and they were in Venetian-protected waters. They arrived in Venice by the end of September.

Within hours of their arrival, the news of their escape from the Ottomans had spread throughout the city. The doge of

Venice, Francesco Foscari, came to visit them and invited them to stay at his residence while in Venice.

Father Ricardo, like most people who met Aziza, had been charmed by her presence and awed by her knowledge of languages and history. While on board the ship for the final leg of their trip to Venice, Father Ricardo, with help from Aziza, who had kept a meticulous diary of her experiences as well as stories related to her by others, had prepared a detailed report of their mission for his uncle, Pope Nicholas.

As soon as they had disembarked in Venice, Father Ricardo, with Petros and Antonio, took the True Cross to the bishop of Venice for safekeeping. For his part, the bishop sent Father Ricardo's letter to Rome that very day by fast messenger.

* * *

By now, most people in the Vatican, with the exception of Pope Nicholas, had given up hope of seeing Rodrigo or his men again. The True Cross, they assumed, was irrevocably lost. The pope, who had more faith and was gifted with sensing future events, thought otherwise. He repeatedly assured his friend, Cardinal Alfonso, that his nephew would come back alive.

Finally, one day in late September, the message from Father Ricardo arrived. There was jubilation at the Vatican that the True Cross had been saved and the Lord's men, who had risked their lives, were still alive. Father Ricardo's letter had given a complete account of their journey, including the ambushes and treacheries that they had encountered during their long trip.

According to Father Ricardo, Rodrigo's fate was unknown. They awaited instructions from the pope.

Nicholas called a conference of his cardinals. After the meeting, he sent a fast papal messenger to Venice with letters of instructions for Father Ricardo, the doge, and the bishop.

* * *

Like other rulers, Pope Nicholas was hampered by the lack of fast communication between different cities of Europe. There were way stations and rest stops between major towns so travelers and messengers could change horses or rest. However, they were not always open and at times they were overrun by highwaymen or invading forces. To address this problem, Cardinal Alfonso Borgia had created a new papal messenger service. Each messenger was given two fast horses. He rode one and tied the other one behind, to his saddle, as a spare. When his mount got tired, he would change to the other horse. Therefore, the horses could go much longer distances before they were exhausted and had to rest or be replaced by fresh horses at a way station. The pope also dispatched a group of twenty Swiss soldiers to Venice to guard the True Cross on its way to Rome.

The messenger arrived in Venice within four and half days, exhausted and very happy to have set a record. The instructions to Father Ricardo and the bishop were to guard the Cross and wait for the Swiss detachment to arrive to help them bring it to Rome.

The instructions to the doge, Francesco Foscari, were similar. Pope Nicholas made him responsible for the safety of the

True Cross and for the emissaries. In a separate letter, Nicholas reminded the doge that the Venetians had been holding the Byzantine crown jewels as collateral on a loan they had made many years ago to the emperor of Byzantine. The pope told Francesco Foscari that he and the people of Venice were responsible to provide for Elena and any other members of the imperial family who may have survived the Turkish massacre.

Venice, as a republic, was controlled by a select group of noblemen known as the Council of Ten. The Council was constantly at odds with Francesco Foscari and his son, Giuseppe. However, Francesco and Giuseppe were very popular with the people of Venice.

The budding relationship between Elena and Fabrizio blossomed. One night, Elena confided to Aziza that she had known deep down that Christopher was not interested in her sexually but she had never wanted to admit that to herself. The defining moment had come at the party in Loukas Notaras's mansion when she, like Aziza, had noticed the adoring way that Christopher looked at Rodrigo. Aziza was happy that her dearest friend and confidant had finally found the love that she deserved. Before they left Venice, the doge announced that he and the other members of the Council of Ten would provide a princely dowry for Elena when she married. They also would pay her a stipend from the difference between the value of the Crown Jewels of Byzantine that were held as collateral in Venice and their true market value.

* * *

After two weeks, the Swiss soldiers arrived. Finally, they set out for Rome. When they were a few hours away from the Vatican, they sent word to the pope. Pope Nicholas was waiting for the cross at the foot of the stairs of the old Vatican as they arrived. The cross was carried in a carriage with an honor guard of Swiss soldiers. All cardinals and leading members of the Roman society including old enemies-the Contis, the Orsinis and the Colonnas- were present. Dignitaries fell to their knees and kissed the old blanket that had covered the cross for so many centuries in that dark room in the great church of Hagia Sofia. The pope wept with the joy of a man who has achieved the impossible.

After a few days, Cardinal Alfonso called the group together. There was still no news of Rodrigo and Zangi. The pope had decided to grant titles and property to all of the men. Antonio and Lorenzo were free to go, since their work was done. Petros, as a physician, could stay and set up practice in Rome. Aziza, as Rodrigo's lawful wife and the mother of his child, was now the senior woman in the cardinal's household. Elena would stay with her as a guest.

CHAPTER FORTY-FOUR

THE RAPE OF THE MILLENNIUM

Like most armies of the day, Mohammed's force was a slow-moving, lumbering juggernaut. It only marched during daylight hours and usually stopped well before sundown to set up camp and prepare food for the troops. Camp followers were legion. Some soldiers took their wives and children with them if they could not or would not leave them behind. For some, it was a necessity since they did not have homes of their own. Traders, pimps, con men, and prostitutes also numbered among the camp followers.

Since Muslim law prohibited prostitution, temporary marriage or concubinage—with its more lenient rules of engagement—had been invented to take its place. A Muslim man could not take a Jew or a Christian as a wife unless she first converted to Islam. But he could take a woman of any faith as a concubine, upon paying a fee, for a temporary marriage as brief as fifteen minutes. The man or a mullah would simply repeat the Muslim incantation of the marriage ceremony, which would temporarily change the relationship of two strangers into that of a husband and a wife. During those fifteen minutes, they were considered legally married. After the time expired, the woman was auto-matically divorced and she could marry again. In contrast, if a permanent marriage ended in divorce, the woman had to wait one hundred days before she could marry another man.

After a city was conquered or an army was defeated, the camp followers often were more vicious and greedy than the conquering soldiers. In fact, instead of following the vanquished soldiers and finishing off the battle, a victorious army often fell on the camp followers of its enemy in search of pillage and booty. If the defeated army had a reserve unit of soldiers, this sometimes gave it an opportunity to turn the table on the victors, who were busy plundering, getting drunk, and ravaging the women[3].

Rich merchants also followed Mohammed's army, traveling in style with their slaves and guards. They carried silver and gold coins to buy slaves and treasures from the conquering soldiers and the poorer camp followers. They usually camped at a respectable distance from the army and waited for victory before moving in.

Mohammed's main army consisted of the archers, the peasant Bashibazouks infantry, and the elite Janissaries. The Janissaries were captive Christian youths turned into fanatical and obedient Muslims.

Much to the embarrassment of the Janissaries, the regular peasant Bashibazouks infantry entered Constantinople first

---

3 During the English Civil War, the Royalists lost the final battle at Naseby because many of the Royalist soldiers were attracted to the retreating Parliamentarian's baggage train. This gave Oliver Cromwell the chance to turn the tide and win the battle decisively. If the Royalists had won that battle, the English Parliament, the mother parliament of all democracies, would not exist in its current form today.

through the Kerkoporta Gate. The sultan himself commanded the archers from a safe distance. The Janissaries, despite their superior skills, could have been defeated and thrown back over the Wall if the Genovese had not deserted and if the Kerkoporta Gate had not been breached.

The sultan had ordered some of his elite troops to enter the city as soon as possible to protect certain neighborhoods where Muslims or collaborators lived. He wanted to keep parts of Constantinople intact to keep it functioning. However, in accordance with Muslim law, he had promised his troops three days of unrestricted plunder and rape.

Sections of the city near the Wall had long been deserted. Consequently, 150,000 marauding soldiers and tens of thousands of camp followers poured down the central boulevard and fanned out in all directions. Even the Turkish sailors guarding the Golden Horn abandoned their ships to join in the great pillage.

What they did that day was not pretty. Older men and women were impaled or had their throats cut or were disemboweled with the sharp Turkish scimitars. Younger women and boys were raped first by men and then by whatever object they could find and left to bleed to death. The savages had no mercy for pregnant women, either. They were cut open and left to die along with their stillborn babies. To them, unborn Christian fetuses were like cockroaches to be pummeled to death.

Young girls and boys were of primary interest, especially virgin girls and nice looking boys.

The invaders had a map pinpointing every convent in the city. The Muslim imams wanted to eradicate the idea that women could be equal to men and perform godly work. The nuns, unlike harem-bound Muslim women, looked after the sick and the needy. They even tended to Muslim lepers that no imam would go near. The convents were targeted systematically, their gates wrecked and the nuns ravished in front of the altars as they prayed and wept. Muslim historians report that four thousand nuns were raped and many killed on the day Constantinople fell.

Churches were sacked and crosses and statues of the Virgin Mary and child were hacked to pieces and burnt.

With the emperor dead, there was no one to protect the Palace of Blachernae. The remaining inhabitants were killed or raped and the great palace was emptied of its contents within two hours of invasion.

The greatest slaughter took place at the Church of Hagia Sofia. There, thousands of people, men, women, children, and infants had gathered seeking sanctuary from the people who did not believe in compassion. They had closed the great bronze doors, hoping for divine deliverance. The Turks broke down the doors and fell upon the people, indiscriminately killing and beheading young and old. They even used severed infants heads to snuff out church candles and joked about it. Soon a river of blood ran down the center of the great hall. The priests and the bishops were not spared. By the time they had slaughtered more than half of the people, they had enough blood and they decided to enslave the rest of them. In terms of utter savagery to other human beings, on that day, they managed to surpass what their cousins the Huns under the leadership of Attila had done over a thousand years earlier.

Once the invaders had satisfied their lust for women and murder, they started to gather and hoard goods and slaves. They roped their slaves together in twos and threes and put them into one of houses that they had invaded. They also stuffed all their loot in the confiscated rooms.

The sultan, soon realizing that the city had a smaller population that he had thought, ordered an immediate halt to the pillage. He told his grand vizier that he did not want to rule over a ghost city.

That afternoon, after looters had removed crosses and other religious artifacts from Hagia Sofia, the sultan and his entourage arrived at the great church. They stepped through ankle-deep blood and passed hundreds of mutilated corpses. The great imam of the Ottomans mounted the altar to declare the church consecrated as a mosque—a bloody mosque.

The slave traders and merchants were quick to enter the city and set up shop in the Spice Bazaar.

That night, down in the cistern, Rodrigo and Zangi could hear the screams of agony of people dying and being tortured as the invaders started enjoying themselves with their captives. Young girls and boys screamed in vain while being ravished, their tiny genitals stretched by huge men. Other more sadistic soldiers tortured and dismembered their captives.

In the morning, the merchants of doom were ready for business, exchanging the silver and gold household items and jewelry for gold and silver coins. Slave traders sorted their human goods into separate categories, the most precious being young white girls who were still virgin. They were examined thoroughly. They would be sold in the slave markets of Ankara, Edirne, or Damascus, or even as far away as Zanzibar in Africa. Young, nice looking boys were destined to be household slaves or sold to the male brothels of the Orient. Strong men capable of hard physical work would be sold in the European parts of Ottoman Empire to the Turkish farmers who had taken over Christian lands.

Older women were not much in demand so, if they were not killed or were not deemed capable of housework, they might be released. There was also a demand for educated men to become tutors for rich Turkish families. The rest of the men and women were sold as household servants.

The people who escaped capture or enslavement before Mohammed called a stop to the massacre were free; however, they were now subjects of the sultan. Many of them managed to buy the freedom of their friends and relatives, if they could find them.

* * *

Rodrigo and Zangi dug a shallow grave in the tunnel that led to the old palace and, after wrapping the bodies of the emperor and their friend, Jean, in blankets, buried them next to each other. Rodrigo removed the blood-stained purple tunic of Constantine to take back to Rome.

After two nights, they surfaced just before dusk. They were astonished at the bloated corpses and the dried blood that seemed to cover the city. The stench was overpowering. They could still hear the whimpers and moans of the injured men, women, and children who had been left to die slowly. Rodrigo tried not to look at the human tragedy around him. He said to Zangi, "I wish the kings of France and Germany and the emperor of Austria could be here to see what these savage rascals have done. Then, maybe they'll know that they will be burning in hell along with Mohammed for helping him do this to these innocent souls."

Now that the emperor and Jean were dead, Rodrigo and Zangi had only two goals in life. One was to find Renaldo and dispatch him to hell. The other was to get out of the city. They knew that the Italian settlements of Galata were largely intact. Many of the Genovese had fled Galata but the Venetians had stayed because they had special commercial treaties with Mohammed. If they could find a boat to take them across the Golden Horn, they could get a passage to Rhodes or even Venice. Since the pillaging had stopped, no one was bothering them and the streets were relatively safe.

Rodrigo and Zangi went to the Spice Bazaar and watched the slave traders buying beautiful young maidens and boys for shipment to the East to uncertain futures. What really infuriated him was seeing the young nuns, still in their habits being traded in such a manner. He felt more hopeless than he had ever felt in his life. He watched as nun after nun was sold to traders and sent into the back rooms to be loaded into carts for the voyage to the Muslim slave markets of Asia and Africa. He could not forget their innocent, pleading eyes that hoped for a miracle that never came. The lucky brides of the Church would be forced into slavery and fornication with Oriental men and made to bear their half-breeds. The unlucky ones would be sold to brothels across Africa and Arabia.

Zangi, seeing Rodrigo's emotional state, suggested that they visit their old mansion. They found the door standing wide open. They stepped inside. The place had been ransacked. The books in the magnificent library, some dating back hundreds of years, were strewn all over the floor. Then they heard a noise and were surprised to find one of the servants, Alexis, alive, hiding in a corner.

He was happy to see them. He came out and kissed Rodrigo's hand, repeatedly thanking God that he was alive. Rodrigo asked if he knew what was happening. The servant did not know but he said that since he felt it was now safe to go out, he would find out. They closed and battened down the door after he left.

Alexis returned around midnight full of news. "Loukas Notaras was the traitor who arranged for the Kerkoporta Gate to be left open for the Ottomans," he said. "He also handed over the Byzantine's treasury of gold and artifacts to the sultan and is now living safely in his palace with his family." Alexis also reported that the Turks were destroying all the evidence of Christianity; Most churches were going to be converted to mosques or presented to high-ranking noblemen for use as mansions. Mohammed was planning to leave a few churches open for the remaining Christians that his troops had not slaughtered. Alexis did not have any news of Renaldo.

They stayed the night at the mansion. Food was now available at a high price from the camp followers. Rodrigo gave Alexis some money to get food the next morning.

~ CHAPTER FORTY-FIVE ~

TRIUMPH OF EVIL

On the fifth day after the invasion and rape of the magnificent city, Mohammed arranged a grand feast in the Palace of Blachernae. Someone had told him that Loukas Notaras had a son and a nephew who were as attractive looking as girls, with dark curly hair, white skin, and perfectly shaped limbs. After a few drinks, the sultan sent for Loukas Notaras.

Loukas arrived with his slaves and paid homage to his new master. Mohammed asked him if it was true that his young son and nephew were the best-looking boys in Constantinople. To the Turks, sex was about the dominance of men. It did not matter if the subject of their desire was a girl or a boy. They did not classify human sexuality as homosexual and heterosexual. Hundreds of years of tribal traditions had shaped their perception of superiority and dominance of men. The head of a Muslim household was always a domineering figure who seldom smiled or showed his soft side in front of his own family. In fact, smiling or showing happiness to underlings, wives, or young children was considered a sign of weakness. Frowning was the hallmark of superiority, as portraits of scowling men attest.

As Loukas well knew, many Muslim men had sex with women just for procreation. They believed the anal muscles of boys and young men were much tighter and stronger than women's were and therefore more enjoyable. As such, they preferred a homosexual lifestyle.

Loukas, suddenly taken aback and fearful, replied that those were malicious rumors and there was no truth to them at all. Mohammed then asked Loukas to send for the boys. Loukas, suddenly finding his courage, begged the sultan to spare his family.

Mohammed, who was already under the influence of wine, ordered him to bring the boys to him immediately for his pleasure.

Loukas, the man who had opened the gate to let the Ottomans in, suddenly developed a backbone. Loukas had detested the Catholics so much that he had started the riot in the city that eventually stopped Constantine from uniting the two churches. Now, the reality set in.

The infuriated sultan had no choice. He could not show mercy to a defiant subject and, as he said later, he did not like traitors anyway. Mohammed ordered the immediate beheading of the former Grand Duke Loukas Notaras. The executioner, who always lurked in Ottoman courts lest he be needed, appeared and with his scimitar beheaded the unfortunate Loukas. Then, as was the custom, he picked up the still warm head of Loukas and with his thumbs plucked out Loukas's eyes and tossed them at the feet of Mohammed.

The sultan ordered his guards to fetch the two young boys. He was astounded by their good looks and sent them to his quarters. Since Loukas was no longer considered an ally of the sultan, Mohammed ordered that his mansion be confiscated and added to the royal holdings and his servants sold into slavery.

Later that night, the twenty-one-year-old sultan, using fragrant ointments, penetrated the two boys and discharged his semen inside both of them to prove his virility and the supremacy of the Turks over the Greeks. It was a dominance that would last almost four hundred years.

* * *

It was two days later that Rodrigo heard some welcome news. Renaldo had entered the city as one of the conquerors alongside his master and was given one of the deserted Greek mansions.

That night, after dark, Alexis took Rodrigo and Zangi to Renaldo's new residence. The lights were burning in the house and laughter and strains of Turkish and Greek music drifted from the windows. It seemed that Renaldo was entertaining Turkish friends.

They circled the mansion several time to identify the best point of entry. There was no reason to go into the house yet, since Renaldo's guests undoubtedly had bodyguards. So Rodrigo, Zangi, and Alexis returned to their own mansion.

~ CHAPTER FORTY-SIX ~

RENALDO TRIUMPHANT!

A few days after the invasion, Renaldo threw a party at his newly acquired mansion for his Turkish friends, among them several *beys*, high-ranking officials, and court luminaries. Being related to the sultan by marriage, Renaldo was considered an important dignitary himself. The soldiers who had plundered the city had saved some of their choice loot for the high-ranking officials. Renaldo received several young boys and girls, mostly untouched, for his pleasure. He also received a share of the jewelry and gold that was taken during the sack of the city. His prize possession, however, was the attractive wife of Loukas Notaras.

After Loukas was slain, the sultan divided his properties among his own family and friends. Duchess Alexandra, being the highest-ranking captured woman, was given to Renaldo. Now Renaldo was going to demonstrate his largess by sharing her with his guests.

Alexandra had been in a state of utter denial and shock for days. Some women achieve the height of sex appeal and beauty after the age of thirty and that was certainly true of her. Renaldo's slaves bathed her and applied makeup to her face to make her look even more appealing.

Renaldo had seen Roman festivities and orgies depicted in frescoes and had always fancied himself a Roman nobleman. But he'd never had the money to realize his fantasies. For this feast, he used the mansion's large hall, where wide soft cushions, pillows, and short tables loaded with fruits, dried nuts, decanters of wine, and sherbets were arranged around the perimeter. Renaldo sat at the top of the horseshoe with his guests arrayed to his left and right.

There was plenty of food and good Greek wine was flowing. The center of the hall was left open for musicians, dancers, and acrobats to perform. Even subjugated people need to eat, so it was not difficult to find eager Greek performers who, despite their misery, were willing to put on a show to earn some money.

Renaldo had arranged this fête based on his knowledge of the Roman stories. A very attractive hostess, who was practically naked from the waist up and wore flowers to cover her nipples, greeted the guests. She had a small, jeweled rose in her navel and wore lace pantaloons and gold sandals. As guests arrived, she handed each a small glass of wine mixed with Turkish *raki*, which is a very potent, twice-distilled anise-flavored hard liquor, similar to the Greek ouzo. It was sweetened with grape juice so it tasted like a sweet sherbet. The hostess seductively suggested they drink it down in one gulp before she guided them to their designated cushions. As soon as they sat down, two attractive, teenage slaves, a boy and a girl, offered wine and sherbet and would continue to serve them until the end of the festivities. These companions were instructed to make sure that the guests were pampered and kept fully satisfied. Several bedrooms around the mansion were set up to receive these men and the slaves and provide privacy. Renaldo had only invited the people who were wine drinkers.

A band played Turkish music and some popular Greek songs. In keeping with Roman traditions, the first group of performers were the acrobats. Two male and three female acrobats, all dressed scantily, performed daring acrobatic acts. Renaldo, being a bragger, tried to impress his friends with his knowledge of history and said, "Did you know that Theodora, the wife of the greatest Byzantine emperor, Justinian, was an acrobat? In those days, as now, acrobats were also prostitutes and Theodora had a tremendous appetite for sex. She once complained that she only had three orifices for sex and wished she had more." They all laughed.

Next, a skinny clown poked fun at a very fat clown. Then the chefs, who personally served each guest, served a sumptuous dinner of lamb kabobs and chicken with rice and vegetables.

After dinner, several of the men, feeling aroused, retired with their companions to the bedrooms. Renaldo stayed behind, as a gracious host should. He had with him one young boy and one young Greek girl but he did not seem interested in either of them. He had told his guests not to wear themselves out because he had a real treat planned for them.

The next show was based on the Greek and Roman mythology of semi-gods and young nymphs and fairies. In those shows, a satyr, a humanlike creature with hoofs and horns and a tremendous sexual appetite, hunted for nymphs, the innocent, fairy-like creatures of Mother Nature who looked after forests, lakes, flowers, and wheat, among other things. The satyrs, sometimes working in pairs, would capture or seduce an innocent nymph and ravish her in full view of the audience. For Renaldo's show, a tall, wiry, naked African played the satyr and a young, innocent-looking blonde was the water nymph in a pornographic display of raw human sexuality. The uneducated, sex-starved Ottomans watched the show with their mouths wide open.

Beer and wine flowed freely. It was then that Renaldo announced that he had saved the best for last. They doused some of the lights to make the room darker and while the musicians gently strummed their instruments, two burly slaves led a beautiful woman to the center of the large hall. Even the Turks could see that she had class and breeding by the way she carried herself.

Alexandra had been dressed in a long lace robe. Her red hair was combed neatly and her eyebrows, lips, and cheeks were carefully made up. Renaldo's slaves had painted her fingernails and even her toenails. She stood barefoot in the middle of the great hall, staring into nothingness. The music stopped.

Renaldo addressed his guests. "This trophy is the chaste wife of the late Duke Loukas Notaras, who dared to defy our sultan. The sultan has been gracious enough to give her to me as a slave. She has not been touched by anyone, and knowing how the duke was more interested in politics and intrigue than in women, she probably has not had a man for many years. I am aware that you all want her, so we will have a drawing to be fair to everyone." Murmurs of interest rose around the room.

"I also know that not all of you are interested in women, but if you are interested in possessing this Greek goddess, please deposit your dagger in the basket that my servant is passing around," Renaldo said.

One of the guests, MirGhozlou, laughingly protested that they should be able to see her body properly before entering the drawing. Renaldo motioned to the two slaves, who approached Alexandra and removed the lace and silk gown from her body. She stood there stark naked, except for a golden chain around her right ankle and a broad, jeweled bracelet around her left wrist. It has always been said that Greek women have the fairest skin in the world and she was no exception. Her red hair flowed down to her shoulders; her breasts were firm with their nipples pointing up in a smooth curve. She had a flat stomach and fiery red pubic hair. She was not the youngest woman that they had seen that night but she was the most attractive.

Guests shouted, "*Merhaba!*" Bravo!

The slaves covered her again and led her away. Renaldo put his own dagger into the basket with those of his guests and asked a slave to pull one dagger from the basket.

The first dagger belonged to Muhtar Bey, a man of about fifty who had already been to a bedroom with his companion girl. He happily jumped up and with the encouragement of the rest of the guests, left the main hall.

When Muhtar Bey entered the dark fragrant bedroom, he found Alexandra on her back on the bed. Being a crude man, he did not waste any time in foreplay. He roughly removed her gown, pushed her legs apart, and entered her. In less than one minute, he was finished. He pulled up his pants and went back to the hall triumphantly to the applause of his friends.

Renaldo's dagger was pulled from the basket next. Renaldo did not hide his enthusiasm. He told his guests that he would

403

be gone for some time and they should continue to enjoy themselves. They leered knowingly.

By the time Renaldo reached the bedroom, the slave women had already cleaned up the bed and Alexandra was a little drunk on the wine she had been forced to drink. Renaldo was gentle with her. He spoke to her softly in Greek and gently removed her gown. He skillfully caressed her body, starting with her earlobes and continuing with her firm nipples.

Renaldo was a master of arousing women. Within a few minutes, she began to respond despite herself. Renaldo continued caressing her gently with his experienced hands. He tenderly opened her legs and inserted himself into her. Years of experience had taught Renaldo how to make women passionate. He was a master of slow penetration, which would make the women want more, and more. Unlike the crude Ottoman before him, Renaldo knew how to control himself and elongate the session.

His technique soon had its desired effect. Because of the wine and Renaldo's expertise, Alexandra's body betrayed her. Her knees tightened around Renaldo's. She let out a series of subdued moans and had multiple orgasms with such intensity that she was soon a spent force. She went limp; her eyes glossed over.

Renaldo grinned wickedly and muttered out aloud, "Even a duchess could not resist this old fox."

After Renaldo, other men possessed Alexandra. She was now a used property and after the last guest, Renaldo sent her to the servant's quarters for the servants and the slaves to have fun with her.

Way after midnight, Renaldo's guests eventually left. He told them to take their companions if they wanted to and some of them did. Renaldo, who was by now quite happily drunk, took his young serving attendants to his bedroom and soon the house fell quiet.

After her horrible ordeal at the hands of the Ottomans and the servants, Alexandra was dumped into the slaves' quarter. An older woman by the name of Zephyra, who had recognized her, took it upon herself to clean her and comfort her. Alexandra was still in a state of shock and in the morning, when the effects of the alcohol wore off and she finally realized where she was and what had happened to her, she went completely berserk and tried to kill herself by cutting her wrists.

The other woman calmed her down. For a while, Alexandra sat in a corner whimpering, and then she tried to hang herself. Again, Zephyra saved her. Later that day, Zephyra removed the bracelet from Alexandra's wrist and gave it to Renaldo's personal servant as a bribe to leave Alexandra alone.

CHAPTER FORTY-SEVEN

REWARD FOR A TRAITOR

After a few more days of waiting for an opportunity to strike at Renaldo and escape from Constantinople, Rodrigo asked Alexis if he wanted to accompany them to Rome. Alexis, whose family had been slaughtered during the invasion of the city, was very grateful and said that he would follow Rodrigo to the end of the world.

By now, it was possible to purchase many goods in the city. Muslim merchants had taken over the businesses of the murdered or enslaved Greeks. Rodrigo gave Alexis some money and told him to buy three large horses and a smaller horse or a pony. The pony would carry their supplies, since Rodrigo did not like mules. That afternoon, a half-shaved Muslim with rotten teeth delivered the animals. They corralled the horses in the yard behind the mansion and waited for nightfall.

Around ten o'clock that night, Rodrigo and Zangi went back to Renaldo's house. The mansion's massive door was closed and no guards were visible outside. Constantinople was already in Turkish hands so the conquerors did not feel the need to protect themselves against a vanquished enemy.

Rodrigo and Zangi hid in an alcove of an old ruin and watched until activity ceased in the house and the master had gone to bed.

Then Zangi used the rope with a grappling hook that they had prepared that afternoon to climb the wall. Within a few minutes, he opened the door to let Rodrigo in. Rodrigo walked past the lifeless body of the servant who had guarded the front door from inside and together he and Zangi quietly made their way to the second floor. This building was similar to their own mansion so they knew where the master bedroom would be located. Zangi silently sneaked into the room in which Renaldo's bodyguard was sleeping. Soon, he was back, wiping clean the blade of his dagger on the curtains. They then crept into Renaldo's bedroom.

Renaldo, who had just retired, was noisily engaged in an act of sex with one of his new slaves. His back was to the door and he was in the throes of passion. The frightened young girl, perhaps no older than twelve, who was on her back suffering Renaldo's poundings, saw them. But before she could say a word, Rodrigo motioned her to be silent.

They slowly crept forward and pulled the satin sheet away from Renaldo's naked body. It was only then that Renaldo turned and saw that his nightmare of nightmares had come true. He pulled out of the girl, who quickly got up. She was covered with bruises. Rodrigo told her to go outside and wait for them.

Renaldo was so frightened that he lost control of his bladder. "Please have mercy, please forgive me. I did not want to hurt you!" he cried.

Zangi had his sharp dagger out, ready to cut Renaldo's throat. With his right hand, Rodrigo waved him away. "First, I want to know where your money is," he said.

"There," Renaldo said, pointing to a chest in the corner of the room.

Rodrigo continued, "I have been wondering why any man would throw his lot in with those Asian savages." With his temper rising, he went on, "This was a civilized city. Why did you and your masters rape and murder the old, the young, the infants, and even the pregnant mothers for no reason at all? Did you enjoy it? They were not enemy combatants. They just wanted to live in peace."

Renaldo had no answer. He stammered his request for mercy and suddenly tried to make a run for the door. Zangi kicked him in his unprotected testicles, which made him howl in pain and drop to the floor. Zangi dragged him back to the bed.

Rodrigo motioned for Zangi to hold Renaldo down. He then took his own stiletto out. With its sharp point he, pierced Renaldo's skin two inches to the right side of his navel. Renaldo cringed and a few drops of blood oozed out. Rodrigo hesitated for a moment. Zangi, seeing Rodrigo's reluctance, asked, "Signor, do you want me to do it?"

Rodrigo was not afraid of blood and he knew what a monster Renaldo had turned out to be, but Renaldo was defenseless now. Rodrigo closed his eyes, took a deep breath, and pushed the stiletto deep into Renaldo's belly. Renaldo screamed in agony. Rodrigo twisted the blade and cut a ten-inch semi-circle all the way to the left side of Renaldo's navel.

He pulled out the bloody knife. Renaldo was in pain but Zangi's powerful hands held him down. Pointing to Renaldo's abdomen, Rodrigo said, "A gut wound like this will not kill you right away. In fact, the pain might go away after a few hours. You will last perhaps a week, or maybe two. There is no remedy for a stomach wound like this, since your intestines are all cut up and cannot be resewn. I once saw a man in Spain who had received a gut shot from a musket. His flesh became putrid and his feces came out of his stomach, attracting flies and maggots. You will die while you are being eaten alive by the worms and flies and the germs that will make you sick. Eventually, gangrene will set in. You know that you will die. I am doing this for Jean and the emperor, who died fighting, for Zangi and for all my friends. But most of all, it is for me.

"Now, Zangi will cut your tongue off so you cannot tell them who did this to you. He will also cut your fingers off so you cannot write with them. We are going to give you a taste of the Oriental torture that you were so proud of."

A horrified Renaldo said, "Please have mercy! On my children's head I promise I will not tell them about you." Rodrigo strode to the door as Zangi pull out his dagger.

The young Greek girl was still waiting for them outside. She stammered, "Alexandra" and pointed downstairs. It dawned on Rodrigo that she might be trying to tell them where Alexandra was being held captive.

They followed the young girl down to a small dark room, where they found Alexandra squatting in a corner, pale and haggard, and mumbling to herself. The older woman Zephyra approached them and explained what had happened to Alexandra.

During the last few days, Rodrigo had seen too many scenes of cruelty to be surprised any more. He asked Zephyra to get the senior Greek slave. Zephyra fetched Korolos, a man over fifty, who had been a courtier in the court of Constantine and was now a slave. Renaldo had purchased Korolos to use him as a tutor for his children. Korolos knew what had happened to Alexandra.

Rodrigo asked him if there were Muslim or Turkish servants in the household. Korolos responded that since Zangi and Rodrigo had already killed two of them, the Greeks had killed the other two as soon as they found out about Renaldo's fate.

Rodrigo suggested that instead of escaping, the Greek slaves should stay in the mansion and tell any visitors that Renaldo had gone hunting. People did disappear during hunting trips and, in time, people might even forget about Renaldo. Perhaps, the Greeks could stay in the mansion indefinitely.

They would have to get rid of the Turks' bodies and when Renaldo died, they would have to dump his corpse somewhere else in the city.

Korolos said, "I agree with you and I also think that you should take the duchess with you. If she could go to Italy, she could become a rallying point for the Greeks and it would give them hope to live and maybe one day rise up again and fight the Ottomans." Korolos nervously fidgeted for a moment and with his head bowed he added, "It shames me to say this, but some of the Greek slaves assaulted her too. So it would be difficult to keep her in this household."

Rodrigo did not want to take a half-crazed woman on a hazardous journey but he felt sorry for her and did not want her to fall into Turkish hands again.

Rodrigo gave most of the money from Renaldo's chest to Korolos and left the mansion with Zangi and Alexandra in tow.

The elegant, attractive duchess of a few days ago was no more. She had lost her husband and her children in a matter of days. After repeated rapes, she had difficulty walking. Zangi picked her up and carried her on his strong back.

Hagia Sophia. Note the four minarets that
were added after the capture of the city.

Interior of the Hagia Sophia today

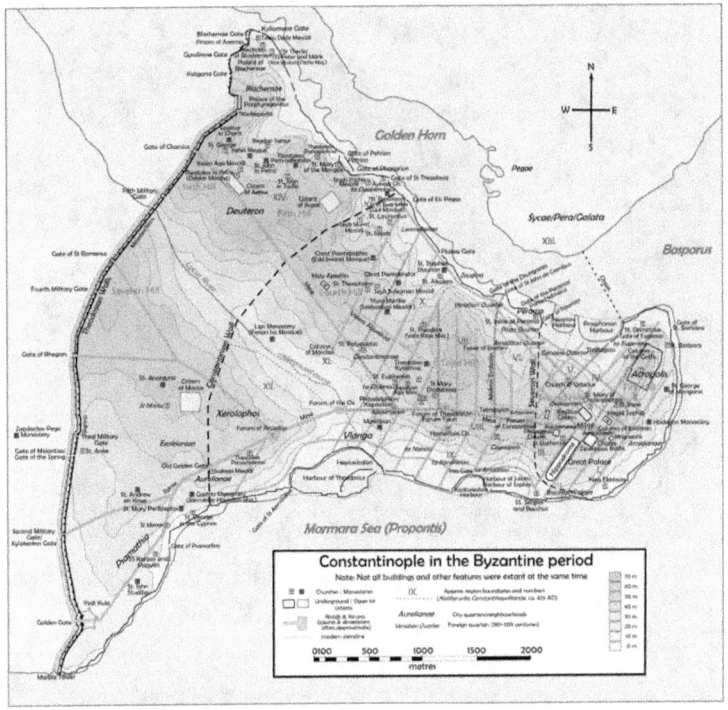

Map of Constantinople at the time of invasion. Note the location of
Kerkoporta Gate and the Blachernae Palace in the upper left.

Mosaic of Hagia Sophia dating back to the
Middle Ages before the conquest by the Ottomans

Ottoman emperor and his army

Rodrigo Borgia as Pope Alexander VI

Fig. 370.—Gipsies Fortune-telling.—Fac-simile of a Woodcut in the "Cosmographie Universelle" of Munster: in folio, Basle, 1552.

Woodcut of Gypsy fortune-tellers in Medieval Europe.

Note the bear training in the background.

Cardinal Alfonso Borgia became Pope Callixtus III

CHAPTER FORTY-EIGHT

ESCAPE FROM HELL

Rodrigo and Zangi had no choice but to carry Alexandra all the way back to their mansion. Alexis was anxiously awaiting their return and after seeing Alexandra in her frail condition, he fell on his knees, kissed her hands, and brought her some hot soup.

She did not want to eat but Alexis told her how the Ottomans had butchered his own family and that he was going to go with Rodrigo so he could fight the infidel sultan. The thought of vengeance and retribution seemed to give Alexandra the will to live. She drank some soup and a cup of wine; put her head against the wall and, for the first time in many days, fell into a deep if fitful sleep.

They all knew that they had to leave Constantinople soon. Their mansion belonged to the sultan now and as such, Mohammed would assign it to a new Turkish owner. They were also wary of spies in the city. Even the Muslim merchant who had sold the horses to them could be reporting on them at this very moment. Rodrigo decided to leave at dawn. They gathered up their belongings that night and prepared to depart.

When it came time to mount the horses, they realized that the duchess had never ridden a horse before. She had ridden sidesaddle, but this was no county tournament. They did not have sidesaddles, and in any case, it would look odd to leave a Muslim city with a woman sitting sidesaddle on a horse.

To solve their problem, Rodrigo decided to mount the horse first and have Alexandra sit in front of him. To prevent her from falling off or jumping off—since they were not still sure about her mental state—Rodrigo instructed Zangi to tie them together at the waist. To make her look inconspicuous, they gave her some plain clothes to wear.

It was early June and the sun would rise at half past four in the morning. They started their trip just before four; riding slowly lest they attract attention. They reached the Golden Gate, which was now open to traffic, as the sky was beginning to glow by the light of early dawn.

Before leaving Constantinople, Lorenzo had drawn a rough map for Rodrigo. There were two possible routes to Salonica: the coastal road that they had taken previously and a road that wound through the mountainous badlands. On the direct coastal road, the journey to Salonica would take two young men traveling alone a week or so. The other road would roughly double their travel time but reduce their risk of capture. Either way, Duchess Alexandra was sure to slow their progress.

Rodrigo was inclined to use the safer, more remote road but he wanted to see the traffic and the conditions for himself before making a final decision. They had bought enough provisions to last for quite some time and were not worried about food, water, and wine.

There were no guards to be seen at the Golden Gate. The bulk of the Ottoman army was encamped outside the Wall and the city was well protected. Rodrigo led them gingerly passed rows and rows of Ottoman tents. The soldiers were either still sleep or getting up for their dawn prayers. What Rodrigo had never noticed before was the particular stench of an army camp. During battles, the smell of gunpowder and sulfur covered the odor. But since the hostilities had ceased, the reek of raw sewage, human sweat, the decaying flesh of the dead and injured, and stale cooking hung in the morning air.

The rear of the campground was given over to the camp followers. Here were the tents of the harlots, the families of the soldiers, and the scoundrels who followed every camp. Drunken soldiers who had passed out were sleeping by the side of road.

Eventually, they left the campsite behind and turned on to the coastal road to Tekirdag. The coastal road was busy with carpetbaggers moving in and soldiers laden with booty and slaves moving out. Rodrigo decided to stay on that coastal road instead of taking the long road through the countryside. He reasoned that people would assume they were Christian renegades who were going home and Alexandra was their slave. Nevertheless, it was hard for Rodrigo to look at the long lines of young and old slaves trudging behind their new masters.

That night, they stopped at a little inn just off the road. There was only one unoccupied room available. It would have looked suspicious if they let Alexandra, who was supposed to be a slave, stay by herself in the room. Besides, Rodrigo was worried that she might try to commit suicide again. He took the room for himself and his slave and the other two slept outside. It was June and the night was quite warm anyway.

Rodrigo led the docile woman to the room, which had only one bed. She had lost all her will to fight. Later, when she wanted to go to the bathroom, Rodrigo followed her and stood outside waiting for her. Ismat, the wily Turkish proprietor, grinned knowingly at Rodrigo and said, "Don't worry, my friend, she cannot run far. We always keep an eye out for the slaves of our customers."

Ismat was eager to hear about the battle. Rodrigo, pretending to be a renegade knight at the service of the sultan, spoke about the big gun and the heroics of Christians and Muslims fighting together to free the city from the Greeks. He knew all the details, of course, but changed the story to please the Turkish owner. Ismat asked if Zangi was Rodrigo's slave also. Rodrigo responded that he was but he was tame and had no place to go. Alexis was his personal servant, he said.

Ismat smirked again and pointing to Alexandra said, "Listen my friend, give her few lashes every now and then and she will soon be tame also."

Rodrigo took Alexandra back to the room. It was getting warm so he took his outer clothing off and told her to do the same. She really was an attractive woman with a very youthful body. Rodrigo hated to tie her to the bed to stop her from running away or trying to kill both of them, but he had no choice. He told her to get into the bed and tied her hands to the bedposts loosely so she could move but not get away. He very gently told her that she would be safe. Then he covered her limp body, took one of the pillows, and stretched out on the floor with his feet against the door. Soon, they were both asleep.

He got up at dawn the following day. Alexandra was still asleep and must have had a restless night since the covers were pushed aside, revealing her tantalizing curves and creamy white flesh. Rodrigo could see trauma bruises all over her body. He covered her and left the room.

The journey to Salonica took another five days. After the first two days, Alexandra began to acknowledge Rodrigo and Zangi and began the long process of facing the facts. The physical healing had started and her bruises were getting paler but the mental healing would take much longer. She started to eat voluntarily and drank some wine since water was not very safe. After the third night, Rodrigo did not tie her hands anymore but still slept by the door and kept all sharp instruments out of her reach. He was not sure that she was any less insane now than when they had rescued her from the clutches of Renaldo.

Then, two nights before they reached Salonica, it happened. It was about two in the morning and Rodrigo was fast asleep, dreaming of happier times, when he felt her weight upon him. He opened his eyes and in the dim light of the candles he had left burning, he saw her face, colored beetroot red with insane passion. She licked his face and asked him to have sex with her, moaning that she was a whore and a slut and she needed to be treated as such. She rubbed her naked body against his loins, moaning wildly.

Rodrigo thought to himself, "Why now?"

Nevertheless, she was going wild and he had to stop her. He slapped her hard across the face several times and told her to control herself. She suddenly broke down, collapsed on top of him, burying her face against his chest, and sobbed like a wounded animal. Rodrigo gently stroked her hair and whispered words of comfort to her. She cried hard, uttering almost incoherent sentences about the tragedies of her life, until his shirt was almost drenched with her tears. Eventually, she fell silently asleep on his chest. When Rodrigo woke up, it was daylight and the sun was shining through the window. Alexandra lay naked next to him with her arms wrapped around him. He gently extricated himself, covered her, and left the room to get some breakfast.

He ran into the proprietor, who snickered sarcastically and said, "We all heard the noises from your room. Did she enjoy it when you gave her a taste of your manhood?" Rodrigo wanted to hit the man across his rotten mouth but controlled himself and smiled back through gritted teeth.

The episode of that night seemed to bring some normalcy back to Alexandra. She did not fully remember the events of the night and was somewhat surprised to wake up naked, on the floor next to the door. She was not even sure whether something had happened between the two of them but she was much more relaxed. For the first time, she managed a weak smile.

Two days later, they were in Salonica, which had been a major Greek port for many centuries. The city was now under Turkish control but most of the populace was Greek. There was also a large population of Jewish immigrants who had escaped from Spain as the fanatical Catholics took over, pushing out the enlightened Muslim rulers.

Alexis had distant relatives in Salonica and was dispatched to find a safe haven for them.

Salonica, a hilly town with a long harbor, had been a major port of trade for landlocked Bulgarians and Hungarians to the north since ancient times. At the time of Rodrigo's visit, Salonica had been in Turkish hands for less than thirty years, yet there was already a sizeable population of Muslims in the city.

They found a large house overlooking the harbor, where they could wait for a ship that would take them to Italy, or at least to Dubrovnik. Zangi and Alexis shared one room and Rodrigo and Alexandra had their own private bedchambers. Rodrigo paid a month's rent in gold.

In Salonica, Rodrigo posed as a wealthy merchant from Italy who was on his way back to Venice along with his wife and personal servants. They hired two women to do the housekeeping and cooking, although Alexandra proved to be a very good cook herself.

They had been in town for about three weeks, when one afternoon, a troubled Alexandra asked to talk to Rodrigo in private. She explained that she had morning sickness and she feared that she was pregnant with the child of one of her ravishers. Candidly, she said she did not want to keep it since she believed it was the child of Lucifer. Rodrigo was afraid that she might try to commit suicide again, so he had to find a way to help her. Rodrigo knew that abortion had been a fact of human life from before biblical times. Wives who got pregnant while their husbands were away or unmarried daughters or sisters who were seduced or raped had to find a way to get rid of their unwanted babies. The alternatives were dishonor to the families and possibly death for the women by stoning. Therefore, there had always been abortion providers who could step in and perform their work for gold.

Rodrigo remembered that his father used to say that Jewish doctors and surgeons were the best in their fields. He was reluctant to visit the Jewish quarter of Salonica since he was Spanish and worried that they would hate him for what the Catholic invaders had done to them.

Contrary to his expectations, the Jews received him warmly and it felt good to speak in his native tongue. Eventually, after making some tactful inquiries, he found a Dr. Ephraim and put his case to him openly. The doctor explained that he did not perform abortions himself but he could tell Rodrigo how to proceed.

There were three methods of aborting a fetus, Dr. Ephraim explained. The first choice was to digest semi-poisonous herbs that would kill and abort the baby during the early stages of pregnancy. A different method was for the pregnant woman to exercise violently or allow herself to be hit repeatedly in the stomach with heavy objects. The final method was inducing an abortion by inserting a long serrated metal object to abort the fetus and clean the interior of the womb. All of these methods were dangerous.

The doctor gave Rodrigo a mixture of herbs and told him to have Alexandra boil and strain them and drink a glass of the liquid every morning on an empty stomach for seven days, and then maintain a fast until mid-day. He warned Rodrigo not to exceed the dose because it would kill her.

Alexandra followed the instructions. The juice tasted vile and it gave her terrible headaches. While she was taking the liquid poison, she found a wooden mallet and repeatedly struck her own belly with it, as well. She tried jumping down from the bed and landing on her stomach but none of those methods aborted the unwanted fetus.

Rodrigo took another trip to the Jewish quarter and asked Dr. Ephraim for help. The doctor, after warning him about the dangers one more time, said he knew of a midwife who could perform abortions and would send her to their home the following day.

To keep the operation a secret from his friends and the servants, he sent Alexis and Zangi to check on the condition of the roads going north and gave the day off to the servants.

Monavar, the Jewish midwife, arrived at ten in the morning. She was a woman in her forties and wore the Jewish costume of long pantaloons and a headscarf. She examined Alexandra thoroughly and confirmed that she was with child. Rodrigo asked her if she could get rid of it.

Monavar looked puzzled. She wondered why a husband would want to get rid of his own child. Rodrigo did not offer an explanation and asked her again if she could perform the operation. Monavar said that she could and asked Rodrigo to leave the room.

Before leaving, Rodrigo whispered in Greek to Alexandra, asking if she still wanted to go ahead with the operation. Her response was emphatic. Rodrigo hugged her and, to keep up appearances, kissed her on the lips before leaving. This was their first kiss.

Rodrigo stood outside the door and listened in while Monavar took out her crooked metal instrument with its jagged edge, inserted it inside Alexandra, and first destroyed the fetus and then scraped her womb clean. It was over within half an hour. She gave some opiate capsules to Rodrigo for Alexandra's pain, took the gold coins, and was gone.

Rodrigo went back into the room. Alexandra was in tears of pain and guilt. He hugged her and gave her one of the tablets with a glass of wine.

For the next two days, Alexandra survived on opiate capsules and Rodrigo's affection. The bleeding eventually stopped and she regained her health.

Alexandra gradually got over some of her grief. She would still burst into tears unexpectedly while eating dinner with the men or weep quietly alone in her bedroom at night. As far as the servants and the neighbors knew, Rodrigo and Alexandra were husband and wife and, as such, they had to keep up the appearance in public. Gradually, a friendly bond developed between the two. Every now and then, they would laugh together and Rodrigo would give her little hugs as a gesture of support and friendship.

After six weeks of living as man and wife, it had become difficult for them to control the affection that was developing between them. One morning, while walking around the house, Rodrigo noticed that Alexandra was sad and tearful. He approached her and tried to comfort her. She put her perfume-scented red head on his chest, held him tight, and sobbed for a few minutes. Then she looked up at his big brown eyes. He lowered his face, their lips met, and it felt like their first kiss ever. The kiss lingered, becoming more passionate. She could feel his arousal through her dress and was herself in no better shape.

Before Renaldo and his friends ravaged her, she had not had a sexual relationship with her husband or any other man for many years and now her long suppressed sexuality flared within her. Rodrigo had not had a woman for over two months now and he was about to lift her off her toes and carry her to the bedroom when they heard a servant return from shopping. They disengaged quickly and tried to act normal.

The servant, a woman of about Alexandra's age, smiled and gave a knowing wink when she saw her blushing.

Alexandra dreaded the time that they would have to leave all of this behind and board a ship for Italy. Some nights, Rodrigo wanted to go to her room and possess her body and soul. Alexandra often woke up and listened for a knock at her bedroom door.

It was easier for Rodrigo to handle his sexual frustration. Soon, he found Ruth, a Jewish courtesan, with whom he relieved his pent up passion. The first time that he coupled with Ruth, he was so lustful and passionate that she half jokingly asked if he had ever been with a woman before. Sadly, Alexandra found out about his relationship and became depressed and quite jealous.

After eight weeks of living in Salonica, the city had almost become their home. They had made friends and had been living as a family for what seemed like a long time.

Then one night after dinner, Zangi and Alexis went to town to visit a *taverna*, as had become their custom. Rodrigo and Alexandra were sitting together, talking about what they would do in Italy. Suddenly, she burst into tears. Rodrigo moved close to her and asked why she was crying.

Through her tears, she said, "Don't you realize why I am crying? I am scared of losing you and once we get away from here, we may never see each other again. Even though I know you are sleeping with that Jewish harlot, I will miss you so terribly. I love you more than I ever loved my husband."

Rodrigo took her small, shaking hand in his warm hands and said, "Of course, we will see each other all the time. We will be friends forever"

Before he could finish his sentence, she jumped into his arms and held him tight.

The thought went through Rodrigo's feverish mind that since they were living as husband and wife, would it be so wrong for him to discharge his conjugal duties? Tenderly, he lifted her chin up, looked into her beautiful tear-laden eyes, and kissed her. This time Rodrigo did not try to hide his arousal. He let her feel the heat and the shape of his manhood, which was trying to reach her through all their clothing.

After a while, he lifted her up, saying, "Let's be like man and wife tonight," and carried her to her bedroom. He wanted to strip her of her clothing himself and, starting with her long dress, he took her garments off piece by piece, marveling at her beauty. The last piece to come off was the lace underwear that she had bought at a local store in anticipation of such a night.

The bruises were gone. Her creamy white thighs were crowned with the fiery red rose of her pubic hair. He knelt down, kissed the red rose, and inhaled her aroma of arousal. Then he held her tightly again and kissed her passionately before disrobing himself and lying next to her. The Mediterranean night was warm and balmy and there was no need for a blanket. The lovers wrapped themselves in each other's arms, caressed, and kissed while uttering words of love and affection.

She whispered seductively, "You are my husband tonight, so do your duty." Soon, he entered that fiery red receptacle of pleasure. She pushed her pelvis hard against him as if to absorb every inch of his maleness into her hungry womb. No one was around and they were not afraid of making loud noises of passion as they consummated their love.

After it was over and they were resting next to each other, Alexandra held Rodrigo's face in her slender hands, looked into his eyes and said, "Tonight, my love, your seeds have purged and healed my body from the semen and the wounds of those evil savages. Thanks to you, I feel cleansed again."

When the first light of dawn appeared in the East, he kissed her goodnight and went to his own bedroom.

CHAPTER FORTY-NINE

RODRIGO AND THE GYPSIES

A few days after Rodrigo and Alexandra's night of passion, Alexis arrived at the house out of breath and bearing disturbing news. Apparently, the sultan's men were lurking about town and asking about them. Either the soldiers had tracked them to Salonica or they were making a wide search of the territory to make sure that they were dead or captured.

The Muslim population of Salonica was growing daily and Rodrigo feared some of the new inhabitants would discover them. He made a trip to the wharf to secure passage out of the city. There were many boats in the harbor, mostly fishing vessels.

He went back to see Dr. Ephraim and asked him if he knew of any fishermen who would take them away from Salonica. Ephraim had come to realize that unlike many Spanish noblemen, Rodrigo was not a fanatic. He had taken a liking to him. He mentioned that he knew of a fishing vessel that had helped many Jewish families who had landed in Cyprus or Crete after fleeing Spain, and wanted to get to the relative safety of Muslim lands. Somewhat relieved, Rodrigo asked to meet the captain of the boat.

The captain of the smallish vessel was a grizzly old Sicilian sea dog by the name of Armando. Armando agreed to take them as far as Candia on the Isle of Crete, which was about three hundred miles away. In Candia, which was under the control of the Venetians, they could find transportation to Venice or other ports in Italy. However, Armando warned them that during his last few trips, Ottoman sailors hunting for fugitives had boarded his boat.

In particular, Armando said, they were looking for Emperor Constantine, since his body had never been found. Rodrigo paid Armando some gold and told him that he and three of his companions would be on the wharf the following night. Armando advised him not to bring too much luggage, since the boat could not carry his crew, four passengers, and a lot of cargo.

That afternoon, Rodrigo walked around the town for a long time trying to organize his thoughts. Now that the sultan's men were closing in on him, it was tempting to get away from Salonica, but he had a nagging feeling that if Ottomans boarded Armando's boat, they would all be captured and the fragile Alexandra would be sold into slavery.

It was almost dark when he got back to the rented house. He called his friends to discuss the matter and explain his decision to them. If he went with them and they were boarded, the Turks were sure to capture and imprison all of them. However, if he stayed behind and the rest of them embarked for Candia, with Alexis posing as Alexandra's husband, suspicions would not be aroused and they would pass safely through the blockade to Candia.

No one wanted to go without him but Rodrigo insisted that it was their only chance of escape and by doing as he advised they possibly would save his life as well their own.

Alexandra cried that night as Rodrigo joined her in her bedroom for a last night in each other's arms. To Alexandra, it was the happiest and yet the saddest night of her life.

The following morning, they gathered up most of their important belongings and prepared to leave at nightfall. After dark, Rodrigo led them to the wharf and Armando's fishing boat. It was small and stank of fish. Rodrigo shook the hands of the men and hugged Alexandra as they said their farewells. Rodrigo told Armando that he would be staying behind and Zangi would pay him the balance of the fare upon their arrival in Candia. Knowing Zangi, Rodrigo was certain that he would look after Alexandra and probably would not sleep a wink until they arrived in Candia in three or four days' time.

Rodrigo watched sadly as the boat pulled away and soon disappeared into the dark horizon. He went back to the suddenly dark and desolate house. Tears pushed against his eyes and though he thought it unmanly, he wept for the loss of his friends and his loved ones.

The following morning, he went out in search of another way to leave town. He had given almost all of his gold to Zangi to ensure that they had enough money for the passage to Venice and that had left him with no money to book another passage to Venice or even Candia.

That was when he came across a Gypsy troupe performing near the western edge of the city. Peasants and poor farm laborers crowded around horse-drawn wagons, watching girls in colorful dresses dance to their companions' music. Others traded coins for Gypsy potions, talismans, and lucky charms. Rodrigo watched haggard men—possibly refugees from Constantinople—show their palms to the fortunetellers or sit with tarot card readers, praying for a ray of hope in a bleak future.

Rodrigo strolled through the throng, Gypsies offering him a glimpse of the bearded woman and the snake girl, or even a whore for a few coins.

Suddenly Rodrigo had a revelation. No one would be looking for him inside a Gypsy camp and he could use these Gypsies to get away from his Turkish pursuers.

Rodrigo asked for the headman and was introduced to a short, very dark-skinned man by the name of Laszlo. Laszlo was a man of about fifty with curly grey hair, large droopy mustache, and penetrating dark eyes. As all Gypsies did, he sported a large golden hoop earring on his right ear and several rings on his fingers.

Rodrigo came right to the point and asked if he could travel with them. Laszlo did not ask why a tall, noble looking man would want to travel with a band of Gypsies; he assumed that he was running away from something. Instead, he asked, "How much are you offering me?"

Rodrigo had only a few gold coins left and he needed that to pay the servants. He asked if instead of money, he could do some work while he traveled with them. An astonished Laszlo laughed so loudly that Rodrigo thought he might split his sides. "Obviously, you do not know anything about the Gypsies," he said, wiping his eyes and getting control of himself. "We were put on this earth by the Lord to take from people like you, not to give, and here you are asking me for a job! I never dreamed of anything like this. Except that I need a strong tall man like you to do certain work, so I am willing to take a chance on you. The work is hard and I may have to ask you to do certain things that you have never done before or may not be pleasant to you. If you still want to come with us, you must be here by tomorrow afternoon, since we will be leaving the day after tomorrow."

Rodrigo was relieved. He was not afraid of hard work.

That afternoon, Rodrigo visited Ephraim and Ruth to say farewell. He told both of his plans and they strongly advised him against getting mixed up with the Gypsies. He gave some of his money to Ruth and kissed the weeping courtesan one last time.

Next morning, he packed up a few personal belongings, paid the servants off without telling them where he was going and by lunchtime, he was gone.

Laszlo was pleased to see him. He introduced him to his wife, Florica, and his daughter, Mirela, and the others. Both the wife and daughter were attractive women. Florica, who was about thirty-two, wore a wide yellow bandana with little pink flowers on her head. Her hair was tied back with a red ribbon. She was wearing a yellow blouse with large puffy sleeves. A red shawl covered her shoulders, crossed over her chest, and was tied around her waist. She wore a long, green-striped skirt and red sandals. Several rows of gold bangles with gold coins and lucky charms decorated each wrist and she wore a long, coin-studded chain around her neck.

The girl, Mirela, was probably fourteen or fifteen years old. She had black eyes and her jet-black hair was straight and hung to her shoulders. She wore a red dress with faded white and blue flowers that covered her body to her ankles. Her feet were bare. The daughter had little jewelry on her hands and a simple silver cross around her neck.

The Turks, being superstitious, generally left the Gypsies alone. It was considered bad luck to kill a Gypsy because a curse would follow the killer and his family. Rodrigo knew that. He also knew that Gypsies generally did not marry outside the clan and yet there were always rumors of them kidnapping babies to bring up as Gypsies. The Gypsies, on the other hand, always complained that childless couples kidnapped their babies. That mutual distrust enabled Gypsies to roam the continent at will.

That night, Rodrigo dined with them. During the dinner, both women eyed the handsome figure of Rodrigo with adoration.

After dinner, Laszlo and a middle-aged man named Besnik invited Rodrigo to sit with them for a drink of the hard liquor they made from raisins. It was very potent. Two or three shots would knock most people out, Rodrigo thought. Besnik gently played the lute while they laughed and conversed. Later, Rodrigo was given a place to sleep under the wagon. The following day, the caravan pulled up tents and moved west toward the town of Edessa. Rodrigo, being the youngest and the strongest man in the outfit, helped pack and move the props, the supplies, and the other goods.

Every night, after work, Laszlo gave Rodrigo a half a bottle of the hard liquor as his wage. Since Rodrigo, depressed and lonely, had lost his appetite, he usually drank it all.

After a few days and few stops, Laszlo asked Rodrigo if he wanted more. Rodrigo had begun to enjoy the hard alcoholic drink that dulled his senses and obliterated his thoughts. He eagerly accepted the additional liquor and soon he started on the road to becoming a carnival freak.

During the day, as the menacing "Beastman," a half animal, half man with the powers of a giant and constitution of a wild beast, Rodrigo would growl like a rabid animal to scare the audience. He ate insects, worms, and people's vomit to the approving roar of paying spectators. In the finale of his act, he would pluck the feathers from a live, plump chicken and bite its head off. Soon, Rodrigo was a star attraction.

He would drink to perform his wild and disgusting duties and at night he would drink some more and pass out. People would come from afar to see him and that made Laszlo richer and happier.

Mirela, who was attracted to Rodrigo, tried to stop his descent into madness. When her parents were busy or asleep, she would come to Rodrigo and sit by his side, trying to soothe and feed him. One afternoon, she even kissed the surprised Rodrigo. He felt stirrings of emotion and love inside his half-mad body and kissed her hot lips. The young girl was now passionately in love with this handsome, unkempt, and mad stranger. She decided that he would be her future husband.

Typical Gypsy Girls

~ CHAPTER FIFTY ~

THE SEARCH FOR RODRIGO

A few months after Rodrigo's men, Aziza, and Katarina returned to Rome, Cardinal Alfonso Borgia sent a search party to look for his nephew. Lorenzo and Antonio headed this group, which included Petros.

The search party rode to Venice and took a boat to Dubrovnik. From there, they separated. One group, led by Lorenzo, went north and west all the way to Edirne; and the other, south to Athens. They found no sign of Rodrigo and came back empty-handed in June 1454.

Aziza's baby girl was born in January 1454. Aziza named her Ariadne in honor of her mother.

Late in December 1453, a distressed Duchess Alexandra had arrived in Venice with Zangi and Alexis. Francesco Foscari, the Doge, went to see her and to put his palace at her disposal.

Alexandra, weary and pregnant, soon became the focus of attention and hope of the Greek émigré community in Italy. She bore a son, whom she named Christopher, and she became a fixture of Venice's high society life. Alexis stayed with Alexandra as her faithful servant.

Alexandra sent Zangi to Cardinal Alfonso with a message informing him that Rodrigo was still alive. Zangi had an emotional reunion with Aziza and Katarina, and Rodrigo's men who had accompanied them to Rome. For the first time since he was abducted as a young boy, Zangi felt he was more important and happier now than he would have been if he had remained with his tribe.

The Cardinal and Aziza did not give up easily. In September 1454, they dispatched another group of Greek-speaking mercenaries under the leadership of Suleiman, who was a Turkish defector. Zangi went along, since they thought Rodrigo might not trust a Turk. Suleiman managed to find Rodrigo's Salonica residence and locate Dr. Ephraim and Ruth. Based on information gathered from those two, he and Zangi resolved to search every Gypsy caravan in the land for Rodrigo or news of him. Unfortunately, they missed Rodrigo's caravan even though they were very close to it.

* * *

Meanwhile, Pope Nicholas was getting weaker and closer to death.

On March 24, 1455, the saintly Pope Nicholas V died. To the end, he had insisted that Rodrigo was alive but in mortal danger. Nicholas was one of the holiest popes that the Catholic Church had ever had. Even though he did not succeed in keeping Constantinople in Christian hands, he had done his best. He had spent all of the money that was given to him personally on charitable causes and on supporting Emperor Constantine.

On April 8, 1455, less than two weeks after the death of Nicholas V, the conclave of cardinals met to elect a new pope. To everyone's' surprise, they elected Cardinal Alfonso Borgia, who was then seventy-seven years old. This surprised no one more than Cardinal Alfonso. He had not expected to live this long, let alone become a pope at this late stage in his life. Nevertheless, he accepted the honor and chose the name of Callixtus III.

As a favorite of Callixtus, his daughter-in-law, Aziza, was now an important person in Rome. She and her baby girl had free access to the pope and as he grew infirm, he relied more and more on her advice and on her actual physical help to move around. No one ever asked this Turkish princess if she was still a Muslim. Everyone assumed that she was a Christian.

The new pope sent a final team in search of Rodrigo in June 1455. The searchers even went as far east as Constantinople but they did not find any sign of Rodrigo. Pope Callixtus then assumed that his nephew had died, possibly at the hands of Gypsies.

CHAPTER FIFTY-ONE

LOVE AND LIFE AS A GYPSY

Some nights, Mirela would sneak away from their wagon to bring Rodrigo food, lie beside him, and hold him while he was passed out. Sometimes, he would come to, hug her back, and then fall asleep in her arms. She always had to go back before dawn so as not to arouse her father's suspicions. Unbeknownst to Mirela, her young mother, who had not had physical relations with her alcoholic husband for years, yearned for this stranger, too. She knew about Mirela's nightly visits and had warned her about the consequences. The Gypsies had certain codes of conduct about purity of their unmarried daughters. A girl who was not a virgin could not be married to a bachelor. This had been drilled into Mirela's head so many times since she was a child that despite the tremendous passion that she felt for Rodrigo, she never surrendered herself to him completely.

Florica regularly inspected Mirela's underwear to determine if she had had sexual relations with Rodrigo, but the relationship remained innocent. Rodrigo did not deflower Mirela.

One night after Mirela returned to the wagon, Florica, who was in heat, left the wagon and joined Rodrigo. She wore one of her secret Gypsy perfumes to make herself more desirable and tried to arouse Rodrigo by putting her hand inside his pants and caressing his member. Rodrigo soon awoke, fully aroused, next to an attractive, sweet-smelling woman. He did not need to try to seduce Florica, for as soon as he kissed her she rolled onto her back and pulled her skirt up. She was naked underneath.

Rodrigo could not see her body clearly in the darkness but he could feel the soft thighs leading to a shaved love nest. He rolled on top of her and the eager Florica took hold of his hard member and guided it in without wasting a second. He was harder than her husband was and reached deeper inside her than she had ever been reached. She had multiple orgasms and tried very hard to keep quiet.

It was not long before she felt his contractions and expansions as he inundated her, giving her the most intense orgasm she had ever had, and then fell pleasantly asleep on top of her. She gently rolled him over, got up, squatted in a corner to empty his seeds, and climbed back into the wagon to sleep next to her husband.

When she woke up in the morning, she noticed that despite her precautions, the wetness had seeped through her nightshirt onto the mattress and had left a stain of shame. Filled with remorse for breaking her marriage vows, Florica prayed and cried most of the day. She asked God for forgiveness and promised that she would remain faithful to her vows.

Over the next few weeks, Rodrigo drank more and more of the dangerous alcohol that they were feeding him. Laszlo started giving him opiate capsules to calm him down when he was in a rage. The crowds got bigger as they traveled from town to town as word of the big and mean Beastman spread. The two women looked after him as best as they could. He was getting affection from Mirela and carnal pleasures from Florica, who, despite her vows, could not contain her passionate desires and soon became pregnant with his seed. Mirela found out about her mother's nightly visits and was scared that her father would kill her and Rodrigo with his razor-sharp dagger if he ever found out.

Cuckold Gypsy husbands slit the throats of their errant wives and buried them on the side of the road.

After a few months, Rodrigo had been transformed into a wild, addicted animal with almost no memory of his past.

In the weeks and months that followed, the Gypsies traveled throughout the Balkans. They went as far north as Skopje, then to Sofia in Bulgaria, and eventually traveled south towards Athens to spend the winter in the warmer climate of southern Greece.

It was early spring and they were camped near Patrai on the Ionian Sea about eighty miles west of Athens. Laszlo was getting drunk every night and a few times, he had hit his wife and daughter. Rodrigo had always abhorred violence against women and even in his drunken stupor, he would try to stop Laszlo's violence. Even though Rodrigo worked for Laszlo, Laszlo was rather intimidated by the tall, powerful man who was becoming more and more important.

Then one night as Laszlo was climbing down from the wagon to relieve himself he fell down hard on his right ankle and fractured it. Florica was under another wagon a few yards away with Rodrigo inside her. They disengaged when they heard his cry and Rodrigo lifted Laszlo back up to the wagon.

The injury was slow to heal properly and it became obvious that Laszlo could not continue as the head of the clan. Normally, Besnik would have succeeded him, but he was too infirm to keep intruders away from the clan. Florica suggested that they elect Rodrigo to lead them. She was hopeful that he would look after her, her daughter and her invalid husband so they would not starve.

The problem was that Rodrigo had been driven half-mad by the alcohol and the drugs he consumed every day. If it had not been for the tireless efforts of Florica and Mirela, who cajoled him to eat and emptied his liquor bottle when he was sleep, he would have been dead or completely mad by now, as Beastmen before him. Besnik told Florica that the only thing to do was to force him to stop drinking and taking drugs at once. In Rodrigo's advanced case, a gradual withdrawal would not work.

It was now early summer. It had been a long time since a youthful Rodrigo had left Rome on his mission. One fine day, Florica, Mirela, and Besnik took Rodrigo on a short trip to a secluded spot close to the beach. There, after Rodrigo had fallen sleep under the wagon, they tied his hands and feet and pegged them to the ground. When Rodrigo woke up, he could not move. He called Florica, who came running with some sherbet. He refused it. Soon, he needed a fix, which they refused to give him. When he shouted for alcohol, they gave him some wine that, at first, he spat out but then grudgingly swallowed.

That night, Rodrigo had the worst nightmare of his life, even though he was awake. First, he was itching all over but he could not move his hands because they were tied. Then, he had visions of cold slimy snakes attacking him and rats nibbling at his genitals. The rats gnawed at his entrails and maggots ate his raw intestines, just as he had imagined they would do to Renaldo. Ants crawled through his eyes into his brain and built a nest there.

Giant leeches attached themselves to his lips and he feared that if he opened his mouth they would get inside and eat his tongue. He was covered with cockroaches and he felt centipedes marching into his ears and tunneling into his brain. Then a black crow appeared above his head with its beak aimed at his eyes. He tried to close them tightly but he could not. He screamed but his voice would not come out of his throat. He was at the bottom of a well and could not get out. He was buried alive, scratching at the lid of his coffin, and he could see mourners talking and smiling as they left the cemetery, oblivious to his silent screams. This went on all night long.

Mirela sat by his side all night, applying cold water to his brow and talking to him of anything that came to her head, hoping that she would be the one link that would save him from insanity and madness. For three days and nights, Rodrigo went through the nightmares of a madman, trying to kick the habits of alcohol and drugs. He was ready to die. He asked the Lord God to forgive him and take him away, but the nightmares went on.

During the first two days, they gave him wine to keep him from having a seizure or sudden death. After the second day, they offered him plenty of broth and soft food.

By the fifth day, he was too weak to scream anymore and his nightmares were less violent. He recognized his companions and even tried to talk Mirela into giving him some alcohol. Mirela refused. Even if she had wanted to give him a drink, none was around. He started to shake and they covered him with woolen blankets. For five days, he had defecated and relieved himself in his pants involuntarily. The stench was overpowering for Besnik and the women, but they stayed with him.

On the sixth day, they allowed him to sit up while still tied up and fed him some solid food. By the seventh day, Besnik told the women that if he were not cured by then, he would never be. When they released Rodrigo, he was too weak to walk by himself. The day was not very warm, but Florica and Besnik walked him to the sea, where they let him cleanse himself. Mirela boiled water from a nearby stream. They threw his old clothes away and Mirela stood back while Besnik and Florica helped Rodrigo put on some Gypsy clothing.

They then fed him and let him sleep in the wagon. For the next three days, they nursed him attentively until he was strong enough to walk by himself. One day, Florica pierced Rodrigo's right earlobe and inserted a piece of silk thread, which would be replaced by the Gypsy earring of authority. After twelve days, they drove back to the camp.

Laszlo was happy to see them again and within a week, Rodrigo was strong enough to take charge of the clan without being challenged by anyone. Laszlo took off his large golden earring and Florica put it on Rodrigo to announce his status as the new leader of the band. Within a few weeks, they started moving again, zigzagging north and west all the way up the Greek peninsula and into the Balkans. Laszlo, who needed a cane to move around, was happy to have Rodrigo in charge and now that he did not have to worry about handling the affairs of the clan, he drank even more. Besnik was content since, as Rodrigo's counselor, he could maintain his position as an elder. The pregnant Florica was pleased because she still had her family together and she still could meet Rodrigo to quench her thirst for passion. Mirela was grateful that Rodrigo was around and she could look after him.

Gradually, Rodrigo remembered his past life. By now, he assumed, his loved ones and friends had made landfall in Italy and were safe from the sultan. He did not think they would care about him anymore, especially now that he was a Gypsy in all manner and form. Therefore, he decided to be satisfied with his lot.

Near the end of July 1455, a son was born to Laszlo and Florica. They named him Janos in honor of Laszlo's father. The birth was cause for celebration for the band of Gypsies. Laszlo now had an heir and being traditionalists, they all reveled in the fact that life would go on as before. Only Florica knew that Rodrigo was the real father, for Laszlo was an old man and a drunk who seldom had intimate relations with his wife, and when he did, he would often climax before making an entry.

Janos was strong, handsome, and healthy. Mirela suspected that her new brother was Rodrigo's son but kept the idea to herself. Even Besnik suspected as much, but as in any monarchy, the truth of the child's parentage is less important than acceptance. If the populace accepts a man as a king, then he is the king despite the fact that he may be the illegitimate son of a courtier who had an affair with the queen—or in this case, the son of a Beastman who slept with the clan leader's wife.

That summer was one of the nicest summers that Rodrigo had ever had. He was in charge and he had Florica and Mirela who adored him. The clan members respected his leadership and strength, the carnival was successful, and everyone was making money. There were very few troublemakers in the audiences with Rodrigo around. Most people would look at his imposing height and broad shoulders, his drooping Gypsy mustache and the large golden earring, and would back off from causing a disturbance. The few who did not, took broken bones home.

Rodrigo still acted as the strong man who performed feats of might but he did perform disgusting acts such as eating live chickens. This time around, they did not enter Salonica or Edessa, since Laszlo did not want Rodrigo to remember his past and be tortured by it.

By now, Laszlo was happy to have a boy of his own and ignored Florica's infidelity, since he did not have the sexual desire or the physical ability to challenge Rodrigo. By January of 1456, they moved back to southern Greece to camp near the Ionian Sea for the winter. This had been a very successful year and the clan celebrated it in honor or Rodrigo, who had been their ramrod during the last season.

As hot as that summer had been, the winter of 1456 was one of the worst on record. The Gypsies moved as far south on the Greek Peninsula as they could to avoid the cold weather. Then when the spring arrived, the dreaded plague followed.

The Gypsy colony was hit hard. One by one, they died. Laszlo was one of first to go, followed by Florica. In just a few weeks, the clan of fifty was reduced to twenty. Rodrigo, Mirela, the baby Janos and, strangely enough, old man Besnik survived the plague. The tribe could not function as a carnival any longer. As a group, they decided to break up and go their separate ways.

For Rodrigo, it was sad to say good-bye to people who had looked up to him as a leader and a provider since Laszlo's accident. Rodrigo, who had been happy as a Gypsy, decided it was time to return to Italy and salvage what he could of his old life. In addition to his son Janos and Mirela, he decided to take Besnik along with him, since he knew that the old man would not survive without them.

So, it was on a sunny day in late April 1456 that Rodrigo, looking very much like a Gypsy with his turban, long flowing robe, large drooping mustache, and the large golden earring, sold all their belongings except Besnik's lute and headed for Athens, hoping to find a ship to take them to Venice.

CHAPTER FIFTY-TWO

HOME AT LAST

Mirela did not want to sell her mother's bangles and gold necklaces but they had no choice, not that she would disobey Rodrigo, who was the head of the household.

They bought some bread and cheese, dried meat, dried fruit, and nuts and boarded the *Star of Candia*, a Venetian merchant ship bound for Candia in Crete and then on to Venice. They had to sleep on the deck, since this was primarily a cargo ship and did not have room for passengers. Besides, they could not afford a cabin. The journey to Candia took only a few days and then they were off to Venice.

Rodrigo did not know what awaited them in Venice, or in Italy, for that matter. During those days at sea, he assumed that his uncle, Cardinal Alfonso, was dead by now and he hoped that Aziza had survived and had a place to live and raise their child. "What about Zangi and Alexandra?" he thought. He was hopeful that they had made it, too. Would he ever find his loved ones and his friends? And if he did, how would they receive him? Little did he know of tremendous efforts that the cardinal and his friends had made to find him.

Mirela, with Janos in her arms, was beside him most of the time. She had matured under the sudden pressure of losing her parents and having to look after the little boy. Her bosoms had firmed up and she had grown an inch or two. She was even more in love with Rodrigo now and ached to surrender herself to him. She would lie awake at night, under the star-filled skies, and dream about what it would feel like to have him inside her hungry womb. On several occasions, she had spied on her sexually aroused mother moaning with pleasure under Rodrigo.

Usually, Janos slept between Rodrigo and Mirela, and Besnik slept a few feet away on Rodrigo's other side.

When they were only two days from Venice, Mirela decided it was her last chance to quench her unrequited love for Rodrigo. She planned her move. She slipped some of the sleep potion, which her mother used to make and sell to people, to Besnik during the evening meal to make sure that he would sleep soundly. She waited until everyone was fast sleep. They were now in the Adriatic Sea, which was quite safe from pirates and the Turkish naval forces. The seas were calm and no one was on deck other than the sleeping passengers and the lonely helmsman.

It was about midnight. Mirela had removed her underclothing earlier and wore only a long dress. She picked up the purse that held the white linen handkerchief that her mother had given her when she had her first period. It was the custom that she would use that handkerchief on her wedding night to wipe away the blood from the loss of her hymen. It would be proof to her husband and the rest of the world that she was pure and untouched on her marriage bed.

The tingling in her loins was intense and unrelenting. It was now or never. Mirela very gently climbed over Janos and moved next to Rodrigo, who was having a bad dream. Mirela kissed his unshaven face quietly and very carefully untied the cord that held his linen pants together. She reached inside and felt his limp manhood. She stroked him gently and lovingly. Within a few minutes, Rodrigo, still sleep, was aroused. She pulled her long dress up to her waist and put his right hand on her throbbing organ. Rodrigo was soon half-awake. He was dreaming of Aziza and in the darkness did not realize who was lying beside him. He responded passionately to her kisses on that balmy night and pushed her onto her back.

Mirela did not need any prodding. She had waited for this moment since she had met Rodrigo two years ago. She opened her legs wide for him. Rodrigo mounted her and while kissing her, guided himself toward her opening. She was drenching wet with desire but even so, the entry was not easy. He groped and pushed hard but it was not successful. He was awake now and ashamed of himself. He withdrew quickly, not realizing that it was not his fault, and apologized to a frustrated Mirela, whose desire had not been satisfied. She was still a virgin and angry with Rodrigo for failing to give her the supreme pleasure that she sought from her lover.

* * *

They were in Venice two days later. Three Gypsies with a young baby boy landing in Venice did not attract anyone's attention. They were hungry and needed something to eat. Rodrigo had only a few Ottoman silver coins left. Seeking food for Janos and Besnik, he approached a street vendor to buy some bread. The vendor rudely asked to see his money first and refused the silver coins. Sudden anger flared up inside the exhausted and short-tempered Rodrigo. He could not even feed his family, and like a Gypsy, he pulled out his knife and struck the man across the face.

They were arrested and he was badly beaten before being thrown into prison. The Venetians did not have dungeons, since the city was built on water. So, prisoners were housed above ground in a jail, which was adjacent to the doge's palace.

Rodrigo was imprisoned there for three months before his case came before a Venetian magistrate. Meanwhile, Mirela, Janos, and Besnik had been released and were supporting themselves by begging and selling Gypsy charms in the streets. They tried to visit Rodrigo every day to bring him some food. Some days they were allowed to see him. It was then that Rodrigo understood the bond of loyalty had held the Gypsies together for centuries and the depth of Mirela's love for him.

Since Rodrigo had an accent, the Venetian judge, Signor Fantini, did not realize that he was a Spanish nobleman and assumed that he was a vagabond Gypsy. When the time came for sentencing, the magistrate asked if he had any money or knew of anyone who would pay his fines, otherwise he would be indentured into slavery for several years. Rodrigo half-heartedly said that his uncle, if still alive, would pay his fines. They asked him for his uncle's name and location. In his confused state he mumbled "*mio zio è il cardinale Borgia* (My uncle is Cardinal Borgia.)" The moment he mentioned the name, a deathly hush fell over the court, for almost everyone in Venice knew of the multiple expeditions that had traveled through Venice to find Rodrigo.

The magistrate asked him to repeat his answer for fear of having misheard him. A confused but defiant Rodrigo repeated his uncle's name. Signor Fantini immediately adjourned the session. To be on the safe side, he decided not send Rodrigo back to prison. Instead he instructed the guards to give Rodrigo food and wine and guard him in one of the Offices. He sent a messenger to the bishop of Venice, who came over, post haste, with Roberto Orsini, who had actually known Rodrigo in Rome.

As soon as the magistrate discovered who Rodrigo really was, he ordered his immediate release. They were all very apologetic to him and chagrined that he had not told them who he was earlier. Not only was Rodrigo the nephew of the pope, but because of his exploits against the Ottomans, he was already a folk hero. Even the street vendor whom he had struck was apologetic.

Signor Fantini immediately dropped the charges and told the street vendor to disappear before he got something more deadly than a scar.

It was then that the bishop told a flabbergasted Rodrigo that his uncle was very much alive and, in fact, he was the new pope. Rodrigo inquired about Aziza, Alexandra, and Zangi, and was assured that they were healthy and he was the father of a beautiful girl.

Immediately, Rodrigo searched for and found his Gypsy family and they were put up in a house that belonged to the Church. The bishop sent a messenger to His Holiness that same day. A Venetian banker advanced Rodrigo as much money as he needed, and which would be repaid once he got back to Rome.

The news of Rodrigo's miraculous return spread through Venice like wildfire. People of all walks of life came to his house to meet the man who had cheated death and had attacked the Turkish soldiers with four of his knights to save a princess in distress. Rodrigo's exploits in rescuing the Duchess Alexandra were now part of the common folklore.

The news of his escapades had been magnified as they were retold again and again, and Rodrigo discovered that according to popular belief, he had single-handedly destroyed Urban's monster canon.

Later the next day, he visited Alexandra and Alexis. Alexandra had been praying for his safe return to show him their child. Many in the Greek émigré community were referring to Alexandra as the new empress of Byzantine and the child as the new emperor. This was nonsense, of course, since there was no empire left and in any case, Princess Elena, as the sister of Emperor Constantine, would have been next in line of succession.

Venetians have always had a knack for throwing parties and Rodrigo's romantic story and his miraculous return gave them an excuse to arrange lavish festivities. At first, Rodrigo felt ill at ease attending those parties, accustomed as he was to being a nomad Gypsy with a simple lifestyle. The Venetian masquerade parties were notorious as the most promiscuous in Europe. Because the revelers wore masks, it was assumed that any liaison was anonymous and sin free.

One time, in a hallway, Rodrigo saw two men, one, wearing a pink mask with yellow flowers bent over with his hands against the wall and his bottom exposed, and the other, wearing a black and white mask, sodomizing him with great ardor. He knew they were both men because he could see that the man in the front was aroused. They heard Rodrigo's approach and in unison, the two expressionless, masked faces turned toward him. He muttered an excuse and walked away.

Rodrigo, his son, and companions were living in the large house that the bishop of Venice had provided for them. They all had their own bedrooms and they had servants and even a nursemaid for the baby. At first, Mirela did not want to let go of Janos. However, Rodrigo assured her that Janos would not be kidnapped and would be with his nurse at all times, next door to Mirela.

It was also the first time ever that Besnik and Mirela had slept on real beds. Besnik preferred the solid ground, so he moved his blanket to the floor and slept there. It took a while for Mirela to get used to the comfortable Venetian bed.

They had been back for two weeks and were still waiting for a response from the Vatican. Late one afternoon, Rodrigo was sitting in the main sitting room, contemplating his past life and accomplishments. He was reminiscing about old associates, friends, love interests, and enemies. He looked up and saw Mirela, who was sitting across from him, sewing. Every now and then, she would look up and smile at Rodrigo. He got up and walked over to her, took her left hand in his right hand, sat next to her and said, "I have neglected to tell you how important you are in my life. When you met me, I must have looked like an adventurous brute. You loved me and took care of me all those nights that I was drunk and drugged and close to death. You did not know who I was and your love nursed me back to health.

Then, after your parents died, you took care of Janos. When I was in detention, you and Besnik begged and worked at menial tasks to bring me food in the prison. I do not think that I have ever had a truer friend than you."

Mirela looked up at his handsome face and, with tear-filled eyes, she said, "I loved you from the moment that I saw you. I do not love any other man in my life except Janos, who is truly yours." Rodrigo bent down and kissed her.

He said, "You know that I am married and cannot be your husband. And because of your traditions, you cannot marry a bachelor if we make love together."

Tears rolled down Mirela's cheeks. She said, "I was put on this earth to be yours and carry your children."

He took her hand and together they walked towards his bedroom, but before they reached his door, Mirela blushingly excused herself and, giggling like a young girl, went to her bedroom. She returned in less than a minute with a silken purse the size of her hand. She smiled sheepishly and said, "This is like my wedding night. I will tell you about it later."

She grabbed his right hand and kept her eyes on him until they arrived at his bedroom. They both knew that no power on earth was going to stop what was about to happen.

He gently undressed her and looked at her body. It was the body of a very young woman, firm and lithe with a natural dark tan. In Gypsy tradition, she was completely shaved. Rodrigo knew the Gypsy belief that the lower parts of the body were impure and had to be kept clean at all times. While she was stood there looking at him affectionately, he kneeled in front of her and kissed her on those tender spots, which inflamed her desire.

She was so excited that she was getting wet and his kisses made her have a small orgasm. Rodrigo undressed quickly and led her to the bed. It was a warm day. They lay on top of the bed and embraced each other.

While kissing her, Rodrigo used his fingers to explore her private parts. Even though she was very wet, she was extremely tight and it was even difficult for his finger to penetrate her. Mirela was so aroused that her body had clasped his finger tightly and would not release it easily.

Rodrigo mounted her and gently tried to insert his instrument inside her. She was difficult to penetrate and was panting for air as ripples of pleasure traveled through her body. He worried about the pain that he might be causing her and stopped. Mirela, who was experiencing the agony of penetration and the ecstasy of having him within her, did not want a repeat performance of what had happened on board the *Star of Candia*. She sensed Rodrigo's hesitation, and pushed her pelvis forward to force him to complete the act of copulation. Mirela screamed in pain as the thin membrane gave way. Rodrigo kissed her tear-filled eyes and covered her mouth with his.

Despite the scorching soreness, Mirela was soon at the threshold of a major orgasm. Soon the pain subsided and gave way to unexpected pleasure.

Later, much later, when they got up, Rodrigo noticed the amount of blood on the sheets. Mirela smiled happily and said, "I must have bled like a pig!" She opened the silken purse and took out the white handkerchief that her mother had given her. She wiped the fresh blood from her young thighs and her private area until the white handkerchief was almost completely red. She smiled at

Rodrigo again and said, "On wedding nights, both parents stay outside the bedroom and wait for the bridegroom to consummate the marriage. We believe that if one or more of the parents are dead, their spirit will be there. The proof of the purity of the wedding is the bloody handkerchief that the girl keeps afterward for the rest of her life. There is also a conviction—you may call it a superstition—that says that the more blood, the happier the couple will be and the more children they will have. So, please get up and open the door, for I want them to see us together. I am now your wife in Gypsy tradition regardless of what the Church says."

Rodrigo kissed the innocent Gypsy girl on her forehead. How he wished there were ten of him so he could spread his affections to all the women whom he loved.

Mirela, who was ovulating at the time, was already pregnant.

* * *

Meanwhile, the news of Rodrigo's safe arrival was greeted with fanfare in Rome. The frail Pope, who was now seventy-eight years old, nearly had a heart attack. Rodrigo was his only heir and he was very fond of him. He told his fellow cardinals that he could now die happily, knowing that his nephew was alive and well.

The pope sent Zangi and Lorenzo, who had decided to stay in Rome permanently as part of the Cardinal's household, and an armed escort of Swiss Guards to accompany Rodrigo to Rome. Petros was persuaded to stay in Rome since Aziza trusted him more than she trusted the Italian doctors. Antonio, who was back in Florence, heard the news, and immediately headed to Venice.

Antonio followed by Zangi, Lorenzo, and the Swiss Guards arrived during the fourth week of Rodrigo's stay in Venice. Zangi, with tear-filled eyes, bowed down to kiss Rodrigo's feet, as was the custom of his tribe. Rodrigo picked him up, hugged him, and told him that he was like a brother to him.

The men stayed with Rodrigo for another four weeks until they departed Venice for Rome in middle of July 1456.

Upon arriving in Rome, Rodrigo went to see Aziza and Ariadne first. It was an emotional scene. They both wept while hugging little Ariadne. The pope arrived at his old mansion, which was now Aziza's house, shortly. The old man wept with joy at seeing the matured Rodrigo once again.

Rodrigo had already sent Antonio and Lorenzo ahead to find a suitable accommodation for Mirela, Jason, and Besnik.

During the weeks and months that followed, Rodrigo, who was given papal lands in addition to the fortune that he had inherited from that grateful widow in Spain, settled into a normal nobleman's life. Normal was not exactly what providence had planned for him, however. Soon the pope asked him to run more errands for his office.

Rodrigo had made two promises that he intended to keep at all costs. One was his promise to Jean to clear the name of Joan, the maid of Orleans. The other was the promise that he had made to himself inside the great church of Hagia Sofia on that fateful night before the fall of Constantinople and the massacre of the innocents.

* * *

Joan of Arc had been unjustly convicted by a religious court in 1431. At that time, the English had a false claim to the French throne and Joan arose just in time to save her country. She was betrayed and captured by the English. Joan was tried for heresy, convicted, and sentenced to be burned at the stake. As she was a virgin, however, she could not be executed since it was assumed that virgins were free of sin. To the eternal shame of the English, the prison guards were instructed to rape her before the sentence was carried out.

The court that convened in the Vatican, upon Rodrigo's return to Rome, carefully examined the records of the first trial and overturned the original verdict. Joan was absolved of heresy and the new court condemned her accusers and the evil judges who had conspired with the English to burn her alive. This opened the door to her eventual beatification and sainthood.

Next, Rodrigo arranged to send Zangi, accompanied by Lorenzo and two servants, to Zanzibar in search of Zangi's village and his relatives. They were away for over a year.

After following several false leads, they eventually found the right village in eastern Africa on the Indian Ocean. There they found Zangi's younger sister, who was an infant when the Arab slavers abducted Zangi. She had been left to die, but survivors of the raid had found her and raised her. They brought the young woman back to Rome with them. At least in Rome, she would not be in danger of enslavement by another group of slave traders.

Zangi eventually married Katarina and they had several children. He remained a true friend and servant of Rodrigo and together they had many other adventures.

CHAPTER FIFTY-THREE

THE FINAL CURTAIN

Rodrigo Borgia had an amazing life. For a while, agents of Mohammed II, who had found out that Rodrigo was still alive, tried to assassinate him. They paid the ultimate price for their failure at the tip of Zangi's sharp dagger. After Mohammed II's death, the new sultan, Bayezid II, proved to be a more benevolent ruler even though he considered himself the rightful heir to the lands once held by the Eastern Roman Empire, which meant most of Europe. He sent gifts to his niece, Ariadne, and tried to maintain a level of friendship with his relatives.

Many years later, Aziza died of the plague, which afflicted most of Europe from time to time. After her death, Rodrigo secretly married Mirela, who had given him several children.

After Aziza's death, Rodrigo rejoined the church as a clergyman and was soon elevated to the rank of cardinal. During the 1480s, a rivalry developed between Rodrigo and another cardinal, Giuliano Della Rovere. Giuliano was about twelve years younger than Rodrigo but he was a master politician and had managed to get himself appointed a cardinal by allying himself with the French king.

In July 1492, almost forty years after the fall of Constantinople, the current pontiff, Pope Innocent VIII, died. Cardinal Della

Rovere used every trick at his disposal to get himself elected pope. However, he failed and to his dismay, Cardinal Rodrigo Borgia was elevated as the Pope to lead the Roman Catholic Church in August 1492. He took the name of Alexander VI.

Cardinal Della Rovere accused Rodrigo of rigging the election and encouraged the French king to invade Italy and usurp the pope. The plan did not work and Rodrigo Borgia lived as a pope for over ten years. He was a patron of the arts, sciences, and knowledge. He had many children before becoming a pope, the most notable or infamous being Cesare and Lucrezia Borgia.

In 1503, he was poisoned by agents of Della Rovere and died. He was seventy-two.

His successor, Pius III, ruled as pope for only twenty-six days. It was again alleged that Della Rovere had had a hand in his poisoning.

Using bribery and intimidation, Della Rovere finally achieved the office of pope in November 1503. It was customary for a new pope to select the name of a saint or a previous pope. Giuliano was so vain and arrogant that he kept his own name and, with a slight modification, became Pope Julius II. Julius undertook many military campaigns to conquer the Italian city-states and annex them to the papal state. That is why he was called *Il Papa Guerriero,* the warring Pope. His actions bankrupted the papacy and left a lasting legacy of weakness, which eventually destroyed the vast papal state and left us with the Vatican as we know today.

Julius hated the Borgias and set about fabricating false stories that were published during his reign to malign and besmirch the Borgia family. He was extremely successful in rewriting history. Regrettably, to this day, many people think of Borgias as an evil dynasty of poisoners and assassins. The only decent legacy of Julius II is the paintings in the Sistine Chapel by Michael Angelo, but the truth behind that is another story.

Slandering and smearing the name of a previous king or pope or ruler has always been a fact of life. It is difficult to disprove misinformation once it has been widely circulated. For example, in England, Shakespeare rewrote the history of England by depicting the heroic Richard III as a cruel and treacherous buffoon who was guilty of infanticide. Why? Shakespeare lived during the rule of Queen Elizabeth I, whose grandfather, Henry Tudor (Henry VII), had usurped the English throne by killing Richard III, using deceit, in the battle of Bosworth in 1485. Obviously, if Shakespeare had not sided with the Tudors, he would have been killed or imprisoned. It is unfortunate that his play, Richard III, has distorted the true history of that period.

Borgia was not an Italian name. It was originally Borja in Spanish and since the Italian language does not have the guttural "H," sound Cardinal Alfonso modified it. Therefore, most Borgias in the world today are likely descended from Rodrigo Borgia or more correctly, Pope Alexander VI. So, if you are a Borgia, wear the name proudly!

The End

APPENDIX A

Author's note: The ancient Romans were masters of carnal desire and debauchery. Like their love of violence, they had an appetite for different forms of sexual gratification. They had devised various shows to depict sexual indulgences.

After the advent of Christianity, that knowledge was lost to Europeans. The Germans and Huns who invaded Europe were just interested in killing and raping as many women as they could and then selling the rest as slaves. As uncivilized barbarians, they did not have the interest in the intricacies of various sexual acts between men and women. By the fifteenth century, most Europeans only indulged in one or two positions of lovemaking and anything else was considered immoral and sinful.

The Arabs, having learned new techniques from their sophisticated conquered subjects in Persia, Egypt, and Syria, popularized a wide variety of sexual positions and activities. They actually produced erotic plays that depicted seduction and sexual activities. The famous explicitly erotic book, *The Perfumed Gardens,* was written by an Arab sheik in the fifteenth or sixteenth century and, interestingly enough, was banned in the West until the 1950s. Some plays like the *Virgin and the Sheik* have survived to this day and are performed in private clubs in Europe.

In the East, sexual plays were allowed, as long as the performers were non-Muslims. This rule also applied to brothels. As long as the women were not Muslims, there was no penalty for being a prostitute.

When the Muslims invaded Spain, this quiet sexual revolution was part of their culture. However, after the Muslims were expelled from Spain, Catholic Puritanism, at least on the surface, was re-established. Then that country descended into a period of fanaticism marked by the Inquisition, during which new methods of tortures were invented to extract false confessions and condemn tens of thousands of innocents to horrible, painful deaths. If the English were guilty of murdering an innocent young girl, Joan of Arc, the Spanish were guilty of thousands of cases of homicide. What is even more shameful, they imported Christianity, which, like Judaism and Islam, is a Middle Eastern-based religion, into the new world and forced it on people who, to this day, have a different concept of the universe.

Civilization is only skin-deep. Extreme violence by men against men and women has been a fact of life sine men emerged from the primordial soup of evolution.

RECOMMENDED READING

For those interested in medieval history there are a number of good books available. I have listed some of the best below:

The Civilization of the Middle Ages. Norman E. Cantor. The definitive book about the Middle Ages. The book actually covers the period from around 400 AD, through the Dark Ages and ends up around 1500. Even though Norman Cantor is a historian, his work is very easy to read and understand.

A World Lit Only by Fire. William Manchester. A fascinating account of the decline and rise of civilization from the fifth century to the 16th Century. The section on the origin and rise of Lutheranism is alone worth the price of the book. Manchester is obviously intrigued by Ferdinand Magellan, who was the first to circumvent the globe and gives a riveting account of that famous journey.

Chronicle of the Popes. P.G. Maxwell-Stuart. An easy concise encyclopedia of the Popes from the first pope to the latest one. It even mentions Pope Joan.

The Inheritance of Rome. Chris Wickham. The Dark Ages 400 AD to 1000 AD have always fascinated me. There is scarce information available about that period and this book shines a bright light on that age.

The Middle Ages. Morris Bishop. Another Easy to read and somewhat tongue-in-cheek book about the Middle Ages. Wonderful read.

The History of the Medieval World. Susan Wise Bauer. Historian Extraordinaire! Very informative and yet somewhat concise book about the Medieval World. However, she concentrates rather too much on the history of India and China during those ages, which had hardly any impact on the entwined history of Europe and the Middle East.

History Of England. Arthur D. Innes. This book has been out of print for many years. It is a concise history of England from the beginning of time to the twentieth century. A very good insight into life and politics. England was never typical of the rest of Europe; nevertheless, it was intertwined with it from the Roman Times.

History of English Speaking People. Winston S. Churchill. A concise history of England and its rise to world dominance from the Dark Ages through contemporary time. Churchill is a good storyteller and yet he is not an impartial historian. His royalist bent shows through as in the way he portrays Oliver Cromwell as an incompetent usurper and revels about the restoration of monarchy in England.

The Time Traveler's Guide to Medieval England. Ian Mortimer. A delightful book. You can learn about the language, the customs, the classes and the people in general in the Middle Ages in England.

The Knights Templars. Frank Sanello. A Pocket sized book full of information about the Origins and the missions of the Knights Templars and their eventual demise.

A Distant Mirror. Barbara Tuchman. A somewhat sad but detailed look at Europe in the 14th Century. Barbara Tuchman is an accomplished historian. However, she has a tendency for verbosity. The book is mostly about France, England and the 100 years war.

Wikipedia. Perfect online tool for cross referencing and fact checking.

www.ingramcontent.com/pod-product-compliance
Lightning Source LLC
Chambersburg PA
CBHW051428260626
47162CB00001B/7